PLAIN JAYNE

BREA BROWN

WAYZGOOSE PRESS

PROLOGUE

Permanent pause. That's what's become of the moment I first saw the burned-down ruins. I'll forever be standing there on that roughly asphalted and pot-holed road, clutching the slick polyester of my graduation robe, feeling and seeing my hair tremble in time with my knocking heart and ragged breath.

Up there is where my window used to be. The night before, my hot pink polka-dot curtains probably reached through the broken glass, trying to get away from the flames devouring them. The aluminum siding around the window burned white-hot, warping and melting, and black smoke competed with the orange flames, as both desperately sought oxygen.

There's a poem in there somewhere, or at least a haiku. If it hadn't been my gutted house, and my dead family, I probably would have sat in the grass verge next to the road and scrawled some words to add to the bulging accordion file that served as my writing portfolio. Maybe I'd have run home and eagerly shared the new scrap with my mom. Or, if she was too busy, I would have pestered one of my sisters, neither one of whom understood my zeal for the written word but both of whom humored me, nonetheless, when I was bursting with inspiration.

But it *was* my family. It *was* my house. Gone. Forever.

That doesn't mean I didn't eventually write about it. My family, of course, will never read it.

CHAPTER ONE

E xactly twelve years after my high school graduation and the fire that killed my entire family while they slept, I nervously fidget outside the office of my brand-new editor at Thornfield Publishing in Boston. If someone wrote this detail into a book I was reading, I'd laugh and put the thing down. Twelve years to the day? Really? The coincidence is too hokey, too cheesy, too *twee*, as the English say, to be believed. If I were to write another book based on my life (continuing where I left off in the book currently being published), I'd change this detail to make it more believable. I'm pretty sure any editor worth his or her salt would force me to change it, anyway.

What is it about May 23 that brings about such massive change in my life? Is it fate? Is it destiny? Is it the result of a curse? Or is it merely what it seems to be: an eerie coincidence? Perhaps I'm being too dramatic or putting too much stock into today's meeting.

Maybe my friend Gus is rubbing off on me, even though last night was the first time I've seen him since graduate school. As much as I love him, I'd hate to think I was turning into him. He gets all a-twitter and sees signs and omens at the slightest provocation and flaps his hands and croons, "Oooooh, creepy!" about fifty times a day, for occurrences as mundane as his Burger King order ringing up as an even dollar amount. He has a regular tarot card reader and psychic, despite the fact that he sometimes has trouble paying the rent on his postage stamp-sized studio "apartment" in a trendy part of Beantown. Let's just say that staying with Gus is bringing back many of the reasons that graduate school was a stressful time in my life.

Back then, I thought it was simply the nature of the beast, but having been long-distance friends with Gus for the better part of the past five years, I've had an epiphany since reuniting with him last night: he's one high-maintenance drama queen. It makes for some hilarious Facebook status updates, but it can wear a girl down to be in the presence of the real Dupuis.

We parted ways for the day at Starbucks a few minutes ago, and I'm still shaking. I have a feeling it's not from the half-caf latte, either. I knew from earlier research that the publisher's offices were less than a mile from Gus's apartment. All I needed was a verbal refresher and maybe some landmarks so I'd know I was on the right streets. But, as was typical, he turned it into a recitation that sounded like something coming from an auctioneer on speed.

"You're gonna go out there and then you're going to make a right at the light... right at the light, right at the light, right at the light.... Going straight, going straight, going straight... past the fruit stand, which is *not* a fruit stand in the winter, but it is right now...straight for a while, straight for a while..."

So far, it sounded a lot like his love life in college.

Then he startled me with a loud, "Stop! At the butcher's

that looks like a bakery—I totally thought it was a bakery for, like, the first three years I lived here, until this one day, there was a hog-pig-thing hanging in the front window, and I was like, 'Huh? What does that have to do with cupcakes?' Anyway, you're gonna cross the street there, because... well, trust me, this is the easiest place for you to cross, because they've got all these shrubs they're growing in the middle of the street, in the median-like—probably some environmental effort, which I'm all for, but sheesh! Sometimes it makes it hard to get around. Then when you get to the other side, you're going to walkwalkwalkwalkwalk, past the shoe repair place—the nice one, not the crappy place—past a ton of law offices, a church, a church, and another church."

At this point, he paused to suck in a huge breath, and I almost told him that I'd look it up on my phone. Then I noticed he was actually sweating, and I didn't have the heart to tell him that he was going to a lot of effort for nothing. Plus, I had to admit it was impressive how he had such a vivid recall of all the places in his neighborhood.

"Now you're almost there; you just have to wait at two more crosswalks, and don't be confused when there's a Starbucks at one of the intersections—you're not walking in circles; it's a different one; this one's *so* much better, though, or I would have taken you there this morning, because then all you'd have had to do was walk next door and voila! Thornfield Publishing! Where your future awaits!"

I smiled weakly at his enthusiasm, feeling gray and lackluster next to him. "Okay. Got it," I fibbed, giving him the thumbs-up.

Grabbing his messenger bag from the back of his chair, he stood, giant coffee in hand, and said, "Now, I gotta scoot. My new boss is about to flip her lid at what she calls my 'little tardiness problem,' and when I joked, 'No one's complained 'til now, little missy,' she said she did *not* appreciate my familiar tone, so I guess I'm on some sort of probation and *woooo, Mama,* I do *not* want to test this girl's temper. You can tell she's one of those people who keeps such a tight rein on her emotions that someday she may surprise the heck out of us all and poop a diamond during one of our story idea meetings! If that's the case, I wanna be on her good side, if you know what I mean." Suddenly, he tilts his head and smiles, "She kinda reminds me of you, come to think of it." That makes him laugh so hard that he rocks forward at the waist and almost spills his coffee. "Oh, shit. Now I really gotta go. Good luck! I'll call you on my lunch break—if I get one—to see how things went. Ta-ta!"

He was gone, leaving a residual shaking in my hands and the faint scent of cologne probably inspired by David Beckham or someone equally sporty-yet-metrosexual and costing about $100 an ounce.

As soon as he was out of sight, I put the publishing house's address into Google maps and got some straightforward walking directions. It told me that my walk would take less than fifteen minutes, but I left the Starbucks with thirty to spare, not wanting to be rushed and panicked if something kept me from getting there that quickly.

Big mistake. I would have rather rushed than sit out here with too much time to think about what might happen behind that huge wooden door. The brass nameplate pronounced the room beyond to be the professional domain of:

Lucas A. Edwards, Ph.D.
Senior Editor
Editorial Arts

Lah-dee-dah.

I talked to my agent, Tullah, this morning, before my hair-raising coffee shop tête-à-tête with Gus. She was extremely supportive and encouraging, although something she let slip has been nagging me all day: "So what if he's not thrilled about this new assignment?"

When I'd questioned the statement, she'd laughed nervously and played dumb. "What? Oh! Nothing. Sorry, I have you confused with another client. My bad. Listen, Jayne, I have to go. Big meeting." Never mind that it was four a.m. in her West Coast time zone and hardly prime time for "big meetings."

Now only a wall and a door separate me from a guy who's pissed off at me before we've even met, for reasons I'm not clear about. This guy is most likely a person who's used to getting his way, and despises anyone who prevents that from happening. He's probably a crotchety old crone who farts dust, is set in his ways, and always on the verge of retirement but never leaves, much to the chagrin of his colleagues.

I can tell by the nervous look of his administrative assistant that he's a real piece of work. Her face looks frozen in permanent apprehension, waiting for His Nibs to outline his latest demands. He probably shouts them at her, too, standing uncomfortably close, breathing his halitosis into her face, daring her to make even the slightest grimace, even when the spittle starts to fly.

I'm wincing sympathetically for the young woman—who introduced herself earlier as Sally—when the door swings open as if by remote control. Nobody comes forward, but Sally glances at the open door and then says pleasantly to me, "You can go in now, Ms. Greer." As I pass her desk, she asks, "Are you sure I can't get you a glass of water, a can of soda, anything?"

I stop and look at her, trying to interpret the motivation for this repeated offer. Is it my imagination, or does she look like she pities me? Like she's mercifully offering me what could be my last beverage ever?

There's absolutely no need for that. I'm a strong woman who can take care of herself. I've done that since I was eighteen years old. Buried my parents and my little sisters. Worked my way through college and graduate school. Beat out sixteen other applicants for a special fellowship in London as part of my post-graduate work. Waited tables and delivered pizzas. Scrubbed toilets, picked up trash, and schlepped popcorn at a movie theater so that I wouldn't have to touch the money my parents left me.

Money that I want nothing to do with, by the way.

If this Mr. Edwards (or Dr. Edwards, I suppose) thinks he's the most terrifying thing I've ever faced, he's sorely mistaken. Maybe. His intimidation tactics are wasted on me. Mostly.

As I enter the office, which is surprisingly devoid of the expected dusty books, autographed author photos, and ostentatious, cut-crystal awards, he turns slowly from the window.

"Ms. Greer," he says flatly, giving me a half-hearted wave.

I missed the mark on the "old and crotchety" bit. He's decidedly youngish and un-crotchety-looking. He's a snazzy dresser, too, in his gray three-piece suit, though the jacket is draped over the back of his chair. I'm treated to a pair of solid-looking arms in a white dress shirt and a broad chest covered by a dapper vest. If it weren't for the scowl on his cleanly shaven face, I'd say he was quite handsome, if you like that brooding look. Which I don't. Not really.

He sneers, and he has nice teeth, although they're wasted on someone who can't even muster a smile when meeting someone new. *Fake it for me, okay, Dr. Edwards? Just this once. Then at every meeting we have after this, you can show your true colors.*

A stickler for manners, I step forward and extend my hand, forcing him to either shake it or offend.

"Dr. Edwards," I return his curt name-only greeting.

"Nobody calls me that," he says, offering no alternative. He seems to consider not shaking my hand, but then takes a tiny step forward and gives me one of those cold-fish hand-shakes that men are so fond of giving to women. I make a point of grasping his hand firmly and pumping our hands with feeling. He withdraws and waves me in the vague direc-tion of a group of chairs and a sofa centered under a hideous light fixture made of deer antlers.

When he sees me eyeing the chandelier, he mutters, "Gift from Tom Ridgeworthy. Supposed to be a joke, but it's kind of grown on me."

He turns his back to me as he searches his messy desktop for something, He doesn't see the shocked look on my face at his mention of one of the most successful writers of polit-ical thrillers today. He didn't say it in a name-dropping manner. The nonchalant way he said it made it sound as if he wouldn't be surprised if I told him Tom Ridgeworthy had given me an equally bizarre gift once, as if everyone's received a gag gift from the bestselling author.

He eventually finds what he's looking for. With pen, notebook, and iPad in hand, he crosses the room and sits opposite me in the grouping that would be cozy if it were in the office of someone a bit cuddlier—like Ebenezer Scrooge.

"Well, then," he says. His attention is on the touch screen of his little toy as he swipes and taps away with long, graceful fingers. "Here we are."

At first, I think he's stating the obvious, at a loss for anything else to say. Then I realize he's arrived at his iPad destination. Turning the gadget around so that I can see it, he shows me a screen with a lilac and yellow book cover. The title of my book, *The Devil I Know*, rests in the center of the cover, the words nestled in the slender pale arms of a faceless woman.

In response to my wrinkled nose, he says, "Not to your liking? What about this one?" With a swipe of his finger, a different book cover slides onto the screen. It's mint green with the title in hot pink letters. It's positioned between some tire marks behind by a 1950's convertible. A red-haired woman sits in the driver's seat, a yellow headscarf trailing behind her in the wind, coming loose from her hair.

"Hmm," I say. I try to figure out how to diplomatically phrase my question after seeing both cover designs.

"These are preliminary." He swipes to the next one. "No?" he asks again, as I barely glance at a cover featuring a rearview mirror with pinky fuzzy dice dangling from it. It reflects the eyes of a woman in dark Jackie O. sunglasses.

Before he can continue with this nightmare slideshow, I say, "But those don't have anything to do with what happens in my book."

"They don't?"

I narrow my eyes at him. "No."

Puzzled, he turns the iPad around so he can look at the images right-side-up again. "Hmm… Interesting."

"Of course, you've read the book, so you know that, right?"

When he continues to stare at the fuzzy dice version, I prod, "Right?"

Startled, he looks up at me and blinks. I think the animals who donated their body parts to his light fixture must have worn the same expression in their final moments. He answers after he recovers his usual bored look, "Well, yes. I've skimmed the first few—"

"Chapters?" I finish.

"Pages."

"You're kidding!"

He redirects my attention to the horrible cover designs. "You're right—these are hideous. As soon as our meeting's over, you can bet I'll be having a stern talk with the art team. These covers are absolute shit, no matter what's between them."

I tense. "What do you mean?"

He sets the iPad aside and scribbles a note on his pad of paper. "I mean, I'll tell them I'm not happy they wasted my time with irrelevant covers."

"No. Not that. Although, they've wasted my time, too." When he stares blankly at me for pointing that out, I continue, "What I was referring to was your comment about 'no matter what's between' the covers. Like my book deserves a nice cover in spite of its inferior contents."

He waves away my claim and says irritably, "What? I didn't say that. You're putting words in my mouth."

I sit back and regard him skeptically. "Yes, I must be," I pretend to concede. "Since you've only skimmed the first few pages, you wouldn't be able to make a fair judgment of it anyway."

"I'll have you know," he replies, puffing out his chest,

"I've been in this business nearly twenty years. I can spot a bestseller from the first sentence!"

"Impressive," I say. "Then I guess you've read all you need to read of my book. You know it's a winner." At least, that's what everyone's been telling me for the past few weeks.

"It has potential," he says.

I want to punch his handsome, square jaw. Instead, I snap, "Do tell."

Returning to the iPad, he pulls up some text, which I immediately recognize as the middle of the first chapter of my book. Using his finger, he highlights one long sentence in yellow.

"Your sentences are too damn long."

"I *will not* dumb it down for any reader," I bristle.

Ignoring me, he continues, "In emotional passages such as these, short, brisk sentences are more powerful. They make the reader read at the same pace that the protagonist is thinking—or even breathing. Think about it: when you're upset, do you *feel* in long, prosaic sentences? No. You think like this: *'I hate this asshole. Who does he think he is? When can I leave?'* I know I think in short bursts when I'm angry or annoyed. *'I can't believe this. Saddled with a no-namer. She writes fluff, for fuck's sake!'* See?" He looks up at me and holds my eye contact, as if we're talking about the price of unleaded gas.

I blink in a way that probably makes me look insane. I honestly don't know how to respond to what he's said to me. To my chagrin, what finally falls from my lips is a lame proviso about the version of the book to which he's currently referring. "I've changed a lot since that version. I tweak it all the time. I like to tweak."

"Not anymore, you don't," he informs me. "From here

on out, you don't touch a damn syllable in this manuscript unless I tell you to."

"Anything else?" I say.

"Since you've pointed out I don't have the most current copy, you need to email that to me by the end of the day. Preferably by 2 p.m. Or if you have a copy with you," he nods toward my ever-present laptop bag, "you can leave it with Sally on your way out."

Dismissed, he effectively says by standing up.

"Are you actually going to read it?" I ask. I take my cue from him and rise from the sofa. There's no way I'm going to let him look down on me.

Disgusted with my childish question, he sighs and answers, "Of course I am. It's my job, isn't it? If you get it to me by two, like I've asked, I'll have my first run-through completed by the end of the day."

"How gracious of you."

Maybe it's my sarcasm, or the traitorous wobbling of my voice. Either way, he seems to soften.

"Listen. Ms. Greer. Don't take it personally. Your manuscript doesn't fit into my usual genre. I'm a bit annoyed that I have to divert attention from my other authors—established writers with proven selling power—to hold your little freshman hand." When I say nothing, he finishes in the same patronizing tone, "Surely you understand."

I loop my laptop bag over my head and drop it. I grunt when the weight drops onto my shoulder. "Totally," I tell him. My voice is as cold as stone. I walk alone to his office door. I open it before I turn back and loudly say, "You are an asshole," before stalking from the room with my nose in the air.

CHAPTER TWO

While I wait for the slowest elevator in the world to arrive, I seethe and try to recover my composure. Then I remember Editor Douchebag's request for my manuscript and mutter, "Shit." A guy standing next to me tries to pretend he's watching the floor numbers light up, but I can tell he's looking at me from the corner of his eye. Ignoring the tiny smirk my outburst has produced, I turn on my heel and return the way I came.

Sally smiles politely and blankly at me when I stop in front of her desk again. "Ms. Greer," she says pleasantly. "Did you forget something?"

I dig a thumb drive from my laptop bag and hold it out to her. "Would it be possible for you to copy a file from this and get it to Mr.—" I stop myself right before calling him one of the dozens of rude nicknames I've invented for him since storming from his office a few minutes ago. "Edwards?"

As she's taking the plastic device from me and plugging it into her computer, the man himself emerges from his office. When he sees me, he pauses as he shrugs into his suit jacket, but he quickly recovers, pretending I'm not there as he continues on his path across the small public area to one of the other office doors, which is marked, *"Blanche Turner, MA, Ph.D., Senior Editor, Creative Design."*

I also pretend to ignore him, going so far as to turn my back on him as he raps his knuckles perfunctorily on Ms. Turner's door before opening it and saying without preamble to the occupant, "Who the hell do you have working down there on cover art, anyway? That painting elephant that's always in the news?"

A tinkling laugh spills from the office. "God, I wish! Maybe then we'd get something original once in a while." There's a pause and then a teasing, "Sheesh, Luke. Rough morning? You look like someone called and told you your pet turtle died."

Instead of answering, he grumps, "Are you coming with me for coffee, or not?"

"Not, if you're going to be an ass-face the whole time," she replies, but I can hear her opening and closing a desk drawer and her voice coming closer to the reception area saying, "Does Lukey-Pookie need a hug?"

At this, Sally focuses all of her concentration on her computer monitor and tries valiantly to hide a smile. I can't resist turning to see his reaction to such a horrible pet name said in such a baby-talk tone in earshot of other people.

I'm surprised to see that he's trying not to laugh. His face looks completely different when it's not so stormy. Before he catches me watching, though, I look down and pretend I'm reading something on my phone, which I've had out of my pocket since leaving his office, preparing to call Tullah as soon as I'm clear of the building.

"I'm about to take back my invitation," he threatens

impotently, pushing playfully on her shoulder as they stroll toward the elevators. "I hate when you get like this."

"No, you *love* it," she accuses.

Then he says something too low for me to hear as they move further away, but whatever it is makes Blanche (who could be the model for the woman in the convertible on the mint book jacket) throw her head back and laugh so loudly that people poke their heads from their offices to see what's going on.

Returning my thumb drive to me, Sally mutters, "Thank God for Blanche, or we'd all be walking on eggshells around here all the time."

"Yeah," I commiserate with her, even though I'm not sure I feel exactly *thankful* for flirty Blanche.

She's one of those women that I generally distrust—the kind who's beautiful and knows it; who struts her stuff and uses her looks to get her way with everything—and every man. I don't have much respect for women like that. Or, maybe I wish I had a bit more of that in me. Life sure seems easier for people like her.

Trying to ignore my jealousy, I focus my attention on my original target and say to Sally, "He seems like a real winner. I don't know how you work with him."

"Oh, he's not all that bad." It sounds like she's worried she's being recorded, and anything she says can and will be used against her. "We try to keep him as happy as possible. He has a bad temper, but other than that, he's a good boss. Anyway, he's the best in the business, so he's allowed to be somewhat volatile."

I roll my eyes as I zip my bag. "Well, so far, I'm not impressed. He needs to work on his people skills." He's probably had people like Sally making excuses for him his whole life, though, so there's fat chance of that.

Now the administrative assistant smiles more warmly. "You caught him on a particularly bad day, which is your bum luck."

"I think I'm the *reason* for his particularly bad day, unfortunately," I tell her, on the outside chance she doesn't already know. "Next time I'll know to bring him a lamp made out of dead animal parts, and maybe then I'll be on his good side."

This statement earns me a laugh almost as loud as Blanche's. Sally surveys me and says, "You know what? I'm sure you're going to be just fine with Luke. As long as you keep your sense of humor. Dish it right back to him." When I raise my eyebrows at her, she blushes. "Well, obviously, *I* can't do that, but there's no reason you can't. You two are equals. It sounded like you were holding your own in there earlier."

"With less-than-perfect results," I point out, but I appreciate the encouragement from someone who obviously knows what I'm dealing with. "Thanks, Sally. Thanks for getting that file to Mr. Edwards. He said he wanted it by 2:00."

"Then he'll get it at 2:00," she replies with a wink. "No need rushing it and making him feel like you're going to jump every time he snaps, right?"

I like her.

If one more person tells me how brilliant Lucas Edwards is, I'm going to puke. They're supposed to be telling me how wonderful *I* am. When I slip and say that on the phone to Tullah, she laughs.

"I think it goes without saying that I think you are. I

think it's even more obvious that Thornfield thinks you are, since they assigned you to Luke. Trust me—he's the best."

"He's an A-one dickhead," I say. "He insulted me about six hundred times in a fifteen-minute meeting that was more perfunctory than a gynecological exam. He used the word 'fluff' to describe my book!"

It was almost a week ago, but the memory of it still upsets me. I haven't been able to get in touch with Tullah to tell her about it until now. Even my condensed retelling of what happened brings it all back like it happened yesterday.

I can hear the indulgent smile in her voice when she says, "Well, that wasn't very nice. I'd be more than happy to talk to him about it, but I'm afraid that's not going to help your cause. Remember—you don't have to be friends with the guy. He's a pro and knows what he's doing, though. If you cooperate with him, you may be surprised at how much you can learn. Now, I have to go. I'm sitting in on a meeting between Thornfield and a studio that wants to option your book."

She says it so matter-of-factly that I almost say, "Fine. Bye," without blinking. When my brain catches up to my ears, I stutter, "Fi—what?!"

"You heard me. Now be a good girl and do your job, which right now is doing what the rest of us tell you to do." Her tone is gentle, but the message is clear: *You're the new kid and should probably do more observing and less talking until you figure out the hierarchy in this process.*

I feel about six years old when I hang up, but with the words "option your book" bouncing in my head like a ping-pong ball in a lottery machine, I soon decide it's petty to dwell on certain slights perpetuated by a bit player in my professional life. A life that seems like it's finally about to take off after years of stagnating. Suddenly, it's a lot easier to put Mr. Edwards in perspective.

I mean, what did I expect? Did I think everything was going to be perfect? Did I feel that once I procured an agent, who in turn found a publisher for me, that everyone would bow down to me and kiss my feet? Is that what I deserve? My grown-up, logical side tells me that's ridiculous, unrealistic, and egotistical. The six-year-old in me says, "Yes! I've been through a lot! I'm ready for some happiness! I've earned this success! I shouldn't have to put up with insults at this stage of the game! It's not fair!"

Too many exclamation points. One of my weaknesses. In addition to long, rambling sentences, apparently.

That thought makes my brain itch. I want so badly to find the nearest bench, crack open my laptop, and find every instance like the one Lucas Edwards circled in my manuscript. I'm under strict orders. First of all, I'm not allowed to do any more tweaking until I get my marching orders from the red pen of Mr. E. Second, I'm supposed to be cooperative and follow all orders given by the publishing pros, including Mr. E., even if I'd rather willfully disobey him while sticking out my tongue and taunting, "Nah-nah nah-nah boo-boo!"

I'm a professional writer now. Emphasis on "professional." I've almost attained a goal that I've been dreaming about since… well, I can't remember a time when it wasn't a dream of mine. So, I'm willing to do anything to see it through. What could Mr. Lucas Edwards possibly say or do to stop me now?

CHAPTER THREE

"Shut the front door!" Gus shouts when I tell him what Tullah said. Then he quickly and dramatically covers his mouth with his palm as several heads turn our way. Obviously, the other visitors to the John F. Kennedy Presidential Library aren't interested in Gus's interjections.

"Sorry," he muffles behind his hand. After removing it, he continues at a much lower volume, "That's bajiggity. What a situation!"

I sigh, feeling twenty years old again, and not in a good way. Being transported back in time several years by this conversation is making me feel queasy. Suddenly, I get a flash of the two of us in the library at Indiana University, where we met while getting our undergraduate degrees. He was always talking too loudly there, too. Or laughing. Or crying. Or otherwise making a scene. We even got kicked out once. Maybe twice.

What's giving me the biggest feeling of déjà vu at this moment, however, isn't the threat of being kicked out of the JFK Presidential Library (although that would be an embarrassment on a whole other level). No, it's the fact that after all these years, Gus still talks—and acts—like he did as a college student. He uses the same made-up words and a vernacular that's unique to him in an overly dramatic way that's a transparent ploy to grab as much attention as possible. I'd forgotten how maddening it is. I'd hoped—although I know otherwise from keeping in touch with him since we went our separate ways for our respective careers—that he'd outgrown it.

Even though he gets on my nerves after the smallest of doses, he's the closest thing to a brother—or any family— that I have. He's like a case of athlete's foot: persistent, recurrent, and impossible to ignore. I have to admit, he's the only one who's shown that he cares enough to stay in my life, no matter how often I try to shake him. That's meant a lot to me.

It's not that I can't make friends; it's simply that I generally don't *want to* make friends or get close to anyone. That's one of the many charming byproducts of losing almost everyone near and dear to you at the age of eighteen. Life is too fickle and fragile to believe for an instant that it won't happen again. It will. That's why when I find myself getting attached to someone—platonically or romantically—I withdraw.

I make it sound like I've had lots of opportunities— hardly. I've viewed dating (and sex) similarly to how I viewed drinking in college. It's something I felt I needed to try, so I could say I'd done it. When it wasn't as great as everyone made it out to be, I checked it off the list and moved on. As for friends, there are very few people I can tolerate. Oddly enough, one of the most challenging people I've ever met is the one whose friendship has stuck.

Now, keeping my eyes pinned on the actual television camera used to capture and broadcast the first Nixon-

Kennedy television debate, I inhale deeply through my nose and count to five before responding to Gus's melodramatic response to my announcement. After all, a small part of me would have been either disappointed or worried if he'd replied with something bland like, "Oh, that's nice." This news *is* big. I'm too new to the whole publishing experience to pretend otherwise.

"I'm trying not to get my hopes up, but it's an amazing prospect," I say with a grin and a pleasant little shiver.

"Who do you want to play Rose?" he asks eagerly. Before waiting for my answer, though, he rushes in with, "I'm seeing Scarlett Johansson. She's the perfect blend of vulnerable and spunky, don't you think? Plus, you kind of look like her.

I resist the urge to insist that the protagonist isn't me. Must not protest too much. Besides, everyone thinks writers base their main characters on themselves, so it would seem over-the-top for me to question Gus's assumption. *Play it cool, Jayne.*

I wrinkle my nose at his choice. "I don't see the resemblance."

"Stop being humble, girlfriend," he scolds. "Trust me; I've given this a lot of thought. By the end of my first reading of your manuscript, I had the Hollywood cast figured out. I knew it was going to be a hit."

His confidence is touching, and it's a much-needed injection to my self-esteem after the week I've had going back and forth on the phone with Lucas Hard-Ass Edwards. To my dismay, I feel tears sting my eyes.

When I don't say anything right away, he assumes I'm still hesitant about his leading lady choice, so he continues, "I know she's getting older, but I think she can still pull off a wide range of ages, including the youngest parts of the story.

I mean, if Tom Hanks could play a high-school kid in *Forrest Gump*, then really…"

I laugh shakily and blink to eradicate the tears. "You know, I think you might have something there. She was good in *Girl with a Pearl Earring*. Like you said, the perfect blend of vulnerable, yet strong." When it's clear he hasn't detected my sentimental reaction, I relax and get into his game a little more, focusing on the character in the book that most closely resembles the "Gus" in my life. "And for Jack, I'm seeing…". I pause for dramatic effect, pretending to think hard about it, but I know exactly what he wants to hear. "Nicholas Hoult. Boyish, sensitive, and bespectacled, of course."

"*A Single Man* Nicholas Hoult, not *X-Men* Nicholas Hoult," he clarifies.

"Exactly," I agree firmly with mock-seriousness.

He nudges me with his shoulder. "I'm serious!"

"I know!" I nudge back. "Who else?"

By silent agreement, we walk toward the exit, both of us having lost interest in the museum. Gus shifts his messenger bag for a more comfortable position on his shoulder. I pull my lip balm from my jeans pocket and moisturize my dry lips before passing the tube to Gus, whose upturned palm awaits.

He quickly applies a layer to his lips and presses them together with a "THWOCK!" Returning the stick to me, he states as we push through the exit doors and breathe in the salty late-spring air that holds the faint promise of summer, "Mom and Dad will be Joan Allen and John Schneider, respectively."

At this point, Gus has no idea he's "casting" real people, because I've flat-out told him (okay, *lied*) that Rose's family is a complete figment of my imagination. So he pins his eye to the blazing skyline and rabbits away, "Then the sisters. That's a tough one. I'd say Dakota Fanning and Abigail Breslyn, but that's probably because they're the only two actors of the right age whose names I know, which is probably a depressing sign that I'm getting old and out-of-touch with the younger generation. But, even they're probably too old. I pictured them as the young versions of themselves when I read the book the first time."

My silence draws his attention, and when he sees that I'm simply nodding and trying not to cry out loud, he says in the southern-accented Ebonics he often slips into, despite originally being from New York and being one of the whitest people I know, "Oh, snap! Whatsamatter, Sugar? Are you thinking about that mean Mr. Editor again? Don't let him upset you! Do I need to go down to that fancy office of his and bitch-slap him?"

He sounds a bit too hopeful that I'll take him up on that offer as he flops his arm around my shoulders and pulls me up against his side. I shrug him off and add a couple of feet of space between our bodies.

I don't correct his incorrect assumption for my sudden emotional state. "It's fine," I insist, following up my claim with a brisk clearing of my throat. "It's been a long day, that's all." I leave it at that, unwilling to admit to him—or anyone—the true reason for my tears, that thanks to tabloids and entertainment magazines, I can picture those two actresses more clearly than I can my sisters' faces. All of our family photos were destroyed in the fire, so all I have are my memories, which are fading more and more every year, despite my desperate efforts to cling to them.

Thankfully, Gus's allergy to silence and his innate narcissism compel him to keep talking. "So what are the chances I'll get to meet Nicholas Hoult when he's playing the literary version of me in the movie based on your book?" he asks at his usual thousand-words-per-minute pace.

"Hard to say," I reply vaguely. "The only things standing in your way are the long odds of this movie ever being made, coupled with the fact that I probably won't have a say in casting, and even if I do, Mr. Hoult may not be available or willing to *be* cast in our movie."

"Well, as long as you keep such a positive attitude, I'd say it's a sure thing," he jokes.

"I don't want you to get your hopes up."

He snorts. "Yeah. God forbid I have something to look forward to in life!"

I link arms with him as we walk in the dappled shade of adolescent trees lining the walk. "Oh, poor you. Your life is so rough." When he mumbles his insistence that his life *is* rough, I defend my cynicism. "My biggest focus right now— as fun as it is to fantasize about Hollywood—is to get this thing to print. *Then* I'll worry about other things."

"You're no fun," Gus gripes.

"If you met my esteemed editor, you'd realize that fun has no place in this process from here on out."

"Oh, yeah. I almost forgot about him." His pensiveness lasts about four seconds. "Well, Honey, you can hardly let him get you down. Not after you've come this far. Anyway, I think what you need is a bowlful of Gussy's world-famous tiramisu."

I have to admit, his suggestion sounds wonderful. It may not solve all the world's problems, but it's a good start.

CHAPTER FOUR

"I won't do it," I say stoutly, at first barely loud enough for it to be technically deemed "aloud." Then, emboldened by saying it once, I repeat myself, this time turning around and facing the person to whom I'm directing the statement.

He sighs and cocks his head, but he sounds more resigned than angry when he replies, "I knew you were going to say that."

Because he knows me *so* well already. After being in the same room with me for a total of twenty-five minutes. Right.

I hold up the manuscript, which is saturated with red ink. "It won't even be the same book if I do what you're suggesting."

"True. It'll be better."

The only thing that stops me from crossing the room and strangling him is that he didn't say it as smugly as he could have said it. He's still very sure of himself, which has the same effect on me as the grating sound of bagpipes.

Rather than give him the satisfaction of showing that I'm annoyed (which I'm starting to believe is his goal), I coolly flip through the sheaf of papers in my hand, a bundle that was delivered to me at Gus's place via bike messenger earlier today, and state coolly, "Your insights are interesting, but that's not what I'm going for."

His jaw tightens. Then he plops himself into the huge leather chair behind his desk, grabs a large pen, and furiously clicks it. He starts to say something, seems to think better of it, but then opens his mouth again and says, "Funny—at this stage, I assumed you were going for whatever it took to get your book on store shelves."

The threat is more than implied. I don't know how to respond, though. I feel like every conversational opening he gives me is actually a crude trap. No matter how poorly disguised it is, though, I have no choice but to step into it. Or my unwillingness to respond becomes its own, more sophisticated trap, as is the case in this instance.

He slides into my silence, "More accurately, I thought you'd want your book to be flying *off* the shelves. Which it's not going to do, the way it's written now."

As he waits for my reaction, one that I'm struggling to moderate, he studiously avoids my eyes. I wonder if he can see how much I'm blushing as he purposefully types something on his computer and hits "enter." Soon after, I hear a musical "ping," and then he appears to be reading from his monitor. His features soften, but he reins in his expression before it becomes a smile.

Now he seems to remember I'm still standing in the middle of his office, doing my best impression of a statue of the patron saint of open-mouthed breathers. Glancing up at me, he lifts his eyebrows quizzically, creating a washboard effect on his forehead. "Hmm?" he questions, as if I may have said something he merely didn't catch while playing

Words with Friends with his mom, or whatever he's doing besides paying attention to *me*.

That thought makes me blurt completely off-topic, "Would you be acting like this if you were in the middle of a meeting with Tom Ridgeworthy?"

"Excuse me?"

I have his full attention now, but I have to admit, I liked it better when he was half-ignoring me. Under his stern glare, I stutter, "I mean, it's just that you don't seem to be focused on…" Reconsidering this suicide mission, I try to back out. "Whatever. Never mind."

Coldly, he says, "No. Please, continue. I'm curious to know what you mean. Because, obviously, you're *not* Tom Ridgeworthy."

"I still deserve some respect!"

In a flash, he's on his feet, crossing the room in two quick strides and standing inches from me. As he towers over me, he says, "You 'deserve' nothing. Got that? I know you're from a generation that wasn't taught that, but allow me to enlighten you. Respect is earned. So far, you've done nothing to earn mine. So you've managed to string a few sentences together into paragraphs, and paragraphs into chapters, and chapters into a novel, but so what? That gives you something in common with millions of other people."

I edge away from him, but the back of my foot bangs up against the leg of one of the chairs under the antler chande-lier, and I almost fall backwards over the arm and into the seat. This doesn't distract him at all, unfortunately.

I can smell his soap (or is that aftershave?) as he looms ominously. "I'm giving you exactly the amount of attention you've *earned* in your thirty-minute writing 'career.' When you prove to me that you're not a flash in the pan, like I suspect, then I'll reevaluate the amount of time I budget to *deal* with you."

"You're not that much older than me," I mutter sullenly. When he straightens and stares at me like I've lost my mind, I skirt the chair to put some distance—and a very solid object—between us and explain, "You mock my 'generation,' but I'm pretty sure yours is the same—or very similar."

"We might as well be from different planets," he says with a sniff. "I don't identify at all with the norms and values perpetuated in my peers."

I roll my eyes. "Oh, buh-rother!" I drawl. "Excuse the hell out of the rest of us."

"I'm simply stating the facts."

"Well, good for you. You know, I don't appreciate being reduced to a stereotype by someone who's less familiar with me than he is with the barista at the Starbucks downstairs."

Dismissively, he waves his hand and returns to his desk chair. "Can we get back to discussing *your book*? Your *raison d'être*? Your *raison d'être* in my face?"

His rudeness momentarily stuns me into silence again, but I recover more quickly this time. "My reason for being in your face is that *you* summoned me here," I remind him. "And I was *trying* to discuss it with you, but you seem to confuse 'discuss' with 'dictate.' As I was saying before, I'm not comfortable with some of the changes you're demanding."

"Be specific. Name one." He points to a chair. "Please, sit. You constantly look like you're about to sprint for the door."

Probably because I am.

I hesitate, but since he used the word, "please," a word I didn't think existed in his vocabulary, I feel obligated to reward him by honoring his request. I choose one of the armless, fabric-covered seats directly across the desk from him. He leans back in his own chair, folds his hands, and rests them on his flat tummy. His expression is one of both boredom and tolerance. I guess I'm supposed to feel grateful that he's granting me an audience.

"The biggest problem?" I begin, waiting for his terse nod. "Well, this suggestion about changing the fire to a tornado…"

When I falter, he prods, "Yes?"

Truth is, my only defense of the fire is that it's what *really* happened, but he doesn't know that. I don't want him to know it, either.

Plus, fiction isn't about what *really* happened; any writing teacher will tell you that. Simply because something happened in real life doesn't mean it makes for good fiction or that it's even believable, in some cases. If you can't sell it to the reader, it's worthless, whether or not it happened. I know all these things. Sometimes it feels as if I was *born* knowing these things. Just as my writing skills feel innate, my instincts tell me it would be wrong to change the fire to a tornado. I don't, however, think Mr. Editor Supreme Douchebag Edwards will defer to my intuition.

Finally, I settle on, "It changes so much."

He smirks. "That's kind of the idea, Jayne."

"If it's change for change's sake——"

"It's not! Trust me." When it's obvious by the mutinous look on my face that I *don't* trust him and probably never will, he sighs. "God! You're going to make me explain every single proofreader's mark in that freakin' manuscript, aren't you?"

I bristle. "No. I'm a professional; I can take constructive criticism. I know a good suggestion when I see one."

Tossing his hands in the air, he retorts, "Obviously not. Or else you'd realize that fires are so cliché." He leans forward, his hands splayed on his desktop. "*Jane Eyre.* Faulkner. Jack London. Fire, fire, fire. It's the only tragedy that writers seem to know how to write about. If it's used symbolically, it's somewhat excusable, but in your book, the fire is simply a means to kill off characters and yet another fire to get confused with all the other fires that have come before it in literature. Boring! 'Flames licking' and 'smoke choking' and 'beams collapsing.' Yawn City."

During his rant, my eyes fill with tears as if the room *is* filling with smoke. I even clear my throat a couple of times before a full-blown cough explodes from my lips. The noise brings him up short, but I turn my head and bend over, pretending to dig for something in my computer bag, which is resting on the floor at my feet.

With a flat, emotionless voice, I say, "I take it you've never experienced a house fire. Or lost someone in one? Because it's not boring. Probably," I add hastily so as not to give too much away.

"Well, it is on paper," he quickly claims, oblivious to my anguish. "At least it is on *your* paper. It's like you imagined what it would feel like and then sucked out all the emotion from your imagination and typed it up, like a robot. Frankly, it left me underwhelmed. It doesn't make any sense, considering there's so much raw emotion in other parts of the book—maybe *too* much. The imbalance is jarring."

Confident that the tears have passed and that I can face him without giving him any clue as to how close to a nerve he's hitting, I straighten, holding the pen I was ostensibly searching for, and sniff. "That's what I was going for," I inform him. "I wanted it to be remarkable to the reader how clinical the description of the fire is. Because that's how the authorities describe it to Rose. Without feeling. She's expected to take in the information as fact, never mind that her *family members* died horrific deaths in the fire. It becomes a part of her history, her life story, but a part that she's never allowed to be emotional about." I tilt my head and narrow my eyes. "Seems like a discerning reader like you wouldn't need something like that spelled out for you."

Not at all fazed by my insult, he points to me and says, "Bingo. If a discerning reader like me doesn't get it, then you've failed."

Aw, shit.

"But—"

"Enough!" He says it loudly enough to drown me out but without any heat. Digging around on his chaotic desk, he comes up with his own copy of my manuscript. "Either rewrite it so that the fire makes me feel something, or change it altogether. Your choice. Next."

I hate this fucking asshole.

CHAPTER FIVE

I'm not going to reach my goal. I'm not going to see one of my books on a shelf in a store before my thirtieth birthday. I have someone in particular to thank for that. I hardly need to even give you his initials, surely. It's obvious who would stand in the way of a dream I've had since I was old enough to realize it would probably be more realistic to shoot for "thirty" than the original "twenty-five" goalpost I'd set in high school. There was nothing (or no one)—until now—to make me think it wasn't a completely attainable goal, despite the challenges I came up against time and again.

I blew off friends, eschewed romantic relationships, and told myself that human contact in general was overrated. Sometimes I worked for so many hours on end that I couldn't even see the computer screen clearly. Eating became a chore that I tried to do as often as possible in front of my computer, with bites in between long passages of prose. I wrote like a woman possessed, as if I could erase the pain with a few million keystrokes or, at the very least, put my grief to bed like an edition of a newspaper. I slept in two-hour intervals, but only when it was physically impossible to sit, type, and think.

Once, before I became religious about backing up my work in three places after each prolonged writing session, my computer contracted a virus—I was "researching" uncircumcised penis pictures, having never seen one in real life, and I stumbled on a site that had a cyber STD—that wiped out a solid week of writing, including the scene in which Rose finds out her sisters and parents have all been killed in the house fire. In reconstructing those chapters—which still aren't as good as the originals—I had to go through the emotional sandblaster yet again.

I also felt the sting of rejection over and over again as every agent I queried told me, "Not for me." Gus, and everyone else who was familiar enough with me to know that I was trying to publish a novel, told me to forget conventional publishing and self-publish or e-publish. Every time I opened my email, it seemed there was a message in there from Gus about another unknown author who had given the publishing industry the middle finger by becoming a bazillionaire via Kindle or Nook or both. I persevered. I was as relentless as a millionaire thrill-seeker with too much time on her hands, obsessed with climbing the world's highest mountain the old fashioned way, simply because she wants to cross it off on her Bucket List.

Because my dream is to hold a hardbound book, complete with shiny jacket and delicious-smelling *paper* pages, bearing my name on the cover and my little author's blurb on the inside jacket flap. *Not* to see my name staring coldly at me from a computer or phone or tablet screen. I've already seen that a hundred times on my own laptop. It isn't the same. Despite how old-fashioned and outdated the concept is, I want something more tactile than what the e-publishing world can offer me.

"There's nothing more tactile than cash, Sweetie," Gus said to me when I tried to explain my obsession with having my novel made into a "real" book. It would have been hard to argue with that, if I was strictly in it for the money. Bigger, more nebulous motivators were pushing me along.

Now, elated and oxygen-deprived, I'm standing on the apex, and my Sherpa, Mr. Lucas Fiddlefart Edwards, is telling me I haven't toiled or sacrificed enough for his liking, and I need to do *more* before I can celebrate and enjoy my accomplishment. He actually wants me to climb down all by myself to get back to base camp. I was hoping for more of a helicopter lift.

What's worse is that the climb down seems like it's going to take almost as long as the climb up, and with my thirtieth birthday in less than a month, there's no way I'm going to realize my dream. The disappointment is crushing. I think I'm being fairly adult about it.

"Damn him! Damn him and the horse that inseminated his mother to conceive him! He's a rotten, stinky shithead! I want a new editor! I'm calling Tullah and telling her I'm not going to do a single one of his lousy edits, and I'm not going to do another thing until she finds me a new editor. Period. End of story."

Gus dispassionately twirls one of his chopsticks along his knuckles while I throw my temper tantrum across the coffee table from him.

"Lucas Edwards is a pompous, old-before-his-time fart with a broomstick so far up his ass that you can see the tip of the handle when he opens his mouth wide enough. Which he does often, because he never shuts the hell up, since he's enthralled with the sound of his voice. I can't believe I ever thought for five seconds that he was attractive." My cheeks flare at that admission.

My friend immediately picks up on it, and his eyes sparkle when he says, "Oh? This is the first I'm hearing of this. Details, please! Is he, like, good-looking in a brooding, scary way? You know, like Michael Fassbender in *Jane Eyre?*"

His mention of the same literary work Mr. Buttface Edwards used to disparage my fire scene causes a pang that's almost physically painful. I sneer. "Not really. Well, sort of. He has a nice body, I guess. And pretty eyes. But, then he speaks."

Gus nods knowingly and goes back to twirling his eating utensil, his mouth slackened in concentration. "Oh. Thinks he's God's gift to women, huh?"

"He thinks he's God's gift to writing! Well, why doesn't he write his own damn book, then? Huh? Huh?"

His mouth closes with a snap before he replies somewhat dully, "Yeah. This is a situation to end all situations, sister. He's a bajiggety boo-face."

For a second, I'm disappointed by my friend's going-through-the-motions tone, but then I realize that when we're not talking about something that directly affects him (or dishing about a hot guy), he's not nearly as passionate as he would be when, say, someone tries to edge their way in front of him in line at the grocery store.

To get him back into the conversation—and on my side —I point out, "Well, this is going to push back any plans for a movie, too. After all, you can't write a screenplay from a book that's not finished. Even though it *is* finished. Just not to *somebody's* liking. Ten people before him have read the damn thing, and it's passed muster, but no. Mr. Tight-Ass Editor has to make sure his bosses don't think he's obsolete. He has to somehow put his stamp on something that's not his. Then he can take some credit when it's a bestseller. He doesn't realize he's holding up the entire process! Half the actors we have in mind for the characters in the book are going to be way too old by the time Lucas Dingleberry Edwards is satisfied enough to send the book to print."

Now Gus straightens, and annoyance flashes in his eyes. "Oh, my God! I hadn't even thought of that, girl! Who does this Lucas Ass-Loogie Edwards think he is, anyway? As if you didn't consider other tragedies besides a house fire when you wrote the damn book?! Of course, you did! You're a writer. I'm sure you researched tornadoes, earthquakes, terrorist attacks, floods, hurricanes, you name it! Why can't he trust your judgment and realize that you had very good reasons for choosing and sticking with the house fire thing? I mean, c'mon!"

I dip the tip of my chopstick in a puddle of soy sauce and use it like an old quill pen and ink on my paper plate. "Actually, no. I didn't consider anything other than a house fire," I admit quietly.

Doggedly, Gus says, "Well, anyway. Whatever! It's your damn book. Like you said, no one else has had a problem with it 'til now." Picking up a stray grain of rice with the tip of his finger and examining it up close with one eye, he asks cautiously, "Although, would it be *so* horrible to *consider* his suggestion? You know, kick it around to see if there's something that jumps out at you?"

At my incredulous look, he hurries on. "Well, he's kind of a dickhead."

"Yeah, we've established that!"

"But he's a successful dickhead with a lot of experience." He flicks the grain of rice in my direction. It sails over my shoulder.

"So, he's read a lot of books. So has your grandma.

That doesn't mean I'm going to call her up and change my plot to whatever she's in the mood to read." I huffily start to gather our trash and stuff it into the white paper sacks strewn around us.

"No, no, no! Leave my Nana Dupuis out of this. Anyway, that's not what I meant. Let me put it this way." He sighs and seems to be reading from the inside of his forehead. "If you do what he says—or at least try—everything goes more smoothly? *Oui?* So you slop an alternate disaster scene together, and if it flows and feels like it works, you consider the next step, which is blending it in with the rest of the story and replacing the fire with the tornado or earthquake or what-have-you. If it's crap—which you can always guarantee it is, if that's the route you want to take—then you show it to him, shrug your shoulders, and say, 'See? The original is better.' Mea culpa and all that jazz. Capice?"

His misuse and mixing of languages and colloquialism aside, it's still a shitty idea, but I don't have anything better. I'm too angry to come up with a plan other than, "Find a new editor," and I'll need the cooperation of my agent to do that. An agent who thinks the sun shines out of Lucas Edwards' ass. An agent who's already told me in not so many words that I'm stuck with this d-bag, 'til publication do us part.

If the fire/tornado debate were the only toxic soup simmering between Lucas Edwards and me, that would be enough to feed an army, but there are about six other broths and stews bubbling on the literary stove that is my manuscript. We only had time to discuss three or four, which means I have the pleasure of another meeting with him to look forward to. He told me straight out that he expects to see the changes we discussed (again, the word "dictated" is more appropriate here, but Lucas likes to pretend that his mandates are "discussions," during which I see the light and decide to do exactly what he wants me to do) at our next meeting.

When I don't say anything in response to Gus's seemingly disloyal speech, he says, "C'mon, Jayne. Big picture, girl. Big picture."

I glare at him. I used to use those words when imploring him to keep things in perspective when we were younger. I don't appreciate him throwing them in my face now. Through gritted teeth, I say, "I *am* thinking of the big picture, Gus. Thank you."

He shows me his palms in a gesture of surrender. "Okay, okay. Just checking. Books on shelves, right?"

"Yeah, *my* book. The way I wrote it."

"Yeah, yeah. It *will* be the way you wrote it, no matter what happens between now and then. *You're* going to write it." He catches the balled-up bag I throw at his head. "Hey! I'm just sayin', Chicka-Boom-Boom! Think about it. You have control here."

"How do you figure?" I ask miserably. Honestly, I don't want to be reassured or cheered up or mollified at this juncture. All I want him to do is curse Lucas Edwards, his family, and any current or future descendants of the man. Is that so much to ask? Apparently so. Because my friend is a frustrated queen who's always wanted to be a cheerleader. Who wants me to stop pouting, get my book to print, and get a movie in the making before his beloved Nicholas Hoult outgrows the role of Jack.

"I know you don't have as much experience with men as you should, but take it from me, Honey-Buns. All you have to do is make your grouchy editor *think* that every idea is his. He wants a tornado; you want a fire. You punch up the descriptive details in your fire scene, including mention of a *tornado of fire*. Then you thank him profusely for the inspiration. Are you pickin' up what I'm puttin' down?"

Despite my foul mood—and a blooming headache, thanks to my self-destructive addiction to soy sauce—I feel a slow smile spreading across my face. "Yes. I think I am."

"This jackleg's just another picky professor with a syllabus of tedious assignments. You never shied away from those challenges back in the day. What's the diff?"

I chuckle bitterly at this comparison. "Appeasing a professor for a grade is one thing; but making fundamental changes to my novel—a project that's like a child to me—feels like selling out."

"Oh, good gravy!"

"What?"

He launches the bag of our dinner waste toward the trash can and seems to consider it a win when it lands on the floor next to the bin. Standing, he stretches, making his checked button-up shirt ride up and show an expanse of flat, hairless belly and a perfect innie belly button. "Sister-friend, you already done sold out!"

"I beg your pardon!" I stand, too, ready to hurdle the coffee table and scratch out his eyes if he persists with his offensive accusation.

Tugging his shirt into place, he tilts his head at me and blinks pointedly. "You're getting paid for this, right? Then, bam! Sell-out. I completely approve, by the way. What's the point in producing art if you can't profit from it? Then you can't get up on your high horse, either."

Damn if he doesn't have a point. Can I win even one argument today? If I were willing to tell him that I felt like I'd be betraying family members that he doesn't even know existed, I might score a measly point, but using my personal tale of woe as inspiration for my novel is admittedly the epitome of selling out. Anyway, I'm not desperate enough to win that point; I won't be telling Gus—or anyone—how close my debut novel follows the story of my life.

After much consideration, I retort lamely and without rancor, "Bite me."

He grins, showing off his magnificent, orthodontist-perfected choppers. "I would, girl, but you know I don't swing that way. Now I don't know about you, but I need to spend an hour or two in the little boys' room after that meal and then head off to the Land of Nod, if you know what I'm sayin'."

Unfortunately, I speak fluent Gus-ese, so I do know exactly what he's sayin'.

The next morning is an exercise in ignoring. First off, I use supreme self-control as I ignore my dialing thumb, which is itching for me to call Tullah and appeal to her human side about finding a new editor for me. Coffee helps. Thinking about the monumental task of complying—or pretending to comply—with Editor Mussolini's changes to my manuscript brings the itching back full force.

Must resist.

Cure for every ailment or problem I've ever had: writing. Oh, the irony. *Well*, I tell myself, *I'm not going to get anywhere until I get started* (thank you, Captain Obvious), so I slide my laptop from its case, boot it up, and open the most recent version of my manuscript. Breathing deeply through my nose, I close my eyes and then scroll to the fire scene. Fire tornado. I can do this.

This is when I have to ignore the screaming in my head: You can't do this!!! That's why you purposely made the fire marshal tell Rose what happened. To keep it clinical, unemotional, and brief, and to avoid any chance of your graphic imagination running away with you.

Right. Well, the first time I wrote this was five years ago. It's been twelve years since the actual fire. Surely, I can detach myself—as a *professional*—enough to do what's required here.

Right?

A tingle at my hairline alerts me to the cold sweat breaking out there. Chills run up and down the backs of my thighs. My vision narrows, and my breathing quickens. The walls of Gus's tiny apartment close in further.

Must not panic.

I take several slow, deep breaths until my facial features feel like they're in proportion with the rest of my head again before focusing on the blinking cursor in front of me. Professional detachment. That's what I'm going for here. I summon the disclaimer I've read inside so many books and before countless movies. *This is a work of fiction. Any similarity to persons living or dead (unless explicitly noted) is merely coincidental.* Yes. They're characters, not my family members.

After all, that's what I need everyone to believe.

I ignore the voice in my head that calls me a fraud.

It's drowned out, anyway, by the couple next door, who is having a very loud argument. From what I can tell, the male half of the partnership left the seat up on the toilet "for the thousandth time," and the female half fell in, because she doesn't have her contact lenses in, which—according to the offender—isn't his fault. It's glimpses like this into coupledom that make me thankful I'm a hermit-in-training and don't have to deal with anyone else's bad habits and idiosyncrasies.

Well, other than Gus's, but that's only temporary, until I

find my own place. Or am driven by his interesting lifestyle to a hotel, whichever comes first. He was so generous to allow me to stay with him, but he didn't tell me that he lived in a sardine can with a futon serving as his bed (and every seat other than the toilet) and a coffee table serving as every surface. I guess it's a testament to his generous nature that he felt obligated to offer me accommodations when he literally doesn't have an inch to spare here. I've seen bigger walk-in closets in college dormitories.

I didn't want to settle down in this part of the country without making sure this could be my true home. As a writer (at least I *think* that's what I am), I can live wherever I want, so I think it's important that I find a place where I feel comfortable and—at the risk of sounding too arsty-fartsy— inspired. This is the first time I've ever been to this area of the country, but based on what I've read and seen so far, I think it'll be a good fit for me, especially if I can find a way to live near the water. I've had my fill of land-locked, drought-prone tinderbox states.

Good news: the couple next door isn't fighting anymore. Bad news: they're having very loud make-up sex on the other side of the wall, about ten feet away from where I'm sitting, from the sound of things.

That settles it. I have to get out of here if I'm going to get anything done. Some things are impossible to ignore, and loud sex is probably number one on the list.

The laptop goes back in its bag. I check to make sure my wallet's still tucked in there, too, pocket the apartment key that Gus left for me on the coffee table/desk/dining table, and vacate the premises before thinking about where I'm going to go. I'll figure it out when I get to a place where I can hear myself think.

~

This is hopeless. Having never tried to write anywhere but the comfort of my own home, I never realized how particular I am about the setting in which I work. I don't have any weird physical rituals that I perform before each writing session (turn around three times before sitting in the chair; close eyes while rubbing pencil between palms; take a deep breath; open eyes; toss pencil; type), but the conditions have to be right. Some of those conditions aren't conducive to public venues.

For example, I can't exactly set out my favorite sugar-cookie-scented LED flameless candle in the Boston Public Library. Somehow that smell has become an olfactory muse. As much as I love the smell of books and polished wood, it's not as inspirational to me.

If that were the only idiosyncrasy I had, I'd probably be able to work around it. I've also become dependent on another crutch: the large fleece blanket that I usually drape over my lap, legs, and feet. It seems like an insignificant thing, and, indeed, it started out that way. One day I was cold, so I grabbed the fleece blanket from the foot of my bed. That would be the end of that story, if not for the fact that I had one of the most productive writing days ever!

The next day, when I was stuck on a plodding plot point, I spotted the blanket from the corner of my eye while I was staring into space. It was exactly where I'd left it, in a heap in the middle of the floor, where I'd dropped it on my way to bed the night before. On a whim, I snatched it from the floor, arranged it evenly over my legs, and then tucked it under my thighs and feet. Immediately, a feeling of security and warmth—both literal and figurative—came over me. I relaxed, the ideas flowed, and I had another 20,000-word day that stretched way into the late night. Since then, the blanket has been my constant partner.

And, yet, I brought neither of them with me on this trip.

I must be getting cocky.

Did I think an *editor* wasn't going to require me to do any re-writes? Am I starting to believe too much of the praise that's been heaped on me by Tullah and everyone at Thornfield Publishing besides Lucas Edwards?

No, I think the real issue is that I didn't realize how dependent I had become on my candle and my—gulp—blankie. It's embarrassing.

It supports my theory that I'm a hack. I'm an imposter, and it's all going to come crashing down around me. They're all going to find out that I can't write. This book is a fluke, and the only reason I was able write it is that I've lived with the pain for so long that it was clawing to get out. It wrote itself. I was merely the medium. The three-book deal I signed with Thornfield is going to be my undoing. I'm not going to be able to fulfill it. Then everyone will know.

That thought triggers my second panic attack of the day, which attracts quite a bit of attention my way. I haven't been able to write anything at the Boston Public Library, anyway, but the anxiety and curious stares are the deciding factors in my leave-taking. It's safe to say I won't be back to this branch, either. Ever. I don't think that's going to break the heart of the librarian who looked like she didn't know whether to call 911 or Homeland Security as I was wheezing my way toward the exit.

On the sidewalk, I sweat, trying to avoid the stream of pedestrians giving me no more notice than water would give to a rock. Slowly, I edge my way to an unoccupied piece of cement against the side of the building, where I pause to catch my breath and figure out where to go next. Just because the library was an epic fail doesn't mean I'm ready to give up so easily. I have an editor to trick into thinking I'm complying with his editorial requests. If I can pull that off, then maybe I can feel like I truly deserve to be a successful writer.

I have to find a place to write, though.

CHAPTER SIX

I am a nut job, and a hack (but we've already established that). By the time Gus gets home from work, I'm in tears.

"Geez-oh-man! What happened to you?" he asks as he parks his bike between the futon and the wall, removes the metal bike clips from his pants, and lifts his messenger bag from his shoulder and over his head. "This doesn't look like a good situation."

Normally, I'd do nearly anything to avoid having someone see me cry, but after the day I've had, I don't have the self-control to prevent making a spectacle of myself.

"I can't do it!" I wail.

"Can't do what, Sugar-Booger?" Gus asks, daintily blotting perspiration from his forehead with a linen handkerchief he produces from the back pocket of his khaki pants.

That's when I wetly tell him about the loud neighbors and the library and my inability to write without all my familiar comforts and surroundings.

"So I went to a coffee shop, because I thought that

there'd at least be some yummy smells from the coffee and pastries and stuff."

When I stop, he urges me on with his crystal blue eyes, but he doesn't say anything.

I miserably say, "It was horrible there, too! Too loud!"

He sighs. "Have you ever heard of earbuds, Babushka? Criminey Pete! I don't go anywhere without my earbuds." He edges past me and opens the only drawer in the kitchenette. While riffling through takeout menus, he informs me, "They keep away the crazies. Sometimes I even wear them without playing any music. As long as the people around me *think* I'm listening to something, they won't bother me. Usually. You know, you always get that rogue weirdo who doesn't give a damn what's goin' on. He's gonna talk to you no matter what. In those cases, I point to my ears, give a helpless shrug, and mouth, 'I can't hear you,' before movin' my ass as fast as I possibly can away from him. Or her. It's not always a guy. Most of the time, it is. In either case, the person generally has more of a beard than I would after a week of not shaving."

As soon as he pauses, I jump in and snap, "Are you finished? I'm having a crisis here!"

He looks up from the menus in his hands. "Oh. Sorry. Yeah." Before I can get back to my problems, he holds up two menus for me to see. "First, though—which one? Mexican or Italian?"

"I can't eat," I state firmly.

"Oh my Buddha! I've never seen you so melodramatic before." Conspiratorially, he mutters, "Between you, me, and the futon, it's not very attractive, Jayne. I mean, really."

Taking me at my word that I'm not going to help him choose which food to order, he tosses the menu with the walking taco on it back in the drawer and squints at the phone number on the menu bearing the Italian flag and a mustachioed man. Or is that a woman?

As he's dialing, I have a change of heart—maybe food is what I need, to feed my brain—and blurt, "I'll have baked mostaccioli!"

He rolls his eyes at me and turns his back as the person on the other end answers, and he begins to give them our order. I move closer to him and hiss so he can hear me, "With a large iced tea!" He swats in my direction, like I'm an annoying fly, and manages to swat my shoulder.

"Oh! Sorry!" he immediately apologizes, whirling and patting me in a conciliatorily. "No, not you, ma'am," he says into his phone. "I hit my bestie without meaning to. *Bestie.* As in, best friend. No, not *crusty!* No! Lady, listen to me!"

I have a feeling half the apartment building is listening at this point. I cover my mouth to stifle my giggles.

Consternation creates two deep wrinkles between his eyes. "Oh, my dear word! This is the most bajiggety experience I've ever had ordering some damn dinner," he says, punctuating it with a huge sigh. "Pardon my Swahili. Listen, I want two orders of baked mostaccioli, an order of garlic bread, an iced tea, plain, and a raspberry iced tea, both unsweet. That's it. Thank you. Sorry for the confusion."

He punches the button on his phone to hang up and turns to me. When he sees I'm laughing, he immediately relaxes. "There's a smile! I was beginning to wonder if it was on vacation."

I choke back a chortle at the memory of the look on his face as he was trying to make himself understood on the phone. "You get flustered so easily," I say.

He fans himself with the menu. "Yeah. I know. That's

kind of my thing. But it's *not* yours, so what's the dealio with you lately?"

Flopping onto his futon and immediately regretting it when the wood frame slams into my tailbone, I wince and say, "Ow! I don't know! This experience is driving me crazy."

"You mean, your dream come true?"

Like a petulant child, I cross my arms over my chest. "Yeah. Well, it's not how I imagined it was going to be."

"As in…?"

I feel silly saying it, but I do anyway. "It's not as fun. I thought it'd be easier than this."

"You mean, you thought everyone would be kissing your ass more?"

His blunt interpretations are too spot-on to be insulting. I'm relieved he understands and isn't going to make me say it myself. "Yeah! I mean, I didn't think it was going to be all, 'Dahling' this and 'Dahling' that, but I definitely didn't imagine myself in a stupid stalemate with an editor."

"Oh, not him again!" he despairs. "I thought we got all this figured out last night. Is this going to be like that awful Bill Murray movie, where he keeps reliving the same day over and over again? Is that what my life has become? Because, Honey, I don't know if I can handle that. Two hours of it on DVD was enough to drive me ape-shit."

When he starts to dig around in his messenger bag, I do the same in my laptop bag, and we come up with our wallets at the same time. Grinning at each other like idiots, we both slap twenties on the coffee table like we're playing a card game with cash in place of cards.

"I've got this," I tell him in a non-negotiable tone, knowing he won't argue. He replaces the twenty in his wallet and pulls out a five, which he tosses casually on top of my money.

"For the garlic bread or the tip," he explains, equally firm. I also don't argue with him. It always seems to even out, no matter who pays, so we don't worry about it.

Except for that one time when we each assumed the other had taken care of the ticket and ended up accidentally dining and dashing. It wasn't until hours later, when we were having a midnight snack at a frozen custard stand that we realized, horrified, what had happened.

He said, "Since you were so kind to pay for dinner, I'll let you get as many toppings as you want on your custard." I had laughed at him and said, "You're in the early stages of Alzheimer's, pal. *You* bought dinner, remember?"

"I most certainly am not, and I most certainly *did* not," he insisted, still perusing the custard menu.

"Very funny."

That's when we both looked at each other and realized what must have happened.

"Oh, my gosh!" we gasped together.

He clutched at my hand like someone had told us we had ten minutes to live.

"Jayne, we have to go back there," he said earnestly, turning in impotent circles, as if he wasn't sure in which direction to start walking.

After the initial shock of it, I had laughed. "Forget it," I told him. "It was an honest mistake."

His eyes were so wide that I could see white all the way around his irises. "What?! Of course it was, but it would be *dishonest* not to rectify it now that we know."

"You just wanted to say 'rectify.'"

"It *is* a delightfully disgusting word," he admitted. "I'm serious! Otherwise, we can never go back there again!"

"I'm okay with that," I said callously, finally deciding on the vanilla custard with caramel and bits of pretzel mixed in.

"Oh, my gosh. We're criminals," he'd whispered, but he promptly ordered a banana and butterscotch concoction and stopped trying to convince me to go back to the restaurant to pay.

Unfortunately, the place was practically on the Indiana University campus, so we walked past it all the time. Every time we did, Gus would cross himself and say, "Hail Mary, full of grace," even though he's not Catholic and doesn't know any of the words after that part.

I was blasé about it at the time, but I've been paranoid about it ever happening again. I figure you're only allowed one of those in your life, and that's only if it's not malicious.

Now I stare at the cash on the table and sigh as I contemplate my current situation. "I can't help it," I declare. "I'm disappointed by how everything's gone so far. The publishing process, that is. It's a lot less glamorous than I thought it would be. I thought it would be *fun,* at least. But this is bordering on miserable."

"Motherfucker." Gus even manages to make one of the most vulgar curse words sound silly, like something a sweet Southern granny would say after burning her finger on the cast-iron skillet while making cornbread. "I can't believe you're going to let that ninny ruin this for you!"

"I'm not!" I protest.

"Yes, you are! You said it's not as great as you thought it would be, and you specifically mentioned *him* as the reason. That sucks!"

I jut my chin out. "Well, I can't make the changes he wants. I didn't write a single word today! It's hopeless."

"After one frustrating day, you're declaring it 'hopeless'? Really, Jayne? Really?"

"I don't see how it's going to get any better. I'm not going to wake up tomorrow or the next day and magically be able to do it."

He scrubs his hands through his hair, and tiny, fine stray pieces, stragglers from the fresh haircut he got on his lunch break, settle onto his shoulders. "That's right, because it's got nothing to do with magic. You're going to figure out how to write without your blankie and your candle and your silent apartment. Then you're going to turn in a brilliant finished product, and Lucas Dickweed Edwards is going to sit up and take notice."

"You're crazy. I know what inspiration feels like, and it's nowhere to be found now."

"Well, you'll find it. You're going to see something on TV or hear something on the radio or overhear a conversation on the bus or in the park or in line at the coffee shop, and it's going to click. You know that's how it goes."

His cell phone rings then. After a perfunctory look at the display, he answers. "*Maman!*" Then he rattles off a string of French so quickly that I can't make out a single recognizable word.

Finally, after what seems like an interminable monologue, he stops and then only says, "*Oui*," or "*Non*," occasionally. Then he says, "*Je t'adore, aussi. Au revoir, Maman!*"

After pressing the button on his phone to hang up, he explains unnecessarily, "My mom," and as if the interruption never happened, he cocks his head and jumps back to our previous conversation. "You know I'm right."

"I *don't* know, Gus," I tell him honestly before voicing my deepest fear: "I think I've lost it. Maybe what I've written so far was all I have to give. Maybe that's it; I'll never be inspired again. Maybe I *am* a flash in the pan, like *he* said."

Gus levels a glare at me. "First of all, who uses the term, 'flash in the pan,' anymore? Second, why are you being so insecure? Your book is one of the best things I've read in a long time. A lot better than most of the stuff out there on the bestsellers lists. I'm not saying that because you seem to be fishing for compliments; I mean it."

A knock at the door prevents me from objecting to his accusation. As he pays for the food with the money I gave him, I try to figure out how much I can tell him about my fears without betraying the truth behind the misgivings. With a disappointed sinking in my stomach, I realize I've already said as much as I can.

What started as a therapeutic writing exercise, a way for me to exorcise my demons without turning to drugs and alcohol (although trust me, I considered them first), quickly bloomed into an obsession. Writing it all down was my way of keeping my sisters and parents alive. It's how I remembered all their quirks and personalities. As a matter of fact, one of the few positive comments Lord Lucas Edwards wrote in the margins of my manuscript was, "Vivid characters. You really bring them to life."

Ha! If only!

Before I knew it, I had a book-length memorial, starting with the day my youngest sister was born and ending with Rose (me) receiving an offer letter from a publishing company, promising to make her the next big thing. That's not how it happened in real life, obviously, but I wrote that before I knew what a quagmire the publishing world is, and I never went back to change it, because I liked the fantasy of the publishing process being effortless and instantly gratifying. I know I'm doing a disservice to all those aspiring writers out there by not being more accurate and honest, but even the frankest portrayal winds up glamorizing things, despite efforts to the contrary. So I didn't worry too much about it. Good thing, too, since the real story thus far has been too anti-climactic to make it marketable.

I took some creative license in other passages, too. After all, we didn't lead an exciting life, for the most part. We were average Midwesterners who lived on a working farm. While that may be exotic to someone who's never stepped off the pavement of a metropolitan area, it was difficult for me to see it with fresh eyes and pluck out the events that would be interesting to an outsider. They were there, but I had to dress them up a bit. It's true that my mom almost gave birth to my youngest sister in the car, because it was a long drive from our house to the nearest hospital, but she wasn't out in the corn field when she went into labor. I embellished that part. We didn't even have a corn field.

Then, as other parts of the story unfolded on the monitor in front of me, I realized I didn't need to do anything to make them funnier or juicier or more tragic. They were poignant and heartrending enough in their original forms, and they wrote themselves. In those instances, it became important to me that I *not* alter a single detail.

When I approached Tullah for representation, I deliberately packaged the book as pure fiction and said nothing about it being "based on actual events," because I didn't want to become the story. I wanted it to begin and end on the page. I knew all along that I wasn't going to tell anyone that this "story" was my personal history.

Anyway, if that detail gets out at this stage, I'll really look like a fraud. Everyone will know that my imagination can't compete with the facts. I'm a historian, not a novelist. I don't create characters; as a matter of fact, two of them created *me*.

Nevertheless, I give Gus a brave smile when he returns to the table with the food. "It's nothing a little mostaccioli can't fix, right?" I say.

CHAPTER SEVEN

He's not impressed. Nor is he fooled. Shit. I should have known that the easy (a.k.a., "lazy") solution wasn't going to be the ultimate solution. Now, I've wasted days on material that's going to have to be scrapped.

When he glances up from his iPad, I try to deliver a confident, approval-seeking smile, but I know it falls closer to "grimace" on the continuum of facial expressions. Thankfully, he returns to his reading too quickly to see it. I think he was mostly checking to see that I'm still sitting here, that I have the *nerve* to still be sitting in his presence. Maybe that was a signal that I should leave before he explodes.

But, no, *his* expression—if I had to try to break it down —contains bemusement, mixed with hints of confusion, contemplation, and... what is that? (All the other expressions are getting in the way.) Uncertainty? Yes! As uncharacteristic as it seems, he definitely looks unsure of himself. I have plenty of time to study him to make sure I'm correctly interpreting the look on his face.

Swipe, swipe, swipe. For the third time, he paws at the tablet resting on his knee to return to the beginning of the passage I most recently delivered to him. Scratches his head. Pinches his chin between his forefinger and thumb in the universal gesture of deep thought. Clicks his tongue against the roof of his mouth. Blinks his green eyes and then rolls them as if he's trying to deliver moisture to a pair of contact lenses, which he doesn't wear.

Oh, jeez. This is torture. I'd rather he rant and rave and tell me it's horrible than make me sit here and wait for him to come up with the perfectly devastating words to say. Because that's obviously what's going on. Any old insult won't do. Its severity has to perfectly match the level of my writing's depravity.

I catch myself cringing and then force myself to relax. Isn't that what you're supposed to do before a traumatic collision? Relax, and then it won't hurt as much.

Finally—finally!—he deliberately sets the electronic tablet on the low table in front of our chairs, but instead of returning to an upright position, he remains bent at the waist, his elbows resting on his knees as he lets his head hang, seemingly enthralled with something on the carpeted floor between his shiny shoes.

I refuse to say anything. I'm not going to play dumb and ask if he likes it; but I'm also definitely not going to antici-pate his wrath and put derogatory words in his mouth.

"So," he says more like a sigh than a word after what feels like at least ten minutes of thick, suffocating silence. Now he turns his head to look at me and smiles.

At first, I'm thrown. The smile is extremely cute. It makes me think he actually liked my changes. Then I recog-nize the pity in it. Huh? Pity?! I think not! Anger, I can take. But his sympathy? (I don't even know what it's for yet.) I don't think so.

"Why are you looking at me like that?" I ask warily, the

tension returning to my shoulders, neck, abs, legs, and every other muscle used to keep me vertical.

Before answering, he shifts his weight back and forth from his toes to his heels a few times. Then he purses his lips, sighs for real, and says, "What's going on here?"

"Here?" I repeat so I can stall as the following races through my mind: *Oh shit, he knows I'm lying about everything—well, not everything—but some things, big things. He knows I'm not a writer and that my story is real real.*

On the outside, I'm as calm as the surface of a lake on a hot, stifling day. I have to remain motionless, because if I move, I'll start to shake. And sweat. And blush.

He sits back in his chair and places his hands on top of his head. In this midst of this extremely stressful situation, I manage to notice that he looks tired. He also needs a haircut. Yep. My world may be coming apart, but I can see that his hair is feathering out over the tops of his ears. For some reason, I care.

"Come on," he interrupts my musings on his coif as he curtly gestures with a nod of his head toward the now-idle iPad. His tone is mild as he asks, "What the hell's that about, huh?"

This calm, laidback Lucas Edwards is freaking me out. It's like dealing with a stranger, and trying to figure out the best way to respond to him is quickly exhausting me. He's laying traps, a minefield of them, surely.

"Um," I hum noncommittally.

"That's crap." Again, he nods toward the table so there's no misunderstanding.

Okay. Whew. I know for sure that he hates it now. Which is what I wanted, right? I didn't want him to like the changes. I wanted him to say, "The old way was better."

Still, his blunt assessment stings. I *know* it's crap; I intended it to be crap; but only I can say it's crap.

I lift my chin. "If you say so."

"Oh, I do," he says, making a sound that takes a while for me to realize is laughter.

First pity and now ridicule? Uh-uh!

Instinctively, I find myself defending what I know to be the worst work I've ever done.

"Whatever!"

Okay, it's a lame defense, one used by every person under the age of twenty-five when they have no true defense. It's a defense I should have outgrown by now. I can't think of anything else to say.

His expression turns to one of undisguised scorn. "'Whatever'? That's all you can come up with? Here I was thinking what I read was a well-crafted joke. Now I'm reconsidering. Maybe the person who retorts with, 'Whatever,' doesn't know how to write any better than that."

I mentally shake it off, roll my head on my neck, and take a deep breath. Meanwhile, in reality, I remain frozen, inside and out. Now's not the time to get emotional. I still don't know enough about what he's thinking to let down my guard. I have to renounce my defensive nature so I can see the plan through.

Coolly, I say, "Oh, well, that. Yeah. I mean…" I shrug helplessly. "Your idea didn't work. I wasn't *feeling* it." I try not to sound too eager when I add, "I think it's safe to say the original version was much better."

He rolls his eyes. "I see."

His know-it-all smugness immediately gets my back up. "You don't see anything."

"I see enough."

Suddenly I'm sure he *doesn't* know the truth. He's bluffing, trying to get me to confess to something that he doesn't even know the first thing about.

I laugh at him. "You're so full of it." When he puts his arms down, resting his hands in his lap, relief that my secret's still safe makes me blurt, "You know, I can't *write* in this stupid city."

He raises his eyebrows. "Temperamental?" he questions sardonically.

I don't appreciate his smirk, but I want to take advantage of this rare good mood he's in. "Something like that," I admit. "I'm staying with my friend, Gus."

"Your 'friend'?"

"Yes. My very gay friend. He lives in an apartment the size of a mini-wheat." My description earns another one of his barking, rusty-sounding laughs. "His neighbors have three settings: sleeping, screwing, and screaming. So I tried to write in some other places—you know, coffee shops and libraries and even a park—but it's hopeless. I'm blocked."

"That much is obvious. What do you want me to do about it?" He stands and picks up his iPad, which he carries to his desk and slides into the front compartment of a leather laptop bag that's already holding a computer probably worth more than what my dad paid for my first car. With deft fingers, he zips and snaps and clasps everything closed as he states, "You provide the writing; I provide the editing. That's how this works. I can't help you until you give me something decent."

"I gave you thirty-six chapters of 'decent' to begin with. You're the one who's obsessed with fine-tuning it." I stare at my nails as I say this, so I don't see his reaction to my statement.

I don't need to see it, anyway. The now-familiar impatience in his tone when he says, "That's my job," gives me a good idea of what his face looks like: he's wearing the "something-smells-really-bad-in-here-and-I'm-pretty-sure-it's-your-writing" expression.

Resigned and hating myself for it, I reply, "I know. But…" *Don't you dare say it, Jayne, you stupid idiot. Do not trust him, just because he smiled a few times and has managed to have a conversation with you that doesn't involve shouting.* "I feel like I've forgotten how to do my part of the job." *Jayne, you moron.*

"You're burnt out," he declares as if it's the most harmless thing in the world.

"That's not good, though!" I lament, taking my cues from him and packing up my stuff. He's obviously getting ready to leave. A glance at the futuristic clock on his desk tells me it's after 5:00. "You act like that's something as harmless as being hungry or tired."

"It is," he says shortly. "I'm late. So, here's my advice: no writing for a week. Unless you become inspired, that is. Don't *make* yourself sit down and write."

"But—"

He sweeps past me to his office door and turns off the light. The room is still surprisingly bright, thanks to the west-facing windows. "But nothing. I have to go." He doesn't move, though, until I join him in the empty outer office, which has been abandoned for the night.

"I just want to get this thing to print," I say, my voice on the verge of a whine as we walk together to the elevator.

"You think I don't?" He stabs fiercely at the "down" button and readjusts his bag on his shoulder. "You can't force it. It has to happen in its own time."

"Screw that. Anyway, that sounds very un-editorial of you. You should be cracking the whip."

He waits to reply until we're in the elevator and he's pressed the button for the lobby. "You can't beat a dead horse, Jayne. If you ever use a cliché like that in a book, I'll make you wish you *were* dead."

Okay. So much for the warm fuzzies I was starting to feel.

It's the first day that I can remember that I haven't written anything. Nothing. No edits, no proofreading, no revisions, nothing. I feel like a tweaker who needs a fix, only my dealer is a laptop, and it's sitting across the room from me, tempting me from its padded case.

I know, though, that if I open it, I'll wind up sitting there, staring at the screen, frustrated by my ineptitude. That frustration will eventually build up to the point of panic and then evolve into despair, finally cooling down to resignation that I'm never going to write another word again.

I've realized that—big deep breath—Lucas Edwards was right: I need a break from it. It doesn't have to be a long break; just enough to recharge my batteries. If I stop thinking so much about it, the creative juices will flow once again. (I hate that disgusting term, but my inspirational pulse is so flat that I'm resorting to banalities that nauseate me.) I'm like a person who's obsessed with meeting Mr. Right and looks for a potential husband in every man she meets, until she deems the search hopeless and stops looking. That's when she finds him—or he finds her—in the most unexpected place. At least, that's how it happens in books and movies.

Sitting here, staring at the four disconcertingly close walls in Gus's apartment, is decidedly un-Hollywood. I honestly don't know what else to do, though. Gus is at work.

I suppose I could wander the city and explore, but it's not as fun doing stuff like that alone. I'm alone all the time in my *real* life; here (which I somehow don't count as part of my real life), I don't want to be alone.

Yet, I feel more alone than ever.

When Gus gets home from work each night, I greet him like a dog with separation anxiety would. Last night, I could tell it was starting to freak him out. He took the gin and tonic (his favorite) I had waiting for him and nervously eyed me like I was an escapee from a nearby loony bin who'd dropped in randomly on the first apartment she found unlocked. I could see this, but that didn't mean I was able to keep my rambling mouth in check as I hopped from one unrelated topic to the next.

I know all too well that when Gus thinks you're acting certifiably insane, you've reached an advanced level of nutti-ness. When he refrains from coming right out and telling you you're crazy, that means he's possibly poop-his-pants afraid of you. I've seen him react this way to homeless people on the subway and some of the residents at his Nana's nursing home.

Hence, I woke up this morning determined to stop being the crazy friend that Gus regretted inviting to stay with him. I've been here long enough, anyway. We're starting to develop little weekend routines, which makes our current situation feel too much like a permanent living arrange-ment-in-the-making, so it's time to find my own place, despite my fear of loneliness. Anyway, just because we don't live together doesn't mean we won't see each other. We'll simply have more than ten feet of personal space.

I was excited about the prospect of living independently again, too, until I started inquiring about the cost to rent my own tiny slice of Boston. It's a tad more expensive to live here—or anywhere within a 100-mile radius of here—than it is in the Midwest. Maybe this calls for a shorter-term commitment. But the rates at the hotels I called knocked the wind out of me, too.

I'm sitting on the futon, trying to catch my breath and decide what to do when my cell phone rings. "LUKE-ASS" flashes on the screen.

"Mr... Lucas... hi," I stutter like a moron. I still don't have any idea what to call him to his face. "Dr. Edwards" has already been shot down; "Mr. Edwards" seems too formal; "Luke" is too informal; and "Luke-Ass" is probably inappropriate, although it's my new preferred private name for him, because it works on so many levels.

"How's the writing coming along?" he jumps right in without returning my greeting.

Defensively, I snap, "What? You said... I mean, I'm *not* writing, remember?"

In his usual clipped, serious manner, he replies, "Yeah. I was testing you. Anyway, listen. I've decided what you need is a change of scenery. I'm sure this whole experience is overwhelming, is it not?"

"Well, I'm not some country mouse wandering open-mouthed around the city, if that's what you mean." What is it about this guy that makes me all sweaty and irritable the minute I hear his voice?

"Good God," he says. "Is that what I said? No. I didn't. I was referring to the publishing experience. How it's intimidating to the uninitiated."

"Maybe," I reluctantly admit. "I'm fine."

"Except you can't write, which is sort of a problem."

"Yesterday, you acted like it *wasn't* a problem."

"I was trying to be nice!" His tone is anything but.

This guy is hopeless. "I don't need you to be nice; I need you to give it to me straight."

"You always act like I'm too mean or something, so I decided to go gentler on you yesterday."

"You don't have to baby me, all right? I'm a professional writer. I can take it." I'm already reaching for my laptop bag. I should be writing!

"Okay, okay. Calm down! Good God. What the...? You're breathing right into the phone and killing my ear!"

I freeze and then transfer the phone from between my shoulder and head to my hand so that I can hold it in a position that won't funnel my breath directly into the tiny mouthpiece. With my free hand, I try to stealthily unzip the laptop bag.

"Jayne," he warns.

Giving up the pretense of being sneaky, I go back to frantic mode, not caring how loudly I'm breathing or unzipping or panicking. "Don't 'Jayne' me like I'm a child! I've wasted the whole morning *not* writing because of your crappy advice. By the way, you're *terrible* at being nice, so you should stop wasting your energy trying to be nice and save it for important things, like helping me finish this book!"

"If you'd sit still and shut up for one second. Hey! What do you mean, I'm terrible at being nice? You're impossible to please!"

"I'll have you know my standards are pathetically low when it comes to you."

"Then you'll be stunned when I offer you the use of my currently empty beach house in Marblehead!" he shouts.

Oh.

This statement brings me up short. It takes a few seconds for me to reconcile his furious tone of voice with the generous offer, but when I realize how convenient this is and how it's the answer to so many of my problems right now, I quickly shout back, equally testy, "Fine! I'll take it!"

"Good!" he replies, his voice still crackling angrily. "I'll tell Sally to send a car to come pick you up."

"I'll be sure to be ready then!"

And with that, I mash down the button to hang up on him. Damn, I miss the days of slamming a receiver down in someone's ear! There was no better punctuation mark to a heated phone conversation than the clang of plastic on plastic and the faint ring of the bell inside the mechanism as it dinged its protest at being treated so roughly. These dainty "beeps" that cell phones make for every function are highly unsatisfying.

I hate you! *Beep.* You can't even draw it out to be a *beeeeeeeeeeeep.* It tones for the same length of time no matter how hard you hold down the button. Lame!

I used to be a phone-thrower, but the person you're mad at has no idea you're throwing your phone, so the only person you're punishing is yourself when you have to spend hundreds of dollars to replace your broken phone or what-ever your phone hits (my windshield was the costliest—and last—victim of one of my post-phone call tantrums, which happened—ironically enough—after a conversation with my auto insurance carrier).

Now that I've kicked my phone-chucking habit, I've taken to sticking my tongue out at the device after hanging up with someone who pisses me off. This behavior is less gratifying, but it's also a lot less expensive.

I do it now. Since I'm alone, I yell, "*You're* a marblehead, Luke-Ass!"

Oh, gosh! I have to pack!

CHAPTER EIGHT

W ho is Lucas Edwards, and how the heck can he afford to own one of these places? It's a question I keep asking myself when the houses get bigger and bigger as we drive closer and closer to the water. Knowing what little I do know of real estate prices in this area, I have to assume these mansions are worth millions, maybe tens of millions. Even though the town car pulls into the sand and gravel driveway of one of the smaller homes on the avenue, it's still gigantic, and it's on an ocean-front lot, so I know it's not bringing down the property value of the houses around it.

If I had to guess—and I'm not very good at these things —I'd say the Victorian-style home is five times bigger than the house where I lived with my parents and two sisters. Some of its more impressive exterior features are its huge bay and dormer windows, the giant wraparound porch, and the ocean-view gazebo large enough to fit a dance floor and a five-piece band. That's only what I can see as I peer at the property from the car window.

"Oh my effing gosh," I whisper reverently.

The driver clears his throat, which I take to be my not-so-subtle cue to stop gawking and get my butt out of the car. I open my door and step onto the driveway, which I now see is made of sand and seashells, not gravel.

The driver, who I'm beginning to think is mute, also gets out, but instead of merely standing there, staring, he goes to the trunk and retrieves my two puny suitcases. I shoulder my laptop bag—I'd never entrust it to someone else or stow it in the trunk and risk being separated from it in an accident— and follow Silent Tom up the shiny porch steps that are painted the same grayish blue as the sky before a storm.

I'm armed with a key and the alarm code, but apparently so is Tom, because he doesn't wait for me to unlock the house. He sets my luggage down, opens the door, and expertly disarms the alarm. When he starts up the stairs with my suitcases, I say, "Oh! Don't bother with that. I'll take them up myself when I figure out which room is the guest room."

Speaking for the first time, he answers in a heavy Boston accent, "Miss, I was given specific instructions regarding your room," before continuing up the seemingly endless flights of white wooden stairs.

I hurry to catch up to him, feeling guilty that he's carrying my stuff. I wouldn't necessarily call him "old," but he's older than I am by a couple of decades, at least. Plus, the guy's a driver for a black car service; he's not a butler. This whole thing is making me feel uncomfortably bourgeois.

Again, we resort to silence. The only sound is the clomping of Tom's polished shoes and the slapping of my flip-flops on the immaculate stairs. At the top of the second flight, he looks wearily at me when I mutter, "I would have been content to stay in the basement." I quickly add, "But this is nice. I bet there are some great views up here."

He doesn't confirm or contradict my speculation. Instead, he leads me down a hallway carpeted in a pattern designed to make it look like the rug's been here for years, when it's obvious by its lack of wear that it's brand new. The wide hallway is paneled in more white wood—this time narrow beadboard wainscoting—and the top half of the walls features a pearly gray paint, reminiscent of the inside of a clamshell. Very beachy in a masculine, non-pastel way.

Tight-Lipped Tom seems to know his way around the place. I stiffen when he pushes open a large set of double-doors at the end of the hall and leads me into a bright, airy, *enormous* bedroom with a huge bed (and some other furniture, but the *bed* is definitely the centerpiece). Wide, dark wooden floor planks stretch from wall to wall, uninterrupted save for a ten by ten square of exquisite Oriental rug anchored by the *bed*, which looks like the softest, coolest, snuggliest instrument of sex I've ever seen.

Before I can check my brain, it delivers a picture of Lucas lying naked in the center of it.

I blush and quickly look away from it, as if by doing so I can also avert my gaze from my own thoughts. "Uh, Tom?"

He turns from where he's stowing my two suitcases next to a gleaming dresser. "Yes?"

I pin my eyes to a spot in the middle of the cheery pale yellow wall nearest me. "Yeah. Here's the thing. Tom."

When I'm too embarrassed to go on, he prods, "Yes?"

Gosh, he's going to make me spell it out. "Okay, here's the thing," I repeat, before rushing on, "I don't think it's appropriate for me to stay in the master bedroom. Maybe one of the other sixteen bedrooms will be better."

"There are only five other bedrooms," he flatly informs me and then tacks on, "Miss."

I sigh. "My point is, there are a *lot* of bedrooms."

"It's a big house, yes."

Is this guy for real? What does he know about it, anyway? I'm about to ask him how he knows Lucas when he says, "This isn't *his* room, if that's what you're worried about. His is next door." He gestures in that direction with his eyes. "This is the room he wants you to have while you're his guest."

I can't fathom why it would matter to Lucas which room I sleep in. I also can't figure out why it makes me feel tingly that he thought about it. To cover my increased discomposure, I cross to one of the huge windows and look at the backyard that slopes down to a private beach. "Oh. Well, okay. As long as I'm not imposing."

"You're not. Now, if that's all, then I'll be going. Paulette will be arriving later today. She's the housekeeper, and she can help you with anything you need."

My heart lifts at the idea that I won't be rattling around this huge house alone, but it sinks at the prospect of being put in charge of a staff member. I'm such an outsider in this world. There's no way I can pull off bossing someone around like the mistress of the castle. Tom is hardly the one I need to talk to about this. I'll give Lucas a call and tell him I don't need a housekeeper while I'm staying in his house. It's a little over-the-top, considering I'll probably dirty one towel, one plate, and one glass a day. I'm sure I can clean up after myself.

I wave goodbye to Tom, listen as he trots down the stairs and through the front door, and turn toward that incredible bed again. I have to know what it feels like.

I slink toward it like a cat sneaking up on a mouse. When I'm standing close enough that the fronts of my thighs press against its high mattress, I reach out my hands and smooth my palms across the surface of the cool, soft comforter.

"Oh, my," I say on an exhale.

Moving aside several pillows, I pull back one corner of the bedspread and slide my hand against the sheets. I've never felt anything like them. They look like cotton, but they're almost as soft as silk or satin. Hesitantly at first and then more confidently as I remember no one's here to see me, I lower my face to the bed and bury my nose in the linens. They smell like money. Okay, not the real thing, but if wealth has a scent, it's this. It's a strange amalgamation of the perfume counter at a department store, a bank lobby, leather, citrus, and sea spray.

Suddenly, as quickly as if I've been goosed, I straighten and spin in a circle, my hands covering my mouth and nose.

"Oh, my gosh," I muffle into my hands. "What. The. Figgity?!" I wonder at the entire situation. A house like this one never figured into even my wildest, most-optimistic best-selling-author dreams.

I can't wait to spend some time here, *not* writing. I can't wait to have Gus here for the weekend. I can't wait to have my morning coffee in the gazebo and swim in the infinity pool and walk in the surf. I can't wait to sleep in *that* bed.

Writer's block is the best thing that's ever happened to me.

"What is Tom?"

"You mean, *who* is he?"

Impatient to have answered the question that's been preventing me from relaxing and enjoying myself at this remarkable house, I tap my foot and fiddle with my hair as I interrogate Lucas via cell phone. "Yes. What or who is he to you? Is he your favorite chauffeur at the car service? Your valet? Your hit man?" I'm only half-joking about that last one. I've come up with crazier scenarios while I replay my interactions with the driver.

Lucas laughs. "Uh, no. But it's good to see your imagination is waking up. Tom's my driver."

"*Your* driver? As in, he drives you everywhere?" I know I sound stupid, but the question makes sense to me.

I simply sound stupid to Lucas, apparently. He answers as if he's speaking to a cross-eyed dog, "Yes. That's typically what a driver does."

"You know what I mean."

"I'm starting to think that maybe I don't, actually."

Irritated at my inability to express myself clearly, I say, "I mean, is he on your personal payroll, listed as your chauffeur? I mean, are you the type of person with the means to employ a *staff?*"

"Jayne."

"Yes?"

"I'm busy. Did you call me about something to do with our business together, or have you suddenly decided your true calling is as an auditor for the IRS?"

I realize with embarrassment how nosy and pushy I'm being. "I'm sorry," I mumble. Then in my defense, I explain, "He didn't make it clear to me what his *role* was in your life or how he knew you. I thought he was a random driver with the car service, but then he was unlocking the door and punching in the alarm code and leading me through the house like he knows the place, and then when he showed me to my room—which is awesome, by the way—"

"I'm glad you like it."

"He knew it wasn't your bedroom—"

"Is that something you were worried about?"

"Sort of. But before I could ask him, 'Hey, how do you know all this stuff?' he was telling me about some lady named Paulette—"

"She's my housekeeper, yes."

"—which, by the way, I don't need a housekeeper. That's just too weird."

"I don't want you to think about anything but relaxing and writing, when the inspiration strikes, which it will," he insists. "Now, I can email you my family tree later, if you want to know how I'm related to all the other Edwardses in the world, and I can have Sally send you a full list of all the people on my payroll—"

"You *do* have a payroll, then?"

"—but I really have to go now. I'm late for a meeting with Arthur Thornfield, who—incidentally—lists me on *his* payroll."

I feel embarrassed and awkward again. "Oh. Yeah. Okay. Well, I'll go swimming or something, then."

I can tell he's smiling, and I can even picture what that looks like when he says, "You do that. Goodbye now."

"Bye."

It's not until after I hang up and have been standing in the middle of the gleaming white and stainless steel kitchen for a while, staring off into space, that I realize we just had our first conversation that didn't include an argument.

CHAPTER NINE

As promised, Mrs. Paulette McGovern arrives later, in time to serve me a light dinner by the pool. I didn't realize she had arrived, and if she hadn't been carrying a tray of food, I may have been alarmed at the sudden appearance of a stranger when I opened my eyes during my impromptu duet with Chris Martin. Instead, I'm merely mortified.

I sit up on my lounger and pop the earbuds from my ears, letting them drop into my lap.

She pretends nothing strange has happened. "Hello there, I'm Paulette. Thought you might be peckish," she says in a delightful English accent.

Taking my cues from her, glad to ignore my embarrassing behavior, I manage to recover with, "Oh, yeah. Thanks."

As she sets the tray of food on the wrought-iron table under the umbrella, I cringe at my ignorant surprise at her attire. She's wearing a linen button-up shirt and a pair of culottes, which are classy and very comfortable-looking, but not what I expected Lucas's maid to be wearing. Unfortunately, I have to admit that I had pictured her more like one of the chamber maids in the BBC period dramas I seem to be addicted to. I feel like an idiot that I thought she'd be decked out in a black dress with a white apron and a silly little cap, like one of the girls in *Upstairs Downstairs*. I'm such a rube!

While I'm beating myself up, she says, "Luke tells me you're quite the writer."

"Quite bad?"

She laughs as if I'm joking, and I don't want to make her uncomfortable, so again, I go along with her. Or, maybe she's laughing because Lucas *did* say I was quite bad, but she's being generous and putting a positive spin on it. While I wrap my towel around myself, I study her through my peripheral vision, but I can't glean anything from her expression. She doesn't have a secret smile on her face that would indicate she's double-speaking. She's not rolling her eyes or doing anything else overtly disparaging. Her expression is blankly innocent as she positions the dishes, cutlery, glass, and pitcher of lemonade.

When I get closer to the table, my stomach growls at the sight of BLT paninis cut into neat triangles, a dainty pot of baked beans, and a generous square of strawberry cheesecake waiting for me. I stop next to the table and gaze down, delighted at the quintessentially summer meal, one that I didn't have to make for myself.

"Oh, blimey! I didn't even think to ask if you're a vegetarian or have any allergies or special dietary needs," Paulette says. "Luke didn't mention any, but that doesn't mean anything, now, does it?"

I think it's hilarious she assumes Lucas knows me well

enough to have a clue about my "dietary needs," but I'm not amused that she's worried about my opinion of the food. I reassure her as I take my seat, "It looks great. I love meat." That hasty declaration makes me blush. "I mean, I'm not a vegetarian."

She looks relieved. Maybe Lucas docks her pay for screw-ups. My heart races at the idea. Once again, I'm terrified at the prospect of having that much power over someone else.

As I'm opening my mouth to make the dangerous statement that I'll eat anything, she sits across the table from me, pours herself a glass of lemonade after pouring mine, and says, "Well, then, you eat up. And let's have a bit of a chin wag. If I'm going to be taking care of you, I'll need to know a bit about you, don't you think?"

I chew and swallow my first bite of sandwich, barely managing to keep from moaning at how delicious it is, and say, "Oh. Well, you don't have to take *care* of me. I'm very independent."

"Not while you're here, you're not," she says sweetly but firmly. "My feelings will be rather hurt if you try to do everything for yourself and ignore me."

"Okay."

"Not that I'll be a pest about it, you know. You won't even know I'm around, if you don't want me around. Luke was clear about that."

That twangs a nerve. Slowly I wipe some mayonnaise from the corner of my mouth and deliberately set the cloth napkin into my lap. "Huh. Well, you don't have to tip-toe around me, either, like I'm a diva. I don't know what Lucas told you about me, but—"

She flaps her hands in front of her chest. "Oh, no, no,

no! That's not it at all! He didn't say a word against you; that's not a bit like him. What I meant was that I'll be here when you need me but out of your way when you don't. That's all."

"Right-o."

After a swallow of lemonade, she smiles at me. "Now, then. Tell me about the foods you detest. That way, I can be sure not to make anything you don't want to eat but are too polite to refuse." When I start to protest and proclaim that I'm not picky, she cuts in with, "Ah-ah-ah! I can tell by the looks of you that you'd eat something you hate before admitting it, so don't be shy. I'm not going to judge you if you say you won't eat anything that's good for you. I can stock up at the market on crisps and sweets just as well as meat and veg."

When the only foods on my list of won't-eats are anchovies, uncooked onions, creamed corn, and beets, she relaxes in her chair, grins proudly at me like I'm a clever child who recited the alphabet in another language, and says, "There. Now that wasn't so hard, was it? I think you and I are going to be great friends."

If every meal she cooks for me is this good, I think we are.

The trouble is, I feel like I have a babysitter. Don't get me wrong; I like Paulette a lot. She hasn't said or done anything obvious to make me think she's reporting back to Lucas about what I'm doing. I have this weird feeling that she's all-knowing and all-seeing when it comes to this house, and if Lucas were to come right out and ask her what I've been up to, she'd feel obligated, as his employee, to tell him. I don't think he'd hesitate to ask her. Not for a second.

Plus, unless she's the most duplicitous person I've ever met, she seems to be under the impression that I'm a great writer. Maybe she doesn't get sarcasm (that would explain her long, happy tenure on Lucas's staff). Anyway, even though I've just met her, she's been so nice to me that I don't want to let her down. I know, that's people-pleasing of the highest, most illogical order, but I can't help it. She's very motherly, and it's satisfying a craving I didn't even know I had. She dotes on me. I haven't had someone do that in, well, twelve years. However, I feel guilty when she serves me while I lounge next to the pool.

To get an idea of what she thinks of me, I say at breakfast this morning while buttering a flaky croissant, "You must think I'm so lazy."

Of course, she denies it. "No! I haven't that opinion at all!"

Washing down a bite with a mouthful of coffee, I smile. "It's okay. I *am* being lazy. I usually write for thirteen or fourteen hours a day."

"Well, you needed a rest, then, like Luke said."

I can't stop myself from asking, "What else did he say about me?"

She doesn't hesitate when she answers, "Only that you're in the middle of publishing your first book—good for you!—and that you need a quiet place to stay so you can relax and polish your manuscript in peace," but she assigns an intense level of concentration to folding the kitchen towel she was using to mop up the area around the sink. When she continues to refuse to look me in the eye, I'm sure he said more than that. I can only imagine.

Eventually she does look up at me. "In any case, it's

good you came here, because no one else uses the house, and I'd much prefer to be here than in the city, where I live alone and only have Luke's apartment to tend. Reminds me more of home when I can be close to the sea."

With such a blatant subject change like that, it would seem obsessive and rude to continue to try to get information about Lucas from her. I dutifully ask where she's from (Dorset) and how she managed to find her way to the States (met and married a Bostonian when he was "on holiday" and stayed at her family's bed and breakfast) and how long she's worked for "Luke" (a vague "quite a while").

I'm out of questions about her, but I still have plenty about Lucas. Feeling that it's not too unnatural a loop back around to our earlier discussion, I ask, "Lucas doesn't stay here very often?"

She scrapes with her thumbnail at something on the granite counter. "Not much anymore. Used to, but he's so busy." She shrugs good-naturedly. "Well, you know how it is. Career before all else when you're young. You always think there'll be plenty of time for other things later."

Lucas has no social life. Big shocker. The guy's about as personable as a porcupine.

Even though I'm a big proponent of hermitism, I egg her on with, "That's too bad. You're only young once, right? Plus, it's a shame this big place is going to waste."

She nods eagerly. "That's what I tell him! He needs to fill it with children." Abruptly, she stops talking. Her mouth takes on a shape resembling a purse that's been zipped closed. After clearing her throat, she continues more moderately, "That is, I also understand where he's coming from. He's a good boss. It's not my place to criticize."

Damn. I was getting into this topic, too. I was hoping she'd tell me something juicy. Maybe a story about a beautiful woman he drove away with his terrible temper and wearying workaholism. Now, heartbroken, he buries himself even more in his work, lashing out at poor, unsuspecting new authors who aren't confident enough to tell him to go do something sexual to himself.

Or perhaps he's secretly pining for the busty Blanche, but he knows she doesn't return his feelings, so his love is unrequited and is eating him alive. That would at least explain his sour attitude.

Or *maybe* he made a pact with the devil that in exchange for his devastating good looks (at least, some people may call them that), he had to give up all vestiges of a personality, so he's cursed to walk through life alone, never having any relationship more meaningful than a one-night stand, because as soon as they get to know him better, women run as fast and as far away as they can. Even though he's physically perfect and a master of the sexual arts.

"Oh, dear!"

Paulette's words register at the same time as the warm wetness in my lap. I startle, spilling even more coffee onto my favorite sundress. "Well, shit!" I scold myself. Paulette passes me the dishtowel that seems to be her constant companion as she goes about her day. I swab at the tan splotch on my cotton dress while trying to hide the red splotches on my cheeks.

Laughing, Paulette watches and says, "You were a thousand miles away. Did you say hello to my sister and brother-in-law while you were there?" Soon, when it's apparent that no amount of towel-blotting is going to help the stain, she holds out her hands, "All right then. Strip to your knickers. I'll take that dress; you go upstairs and find something else to wear."

It doesn't feel strange at all to follow her orders since she's so matter-of-fact about it.

Her attitude reminds me of the woman in the fitting room of a lingerie store I visited with my mom when I was in high school and needed a special strapless, backless bra to go with my prom dress. She had casually stood by in the dressing room while I took everything off from the waist up, and then she handled my breasts like a couple of melons (fine—more like oranges) in the produce department as she took my measurements.

When I blushed and stammered, she said curtly, "There's no need to be embarrassed. I see bare breasts all day long; it's what I do." She wrote my specs down on a spiral-bound mini-notebook and tapped my shoulder with her pencil. "Now, hold tight; I'll be back in a few seconds." And then she'd left me in there to simultaneously shiver and sweat with my arms crossed over my chest.

She returned with a bustier that she wrestled me into as I held on for dear life to one of the hooks on the wall next to the changing room mirror. When she was finished, I had an hourglass shape that most supermodels would have been jealous of.

That's when Mom barged in, eager to get a look. She blinked back tears and fanned her face. "Oh, Jaynie. You're going to be stunning! Look at you!"

At the time, I was supremely annoyed at the crowd around me in my undies, but before we were even home, I'd realized that Mom and I had shared a rare woman-to-woman moment. While it may not be one of my fondest memories, I look back on it wistfully, because it's one of the very few moments like that I ever had the chance to experience with her. I had no idea at the time how precious it was.

Like the woman in the lingerie shop, Paulette is all business after I hand over my soiled dress. She doesn't even give me a second glance in my mismatched Target bra and panties but immediately turns and heads in the direction of the laundry room. Only when I'm climbing the stairs in an unfamiliar house in my underwear do I feel self-conscious, and then only a little bit. After all, there's nobody here to see me.

CHAPTER TEN

Paulette may insist she doesn't think I'm lazy, but I *know* I am, so when I've changed into clean clothes, I grab my laptop and set off in search of a place where I can concentrate and write.

There's a library, complete with dark raised wooden wall paneling, hardwood floors, fusty rugs, and an entire floor-to-ceiling wall of bookshelves, crammed with ostentatious works of Literature with a capital "L." A leather-topped desk sits in the middle of the room. The only thing on it is a green glass-shaded library lamp. The drawers are empty, except for the thin middle drawer, which contains some pens and blank pads of paper. This is definitely not where the man of the house spends time working. There's not even a phone in here.

It should be a perfect, solitary, distraction-free place for me to set up shop. It's quickly apparent, though, that it's not. Too quiet. And the stale air-conditioned air makes me feel like I'm standing in a vacuum.

Out in the hall, I cross to the door opposite the library

and push down on the handle. It doesn't budge. *Hmm, Lucas's private porn room, I presume?* I think with an evil smile. It's the only locked door I've encountered since arriving here. Interesting. I'd ask Paulette, but I don't want to seem too nosy. Anyway, it's not like it's any of my business, right? Even so, I stare at the door for a while, dying to know what's on the other side. Eventually, I give myself a little shake and blink away the possibilities, making my way through down the hall, through the kitchen, and outside.

I realize my options are limited out here, too, thanks to the antique I call my laptop, which runs on its backup battery barely long enough for me to get into a writing rhythm and then promptly dies. So I need to have access to an electrical outlet. That means I should be safe anywhere close to the house. I've noticed its outer walls are dotted with covered outlets, ostensibly for electrical lawn equipment and other outdoor appliances and conveniences.

The pool's too tempting, so I don't even consider pool-side as an option. Too hot, anyway, out there in the direct sun. I scope out the covered balcony outside the bedroom where I'm staying. After climbing the wooden stairs and coming to a shamefully breathless rest next to the railing, I determine that it's breezy, shady, close to an electrical source, and has some comfortable seating options. Yes. This could work.

My eyes land on the French doors a few feet away from where I'm standing. I set my laptop on the chaise longue, cross to the doors, look around to make sure nobody's watching, and peer through the glass at the room inside. It's a mirror image of my room in layout and a photo negative of it in color scheme. The walls are painted a deep navy blue; the baseboards and moldings are a medium gray. The floor's kitted in gray wood planks that are designed to look weathered, but I can tell from their sheen that they're smooth and un-splintered, perfect for skating across on sock-clad feet.

Black and white photographs of various sizes adorn the walls at differing heights. The ones I can see through the paneled curtains that cover the door's glass panes seem to be abstracts of common beach items (I think one is the inside of a conch shell and the other is an extreme close-up of the frayed canvas wrap on an old-fashioned life preserver). Quite artistic. The wooden furniture is painted in a high gloss to match the baseboards and molding.

And the bed. It's a nice bed. Lower than the one in my room. Platform base with a simple, rectangular headboard. Solid medium-blue bedspread with wide navy border edging. I don't let myself look at it for too long. It makes me feel squirmy, for reasons that I don't even want to explore.

Breathless, I scurry back to the chaise and snatch my laptop bag. Nearly at a run, I find the closest set of stairs to lead me down to the backyard, where I try unsuccessfully to catch my breath.

"Ahem." I clear my throat repeatedly while I swipe my bangs from my forehead and turn in circles, looking for an escape. From what, I'm not sure, considering what I want to get away from is in my head.

Never mind. Gazebo. Yes!

I lurch toward the white gingerbread structure under the sprawling oak tree and almost trip up its three short steps to the safety and seclusion it provides.

I don't know why I didn't think of coming here before (especially before I looked through that door). I know it's wired and has electrical outlets, because Paulette snuck in while I was napping here yesterday and plugged in a behemoth antique oscillating fan. It felt heavenly, and the sound of the crashing waves mere yards away was a natural tranquilizer. I probably would have slept through dinner and well into the evening if the mosquitoes hadn't chased me inside.

Now, I look around as if seeing it for the first time. Yesterday, it was just a sweet sleep spot, with the wide padded ledge ringing its inside perimeter and the lattice walls that simultaneously conceal (although it hadn't hidden me from Paulette's view) and provide a fresh cross-breeze. Today, I see it as more of a workspace, with a generous-sized rectangular table in front of one side of the octagon's padded ledges, several electrical outlets embedded in the wooden floor, and a peekaboo view of the ocean that should be compelling without being too distracting. Perfect.

Before I can talk myself out of it, I unpack my laptop and the three-inch stack of paper that is the marked-up hard copy of my manuscript from Lucas. Once I'm plugged in and booted up, I adopt the new writing strategy I've been developing in my head during my lazy poolside tanning sessions. It's always been my habit—with school work, household chores, and the various jobs I've held down to pay the bills while I've pounded out this book—to tackle the toughest part of a job first and then work my way to the easier, less taxing tasks. While that may make sense when it comes to cleaning a bathroom, it's not getting me very far with these revisions. As a matter of fact, starting with the hardest job—rewriting the fire scene—is overwhelming and defeating.

I've been toying with the idea of starting with the easy stuff (the things I would normally leave until the end) and working my way up to the Herculean task of the fire scene. Starting at the end works for solving mazes. Why wouldn't it work on difficult editors' revisions? If nothing else, it will give me a feeling of accomplishment, like I'm actually getting something done, instead of spinning my wheels on one seemingly impossible assignment. Then everything will be done but the fire scene, and I'll be able to fully focus on it. Who knows? Maybe I'll even stumble across some inspiration along the way, and I'll be eager to do the re-write.

Probably not, but I have to take my optimism where I can get it, at this point.

Without further ado, I start on page one and methodically make the changes Lucas has suggested, nay *demanded*, bookmarking and skipping over anything that gives me pause or seems complicated and time-consuming. My goal today is to get stuff done, not sit and agonize and contemplate. If I notice that familiar feeling of dread slipping in, I move on to the next comment.

In no time at all, I've reached the end of the manuscript, and I can't stop myself from grinning and saying out loud, "That's what I'm talking about!" even though it makes me feel like a goober. I'm a happy goober, and that's all that matters right now.

Quickly, before taking a break, I count how many of Lucas's requested changes I skipped (all instances of bland descriptive prose—another one of my weaknesses) and note with glee that there are far fewer than it seemed there were when I was going through the copy the first time. I'm on a roll and don't want to lose momentum, but I also recognize that I'll run out of gas if I don't refuel with some food and water. I decide I'll choose one scene—Rose's visit to her family's burial plot upon returning to her hometown after college graduation—and think about it during lunch. Notepad and pen in hand and a definite pep in my step, I cross the sunny yard of thick, velvety grass that only money can grow.

It's not a fun thing to remember, but over my tuna salad sandwich (the best one I've ever eaten, thanks to Paulette), I force myself to go sense-by-sense through the experience of seeing my family's gravesite for the first time. I ordered the headstones in the haze that was the week following the fire, but I was hundreds of miles away—probably sitting in a lecture hall, listening to a professor drone on about a subject that I didn't care about but was forced to take to fulfill a general education requirement—when they were placed. I could have taken a trip on any given weekend to visit the cemetery, but somehow it was never a priority. It definitely wasn't something high on the list of things I wanted to do. Until I was finished with college, that is. Then, I felt an almost physical need to go there.

It was technically late spring still. In Indiana, that meant it was already blazing hot. The scorched grass crunched under my shoes as I picked my way to the plot where the people I'd been closest to in the world lay buried in their caskets.

Caskets. An interesting choice I made, considering they were already partially cremated in the fire. I don't even remember making that decision. Maybe I didn't. Maybe that was one of the few things my mom's sister, Chelsea, did before she went back to her life in California and never spoke to me again. Or, maybe that was one of the things stipulated in their wills—they didn't want to be cremated. It's not something we ever sat around the dinner table and talked about. It doesn't matter, I guess, because the result was that their charred bodies were put in coffins and tossed into some holes in a depressing cemetery in central Indiana. Done. No going back.

No going back. That's what I kept telling myself while I walked closer and closer to where I knew their graves were. That, I remembered. Way in the back, almost against the chain link fence separating the graveyard from the private property that would probably eventually be bought by or donated to the cemetery as the population of the dead continued to grow and outnumber the living population in my—literally—dying hometown of Longview, sat the graves. Tangled up in the fence was a small group of honey-suckle bushes. When the wind would gust, the sweet, cloying aroma would waft my way, confirming that I was heading in the right direction. Every step I took, I contemplated turning around and running in the other direction. No going back. By the time I stood in front of the headstones, I was sweating, and it had less to do with the June heat or the relentless sun than the fact that I was wrestling with myself. My fight instinct had my flight instinct on the mats—barely.

My mind was racing as I stared down at the names as if they belonged to strangers. The letters didn't seem to be working together to form the words. Maybe it was the font in the marble. Maybe it was the neurons misfiring in my frantic brain. The cicadas in the neighboring field were deafening. There was a metallic taste in my mouth.

Shannon Lynelle Greer, beloved daughter and sister; Nicole Gayle Greer, beloved daughter and sister; Gayle Barbara Greer, dear wife, mother, daughter, and sister; Robert Leonard Greer, devoted husband, father, and son.

Jayne Ann Greer, cheater of death.

Because that's what I'd done, hadn't I? *I should be here with the rest of them*, I remember thinking miserably. I, too, should be described as the beloved daughter and sister. I would have been, had I not—at my mother's urging—attended the all-night post-graduation party hosted by the Longview High School Student Council. It wasn't really my scene, but all my friends were going, so I didn't want to be the only one who wasn't there, in case something interesting happened.

Of course, nothing did. Nobody in my graduating class was even daring enough to spike the punch or smoke a joint in the bathroom. No, the most exciting thing going on that night, unfortunately for me, was happening ten miles from where I was at the small town's civic center, at my house.

Over the years, I've tried to imagine, in split-screen fashion (like in the movies), what was happening simultaneously at different points of the night. When I was hanging out on the perimeter of the makeshift dance floor, scoffing with my friends at the slow-dancing partnerships while secretly wishing Tanner Kelley would ask me to dance, was the frayed wiring in our old farmhouse smoldering? By the time we'd moved on to the video game room, had flames developed in the walls, while my unsuspecting family members slept? As I participated in the water fight in the wee hours of the morning, was the fire spreading while the defunct smoke alarms looked on silently? At what point did the flames race up the stairs from the first floor, where they originated, to engulf the old wooden staircase, the only means of escape? During the raffle winner announcements? When I was contemplating leaving early to go home and catch a few hours of sleep in my own bed, were my sisters and parents finally waking up to the choking smoke, throwing their legs over the sides of their beds, only to have the soles of their bare feet scorch against the white-hot floor?

No. I know it didn't happen exactly like that. At least,

that's not what the fire chief told me. He said that some-thing—most likely carbon monoxide—killed them in their sleep before the fire ever started. He knows this, because there was no smoke in their lungs. Then the faulty wiring sparked in the laundry room under the stairs. He said the two events may not have been related at all. As a matter of fact, he seemed baffled and almost personally offended that the two things could happen within hours of each other. After all, carbon monoxide robs the atmosphere of oxygen, and fires need oxygen to spread. He mumbled all this under his breath, as if he were thinking out loud, instead of trying to explain to a bereft family member how something like this could happen.

Despite all his doubts about the scientific possibilities, he was my biggest supporter when rumors started to spread about something more sinister bringing about the deaths of my parents and sisters. When theories about murder-suicide (and outright murder, involving yours truly as the killer) crackled in the dry June air, he quickly doused them with his official ruling that the deaths were an accident and the fire that followed a bizarre coincidence. That was his profes-sional opinion, and he stuck by it over and over again, in newspaper articles, reports, affidavits, and insurance deposi-tions. The inconclusive coroner's report neither supported nor refuted his claims.

That's not how it happens in my book, though. Rose's family members aren't victims of a silent killer in cahoots with a tangle of wires and a dryer's full lint filter. Rose's family fights to escape the heat and smoke and flames. They die huddled together, comforting each other, not alone in their beds. I know it's better that my family didn't feel anything. A part of me blames them for not fighting death, even though I know they didn't stand a chance. I want Rose's family to have the chance mine never did.

At the light touch on my shoulder, I bungee back to the present by flinging my half-eaten sandwich into the air.

"Oh, dear," Paulette says mildly, her eyes pinned to the food on the patio stones. "Now look what I've done. And I only wanted to see that you were alive."

More sharply than I mean to, I reply, "Of course, I'm alive!"

Sheepishly, she explains, "I got an email from a friend once that told a story about a man who sat dead at his desk at work for five days before anyone thought it was odd that he wasn't moving, and they discovered that he was deceased. I'd hate for that to happen to someone I know."

I rub my eyes. "You shouldn't believe everything you read in emails."

"No! It was a true story! I've been terrified ever since. I pester Luke by relentlessly checking on him when he's around. He's exactly the sort of person that could happen to."

Yeah, but only because no one would care if he dropped dead at his desk.

I blush as if she can hear my thoughts. "Oh. Well. I'm fine. Just thinking."

"You've been working so hard this morning. Maybe a rest by the pool will do you some good this afternoon," she suggests as she efficiently scoops up the remnants of my sandwich. "Would you like me to make you another sandwich?"

"No," I say in answer to both her statement and question. "Thank you, but I'm going to get back to it. I think. I mean, maybe I know how I'm going to write something."

Not here, though. Swiftly I rise and hurry in the direction of the gazebo, despite my worry that I'll frighten off the words if I move too suddenly. They're like skittish, capricious butterflies that have honored me with their company.

Based on this morning's work, though, I know that they'll still be with me by the time I get to the gazebo. I've felt this way before.

CHAPTER ELEVEN

"**A**nd who is *this*?"

I can't place the haughty voice with the harsh Boston accent. It isn't Paulette, and it certainly isn't the voice of the fire chief who was describing to Rose what had happened to her family in the second chapter I've pounded into my laptop keys since lunch.

With what amounts to a surprising amount of effort, I lift my head on my stiff neck and blink at the silhouette before me. I see hands on hips, elbows flared, and massive sunglasses pushed on top of a cascading mane of dark hair. My shoulder muscles creak as I move from my hunched-over position for the first time in hours.

Before I can decide if I'm going to introduce myself to this stranger, I see the familiar shape of Paulette catch up and hover at the gazebo steps.

She answers for me, "This is Jayne. Luke invited her to stay."

I still can't see any details of the stranger's face, but it's clear by her tone that she's looking down her nose at me. "How generous of him—and ballsy—in my house."

Recovering from my writing stupor, I stand so that I'm not looking into the sun bouncing off the shiny wooden floor. Reflexively, I offer her my hand, even though I think she's insulting me, and it's slightly absurd for me to uphold niceties if that's the case. An introduction is *definitely* in order, if for no other reason than to disabuse her of the ludicrous assumptions I think she's making.

"Hi, I'm Jayne Greer, one of Lucas's writers." I falter on the last word, not sure how to describe myself. Client? Not really. Project? More accurate. Thorn in side? Ding, ding, ding!

"I'm sure you are," she replies snarkily.

"And you are?" I verbally nudge her like a mother hinting to a child that she needs to mind her manners.

Paulette nervously interjects, "Oh! Goodness me! Where are my manners? Caroline, this is Jayne Greer... er, which she already told you. Jayne, this is Caroline O'Shea-Edwards, Luke's... er, right... That is..."

"His wife," Caroline O'Shea-Edwards supplies smoothly and smugly. "At least, legally that's still the case, last time I checked."

"Oh! How nice!" I utter, with all the fake enthusiasm of a reporter who's trying her hardest to make a report about Congressional budget talks sound exciting and glamorous and like something she's interested in. Truthfully, I'm trying not to laugh. What I want to say is, *How absolutely hilarious that Lucas is* married, *and to a nightmare like you.* I manage to simply smile into her ice-cold gray eyes.

My smile fades, however, when she says in an equally phony voice, "Yes, well, I'm so sorry to be the one to tell you this, but you're going to have to leave."

Paulette and I speak at the same time.

"Okay."

"What? Wait. Caroline, Luke said—"

"I don't care what *he* said, and neither should you," she snaps, turning her full attention to the housekeeper. "The house in town is being repainted, and I can't stay there. This is *my* house; my daddy gave it to *me*; and I have the right to stay here whenever I want, no matter what promises Lucas has made to complete strangers. What is this, some sort of charity for him? If he uses the house for 'business' x-number of days, we get a tax write-off, or something?" She tosses her glossy chestnut hair over her shoulder and thrusts her pointy nose into the air and her designer purse into Paulette's arms. "You can put that in the yellow room for me."

She apparently thinks she's finished with me. Which is fine, except I don't appreciate being dismissed. I clear my throat. She turns around and look me up and down as if she has no idea who I am or how I appeared in front of her.

"Hey," I begin with a casual wave, as if to say, *It's me again; still here.* "The thing is, I know this is your house—well, I *don't* know that, but you say it is, and I don't have any reason to question that—but the thing is…"

Now I'm stuck. What *is* the thing? The rational part of me is screaming for me to pack as quickly as possible and get the hell out of here. The creative side of me is sobbing, begging for me to figure out a way to stay in the only place in which I've been able to write for weeks. And not simply write—write *well*. Write *inspired*. Telling something like that to a person like Caroline O'Shea-Edwards is probably the fastest way to get evicted. She'd kick me out for the fun of it.

Desperately, I toss out a lie. "The thing is, I was getting ready to leave tomorrow. Yep. Today was my last day." Sure. That works. I mean, I can pull an all-nighter. I can type all my handwritten copy into my electronic manuscript, get a few hours' sleep, and be on the next train (taxi? Ferry?

Bike?) to Boston in the morning, when I can deliver the finished product to Lucas. Lord knows I don't want to be in the middle of what sounds like a house-custody battle between the scariest couple on the planet.

Unmoved, she says drily, "Good. Then I'm not cutting your visit too short. I'd feel so guilty about that."

I pretend to misunderstand her and act relieved. "Yeah. Exactly. So, I'll leave in the morning, as planned, and then you'll be rid of me. Thanks!"

Before she can object, I gather my things and practically run into the house after Paulette, who's already upstairs in the "yellow room," which—funnily enough—is what I've been calling simply "my room."

I stop short. "Oh. Yeah. I guess this room *is* yellow. She wants to stay in here, huh?"

Paulette doesn't pause in her frantic stripping of the bed. "Yes. Of course. Whatever's most difficult. I'm sure she came up here first to see which room was taken before deciding it was the one she wanted."

Without thinking, I circle to the other side of the bed and pull the sheets from the corner furthest from Paulette. "Yeah, why doesn't she sleep in the master bedroom?" I wonder, taking advantage of the housekeeper's uncharacteristic show of disapproval in a bid to get more information.

The moment has passed. She seems to remember her "place" and merely purses her lips so hard they turn white. Then she says, "Never mind. I'll help you pack."

Even though I'm a little hurt she's not acting more regretful at my imminent departure, I recognize where her loyalties lie—with the family who pays her.

"Actually, Caroline said it's okay if I stay one more night. So I'll move my stuff wherever you think is best."

She stops moving to smile at me. "Oh, good! I'm so glad

you're not rushing off today. It's not fair, anyway. You're not finished with your book, are you?"

I shrug sheepishly. "It'll be okay," I say unconvincingly. "I'm almost there."

A scowl fleetingly crosses her face, but then, just as quickly, it returns to a state of blank innocence, and she stoops to gather the bed linens in her arms. "You can move across the hallway into the lilac room, if you like. It's the closest."

It's not like I have a ton of stuff to move, since I haven't technically unpacked (I'm getting used to living out of suitcases), but I'm all for convenience. The few items that have made it out of my suitcases—laptop, cell phone, MP3 player, paper and pen—now go back in one of them before I zip it and wheel it with its identical twin across the hall into the "lilac room."

It is very *that*. Lilac, that is. Subtlety wasn't an object in the interior design of this bedroom. It's color-themed in a way the "yellow room" never seemed to be. In addition to everything being a light purple, including the wood furniture that at first glance looks white but is, on closer inspection, a very faint hue of, yes, lilac, there are silk approximations of lilacs and lavender in cut crystal vases scattered throughout the room. There are even framed prints of lilacs on the walls and a few dried cuttings in shadowboxes. Well, the good thing is that I can't picture anyone having sex in *this* room, which seems more fitting for a grandmother. The only thing I can picture someone doing in here is having a virtual allergy attack.

Well, it's only for one night, so who cares? The bed is another one of those high numbers that requires a tiny set of steps in order to climb onto it, and the percale sheets under the white eyelet comforter are probably every bit as soft as the ones in the "yellow room." To be sure, I walk over to it and run my hand under the covers. Yep. Six-thousand thread count. Approximately.

Now a faint ringing makes me snatch my hand away from the bed, as if I've been caught doing something naughty. It takes me a second to figure out it's my suitcase making the noise, and then I realize it must be my cell phone ringing, which reminds me that I have to break the news to Gus that he won't be able to come visit here this weekend. That's going to be an unpleasant conversation.

As I'm unzipping my bag and reaching in it for my phone, Caroline swoops past my door and turns into the room across the hall. She's saying to a trailing Paulette, "But then you disappeared on me! Anyway, while you're at the store, make sure you pick up some lobster, shrimp, and steaks for grilling out. Not too many. It'll only be me, but I'm craving surf and turf. None of that aged beef, though. I'm not sure I can handle that in my delicate state. As a matter of fact, maybe seafood's not a good idea. Too much mercury."

"Hello? Jayne? Are you there?"

I've been so intent on eavesdropping that I haven't had the brainpower to multitask and say anything after hitting the button to answer my phone. Now my brain reminds me that the caller ID told me Luke-Ass was calling, and that the proper greeting is:

"What? I mean, I'm here!"

Or not. But it'll do.

He chuckles nervously. "For a second there, I thought I heard someone else and was afraid I'd dialed the wrong number."

I try to tune into our conversation and block out Caroline's continuing loud debate with herself about whether or not to eat seafood ("or is it only shellfish and sushi I'm supposed to avoid? Too many rules! I'm dying for a lobster tail!"). Finally, I close the door and retreat to the end of the bed, which I lean against with my hip.

"Sorry. I was distracted," I explain succinctly.

"Not too distracted, I hope," he replies. "Someone tells me you're doing a lot of writing."

Without the usual annoyance and frustration fueling it, the statement, "I wish you'd stop using Paulette to spy on me," comes out sounding as mundane as a request for him to copyedit something I've emailed to him.

"I'm not spying! I'm simply getting information from someone else so that I don't have to bother you."

"Spying."

"Semantics. Anyway, how's it going?" He sounds the happiest I've ever heard him. Which puts me on my guard.

"Fine. Almost finished."

"You are?! That's great!"

"Yeah."

When I don't expound, he prods, "Well? Are you happy with what you've written?"

"Does it matter?"

"Sure. To some extent. Do you think *I'll* like it?"

"No." I'm deliberately being difficult, because I don't trust his motives for asking. I mean, who is this guy, anyway? Now I find out he has a wife? What about the buxom Blanche? Does *she* know about his wife? Because, really, I don't care. I bet Blanche would. Is he playing her?

"What do you mean?" he asks, refusing to let me get away with monosyllabic answers, his smile no longer audible. "Please don't hand me any more crap and try to pretend like that's the best you can do so that I'll leave you alone and publish your book, as-is. It doesn't work that way. You'll work on it until you get it right."

Hackles: raised.

"I don't think it's crap, okay? It's damn good."

"Oh. Well, good."

"I don't know if it'll be up to *your* standards, but that's a whole different story."

I hear him take a deep breath and then exhale. After a few seconds, he says, "I'll take what I can get right now. So, when do you think you'll be sending me something?" Before I can answer, he rushes on, the enthusiasm back, "Or, I have a better idea! I'll come there this weekend, and we can look over it there. I could use a weekend at the beach."

"Perfect," I say sarcastically. "Only I won't be here this weekend. Would you like me to leave the manuscript with Mrs. Edwards?"

The silence that greets my question is so complete that I think for a minute that we've been disconnected and he never heard the question at all. Which would be a pity, because I'm pretty proud of how seamlessly it fit into our conversation.

As I'm about to hang up and wait for him to call me back, he says, "Shit. Tell me she's not there."

"That would be a lie, unfortunately."

"When did *she* get there? Sonofa… Sally!" he yells a little bit away from the phone but not enough that it doesn't hurt my ear. I hear Sally's faint response in the background. "Get my wife on the phone for me right now… No, not my cell phone, *obviously*, since I'm currently holding that one to my ear; my *desk* phone. Let me know when you have her."

"Listen, I don't want to get in the middle of anything," I say, trying to talk as quickly as possible before a call goes through to Caroline, who's still right across the hall, dictating an endless grocery list to Paulette. "I just thought you should know that I'm leaving."

"Well, where are you going to go?" he asks hotly and then doesn't wait for an answer. "When did she get there?"

"About a half hour ago. I'll go back to my friend's apartment until I find something more permanent. Or I could go back to Indianapolis, and we can conduct our business through email and phone."

At least in Indy, I'll have my blankie and my candle, so I know I'll be able to write. It's no seaside *mansion*, but it's better than Gus's place. I don't know why I didn't think of it before, actually.

Unfortunately, I don't want to go back to Indiana at all. It's *not* better than Gus's place, if I'm being honest with myself. Not at all. It's lonely. I know hermits aren't supposed to feel lonely, but I didn't feel a gaping hole in my life when there was no one there. Now that I've had the company of Gus and Paulette, people who seem to *care* about me, for reasons unknown (although in Paulette's case, it's probably more a matter of her being *paid* to care), I don't want to go back to my solitary existence, no matter how comforting the familiar surroundings would be at first.

How did this get so out of control? I naively thought that I'd pop into Boston, meet with Mr. Editor, and then my book would get published, all in the span of a week or two. Okay, maybe not *quite* like that, but I did think it would be a lot tidier than this.

This is a business trip turned vacation turned writing retreat turned reality TV show.

"Don't go anywhere," he orders firmly.

"Well, I'm not going anywhere today, but she wants me to leave in the morning," I explain.

"No. You were there first."

"It's her house."

"Well, legally, maybe. But we had a deal. Sally!"

I jerk the phone away from my ear and mouth, "Ow," while he asks Sally if Caroline's on the phone yet and then tells her to clear his schedule for the rest of the afternoon when she tells him Caroline's not answering her phone. I've never heard someone actually give the order to "clear his schedule" before. In real life. Not on TV. It makes me snort back a giggle.

To me, he says, "I'm on my way. Don't move."

"That could get very uncomfortable. Even more uncomfortable than I already am, stuck in the middle of... whatever this is. My foot's already falling asleep in this position." When he insists and then hangs up without a goodbye, I have to admit that a tiny piece of me is glad I may not have to leave. A big piece of me. As a matter of fact, I'm pinning all of my hopes on Lucas using his considerable intimidation skills on his wife to get her to go away. My book kind of depends on it.

CHAPTER TWELVE

O h, the yelling! It's been going on for over an hour now. Paulette and I have shared an entire pot of tea (so much for sleeping tonight), sitting across the table from each other, mostly avoiding eye contact, but every once in a while unable to resist wide-eyed looks at each other in response to what they're saying in the next room. It's probably not right to eavesdrop, but since I have a fairly high stake in this, I feel justified.

Lucas and Caroline, of course, have no idea we're in here listening. I was going to wait out in the gazebo, but on my way through the kitchen to the back door, Paulette snagged my arm. She put a finger to her lips and pointed to the wooden table, which she had set for tea for two. Snack and a show. I didn't protest for a single second. I mean, this is riveting stuff.

Unfortunately, they haven't gotten around to discussing *me* yet.

They've been too busy screaming at each other for things dating back to their engagement. It's a wonder the two of them ever got married. It *was* a mystery why they're still together, until Lucas interrupts Caroline in the middle of an old grievance about a broken gravy boat and says:

"Just stop it! Stop! None of that has anything to do with why I'm here!" I can picture him pacing the airy living room in efficient, long strides. "You're trying to distract me, but it's not going to work."

"I want you to admit, after all these years, that you broke that gravy boat—a family heirloom—and then tried to hide it from me. Or, at the very least you're protecting one of the help," she hisses.

The help? I squirm in my chair and fiddle with the cotton ties on the red and white gingham seat cushion. Those two words seem to rest between Paulette and me like a racial slur. We're both doing our best to ignore it so that we don't have to acknowledge the subtle hierarchical differences that exist between even the two of us.

"I'm not going to get into your unhealthy obsession with possessions in general and that hideous piece of pottery in specific. Unless you want to talk about this *house*, which I do. Because we had a deal, Caroline." As his voice lowers, Paulette and I both lean closer to the wall that separates the two rooms. I'm practically hanging off the side of my chair.

"Screw the deal. I changed my mind," she says, sounding like a spoiled brat.

He laughs the most unamused laugh I've ever heard. "Too. Bad. If you don't want to keep up your end of it, then fine. As a matter of fact, great! I'll have my lawyer call your lawyer."

Again, I have to struggle to keep from laughing out loud at all these TV-script lines creeping into his speech today.

I don't need to worry about anyone hearing me laugh, though, because it would be drowned out by the screeching, "No!" that Caroline lets loose.

Lucas doesn't change his tone at all. "Yes. It's up to you. It's an easy fix. I'm perfectly content to continue our agreement, exactly as we've been doing for the past two years. I get this house; you keep our marriage on paper and in public. It's simple."

"You know it's not simple!" She's downright hysterical now, but she may as well be behaving like a rational person, based on Lucas' reaction to her.

"Yeah, it is. What's more important to you? Using a house *maybe* three weeks out of the year or keeping your parents and so-called friends in the dark about the end of our marriage? It makes no difference to me, Caroline."

If I didn't think I knew him better, I'd say he was being *gentle* with her. It almost sounds like he's reasoning with a child in the throes of a temper tantrum over choices. *Do you want to go swimming in the ocean or in the pool? You can't do both. You have to choose.*

When she doesn't answer him, he says more forcefully, "Come on! I have a life. Whatever you choose doesn't affect it either way, but I'd like to get back to it. You want this house back, then we draw up the divorce papers. You leave here, I'll pretend this never happened, and we go on like before. I'll see you a few times a year at your parents' house for Thanksgiving, Christmas, what have you, and I'll make sure I sign the tax return and get it in the mail before the deadline each April. It's not like I ever want to get married again."

Now it's obvious he's merely talking to fill the silence while she comes to the decision he's almost sure will benefit him the most. It also sounds like he's reciting something he's said several times in the past. I peek at Paulette from the corner of my eye and see that she's listening with her mouth hanging open, absent-mindedly rubbing her bottom lip with the tip of her thumbnail.

"I do love this house," Lucas continues. "It's perfect for relaxation in the summer and solitude in the winter, but it's a small price to pay for being rid of you forever. Now I'm not sure which decision I'd prefer you make," he says, sounding surprised. "No house, bad; no Caroline, good. House, good; putting up with your bullshit theatrics for the rest of my life, bad."

"Screw you!" she shouts.

Now he laughs. "Uh, no. That was a major mistake. Moment of weakness not to be repeated, ever. Plus, don't you have *people* for that?"

"You are the biggest dickhead on the planet!"

In this moment, I can't help but sympathize with Caroline. I know only too well how he can drive someone crazy with his smugness.

"How can you joke about that?" she asks in a tortured voice.

"About what?" After a pause, he says, "Oh, come off it! Surely, you're not serious. *You* were the one who made such a big deal about it being wrong. I mean, I was okay with it. It was not the best I've ever had, but it had been a while, so I thought it was fun. Harmless, in any case. You went on and on about it being the biggest mistake of your life, and you weren't happy until I agreed. You hounded me for a week afterwards, first apologizing and then begging me to tell you *I* was sorry. Even though I wasn't. I mean, we *are* married. We used to do it all the time—"

"Enough! Oh my God, my nerves are shot!"

I hear the squeak of leather as someone sits on the sofa, followed shortly after by another squeak.

"Hey, I'm sorry. I'm only joking, you know, trying to get

you to make a decision. Remember how you used to like that?"

"I *never* liked that, Lucas. You know it's always made me furious. And don't touch me."

"Oh. Well, it's hard to tell the difference with you, sometimes. Anyway, what's it gonna be? I need to know what to tell Jayne. She's supposed to be here working, you know."

The ice is back in Caroline's voice as she says, "Oh, yes. Your pet, Jayne."

"Don't be an idiot." More squeaking, and then his voice comes closer to the kitchen door.

Paulette jumps up and grabs the first thing she sees (the teapot), carrying it to the sink, where she dumps out the dregs and makes a big show of looking busy and rinsing it. I remain glued to my chair, paralyzed by panic at the idea of being caught listening. He stays in the other room, apparently standing on the other side of the door while he explains, "She's just another writer. A head case, at that."

Wow. Now it's Paulette's turn to pretend she didn't hear anything. Frankly, I'd rather be called "the help" than a "head case," no matter how accurate his description is.

"I sent her here to get her out of my hair for a couple of weeks, and now you're effing everything up. As usual."

"You've never let any of your other authors use the house. Not even the good ones. Why is that, Lucas?" Her patronizing tone is insufferable. I can only imagine the pounds per square inch of pressure Lucas is exerting on his jaw. "Don't try to bullshit me."

"Wouldn't dream of it, Darling. Now, be a good girl and go pack up your things."

"No. I told you, they're painting the house in town. I can't stay there."

"Shit, Caroline!" What sounds like a punch rattles a

shelf of collector's teacups on the wall three feet away from me. "Do you know how awkward this is for me? I—"

"I don't care! It's obvious your precious Jayne didn't know you even had a wife, so I'm sure you have some explaining to do there, but I have bigger things to worry about than that."

Paulette rejoins me at the table. Twisting a dish towel between her fingers, she stares intently at the kitchen door as Caroline's kitten-heeled shoes click across the wood floor.

Lucas murmurs barely audibly, "As in…?"

Tearfully, and sounding tortured, his wife answers, "I'm pregnant."

When Paulette was unable to hold back her bark of a laugh, and I fumbled the spoon I was mindlessly fingering, the crying came to an abrupt stop, and the door flew open. The two of us couldn't have looked guiltier if we'd been stuffing the silver into a big black bag. I suddenly remembered how to use my legs, though, and took off with my laptop out the back door, practically running toward the gazebo, where I should have been the whole time, anyway. I didn't even stick around long enough to hear how Paulette explained herself.

Well, so much for staying here to finish my revisions. Even if Caroline magically changes her mind—not likely after catching me so obviously listening in on a conversation with her husband—there's no way I can stay here. I'm mortified. Plus, now I know *way* too much about Luke-Ass's private life. His messy, depressing private life. Ick.

Not to mention, he thinks I'm a bothersome head case. I guess I already knew he thought that, but it's another thing to hear someone come right out and say it.

Abandoning the pretense of working on my book, I set aside my open laptop and cross the wooden gazebo floor so that I'm peering through the lattice at the beach below. The water looks hard today. Like the waves are slapping the surf, instead of caressing it. It's not that the water is choppy—on the contrary, it looks as smooth as sapphires—but the waves are breaking with tremendous force, as if they're trying to punish the ocean floor. I wonder what's happening way out in the ocean, where these swells are forming. Is there a storm that's not even visible this far away? Or is the cause something as simple as high winds? Whatever the reason, I can't take my eyes off the waves, even when I begin to cringe as I anticipate their violent breaking.

Here in Marblehead, it's a blue-sky, puffy clouds day, the kind of day that epitomizes the word, "summer." The weather doesn't seem to have a clue that people like Lucas and Caroline Edwards exist or that their toxicity could seep into others' lives. The ocean looks like it has experience with their type.

The sound of footfalls on the gazebo's steps alerts me to company. Expecting to see Paulette when I turn around, my expression is one of mutual sheepishness at our being caught eavesdropping. It quickly shifts to pure embarrassment, complete with blushing and perspiring, when I see that Lucas is my visitor. I was hoping that Paulette would deliver my things to me, with the request from my hosts that I leave as soon as possible. I would have been okay with that. I would have understood. I would have been grateful not to have an uncomfortable confrontation regarding my gauche behavior.

Before I can grope for the right thing to say, he sits down on the top step, turns mostly away from me and says to his feet, "I'm sorry you heard all that."

"I—huh, what?" is the intelligent utterance that plops from my mouth in response.

He's rolled up his shirtsleeves to below his elbows, and the top two buttons of his shirt are undone. He slides off his shoes and peels off his socks, stuffing them into his shoes, which he sets aside on the steps. "I didn't realize you were trying to have tea with Paulette in the kitchen."

I start to confess that we were only having tea in there so we could eavesdrop but hold back, barely, and say instead, "Don't worry about it. Life is... messy... sometimes."

Glancing over his shoulder at me, he clarifies, "No. I meant... I'm sorry you heard us talking about... you."

That's right. I'd almost forgotten that I had a bit part in their drama as the high-maintenance head case. Pretending I don't care, I shrug. "Whatever. It's not like I didn't already know you feel that way."

Shortly, he replies, "I don't, of course. Don't be ridiculous." He clambers to his feet and steps up into the structure. Sand rasps between his bare feet and the floorboards. At my skeptical glare, he says, "I only said that to Caroline so she wouldn't jump to any insane conclusions of her own."

"'Insane' is right."

"Level-headedness isn't one of her strong suits," he replies, incorrectly assuming I'm referring to her, when really I'm talking about her insinuation regarding Luke-Ass's relationship to me.

I refuse to say anything bad about her. I hardly know her or their situation, for one thing. More than that, she's his wife. Sort of. And, apparently, the mother of his unborn child.

I'm trying to figure out if it's appropriate to congratulate him about his impending fatherhood when he narrows his eyes at me. "Why would I think you're crazy, anyway? Is there something you're not telling me? Because as far as I can tell, you're remarkably ordinary."

He makes it sound like more of an insult than anything he said about me to Caroline.

Compared to her, I *do* seem relatively normal. Who bickers about a gravy boat when she's pregnant, her marriage is at stake, and her husband is enumerating all the ways he's willing to continue to perpetuate the sham that it currently is? Lady, forget about the damn gravy boat!

I'm more concerned with puzzling through this than responding to his questions. He eventually gives up on hearing an answer and says, "Well, I'm going for a walk on the beach." He bends over and rolls up his trousers. "Being around Caroline always makes me want to walk into the ocean and never come out again."

I snort at his description.

"You think I'm kidding. Anyway, I have to figure out how I'm going to get her the hell out of here. My usual bargaining chips are nothing in the face of what she said in there."

About that. He's being awfully callous about it. I mean, I can understand that it may not be the best news in the world, coming from someone who makes you want to kill yourself, but I think you'd have to be incredibly jaded not to be moved by it. Even if it's moved in a negative way. Show *some* emotion! He's so flat.

None of my business, I warn myself sternly before calling him on his unemotional state. For all I know, he's a wreck on the inside. He *does* strike me as one of those people who experiences strong feelings but rarely lets anything but anger show. And even when he lets his temper get the best of him (which is often), he usually rapidly recovers and then appears as if nothing happened. Maybe *he's* crazy.

At least some hint of my thoughts must be apparent in my expression, because when he straightens and glances at me, he sighs. As if explaining the situation to someone who spent much of her childhood eating lead paint chips, he says, "She's not, you know. Pregnant. She makes this claim every time we've been... together. She had a full-blown hysterical pregnancy once, because she convinced herself so thoroughly of it."

"TMI," I mutter before I can stop myself.

"Pardon?"

Blushing, I say quickly, "Never mind. I'll pack my stuff. Is there a bus stop nearby?" Marblehead doesn't seem like the type of place to attract too many bus travelers, but it's the first mode of transportation that springs to mind when I think, *Get me the hell away from this dysfunctional nightmare.*

He looks down his nose at me. "No."

"Well, I guess I'll call a cab?"

"I mean, no, you're not leaving." When I flinch at his firm tone, he revises, "Unless you want to, that is."

I gaze longingly down at my laptop, which was mere hours ago the instrument of some of the most inspired, free-flowing writing I've ever experienced. Ever ever. I *don't* want to go. I want to stay here and finish my book. But not if Contemptible Caroline's going to be hanging around, too.

As if he can read my mind, he says quietly, "I promise I'll get her to go away. Somehow. It may take a day or two, though."

"I don't want to get in the middle of this—whatever you two have going on," I tell him for what feels like the thousandth time, "but I *was* writing well before she got here."

He raises his eyebrows. "Oh? Anything you'd be willing to share with me? After my walk, of course. I desperately need to, uh, clear my head."

I'm loath to show him anything yet. Not until I've had a chance to proofread at least three times everything I've written today. "Maybe tomorrow?"

"So you'll stay?" he checks, backing down the gazebo steps and continuing his backpedaling through the grass, toward the beach.

I nod and sit at the table, resting my fingers on my laptop keys. "Yeah. If it's okay."

His smile makes a brief appearance before ducking behind his usual serious expression. "More than okay. And, please, don't worry about this thing with Caroline. Concentrate on your writing, and I'll take care of everything else. Without involving you at all. I promise."

Again, I nod, but I don't know how he can make such a promise. Seems to me like Caroline's the one in control, not him.

CHAPTER THIRTEEN

Why did I agree to participate in this ridiculously awkward farce of a dinner? I feel like the sullen daughter caught in the middle of her parents' rancorous divorce as I poke at my new potatoes and endeavor to get through the meal without uttering a single syllable. My parents in this analogy are arguing and insulting each other without saying a direct negative word.

Lucas started it with, "Darling, make sure you eat your vegetables, especially that spinach. Folic acid is good for the baby, you know."

Caroline added a heaping serving spoonful to the current no-thank-you helping on her plate. "Yes, that's right. And you should double up on your steak portions. Iron and protein will help with that little problem you sometimes have in the bedroom, Dear."

If I didn't believe he was physically incapable of it, I'd say he blushed. "Oh, now don't exaggerate," he said in a cavalier tone. "That's only ever happened in the presence of trolls posing as normal, sane women. It's a brilliant manifestation of natural selection." He smiled charmingly at her.

Back and forth they go until I set my fork down with a clank, pick up my plate, and carry it into the kitchen. Paulette's in here, busy cleaning up. At my entrance, she turns from the sink, where she's scrubbing a broiler pan, and watches me plop into one of the chairs at the kitchen table.

"Everything all right, luv?"

I stab at my food. "Yes. Now it is, since I'm no longer eating in the same room as those two lunatics."

She snickers. "Oh, they're passionate, that's for sure."

"Passionate?!" I nearly choke on my food. After swallowing, I state, "They're horrible. What even possessed them to ever get married?"

Matter-of-factly, she answers, "Money, mostly, I'd say." She goes back to scrubbing the pan. "Although I think they had an affection for each other at first. I know Luke was quite smitten with Caroline. When you're young, it's exciting to be with someone who's a little wild. That excitement wears off once adult life sets in, I'm afraid."

It probably helps that Caroline's movie-star beautiful, too. I don't add that to the commentary, though. It will only prompt Paulette to assure me of my own attractiveness, and the last thing I want is for her to think I'm comparing myself to Caroline, for any reason. Plus, I don't have any illusions about my looks. You can dress up my first name any way you'd like, but I'm still as plain as any regular old Jane, "y" notwithstanding.

Of the three of us sisters, Shannon was the prettiest. Everyone said it. It went this way: I was (I suppose, *am*) the smart one; Shannon was the pretty one; and Nicole was the funny one. I don't think it's allowable to be more than one thing. So "smart" it is. Not pretty. Not funny. Just smart. And not necessarily in the sense of "intelligent." I'd say it's more of a creative smart than anything. Not that I'm complaining.

It's served me well. Until today, that is. Today, I'm cursing it, because it's landed me in this predicament.

Not for the first time, I'm wondering why I couldn't get the standard, kind, grandfatherly—or better yet, grand-motherly—editor, who patiently marks run-on sentences and other minor grammatical misdemeanors and maybe offers some mild suggestions for improvement here and there regarding diction or syntax. No, I had to get peppery, volatile Lucas Edwards, with his demands for major revisions, his gorgeous house on Marblehead, and his train wreck of a personal life. Eff me.

If it weren't for the magical gazebo in his backyard, I'd be running away from this place as fast as I could.

All conversation seems to have ceased in the adjoining dining room, but I'm not going back out there. Their strained silences are surely as bad for digestion as their snarky comments. I'm fine with eating in here, like one of "the help."

I'm swallowing the last bite from my plate when Lucas comes through the swinging door with his hands full of dirty dishes and cutlery.

Paulette glances at him and clucks the admonishment, "I would have gotten those, Luke. How many times have I told you?"

He sets the plates next to the sink and shrugs. "Why? I have legs and hands and arms, and I wanted to see if Jayne had told you how rude and inappropriate Caroline and I were being at the dinner table."

I can't help but smile at his acknowledgment, but before I can reply to his indirect apology, Paulette says with a nervous glance at the dining room door, "Oh, I already knew it. Jayne didn't have to tell me anything. You and Caroline are like two children."

"She went up to bed, so you don't have to worry about her hearing you." He leans against the counter and comes close to whining when he says, "Why won't she go away, Paulette? Why does she insist on making my life miserable?"

Suddenly it occurs to me that he didn't see me sitting over here in the corner when he came in. I want to leave the room or at least signal my presence, but another part of me wants to hear Paulette's take on it. I have to say, as much as I hate that I'm in the middle of this soap opera, I can't help but be interested in what led up to all this.

She nudges him gently away from the dishwasher so she can open it and put the dirty dishes into it. While she bends over to load the appliance, she replies, "It's not my place to say."

"I'm asking you, though. I'm giving you a place," he insists.

Sighing, she says, "If you truly want my opinion…"

"I do!"

"She's always gotten her way. Why should this be any different? She wants this house back, apparently."

He runs his hand through his hair. "What does she want more: the house or her parents' approval? It used to be no contest. The threat of divorcing her—usually the ultimate trump card—seems to be having no effect on her at all this time!"

Paulette simply shrugs. "I don't know what you want me to say, Luke. Other than maybe it's time you stop threatening her and do it."

That statement makes him slouch and stare into space. "This whole pregnancy nonsense is an interesting complication, though," he mutters. "What if she's not lying this time?"

Now Paulette peeks over at me. Lucas follows her eye

line. His entire demeanor changes. Gone is the lost little boy look, the helpless, unfocused stare, and the slack face. His eyebrows ram together, and he draws to his full height.

"Jayne. I didn't realize you were in here. I thought, maybe, you'd gone out to the gazebo."

I nod to my plate. "Thought I'd finish eating first. Unless you think I should forgo eating to finish my manuscript as quickly as possible." I'm half-joking. Which means I'm half-not.

He looks confused. "What?" His expression changes to one of impatience and exasperation. "Of course not. That makes no sense at all. I invited you to dine with Caroline and me."

"Well, that wasn't the most relaxing dinner conversation, as you already know." I take my plate and glass to Paulette. After she receives them from me, I move to the other side of the large kitchen, lean up against the counter, cross my bare legs at the ankle, and stuff my hands in my hoodie pockets.

"I apologize for that. And I started it, so I have no excuse."

"You don't have to make excuses to me. From now on, if it's all the same to you, I'll eat in here. Alone."

His closed-off expression gives no clue as to what he's feeling when he concedes, "Fine. Whatever you like."

I scrunch my shoulders up close to my ears. "Not that I'll be here much longer."

Before I can explain, he jumps on my statement. "Oh? Are you almost finished?"

"No," I relate regretfully. "I can't stay here with all this going on. It's uncomfortable and distracting and none of my business."

He curses under his breath, his face resembling how it

looked when he was talking to Paulette before he realized I was in the room. "Please, Jayne. Give me a couple of days. If I can't get her to leave, then by all means, I'll help you find somewhere else to stay and work."

"You don't have to—"

"I want to!"

From anyone else, it would sound generous. From him, it sounds angry.

I pull my head back at his gruff tone and say, "Whoa. Tone down the intensity, all right?"

Finished with her kitchen cleanup, Paulette quietly slips from the room, leaving us alone.

When she's gone, he begins, "I'm sorry, but—"

I interrupt, "What's your deal, anyway? Why is it so important to you that I stay here to work on my manuscript? It makes no sense. I'm one more complication in this cluttered situation." I hate how Gus's overuse of that word makes me hesitant to use it, even when it's the best option for vaguely describing something you can't otherwise name, like this.

Lucas misinterprets that hesitation as diplomacy. "I know it's ugly here. I know *she's* a hideous distraction." He nods toward me "Look at you. This place obviously suits you. Or did, before she ruined it."

His reference to my appearance makes me self-conscious. I stand straighter and tuck my hair behind my left ear.

"Stop!" he startles me by barking. When I freeze, he explains, "See? You're already tensing up and reverting to that awkward, insecure person who walked into my office and walked back out with a severe case of writer's block. That can't happen."

Before thinking about it, I reply, "Well, no offense, but you and your wife don't foster a sense of carefreeness."

"'Carefreeness?' Oh, boy. This is bad already."

"I'm not writing; I'm speaking! You can't judge me based on un-edited... words... I'm saying off-the-cuff."

"When the words don't flow in your speech, that means they're not flowing in your head, and if they're not flowing in your head, they're not going to flow from your fingers to the screen to the paper. Oh, shit. Why does she have to ruin everything? Everything!" He paces the kitchen, muttering things of which I only hear snatches, like "ants in her bed," and "bad smell."

"I'm writing fine," I insist.

"You were!" he counters, ceasing his pacing. "You *were* writing fine."

"Am!"

He shakes his head and wags his finger in the air. "No. I can tell a definite difference between the stuff you produced this morning and afternoon and what you tried to write before dinner, after Caroline arrived and interrupted your flow."

My blood drains into my feet. "What? What do you mean, you can tell? I haven't shown you anything."

His eyes widen momentarily but return to their bored shape so quickly that I almost wonder if I imagined it. Casually, he says with a wave of his hand, "Oh, I took a peek when I finished my walk, and you had already come inside to get ready for dinner."

"You what?!"

"It's not a big deal. You wrote *a lot* today. And most of it was good. Like I said..."

"You had no right!"

"I'm your editor."

"It's not ready to be edited. It's rough. Rough rough." I feel more exposed than if I were standing naked in front of him. Well, maybe not *that* exposed.

While I'm contemplating that horror, he stubbornly ignores my outrage and offers, "The cemetery scene is excellent... to a point. Your descriptions of the physical surroundings are so vivid that I can *see* the place. It's a horrible place, even on a bright, sunny day, like in the book." He looks down at the floor, as if he can read the manuscript there. Gesturing at his shoes, he continues, "And I'm there. I'm feeling the hot summer sun. I'm hearing the grass crunching under my feet. I'm hearing the cicadas offering up their unholy high-pitched drone in unison." Now he looks up at me, his face blank. "And then... nothing. I'm yanked from the scene by the flat prose that follows. Prose that should be so heavy with emotion that I can almost feel it weighing down my shoulders. I should feel burdened with what this character is thinking and feeling. Yet, I feel nothing. *That's* what you wrote—or tried to write —when I left you to take my walk. I can tell. The shift is obvious."

"Maybe you're the problem, then," I snap, not appreciating his criticism or his invasion of my privacy, even if I was the fool who left her laptop plugged in and out in the open for anyone to see. I don't even have my manuscript password protected.

As if reading my mind, he says, "You might want to think about password protecting that document, you know. As glad as I was to see that you hadn't done so, it's not very smart to leave yourself open to plagiarism like that."

"Nobody even knows who I am," I argue listlessly.

"And they never will unless you learn to write with feeling when it counts. That scene in the graveyard—*that's* your money scene. You ever read anything by Blake Redmond-Womack?" Without waiting for me to answer (because I'm not going to admit it), he says, "Of course, you have. Everyone has. Or at least seen the movies based on his books. Anyway, that's the sort of passage that Womack pumps out before he's even had his morning shit, because he knows women who read chick lit love a good cry."

"I don't write chick lit."

"Whatever. You know what I mean."

I walk to the back door and stare at the reflection of the setting sun in the surface of the sea. "I know what you're implying, and let me clue you in on something. I didn't write this book to manipulate people's emotions and give them an outlet for the 'good cry' they need when it's that time of the month and they're curled up on the couch with their heating pad and a book. I wrote it—I'm writing it—for me." I stop, knowing I'm getting dangerously close to saying too much. "It makes *me* feel something. And if it doesn't elicit the same response in someone else—you, for example—that's not my problem. I can't make people feel what I felt—I mean, what I *feel* when I write it."

"Then you're, at best, a diarist. And you have no business with a publishing contract, because, if what you say is true, then what's the point in publishing your book? If your goal is to make yourself feel something, and you've accomplished that, why do you need to publish it for the world to see? And if you can't make other people feel what you're feeling, then you're a sucky writer."

I whirl around to face him. "Excuse me?"

"You heard me."

"Screw you."

He laughs. "Nah. You heard Caroline earlier; that's highly overrated."

I ignore his attempt to get me off track. "No, I'm serious. I've poured my heart and soul for the past five years into this book, and everyone else who's read it has deemed it brilliant. You're the only one who wants to change it or has a problem with it. So, I think *you're* the problem. And it's not my fault you don't know how to feel."

"I'm the reader. The *real* reader, not one of your friends or your agent or your *mom.*"

His reference to my mother makes me physically flinch.

I wish so much that my mom could read my book. And my dad. And my sisters. I wish this were all a product of my very active imagination. I wish I were spewing theoretical feelings and thoughts into the manuscript. And if sometimes those feelings don't come across as strongly as I'm feeling them, it's only because I'm restraining myself so that I don't cross the line into sentimentality, which I'm sure Luke-Ass would also criticize. I can't win with him, so he can go screw himself. There. That way, nobody but himself has to be punished with his reportedly abysmal bedroom techniques.

Without another word, I yank the door open and speed-walk across the lawn toward the brightly lit gazebo. At the last second, though, I veer away from it and head for the beach.

I wonder if my mom ever saw the ocean. I wonder if she ever sat and watched the waves, like I've done for the past two hours. By the time she was my age, she already had three children, and she was a full-time employee of the family business, farming. It was one of those livelihoods that didn't allow for vacations. We never went on vacation as a family, that's for sure. For the most part, we stayed at the farm. Three hundred sixty-five days of the same routine.

Sometimes Mom would take the three of us girls somewhere for the weekend. Or Dad would go away for a weekend, usually hunting with old buddies from high school. I think my parents went somewhere as a couple once, but I was too young to care about the logistics, so I don't remember how they swung that. I doubt that Mom saw the ocean once she was married to Dad. If I remember correctly, their trip together was to a landlocked city not too far from home (in case they needed to get back quickly). Probably Chicago. Or maybe Cincinnati.

Neither place strikes me as romantic, but what do I know about that? Bupkiss. College flings can teach you a lot about sex, but they're not particularly romantic. At least the ones I had weren't. If I were a romance novelist (or a writer of chick lit, as Lucas keeps suggesting), that would be a professional liability. No, the only professional liability I possess is the inability to make people feel. Or one person in particular.

I've tried as hard as I can not to think about that person since I stormed away from him. I walked for a while, but the breeze off the ocean was getting chilly, and the water was surprisingly cold on my feet, so I turned around and walked on the cool, packed sand back to the Edwardses' private beach. Now I sit on the other side of a dune obscuring the house from my view (and me from the house's view), my knees drawn to my chest, my hoodie pulled over my knees, as I stare at the water.

The sand next to me shifts, and Lucas appears over the gentle rise. He's carrying a blanket and stops short when he sees me. Due to the darkness that only the moon is nervy enough to try to penetrate, I can't see the expression on his face, but his curt, "Oh, there you are," gives me a decent idea of what he's feeling.

I lean sideways and look up at him. Nodding to the blanket, I say, "I've heard of separate bedrooms, but this is pretty extreme."

"What?" he snaps. Then he tones down his annoyance when he realizes I'm joking. "Oh. This is for you, not me." He unceremoniously drops the blanket in a bunch onto my shoulders and sits next to me. "It gets cold down here by the water. Paulette suggested I bring you this, since you've been gone so long. I was expecting to have to traipse up and down the beach, looking for you."

I unfurl and arrange the blanket more securely around me. "No traipsing necessary. See, I'm not so high-maintenance, after all. I'm sure Tom Ridgeworthy is a much bigger diva."

He stares out at the water and says cryptically, "You're definitely nothing like Tom Ridgeworthy."

Under the warmth of the quilt, I uncurl myself and sit cross-legged, allowing my hoodie to return to its original shape. "Thanks, I think." I choose to take it as a compliment, anyway, since Tom Ridgeworthy, dressed in his bomber jacket and aviator sunglasses, as if he's a real-life action hero, looks like a douche on his book jackets. "And thanks for the blanket."

"Like I said, Paulette was worried about you. Not that she'll admit it. And I think she was off to bed when I was on my way down here."

"Okay."

He sifts sand through his hands, watching it fall into tiny mounds next to his legs. "I regret what I said earlier to you."

This statement that sounds somewhat like an apology gets my attention. "Oh? Which part?"

His focus remains on the sand. "You're not a sucky writer. I didn't say you were, anyway. The more I thought about it, the more I realized it sounded like I did. I only meant, if you can't make readers feel what you're feeling, then you're a sucky writer. But I know you can." Finally, he looks over at me and seems surprised that I've been staring at him the whole time. "I know you can," he repeats.

I look away. "Hmm," is all I say.

"What does that mean?"

After thinking about it for a while, I answer, "It means, 'hmm.'" I smile over at him. "I appreciate your vote of confidence, but—no offense—I already know that."

"But—"

"The challenge is—can I make *you* feel what I'm trying to convey? You're obviously a harder sell than the average reader, who is *not* my mom, by the way."

He winces. "That was a low blow, I suppose."

Two sort-of apologies in one conversation? I feel obligated to cut him some slack for his trouble. "Granted, my friend, Gus, is an easier sell than the average reader. He cries about everything. I once witnessed him tear up at a toilet paper commercial, because 'those cartoon bears are just so skip-boppety cute!'"

"'Skip-boppety'?"

"Gusese for 'darned' or the multi-purpose 'fucking,'" I translate.

He laughs. "Okay, then. This Gus sounds like a character."

"He is. He would call this whole thing between you and your wife a 'bajiggity situation.'"

This makes him laugh even harder, but then he stops abruptly. "Wait." He puts his hand over the blanket on my arm. "Where have I heard that? Hang on, Gus *is* a character! Is Gus Jack? Or vice versa?"

For some odd reason, I feel caught. Well, what's the point in denying it? Writers use real people in their lives as inspiration all the time. "Yes. Jack is based on my friend Gus. He's colorful. He deserved to be a character in a book."

Teasing, he asks, "So does that mean you're Rose?"

"No!" I immediately and adamantly reply. Damn. I meant to be a lot more casual and carefree about it if and when he asked me that.

"I see."

"She's really not," I lie insistently.

"That's fine. I was simply wondering."

"Now you know." I stand and wrap the blanket more tightly around me. "Anyway, I'd better go pack up my stuff and head inside for the night." I bend over to retrieve my flip flops and nearly topple over on the uneven surface underfoot.

Lucas catches me. "Careful."

Regaining my balance, I blush. "Sorry."

"It's not a problem. I don't want you to sprain your ankle, though. Maybe I should carry the blanket?"

He reaches for it, but I pull away. I don't want to relinquish the quilt, although I'm not sure why. "No! I mean, it's fine. I'm stiff from sitting for so long. I'm fine now." I slide my feet into my flip-flops and shake the sand from them one at a time before making my way over the dune in the direction of the gazebo.

I glance over at Lucas, who's concentrating on his feet as we walk through the sandy grass that gradually gets lusher and lusher the closer we get to the house.

When I peel off to retrieve my writing supplies in the gazebo, he lifts a hand and says wearily, "G'night, Jayne."

I duck my head. "Night." Then I head up the steps into the gazebo, where I can see my laptop sitting exactly as I left it. Well, almost. It was open last time I saw it, but now it's closed.

CHAPTER FOURTEEN

I can't sleep. Normally, I'd write, but for the first time I can remember, I don't want to write. I want to do something normal. What do normal people do when they can't sleep?

Watch TV.

I creep through the quiet, sleeping house in search of a television. I think I remember what one looks like. I haven't owned one in a long time. I don't watch enough TV to bother with owning one and paying for cable or satellite or any other service. Plus, I can stream online every show I want to watch, like all the period dramas on PBS and BBC.

I stop in my tracks at the bottom of the stairs to the basement when I come around the corner, only to be confronted by the biggest, shiniest, flattest TV I've ever seen.

"Pretty," I breathe stupidly. Plopping down onto the overstuffed couch, I grab the remote from the low coffee table and study the device. It looks like something designed by NASA for use by astronauts (or at least someone much smarter than I am).

Okay—power—that's straightforward.

The TV comes on with a soft click. A blue screen tells me to "press OK." After searching on the large remote, I find the appropriate button. An infomercial blares out at me, "ALL THIS FOR ONLY $19.99! BUT WAIT!"

I quickly locate the volume controls and press firmly on the bottom button until the program becomes little more than a murmur. Holy crap, that was loud. My heart knocks in my chest and thumps in my ears.

When the adrenaline rush subsides, I focus on the remote once more. Channels. Okay. I scan up until I get to the upper channels like HBO and Cinemax. What's this?

"Oh!" I say out loud as my brain registers that I'm looking at two naked people writhing against each other in an elevator. My finger poised over the channel button, I watch for a few minutes. That actually looks nice. Well, that may not be the best word for what they're doing, but it looks fun, in any case. I seem to remember it was somewhat fun, but a lot of work to get to that point. Not that I ever did anything like that in an elevator. Or anywhere close to being public. I just mean... Oh, never mind. I know what I mean.

I reluctantly change the channel when watching the two actors (that's all they are, I have to remind myself) makes me sweat along my hairline. Eventually, I settle on a period piece on the BBC that's decidedly less sexual but will probably put me to sleep as effectively as a good shtupping. I relax back into the couch cushions and pull my knees up to my chest. There's something about English accents that makes me feel all warm and fuzzy.

I wake up on my side, having toppled over in my sleep at some point. My muscles are tense from trying to generate body heat in the chilly basement. On the television is a whimsically drawn cartoon featuring little English characters. The young boy is helping the young girl, Lola, catch a spider from the bathroom sink. She's thanking him profusely in her adorable accent. "Thank you ever so much, Charlie. You know I'm not keen on spiders."

Keeping my eyes on the television, I pull a blanket from the back of the couch and lie on my side once more, settling in to watch the clever show. I'm laughing out loud at another adorable yet grownup-sounding line when a voice behind me startles me.

"I never would have pegged you for a cartoon watcher."

My laugh sticks in my throat, and I stiffen, but I don't move. Finally, I say, "This is the first time I've watched this show. First time I've watched TV in months."

He comes closer, standing behind the couch, looking first down at me and then at the television. "TV rots your brain."

"Precisely. But this show is smart."

"It's a children's program."

"Yeah. I guess that's why it's smart. Adults don't require intelligent programming anymore. We're content with killing our brain cells with reality shows, but this is great."

He comes around the couch and sits at the other end, where he wedges himself into the corner and leans back as if he's studying the show for academic purposes. I curl up more tightly to give him some extra space. He crosses his legs, resting his ankle on his knee. I have no idea what time it is, but he's already dressed, so I assume it's some normal time in the morning and not terribly early. I'd ask, but I'd rather continue watching the show. I want to know what happens to the spider and if Lola ever learns to be more "keen" on spiders in general.

When the episode's over, he chuckles and looks over at me. "You're riveted."

"I love it. It's so quirky. I think I've found a new hero in this Lola character." I stretch and then pull my leg quickly back when my foot nudges his hip.

"Did you sleep down here all night?" he asks, sitting forward and putting his elbows on his knees.

"I've been here since about two," I admit. "Couldn't sleep."

"I couldn't, either," he shares. "I sat up in bed, reading. What on earth did you find to watch at that hour? It's all infomercials and porn."

I will not blush like a guilty teenager. Right. "I think it was an adaptation of *Jane Eyre,* if I'm not mistaken. It didn't take long for it to put me to sleep. Mission accomplished."

He laughs. "Maybe I should have come down here. My reading wasn't much help."

Imagining him walking in on what I was watching for a short time before *Jane Eyre* makes me blush in earnest. To hide it, I pretend to rub sleepily at my face. "What were you reading? Something for work or for pleas—not work?"

"I was actually doing some research, for personal purposes. Anyway, I guess I should let you get some breakfast and get to work."

I can practically hear the whip cracking.

Defensively, I say, "I'll get there. I've never needed a task-master before."

He blinks at me before saying levelly, "That's not what I meant."

"I'm sure. The sooner I finish my book, the better, right?"

"For everyone, most of all, you."

"Most of all, you. Then you can give Caroline her house back."

I move to sit up and set my feet on the ground, but only

one leg makes it before he grabs my other ankle. "Stop worrying about Caroline. I told you, I'll deal with her."

"You wouldn't have to deal with her, if I weren't here." I jerk my foot away from his grasp, sit up, and move as far away from him on the couch as possible.

"I only have myself to blame for that. I invited you to stay here. And it's my fault that this house is even an issue. I should have divorced her a long time ago. I've procrastinated too long." He rubs his jaw. "I love this house. Once we're divorced, it'll go to her, like everything else that I only have because I'm married to her."

"That's a shitty reason to stay married to someone you don't love."

"True," he allows. "She has her shitty reasons to stay married to me, too, though. And until now, it's worked out fine. I knew it wouldn't last forever, though. Nothing does with her."

I'd rather not know any of this. I mean, I *know* couples like them exist, but actually being in the presence of one such couple is extremely depressing. I'm no romantic, but I'd rather be alone the rest of my life than ever be part of a relationship or marriage that's based more on convenience and tax breaks than love. Maybe I *am* a romantic, after all. A closet romantic.

"Well, this is uplifting, inspiring conversation, but now that you mention it, I *am* hungry and would like to try to get some work done, if for no other reason than to decide if it's worth staying here to try to get any work done," I snipe.

He stands when I do. "I'm sorry you got involved in this. I am. It's complicated."

The sincerity with which he says it makes it impossible for me to continue to be too bitchy, but I do say, "You know what? It's none of my business. And I wish you'd quit trying to make it my business."

"Fair enough."

"Thank you." With that, I trudge up to my room to get showered and dressed for what I hope is the most productive day of my writing career, so I can leave my manuscript in his hands as I walk away from this house—and the private horrors it contains—forever.

"I'm not hungry," I say without looking up at the person who's entered the gazebo as I continue to type as fast as I can to keep up with the lightning-quick narrator in my head. Plus, I'm trying to beat the storm that's blowing in off the ocean and should be arriving any minute, if those black clouds are any indication. How symbolic. The constant storm inside that house is why I have to finish this.

The snotty reply, "I'm not offering to serve you," makes my head snap up.

Oh. Shit.

"Hi, Caroline," I say as politely as I can muster.

She sniffs. "It's about to rain, you know."

"Yes, I can see that. That's why I'm trying to hurry and finish this chapter," I hint.

Wrinkling her delicate nose, she asks, "Are you unable to write indoors, or something?"

"Not 'unable,' just not as well." I tuck my hands under my legs and hunch my shoulders toward my ears. "I like it out here."

"Yes, well, don't get too ensconced," she simpers. "I believe I heard Lucas on the phone earlier trying to find somewhere else to send you."

My heart drops. "R-really?"

The fake sympathy on her face is sickening. "Yes. Oh... I thought you knew. After he and I discussed it, I assumed he was coming out here to tell you right away. I don't mean to cause problems between the two of you."

It's all I can do not to laugh out loud. At many parts of her claim.

"There's no 'two of us,' for one thing," I say, but then I realize I don't want to say the other thing out loud, so I stop before telling her that I think she absolutely wants to cause as many problems as possible.

Inspecting her fingernails, she drawls, "I see the way he looks at you. And just because I'm his wife doesn't mean you have to pretend. Although the separate bedrooms are a nice touch. How very disciplined of you both!"

When all I do is glare at her, she takes that as an admission of sorts and continues, "A woman like you should be quite proud of herself. Lucas is picky. As a matter of fact, I think you're the first mistress he's ever had. And I know that's not out of some sense of loyalty to me." She laughs bitterly. "I have to say, though... I'm surprised at his eventual choice." She looks me up and down.

"Our relationship is purely professional," I insist calmly. Thunder punctuates my sentence.

"Oh, my. No need to get testy."

"I'm *not* being testy. Even if I have a right to be, considering how offensive you're being." So much for finishing this section. I sigh as I make my backup copies and pack up my stuff.

Feigning contrition, she says while watching me, "Please, don't be offended. That wasn't my intention. I simply wanted you to know that I know what's going on—Lucas has never offered to have any of his other authors stay at his precious beach house—and that I'm okay with it." Now, ultra-casually she adds, "As long as… Well, I'm going to have to be perfectly blunt with you now. As long as you don't get any ideas about marrying him, because—"

"This is ridiculous!"

She talks over me. "Because O'Shea's do not get divorces. And now that we're expecting a baby, it's even more out of the question. I'll do whatever it takes to make sure he upholds our marriage contract. 'Til death do us part."

The thought of my marrying Lucas—of even *wanting* to marry him—makes me laugh out loud. "You're crazy, lady," I tell her as I loop my laptop bag's strap over my head. "Lucas and I can barely be in the same room together ten minutes without arguing. He sent me here to get me away from him and to finish my manuscript as quickly as possible so I'd stop being a pain in his ass. Period."

"If you say so."

"I do. Now, excuse me. I guess I need to go find him and figure out what's going on. Thanks for the heads-up." I edge past her and down the gazebo stairs.

As I'm crossing the lawn to the back patio, the lackadaisical raindrops suddenly find a purpose: drenching me. I'd run, but flip-flops aren't good running shoes. As a matter of fact, I've sprained my ankle before trying to run in wet flip-flops, and my laptop is protected by its bag, so the worst that will happen—if I keep calm—is that I'll get a little wet and will have to change my clothes. Big whoop. There's something about a downpour that makes me panic. Maybe it's the lack of control. Mostly, I think it's the wet clothes. I don't like wet clothes.

When I finally make it inside the doors that lead to the kitchen, I'm soaked through, and my hair is dripping onto my shoulders. Paulette looks up from where she's preparing sandwiches for lunch and laughs at me.

"I was afraid you'd wait too long to come in. Best get out of those wet things. Lunch will be ready before you are," she says in her typical mothering fashion.

To be safe, I slide my laptop out, before the rain can soak through its bag, and carry it over to the sink, where I grab a towel, wrap it up, and carry it under my arm toward the kitchen door. "Have you seen Lucas lately?" I inquire. "I need to talk to him about something."

"Not before you eat, surely!" she declares firmly. "Anyway, I'm sure he'll be down for lunch any minute now. That man doesn't skip meals when I'm around."

I'd rather not talk to him about my situation in front of anyone else, especially not Caroline. And if I'm leaving, it'd be nice to know right away, so I can pack before lunch and be ready to go. No sense lingering longer than necessary. If I'm no longer wanted here, it'll only be awkward. More awkward than it already is. Yikes. That's hard to imagine. Plus, if he hasn't already found somewhere else for me to go, he needs to save his energy. I'm not a shelter dog that he impulsively brought home and now feels guilty because he's decided he doesn't have room in his life for me. He doesn't need to find me a new home. I can check into a motel. Or go back to Gus's.

Yes. As soon as I'm finished talking to Lucas, I'll call Gus and tell him I'm on my way back, if he'll have me. I'll cook his favorite dinners every night, like a good non-wife.

I'm deeply strategizing, my head down, as I stride briskly down the hall to "my" room to change my clothes, when I run into something—or more accurately, someone—hard and unyielding.

"Oof!" I barely manage to hold onto my laptop as it

slides against the dry towel under my arm and threatens to crash to the floor.

"Jayne! What the fu—I mean, watch where you're going!"

"You bumped into me!"

"I absolutely did not. I stepped from my bedroom and saw you barreling toward me but had nowhere to go, since I can't melt into the wall. If you had been looking up... What happened to you?" He puts a hand on my upper arm and fingers the drenched cotton of my t-shirt sleeve.

I step away from him. "I got caught out in the rain."

"Is it raining?" He cranes his neck to see around me to the end of the hallway, where there's a large window that's being power-washed by nature. "Oh. I had no idea..."

"Yeah. It's thundering and everything. What have you been doing that makes you so oblivious to your surroundings?" I ask more grouchily than the situation calls for.

He gives me a strange look but answers, "I've been on the phone."

"About that... I'll be out of your way right after lunch."

"What are you talking about?"

Self-consciously, I run my fingers through my dripping hair and tuck it behind my ears. "Caroline told me that you and she agreed she'd be staying and I'd be leaving and that you were trying to find another place for me to go to finish my manuscript, but that's silly. I mean, I'll go back to Gus's. Or something. I'll figure something out. Maybe I'll even go home."

"Home? As in Indiana?"

"Yeah. That's where I'm most comfortable, anyway. And since these changes you want are obviously going to take me a while, it makes sense to go back—"

"Wait. Stop. Jayne." He steps closer to me. "I haven't

had a chance to talk to Caroline yet today, so whatever she told you is a lie."

"It is?"

"Yes."

I hate how glad that makes me. Not only because I get to stay here, but because that means Lucas didn't agree to anything with Caroline that involved kicking me out.

He bites his lower lip. "Well, you're cold." Suddenly his eyes widen, and he blushes. "That is, you're probably cold. I can't tell if you are or not. I assume you are. Because you're wet—your *clothes* are wet—and you're standing in an air-conditioned house. So, yeah."

"I am a little cold," I confirm his stumbling hypothesizing. "I'm going to change."

"Good idea. And I'm going to find Caroline and wring her neck."

I smile at that before turning and walking the rest of the way to the room where all my stuff is. When I get to the door and turn into it, I glance up the hall and see he's still standing there, watching me. He jerks into motion, when I smile at him uncertainly, and crosses to the stairs, which he takes at a near-run, shouting, "Caroline!" on his way down.

Oh, great. I'll be eating lunch in the kitchen with Paulette for sure.

CHAPTER FIFTEEN

"*I see how he looks at you.*"

With undisguised disgust? Because that's the only way I've ever seen him look at me. Except in the hallway, but that was a fluke. He quickly understood when I got into the bedroom and started undressing. My nipples were standing out like pencil erasers through my t-shirt and bra. I think even Paulette would have been flustered by that. I wouldn't have been able to talk to myself in the mirror with that going on. They were *out there*. Ka-TOW! He's lucky he still has both eyes.

I'm going to pretend like that never happened, though. Because it was obviously embarrassing to him, and it's definitely embarrassing to me, so what's the point in belaboring it? Anyway, what would I say? "Sorry I almost gave you a permanent disability in the hallway earlier"? Yeah, there's no classy way to apologize for my inadvertent indecency. So... moving on.

I'm decidedly paranoid, thanks to Carolin-a Liar. What a bitch. I'm beginning to think there's nothing worth staying here with her much longer. Sure, I've written some inspired stuff lately, and it's great to be in such a beautiful place with someone to wait on me and take care of me, but when I'm not writing or eating Paulette's delicious cooking, I can't get away from the fact that I'm walking on eggshells around the true owner of the house, who's hell bent on staying here and getting rid of me.

At this point, it doesn't matter what Lucas wants me to do. It's time to give Gus an idea of what's going on and warn him that I may be about to darken his cramped doorstep again.

The text I send him in the middle of the afternoon (*Call me as soon as you get a chance*) elicits a nearly immediate response. Answering his call, I shut myself in the closest unoccupied room, the dim, fussy library.

"What's up, Babushka?" he asks right away. "I only have a couple of minutes before Boss Lady realizes I'm gone."

I fill him in on the highlights, leaving out the most salacious parts (there will be time for that later) and say, "So, can I come back to stay with you for a while? Just 'til I finish these revisions?"

"You know you're always welcome, girlfriend, but…"

I hold my breath while I wait to see if his reservation is a deal-breaker or simply a minor inconvenience that I'd be willing to work around.

"Some filthy tenant in the building who recently got evicted had a major roach infestation, and they have to bomb the whole building. As it is, I was counting on staying out there with *you* this weekend. And then during the week, I'll be staying at a friend's until I can go back to my own apartment."

My first reaction is, "You have other friends?"

"Of course, I do! You are so silly sometimes. If you can

stick it out a week, you're welcome to come back to my place, Sugar Booger."

I sigh. "Hmm. I think I'm going to go back to Indy."

"What?! No!"

"Why not? We have the technology. There's no reason I have to be geographically close to the publishing company to accomplish what needs to be done." I run my fingers along the spines of the books on the eye-level shelf as I pace back and forth. "This is stupid. If I weren't writing like a fiend here, I would have been gone a long time ago."

"What does Luke-ASS say?"

"He wants me to stay, for some reason. I wish you had more time, Gus. I'd tell you all about the messed-up shit going on between him and his wife. As it is, I mostly feel like I'm a pawn he's using to annoy her. Quite successfully, I might add."

"Good gravy! And they say that homosexuals are a threat to the sanctity of marriage? As if! These two prove that you straight folks are ruining the institution just fine on your own. Buh-jiggity!"

I giggle at him. "As usual, you have a good point. I wish you were here to keep this all in perspective and make me laugh about it. It's not very funny usually."

"Well, you were there first! I say, as long as you're still able to write as well as you have been, and Luke-ASS is okay with your staying, you avoid this Caroline creature—sounds like a big enough house that it's possible—and stick to your guns. Hell! Invite me out there this weekend, as planned, and I'll have Caroline out the door in five seconds flat. I have two days to plot how to make it happen. I love a challenge."

Picturing Gus in the mix makes me laugh and groan at

the same time. "I think this is messed up enough. Thanks for the offer, though."

"Oh, sister-friend, I gotta go! I heard Boss Lady ask the receptionist where I am."

"Where are you?"

"In the supplies closet."

"Oh, now, you haven't been in the closet for years, Gus."

"Right? I forgot how claustro-frickin-phobic it is in here. Smooches! Let me know what you decide, whatever it is, but my vote is for you to stay put. Indy is so boring!"

"It definitely is, compared to this place," I grumble.

"Keep writing. Then when you've knocked his socks off, you can go wherever you want."

We say goodbye, and I sink to the floor, where I trace the pattern of the Oriental rug and despair at how the phone call I had hoped would give me all the answers I needed has only made things more confusing. Before I called Gus, my plan was to stay with him or go back home. He's reminded me that the very last thing I want to do is to go home to my solitary life. He's right; it's a big house. There's no reason I have to be in the presence of Caroline or Lucas. And at least here I have Paulette to keep me company when I feel the need for some human interaction. At home, I've often resorted to going to the nearest grocery store and buying things I didn't need, simply so I could talk to someone, usually the checker.

I don't want to be that sad person again.

"She'll be gone by the weekend," he murmurs to me in the corridor outside the library when I finally emerge, still not sure what I'm going to do.

My tummy jumps. At the news, of course, not at the fact that he's standing so close to me that I can smell him. And he smells good. I mean, he's still Luke-Ass.

"Okay," I reply, trying to be cool, when I really want to jump up and down and say, "Yes!" and possibly even hug him. Maybe. "That's good news."

He inches even closer. "She has a family thing to go to this weekend at her parents' place. And then I told her she can stay at my—our—apartment in the city."

My guts go cold. "Oh. I see."

He smirks. "Yeah. I'm making a big sacrifice for you here, Greer, so you'd better deliver. I mean, no pressure." Still, he gets closer. My shoulder's against his chest now.

"HRight. Well, you don't have to do all that for me."

Intensely, he counters, "It's the least I can do. I feel horrible for inviting you here only to have you stuck in the middle of this ridiculous long-term feud between the two of us. She brings out the absolute worst in me. It wasn't always like that, though. I guess the memories of how it *used* to be are still strong enough to make me hope for that happiness again someday. Not with her, though."

When I squirm and shift my weight from foot to foot, he says, "Sorry. I know, you don't want to know. I don't know why I'm telling you all this." Finally, he backs off.

I duck around him. "I don't know, either. Has it stopped raining yet? I'd like to do some more writing today."

"I thought that's what you were doing in there." He nods to the library. "That's why I didn't interrupt you sooner to tell you about Caroline."

I try not to feel or appear guilty when I say, "No. I called my friend, Gus, to ask if I could come back to his place. But, his place is being bug bombed thanks to an unhygienic neighbor."

Drawing his head back, he says, "Wait. What? I thought you said you'd give me a few days to figure out what to do with Caroline."

"I did, but it's so uncomfortable here, Lucas," I whine. "I can't concentrate!"

"I told her to leave you alone."

"Yes, the whole house heard you. I think they heard you down on the beach, too."

"The only way to get through to her sometimes is to shout. I'm not proud of my bad temper, but... she drives me insane."

"Okay, fine. Don't you think it puts me in an awkward position to know that you two are arguing so loudly about *me*? And it's all so pointless. I don't have to be here."

"Yes, you do."

Without touching me at all, he steers me into the previously locked room and closes the double doors behind us. I perch on the edge of a roll-top desk that's open and has quite a few papers scattered on its surface. The papers are littered with aggressive red editor's marks. So *this* is what goes on in here. To find out it's his plain Jane office-away-from-the-office (and not some sacrosanct sex closet) is mildly disappointing. Unless there are secret compartments, storing kinky sex equipment.

"You're a damn good writer," he pulls my attention back to him by telling me what every teacher I've had since the sixth grade has told me (although they may not have used those exact words). "But, the writing you've done here —it's on a whole other plane. As a matter of fact, it's so markedly different that we're going to have to do some considerable blending to make it match the rest of the book." When he sees my face sag, he quickly says, "That's not a problem at all, and I'm sure it won't take long, and I don't want you to worry about that right now." He sits in the desk chair, steeples his fingers, and swivels. "What I'm saying is, you're writing out of your mind. Here. And it's not that I don't think you're capable of doing the same thing elsewhere, but why take the chance? You're here. It works."

I absently rub at a tiny patch of fine stubble on my knee that I missed while shaving this morning. Reluctantly, I tell him, "I know. You're right. I've never written like this before. Ever." I hazard a glance up at him. "I feel like my mind is opening up to creative avenues that I didn't even realize existed before."

My attempt to be vague makes me sound flaky, but what I can't tell him in so many words is that I wrote an entire sequence this morning that had nothing at all to do with anything that happened in my real life. It was entirely made up. Telling him that would probably confuse the hell out of him, though. Actually, he'd likely jump to the conclusion that I've plagiarized the rest of the book. I definitely don't want him to suspect that. I also don't want him to know how non-fiction my fiction novel is.

For one thing, I don't want to explain *how* real it is. "What about this part? And this part?" "Yeah. It all happened." Or "No, I changed that to make it more believable." Then, I don't want to see the, "Oh, shit, you poor thing," look that will inevitably take up residence on his face every time he sees me. Even if it's for only a split second, it'll be there. No, it's better that he thinks I'm a fiction writer who's too unimaginative to come up with a better demise for her protagonist's family than a tired, old fire.

The point is… I'm willing for the first time to legitimately make whole sections of the book fiction. That's something I've never considered before. For the most part,

I've been faithful to history to a fault, possibly to the detriment of the book.

That being said, the tornado idea has grown on me since I've arrived here at the beach house. I'm willing to at least try to write it that way—in a separate document—and see if it still works. He's right that it would be less cliché, as long as I can write it in a non-*Wizard of Oz* way.

"Well, I'm glad your friend's place is unavailable, then," he interrupts my impromptu brainstorm about tornado imagery. "Unfortunately, that means two more days under the same roof with Caroline, but I think she finally got the message about staying away from you."

He leans forward and straightens some of the papers on his desk.

I look over his shoulder out the window and see with dismay that it's still raining. And it looks like one of those storms that takes its sweet time passing through, too. Before I can stifle it, a sigh escapes my chest and rattles my lips.

Bemused, he watches me hop down from the desk and go to the window, where I gaze wistfully toward the gazebo, which is barely visible through the downpour.

"What is it now?" he asks with a slight edge to his tone.

"I like to write out there," I say simply.

"Then take a break while it rains. Read a book." He thrusts a messy handful of papers at me. "Read *this* book. Please. So I don't have to."

I feel sorry for the author who worked so hard to write that, only to have it become someone else's chore. Glancing at the pages, I say, "It'd be difficult to read after what you did to it."

He shrugs. "It's shit. What can I say? Even the bestsellers lay an egg now and then."

My eyes widen. "*That's* a bestseller's work?"

"I wouldn't call it 'work.' I'd call it, 'I think I'm a publishing god, and I'd rather spend my time on the beach in Cabo than fulfill this five-book deal that made it possible for me to afford this one-month vacation, so here's something I slapped together; now, make it work.' That's what I'd call it."

"Oh."

He rolls his eyes. "Makes me wish *I* were in Cabo."

"Well, I *want* to write. I don't want to take a break. I have some good ideas that I want to get down before I forget them."

He stares at me as if I'm mentally deficient. "Then write, Jayne. What do you want me to tell you?"

"Where, though?" I nearly moan, staring longingly at the soggy gazebo again.

"Wherever you want, for heaven's sake! I'm sure you can find somewhere in this house that's quiet and has the correct feng shui to suit your delicate constitution." He scoots closer to the desk. "In my case, it's this room. And I have a lot of work to do. Negotiations with Caroline have set me way back. Not to mention that telecommuting is not ideal for me. I'd rather be in my office in the city. We can't always get what we want, right?" With that, he hunches over the thick stack of paper on his desk, uncaps his red pen, and appears to get back to work.

Since he hasn't explicitly told me to get out, I linger for a while, looking around the large room. It's large and airy, with high, punched-tin ceilings, a fireplace, and plenty of windows. Facing the back and side yards, those windows yield a marginal view of the ocean. The walls are a light brown, reminiscent of coffee with heavy cream. The dark wood accents contrast nicely to give it a masculine but cozy feel. In addition to the roll-top desk and Lucas's mesh office chair, there's a grouping of butter yellow chairs and a sofa around a low, square coffee table, centered in front of the fireplace. It's a calming room.

"Jayne."

His warning tone lets me know I've overstayed my welcome. "Sorry. I'll be leaving now. Good luck with your editing."

I have my hand on the curved door lever when he half-turns toward me and says, "You're welcome to work in here until the rain stops. Caroline definitely won't bother you in here. And as long as you don't do anything odd like talk out loud to yourself when you write…?"

I shake my head vigorously. "No. I'm quiet."

"Then be my guest."

It's worth a try. I can sit on the couch and still get a glimpse of the ocean now and then, when I look up from my laptop. If Caroline never comes in here, that's another huge factor in the room's favor.

"That would be nice," I say. "Thanks, Lucas."

He nods and goes back to his papers. "Just one thing."

I tense. "Yes?"

"Please, stop calling me Lucas. *She's* the only one who insists on calling me that. I hate it."

"Oh, sorry."

"It's not your fault. But, if we're going to be officemates, you should know." When he says nothing else but makes a loud slash through half a page of text in front of him, I figure our conversation is over and run upstairs to get my laptop.

CHAPTER SIXTEEN

This is working out okay. I'm not writing exactly like I was before, but I think that has more to do with the fact that I'm not used to being in the same room with another person while I write than it does with the setting. It's fascinating to observe someone else's work habits.

For the most part, Lucas—er, Luke—is quiet. The only sounds he makes are the scratching of his pen and the occasional fluttering of paper as he flips the pages of the manuscript from the large, even stack in front of him to a smaller, more haphazard stack to his left. Every thirty minutes or so, he straightens the smaller stack. A couple of times, he's abruptly pushed back from the desk, thrown his pen down, and stalked from the room, only to return ten minutes later with a cup of coffee or a bottle of water or, in one case, nothing at all.

After his latest storm-out, I'm shocked when I look at the clock on my laptop to see that two hours have passed, and I've hardly written anything. I guess I've been watching him more than I realized. Time to focus.

When he returns this time, I don't even pause to glance

at him in my peripheral vision. It doesn't matter that I'm writing stream-of-consciousness gibberish to try to get my thoughts flowing (in this case, *I will not look at him, even though he's nice to look at, but he's still a jerk, for the most part, although he has been a lot nicer here than he was in Boston*—).

Before sitting down in his chair, he suddenly whirls on me, points, and says, "Read the last thing you wrote."

My fingers freeze on the keyboard. "Huh?" I gulp and will the blood flow to return to my extremities.

"Read the very last thing you've written," he reiterates more specifically.

"No!" I automatically refuse.

"Yes," he insists. "Read it. You haven't taken a break in hours. Read to me what you're writing. Trust me."

I skim up the page to something safe.

"No! Don't choose the last thing you *like* that you wrote. I want to hear the last sentence to leave your brain."

There's no effing way on this effing earth that I'm reading what I typed. What's he going to do, spank me? *Oh, yes, please.*

I blush at that rogue thought.

"Don't be embarrassed. I don't expect that everything you write sounds great the first time it hits the page. Come on… be a good sport." He half-smiles.

I grit my teeth and read the second-to-last thing I typed, while he was out of the room. "*Tissues with lotion are gross.*" It's inane, but at least it's not humiliating.

He shakes his head. "That's it. You need to take a break."

"No, really. I hit a wall, but I'll get back on track in a minute," I swear.

Physically removing the laptop from my lap while I frantically work to delete the embarrassing line at the bottom, he mercifully closes it without glancing at the screen and sets it on the coffee table.

"Up," he commands.

"Do I get a Scooby Snack if I obey?" I half-gripe, half-flirt.

"Maybe," he flirts back. "You'll have a happier editor, who won't have to weed through a bunch of freewriting garbage after you turn in your manuscript, that's for sure."

"I'll delete all that stuff!"

"Still, there will be some things that may seem critical to the story that you'll keep, but it won't be your best work, because you're forcing it." He yanks on my hand and pulls me to my feet. "Writing a book is not like running a marathon. You don't push through the pain. If it's painful, you stop and take a break."

"It wasn't painful."

He scowls at me. "An analysis about facial tissue is painful. Now, come on. I need a break, too. And not just a walk to the toilet and back. A real break."

Like a sassy teenager, I pull my hand from his admittedly light grasp and say, "What are we gonna do, yoga?"

He pretends to consider it. "Not a bad idea, but I thought we'd take a drive."

"Where?"

"Who cares?" is his rejoinder.

I can think of at least one person who'd probably care a lot. And oddly enough, that thought makes me readily accept his invitation.

As we're heading out the front door, he says, "Don't worry; you can compare and contrast name-brand to store-brand tissues when we get back."

I'm too relieved he didn't see my comparison and

contrast of Marblehead Luke and Boston Luke to put any bite behind my observation: "You are such a dickhead."

The weary way I say it makes both of us laugh.

"I've been told that so many times that I'm starting to get a complex," he jokes as he opens the passenger door to a low-slung silver import and squints down at me through the rain before closing it.

If I thought it were possible for him to care about what anyone else thinks of him, I'd almost feel sorry for him.

We wind up at an old-fashioned tavern, and what started out as a having a couple of beers to unwind turned into drinking several pints of beer (for me) and both of us eating a full meal, which wouldn't have been a problem, except…

"Paulette is going to kill us when we're too full to eat her dinner," I say in the car on the way back to the house.

Gruffly, he replies, "Am I on Paulette's payroll as a professional eater, or is she on *my* payroll as a cook and housekeeper?"

"Well, I know," I reply incongruously, having trouble articulating like an intelligent person. Fortunately, he seems to understand what I'm saying, anyway. "It's still rude that we ate someone else's cooking behind her back."

"She'll get over it. Anyway, we didn't *plan* for it to happen; it just happened."

"Yeah, well we could have shown some self-control. Or at least called her to tell her not to cook dinner for us."

"I refuse to feel guilty about this," he says a lot less bravely than he originally seemed at the idea of disappointing the housekeeper. "Anyway, she still has to cook for Caroline, so it's not like her efforts will be totally wasted."

I bite my lip and stare out the car window, feeling worse and worse the closer we get to home and Paulette's possible wrath. Not that she's ever been anything but perfectly pleasant to me. But I don't want that to change anytime soon.

"Yeah, but she enjoys cooking for *you*," I point out.

He laughs. "Don't put this all on me! You were the one who said you were getting drunk, because your stomach was empty."

"I was. It was!" I giggle and then groan, clutching at my belly. "But now it's so full. And I'm still drunk."

"Then it was all worth it," he mutters sarcastically.

"Wait! What happened to the tough-talker who's not on Paulette's payroll?"

"I think he's still sitting at the tavern," he admits sheepishly.

When all I can do is laugh at him, he rubs his forehead and curses under his breath. As he pulls into the driveway and puts the car in park, he says, "Okay, here's what we're going to do. We're going to go in there and take small help-ings of everything she's—"

"No! If I try to eat another bite, I'll seriously throw up." The mere thought of it is making me feel sweaty and nauseated.

"No, you won't. You'll be fine." He consolingly pats my hand. "Plus, who knows? Maybe dinner's not ready yet. We may have a while to let our first meal settle before we have to eat more."

"Unless we're allowed to wait until tomorrow morning, it's not going to matter. I'm stuffed."

Using the same tone I recognize from when he was first trying to convince Caroline to leave the house, he says, "All right. Then we'll simply tell the truth and let Paulette know we're not hungry, because we already ate at the tavern. We'll bravely suffer the consequences, which may or may not be more severe than being uncomfortable from overeating."

I narrow my eyes at him. "I know what you're doing."

"Laying out our options?"

"No. Presenting our choices in a way that makes *your* way sound like the best way."

He stares through the windshield. "I don't hear you offering up any ideas, so technically both ways are my way. I'm willing to do whatever you want to do. We'll present a united front."

I push on his shoulder. He smiles but refuses to look at me.

Finally, I say, "It's hardly raining anymore. How about we go for a walk and accidentally-on-purpose miss dinner? 'Oops. We lost track of time.'"

He imitates Paulette, "'Then you must be quite peckish. I've kept everything warm for you. Here. Heaping helpings for everyone!' *That's* how that scenario will go down."

While laughing at his inevitably spot-on logic, I consider our three choices and decide, "Yeah, but at least with my option, we'll be getting some exercise that not only buys us some time but could help with digesting meal number one."

"Good point."

"Thank you."

"Walking in the rain, it is."

When Luke's prophecy comes true almost word-for-word, it's all I can do not to crack up. Then I stifle my giggles all through the meal as I watch him choke down every single bite of food Paulette sets in front of him. I take advantage of her not knowing much about my eating habits and push away my plate after a few torturous mouthfuls, with the claim that pasta always quickly fills me up.

I can no longer hold back my laughter, however, when she takes one look at Luke's empty plate and says, "Oh, but Luke always has seconds of my spaghetti and meatballs," and starts to load him up again, oblivious to his bulging eyes and sick grimace.

"What's so funny?" she wonders, looking from him to me.

He pushes her serving spoon away from his plate. "Paulette, I can't eat another bite. I… I think I may be coming down with something. I'm not very hungry tonight." He suppresses a burp behind his fist and rests his head in his hand.

When I continue to laugh at his misery, she gently scolds me, "Now, it's not nice to make fun of someone who's feeling under the weather," as if I'm about a quarter of my age.

As ludicrous as the situation is, I sober at her rebuke and mutter, "Right. Sorry. My bad."

"Perhaps you should go lie down for a while, Luke," she suggests sweetly. "I can bring you something for your stomach. Are you feeling feverish? It probably wasn't very wise to go walking in the rain for so long."

"Good God, woman, I'm fine!" he snaps before obviously thinking better of it and saying more softly, "It's probably stress. I'm sure I'll feel better in the morning."

With that, he rises from the table and trudges up the stairs. I try not to smile at the sound of his slow progress. *Swish… clomp. Swish… clomp.*

When he's gone, Paulette shakes her head at me. "He works too hard. And as if that's not enough, he has to deal with Her Royal Highness and all of her demands and shenanigans. It's no wonder he's short-tempered sometimes. I can't help but want to mother him, though." She carries our dirty plates and the serving bowls into the kitchen, muttering to herself under her breath.

Abandoned, I'm at a loss for what to do next. I go into Luke's study and sit on the couch for a while, but for the first time in a long time, I don't feel like writing anything. I do, however, delete what remains of the embarrassing sentence I wrote before we left for the tavern (*"I will not look at him, even though he's pretty nice to look at—"* is still there for anyone to see). Then, on a whim, after I back up my work for the day, I password protect my computer and my manuscript files. I've been meaning to do it since Luke suggested it after admitting to reading my document without permission. I just keep forgetting. If we're going to be working in the same room, and I'm going to write stupid, mortifying things to pass the time when I run into a spot of writer's block, then I'd better protect myself from abject humiliation.

After I shut down my computer for the day, I consider Luke's earlier idea to read a book. I search through the library across the hall for nearly fifteen minutes before finding anything that remotely interests me (I knew Tom Ridgeworthy was prolific, but holy shit! I'm assuming Luke has a full collection of the man's books; unfortunately, not a single one of the nearly two-dozen novels about political intrigue is my cup of tea). I eventually select a Toni Morrison book I read in college but wouldn't mind reading again, now that I have some more worldly experiences under my belt. Ha! It's probably still going to blow my mind.

All the food and alcohol I've consumed in the past couple of hours has made me sleepy and sluggish, so I decide the safest place to read is in bed, where I can pass out and not have to move any more than to pull the covers over myself when I get chilly in the middle of the night. It's a few minutes before 9:00, but as I make my way up the stairs, the book in one hand and the banister in the other, I'm eagerly anticipating a full night's deep sleep on the heavenly mattress.

At the top of the stairs, a sound brings me to a halt.

Moaning. At first, I think it's *that* kind of moaning, and I almost turn right back around and resign myself to another night on the sofa in the basement. Then I realize how illogical that notion is, considering the only two people up here hate each other.

Or *do* they?

In a matter of seconds, I picture Caroline waiting for Luke on his bed when he came up here to nurse his sick tummy, and yada, yada, yada.

At that thought, I turn to trot down the stairs, but something other than disgust and horror makes me stand firm on the top step. I force myself to identify the feeling. It's not necessarily jealousy, although that's close enough that I keep thinking that must be what it is. No. It's not, though. It's… it's the same feeling I got when, as a kid, I'd go to the haunted corn maze every Halloween. More specifically, it's a combination of feelings. It's excitement mixed with fear, dread, and irresistible curiosity. I know there's likely going to be a hideous sight when I come around the corner, but nothing in the world is going to stop me from looking.

When the next moan drifts down the hallway, I'm resolved to see who's making the sound and why. It's loud enough that I can hear it, but soft enough that I can't tell if the moaner is male or female; if he or she is moaning in pleasure or pain (or both). Must investigate. Have to know. Inquiring minds and all that.

Once I've determined that the keening is coming from Luke's room, I almost chicken out, but when I see the door's not latched shut, I figure it's as much the room's occupant's fault as it is my own if I happen upon something private. Plus, what if there's something really wrong? It would be irresponsible of me to ignore the plight of this poor person, if they're in enough pain to be making so much noise.

I push against the door and cringe while peeking through the widening gap I'm creating between the door and its frame. "Hello? Luke?" I query meekly.

"Jayne?" he weakly calls back.

Since he doesn't ask me to go away, I enter the room and have to cover my mouth and bite down hard on my lip to keep from laughing out loud at the sight before me. He's lying across his bed on his back in his underwear and a white t-shirt, his legs draped over the side of the mattress, his arm flopped over his eyes.

My, oh my. My imagination hasn't been doing him justice. He's lean without being skinny, muscular without being bulky, furry without being hairy, and he fills out those boxer briefs quite nicely.

"Jayne?" he repeats, making me flinch guiltily. "Please, kill me."

"Go into the bathroom and make yourself throw up," I advise, tearing my eyes away from his crotch.

He pulls his arm away from his face and turns his head to look at me. "No! That's disgusting!"

"Yeah, but you'll feel better instantly."

"Why did she give me so much … food?" His hand rubs ineffectually over the engorged belly under his t-shirt.

"I think the better question is, why did you eat it?"

"Because I don't have a dog to feed under the table."

"You might want to consider getting one."

Before thinking too much about it, I sit on the foot of his bed, my back to him (I've gawked at him long enough in his skivvies). Fingering the spine of the Toni Morrison book, I say, "It was sweet of you to make yourself sick eating that spaghetti, so you wouldn't hurt Paulette's feelings."

"Stupid, you mean?"

I knock the book against my knee. "You didn't do it because you were too stupid to know better. You did it in *spite* of knowing better. Because you care about how your actions affect her."

"Yeah, I'm Boss of the Year."

"I won't tell anyone you're nice sometimes. I know you have a reputation to uphold."

He cracks an eye at me. "What are you talking about?"

"Big, mean Mr. Editor, storming around, upholding the laws of grammar and mechanics, the only person standing between misplaced modifiers and the downfall of civilization."

"Have you lost your mind? Can't you see I'm dying here?"

I glance over my shoulder at him. "You're going to be fine. Do you want me to find some antacids for you?"

"Would I have to eat them?"

"Yes…"

"Then, no."

"Okay, then."

"What did you mean about my being big, mean Mr. Editor? I'm not mean."

I laugh at the ceiling.

"What?" He tries to prop himself up on his elbows but falls onto his back after a short struggle and says breathlessly,

"Do I have time to hand-hold? No. I'm not *mean*. I'm firm. And no-nonsense and efficient."

"Cold, scary, dictatorial, and perfunctory."

"Look who discovered the thesaurus function on her word processor," he grumbles.

"Don't make me smack your stomach with this book," I threaten with a smile.

"Feel free, if you want to be showered with vomit."

"Gross!"

"Fair warning."

I stand up and take two steps toward the door.

"Wait!" He holds his arm out toward me. "Don't go."

When was the last time a gorgeous, scantily clad man said that to me? Never!

After several seconds pass without my saying a thing, he says, "Keep a dying man company."

"You're pathetic. I was going to turn in early."

"Please. Don't be *mean*. Stay here and talk to me until the nausea subsides."

"Put some clothes on."

What?! I did *not* say that. Why did I say that?! It's the opposite of what I want him to do.

He groans. "Are those your terms?"

"Yes."

"How about if I cover up with a blanket? Because I took my clothes off for a reason. They were cutting me in half. I felt like a tube of toothpaste in a grubby little kid's fist."

"Lovely."

"I didn't say it was attractive." With what appears to be a supreme amount of effort, he yanks the bedspread up and over himself sideways so only his head is sticking out. "Better?"

"I guess." I retake my seat on the bed. "Do you want me

to read you a story?" I offer, holding up the book in my hands so he can see the cover.

"Rain check?" When I laugh, he says, "Great book, but... not necessarily uplifting and soothing."

"Oh, is that what we're going for here? Uplifting and soothing?"

"Yeah."

"I don't know if I have a grasp on those particular... genres."

There ends the conversation for several minutes, until he moans again with his eyes closed and says, "You have to talk. About anything but food. Because all I can think about is food when you're not talking."

"I don't know what to say."

"Figure it out. Say the first thing that comes to mind. I don't give a shit what it is. As long as it's not about food."

I sigh. "I'm so boring," I lament when I come up blank. We seemed to find things to talk about at the tavern and on our walk this evening, but something about this room is making me freeze up. Maybe it's the fact that it's his bedroom, and this is his bed, and he's half-naked (sort of), and I'm horribly repressed.

"Oh, for the love of ...! Have you seen any good movies lately?" he tosses out.

"No. I've been busy writing."

"Every waking minute?"

"Pretty much."

"You're a publisher's wet dream."

"Thank you?" I reply.

He ignores that and goes back to trying to drum up topics of conversation. "How was your trip out to Boston? Have you had a chance to see any of the sights with your friend, Gus?"

I think back to my travels and almost whoop with excitement when I remember something interesting about me. "Well, it was my first time flying, so that was exciting."

"Ever?"

The way he asks it makes me feel freaky, so I hesitantly admit, "Y-yes. I've always driven everywhere."

Eyes still closed, he says, "Wow. So, what'd you think? Don't tell me—you're already a member of the Mile High Club."

"No!"

He chuckles. "That was a quick denial. I think that's a 'yes.'"

"There was nobody on any of my flights—including the flight crew—who was remotely worthy," I say sniffily to hide my embarrassment, relieved beyond measure that he feels too sick to open his eyes.

He makes a face. "Well, then!"

"Are you saying you're a member?" I ask, failing miserably at sounding casual.

His ensuing laughter obviously hurts his gut. After he recovers, he licks his lips and says, "Nope. I'm much too inept for such small spaces."

"Inept. Sure." I'm dying to change the subject, but since I've already proven I have nothing else to offer this conversation, there's nowhere for me to turn.

Seriously, he says, "I'm not kidding. I'm a spaz."

"Whatever."

My dismissive comment was meant to discourage further disclosure, but he takes it as a challenge to prove it. Opening his eyes, he rolls onto his side and props his head on his hand. "You know that commercial where the guy and the girl are supposedly having a romantic night in, and they end up stumbling around the bedroom, knocking heads and throwing out their backs?"

I giggle and cover my mouth while nodding. "Yes."

"When that commercial came out, I thought someone had gotten the idea from looking in my windows."

"Stop it!"

He widens his eyes innocently. "I swear! There's something about it that gets me all nervous and flustered and turns me into a bumbling idiot. Well, not always, but most of the time. And the harder I try to relax, the worse it is. I knocked out a date's tooth once. With my head."

"Bwahaha!" I explode, falling sideways onto his bed.

"I'm serious! Had to take her to an emergency dental clinic. She was fuh-reaking out, babbling about a recurring nightmare coming true. I was like, 'I only wanted to get laid.' But I paid for the surgery to replace her tooth. This was in grad school, before I had that kind of money to be throwing around."

I swat blindly at his head while I picture the whole thing going down. "Stop it. Just stop! That did *not* happen."

"Yes, it did! Why would I tell you such a terrible story, if it weren't true? Shit. I don't know why I told you at all. It's degrading, but it's not the worst story, by far."

"Shut up!"

"Okay. I'm not going to tell you the worst story, anyway."

The door to the bedroom next door rattles loudly. Seconds later, Caroline's head pokes through Luke's open bedroom doorway. "What the hell is going on over here?" she demands waspishly. "I'm trying to sleep."

Luke looks around me. "Oh. Sorry. I was regaling Jayne with the tooth story."

Caroline rolls her eyes. "Why do you insist on telling

everyone that horrible story? It wouldn't be funny if it was *your* tooth." She touches her left front tooth with her tongue. "I looked like a hockey player."

My eyes nearly pop from my skull. "It was *you*?!" I barely manage to sputter.

Luke laughs at my reaction and Caroline's disgusted expression.

"I didn't tell her who my date was. That's all on you," he states.

"God, I hate you!" she shouts before yanking on the door and slamming it on her way back to her own room.

"Do you believe me now?" he asks after we hear her door bang shut.

"I guess so."

"I'm not bragging about it; merely being honest. What were we even talking about?"

Like an idiot, I remind him, "The Mile High Club."

"Oh, yes! Well, no, I'm not a member. Imagine the mayhem I could inflict in such a confined space. I'm picturing loss of cabin pressure. Not to mention, planes are dirty. I'm too germophobic to attempt something like that." He flops onto his back once more and blinks up at the ceiling. Pushing the blanket away, he bends one of his legs to bring his foot up to rest on the edge of the bed. "Whew… I think the worst is past. I can almost breathe normally again."

Unfortunately, I'm having the opposite experience.

CHAPTER SEVENTEEN

Ha! This is hilarious. Talk about literary clichés come to life. I'm falling in love with stupid Luke-Ass Edwards. Or at the very least, I have a fierce crush on him, which is equally bad, if not worse. How the hell did this happen? A few weeks ago, I didn't even know he existed. Then I met him and *wished* he didn't exist. And now, I can't imagine existing without him.

Oh, shit. That's the mawkish thinking of someone in love. Or in lust. Yeah. Maybe that's all it is. Lust. I'm sex-deprived, so seeing him in his leaving-not-much-to-the-imagination underthings sent me over the edge. *He's* not necessarily the object of my desire; any half-dressed man would do. Yes. That's an excellent theory. Let's test it out with some middle-of-the-night TV watching.

Settled in the basement in a chair with a view of the room's entrance (there will be no soft-stepping lurkers observing me from behind this time), I channel-surf until I get to the naughty channels. The first program I land on started moments ago, so nothing interesting is happening yet. Next.

Okay, this is a bit steamier. What is he *doing*? Oh! Ick. Never mind! Next!

Whew. This looks more… conventional. Nice (for porn, I suppose). Having come in on the middle of it, I have no idea what the story line is (as if it matters), but these two are at least doing something that resembles what I've done a few times in the past. Only this guy's too smooth. I don't mean hairless (although he is disturbingly that, too). It's all so choreographed. It would be a nice touch if they bumped noses or did something that looked semi-unscripted. It's obvious a director has told him to put a hand there and lift his leg at precisely *that* moment so that… Oh, wait. *That's* interesting. I bet that feels weird. Anyway!

I glance at the doorway, my finger poised over the "power" button when I think I hear someone on the stairs. Nobody materializes, though, so I go back to studying the show.

What was the point of this exercise, again? Oh, right! To see if it's as titillating (yep, I said it) or more to see a hot, naked stranger as it was to see my editor in twice as much clothing.

Well, the answer so far is no. BUT I'm not giving up. Because the problem I have with this guy is that I simply don't find him very attractive. He seems to have all the right features in all the right places, but he's too blond. And that cocky look on his face when they cut to a close-up of him is off-putting. It's as if he's saying, "I know I'm good," and that's intimidating. Plus, what if he's not? He actually appears to be a bit robotic. And too muscly. Like bulky, body-builder muscly. His muscles stand out everywhere, no matter what he's doing. I can't stop staring at them.

No, what would be much better is if he had dark hair,

green eyes, and a smile that looks like it only comes out for special occasions, but when it does... look out!

Oh, man!

I feel like crying when I press the button to turn off the TV. This is such a bummer. It would figure that I'd fall in love with the first straight man I've spent any amount of time with in... well, a long time. Why does it have to be *him*? He's complicated and moody and admits to being bad in the bedroom, which should be a major turn-off (I like my teeth and would like to have them for many more decades, if possible), but his self-deprecating divulgences only endear him more to me. They make me think, "Oh, so he's *not* perfect," and it's a relief, although I *know* he's not perfect at all (see: "moody" and "complicated").

And his life is far from perfect. He's married, for Pete's sake! The fact that he's not in love with his wife but stays married to her anyway, for material reasons, only speaks poorly to his character. He should repulse me.

Great. Now I'm starting to sound like a Jane Austen narrator. I think that's a definite sign that twelve hours of sleep are in order.

Sleep isn't restful when it's full of bad dreams (technically, good, I guess) about romantic rendezvous with professional acquaintances. Now that I've resigned myself to my feelings (whatever they may be), I can't think about anything else! This will never do. How am I going to face him today?

When I woke up for the first time, shortly before 8:00, and I heard the rain hitting my window, I nearly had a panic attack. Another day in the same room with him? I don't think I can do it. Declarations about Kleenex will seem profound, compared to anything I'll be able to write today. I was too tired—and paralyzed by fear—to get up at that time, anyway, so I decided to stay in bed, dozing while attempting to hatch a plan. Caroline's leaving this afternoon for her weekend with her parents. Maybe I can convince Luke to leave at the same time.

I ignore the twinge that the thought of him leaving produces and give myself a firm talking-to. It's time to stop screwing around, pun intended. This is a dangerous, stupid game you're playing, with the only possible outcome involving your sitting alone in your apartment in Indianapolis in a few weeks, wiping your eyes and nose on your blankie and writing romance novels featuring the same leading man over and over again. Only he's not your hero. He rubs elbows with the likes of Tom Ridgeworthy and breaks the hearts of every new author who has the misfortune of being assigned to him. Even if he weren't completely out of your league (and he sooo is), he's a married man and possibly a father-to-be, no matter what his claims are to the contrary. Keep walking.

Or writing, as the case may be.

A quiet knock on my bedroom door wakes me from yet another dream about having sex with Luke in the gazebo (porn was a bad choice). Assuming it's Paulette, I sleepily croak, "Come in," only to be shocked, dismayed, and overjoyed when Luke peeks around the edge of the door.

"Are you sick?"

I pull the covers up to my chin and try to subtly smooth down my hair and tuck it behind my ears. "Huh? No."

He shoots me a dubious glare. "Are you sure? Because it's after noon. Paulette asked me to check on you. If you're sick..." He shrinks back into the hallway as if he's afraid of me.

"I'm not sick, just tired."

He takes a step further into the room. "If you're sure…"

"I'm sure!" It's seriously unnerving talking to him so soon after having such a raunchy dream about him. That and the fact that it was only a dream are making me cranky. "I don't have cooties, if that's what you're worried about."

"I wouldn't say, 'worried,'" he defends his paranoia. "Anyway, Paulette's the one who wanted to know what your deal is."

I sit up in bed, hoping my hair's not too crazy but feeling awkward having this conversation while lying down. "Why didn't she come check, then?" I ask, wishing I didn't sound so bitchy.

He shrugs. "I don't know. She asked me to do it. I said I would. We didn't have a ten-minute discussion about it." Edging toward the door, he says, "If you're tired, I'll leave you alone. Unless you want me to have her bring you something to eat…?"

I shake my head. "No. Thanks. I'm getting up. I didn't realize how late it was. It's raining, and I didn't sleep well again last night."

Please don't ask me why, I silently beg.

Before he has a chance to, I blurt, "How are *you* feeling today?"

He looks confused by my question, but then he says, "Oh! That. Yeah. I'm fine. Back to normal. I even ate breakfast."

"Fast metabolism. Lucky you."

"I guess. Hey, about last night."

"What about it?" I ask eagerly and sit up taller. Oh, jeez. Could I be more transparent?

Fortunately, he seems too focused on his shoes to notice. "That's not why you're still in bed, is it?"

"What? What do you mean? No! Why would you think that?"

He looks up, his eyes wide and full of dismay. "I was miserable. But now, in hindsight, it seems like maybe some of what we talked about was inappropriate and may have made you uncomfortable—"

"No! Not at all!" I lie.

"You seem like the type of person who doesn't talk about... things like that. And I totally disregarded that in my efforts to distract myself from feeling so horrible. But now I feel even more horrible. As in, guilty."

"Really. Don't worry. It's fine."

"It's *not* fine. I'm sorry. The last thing I want is for you to get the wrong idea."

Oh.

After a pause as thick and tense as saltwater taffy, during which I stare intently at the bunches of lilacs on the bedspread, he says softly, "I'm such a moron that it took Caroline pointing out to me that you would have every right to report me for sexual harassment and fire me as your editor and—"

"What?! I'm not going to do any of those things," I interrupt him.

"You'd be justified in doing so."

"It was innocent. I totally believe that."

He toys with the hem of his dress shirt, which is peeking out from the bottom of his sweater vest. "Thank you for putting the best construction on it. Because it *was* innocent. I was sick, and you're so easy to talk to, and making you laugh kept my mind off feeling so rotten. I got carried away."

"Yeah. Me, too. It was funny."

All business now, he pushes his shoulders back and says,

"Okay, then. Good. I'm glad. And don't worry; it won't happen again."

Before I can answer, he leaves the room and closes the door behind him. I stare at the door for a few minutes while I brainstorm possible pen names for the bodice rippers I'll soon be producing. Then I burrow under the covers and focus all my energy on not crying.

CHAPTER EIGHTEEN

W eak from hunger and hopeful that the silence in the
house means Paulette and I are the only two people
left, I emerge from hiding when I imagine I can smell
dinner. I feel very mole-like (fitting, considering that's how
unattractive and undesirable I feel), blinking against the
setting sun blazing through the front windows and bouncing
off the slate foyer floor, as I follow the mouthwatering smells
to the dining room.

Luke's sitting alone at the huge table, which is weighed
down with an obscene amount of food. When I merely stare
at it all, he puts down his utensils, wipes his mouth and says,
"Thank God. I was afraid I was going to have to eat all this
myself and suffer through a repeat of last night."

His reference to last night brings me crashing back to
reality. Stiffly, avoiding eye contact, I sit at the other place
setting (I hope it's not meant for someone more important
than me... like Jesus) and pretend it takes all of my concentration and attention to put my napkin in my lap. When he
passes me serving dishes, I keep my eyes on the food they
contain and diligently ensure our fingers don't brush against

each other. I don't want anything to happen that would cause him to think I'm getting the wrong idea.

Soon, it does take all of my brainpower not to eat like an animal, because I'm ravenous. It isn't until I no longer feel faint that I notice Luke has his iPad next to his plate, and he's occasionally reading something on it and then typing. Since it's preventing us from suffering through stilted dinner conversation, I don't mind, but when Paulette comes in from the kitchen and takes in the two of us, she rebukes him after inquiring about my health, "Luke! It's horribly rude to faff around with that contraption at the table!"

He looks up and scowls at her. "I'm working."

"That doesn't make it any less rude!" she maintains, looking over his shoulder. "Anyway, you're not working; you're chatting with Blanche."

Unrepentant, he chuckles. "She's a work colleague."

"I don't mind," I interject after chewing and swallowing my last forkful of mashed potatoes. However, now that I know he's been chatting with Blanche, I mind a little bit. I'd almost forgotten about that busty, highly educated siren of Thornfield Publishing.

"She says the place has gone all to hell since I've been away," he grouses. "I'm not surprised."

"Maybe you should go back," I suggest mildly, closely examining the peas cradled on my fork.

"I plan on it," he replies, pulling the cover over the tablet's screen. "Possibly Sunday, for a few hours."

I don't know whether to feel relieved or disappointed by this news.

Then he adds, "I have to go into the city to pick up some stuff at my apartment to bring back here."

My fork falls from my hand and lands with a muffled thunk on the carpet next to my chair. "Oopsy!" Paulette trills. "No worries, dear. I'll go get another for you." She disappears into the kitchen.

"Y-you're coming back here?" I inquire, fingering my earlobe.

He drains the wine in his glass. "I'm sure as hell not staying at my apartment while Caroline's there. We'd wind up killing each other."

"Don't you have to get back to the office? You said you hated working from here."

Staring steadily at me, he answers, "It's only a forty-minute commute. I'll drive back and forth until Caroline can go back to the Beacon Hill house." He stands and picks up his plate. As he gathers his dirty dishes, he mutters, "Paint fumes, my ass. I know she wants to snoop around the apartment. Well, there's nothing to discover, unless you count my recent addiction to Magnum ice cream bars." Before pushing with his butt through the kitchen door, he asks, "Have you ever had one?"

I shake my head.

"Oh, dear God. They're orgas—I mean, they're awesome. There's a freezer full of them at my apartment. I won't have to worry about Caroline eating them, though. Even in her 'condition.' She'd rather eat a cow pie. Fewer calories."

With that, he backs into the kitchen. I hear him say, "What's taking so long with that fork, Paulette? The poor woman hasn't eaten all day. I could have forged one out of silver for her myself by now."

"Oh, you!" Paulette squawks at him. "I merely got distracted!"

She returns to the dining room with my eating utensil and says, "So sorry, Jayne. My kettle was about to boil over."

She leaves me alone again before I can utter a single syllable.

"Get out of that dishwasher!" I hear her cry on the other side of the door. "You'll be putting me out of a job, you will!"

While they bicker about division of labor, I push my food around on my plate and try to calm myself at the news that Luke's not going back to Boston to stay. It's not as bad as it sounds. Yes, he'll still be here, but only to sleep. He'll be gone from very early in the morning until fairly late in the evening. I may never have to see him at all, if I plan things out just so. Sleeping when he leaves in the morning; working —somewhere isolated—when he returns at night.

Silly me, I thought once Caroline was no longer here, he wouldn't feel the need to stay here to protect me from her (or whatever he was doing). I didn't take into account that they can barely co-exist in a seven-thousand square-foot beach house, much less an apartment a tenth of that size. I wasn't necessarily looking forward to him leaving, but I was hoping I'd be less distracted and get more work done.

And I still will, I firmly tell myself now. That workaholic will never be home.

While finalizing plans for Gus to come out to Marblehead next weekend, the door to the sitting room flies open, and Luke pokes his head through.

"Honey, I'm home!" he bellows. "And traffic was murder. Pour your old man a gin and tonic."

"Who the hell is that?" Gus wonders. I can practically hear him drooling.

I blush and look down to hide my grin at seeing Luke,

who's holding one of his hands over his mouth now that he realizes I'm on the phone. "It's just Luke. Being silly."

"Luke-Ass?"

"Yes."

"Wait a minute. The man who 'has a broomstick shoved so far up his ass that you can see the tip of the handle every time he opens his mouth, which is often, because he loves the sound of his own voice' is being silly?"

I glance up. Luke mouths, "Sorry" and plops into the chair perpendicular to the sofa I'm occupying.

"Yes," I succinctly answer. "Hey, listen. I've gotta go. You'll be here next Friday night, right? Do you need a ride? I could probably ask Luke to have a driver bring you out here." Luke, himself, verifies this is true by nodding before letting his head fall and rest against the back of the chair.

"Uh, yes please! I'd have to be the King of the Dingle-berries to turn down that offer. Oh, girl! This is gonna be so much fun! Mmm-hmm!"

Before he sprains his southern belle tendon, I let him go. As soon as I say bye, Luke magically revives.

"The irrepressible Gus, I presume?" he inquires.

I set my phone on the table next to my laptop. "The one and only. It's still okay for him to come stay next weekend, right?"

"Absolutely. He's welcome to come out every weekend. Or whenever. Mi casa es su casa."

I pull my laptop onto my lap and keep my eyes pinned on the screen while I lie, "He's busy this weekend." I clear my throat and change the subject. "You're home early." I try not to make it sound like an accusation. Or like something a wife would say to a husband.

"Am I?" he replies innocently.

"It's only 2:30," I point out as I back up my work and prepare to shut down my computer.

He stares into space and says, "I dunno. I was sitting at my desk at work, and I looked at my schedule and saw I didn't have any afternoon meetings, and I got this restless feeling, like if I sat there another minute, I was going to scream. And I thought, 'Why do I have to sit here? I don't.' I never take all my vacation in a year, so Thornfield owes me a shit-ton of time. I don't have any tight deadlines. So I left." Now he blinks at me as if he can't believe he did it. He chuckles nervously. "I just walked out."

I raise my eyebrows at him.

"I've never done that," he explains. "Ever. I'm usually the first one there and the last one to leave. Sally looked at me like I'd lost my mind when I told her I was leaving for the day." He laughs harder at the memory. "Her gum fell out of her mouth."

"Well, good for you. Everyone needs a break now and then."

Before I can stop him, he snatches my laptop from me and says, "What have you got here? It's been a few days since you've shown me anything. I'm beginning to think you're lurking on Facebook and playing Words with Friends instead of writing."

"Hey!" I object to all aspects of this scenario. I don't like that he's commandeering my computer or that he's accusing me of slacking off. "Don't read anything I wrote today. It's not right. Yet."

He systematically ignores me as he opens the file on my desktop that he already knows is my manuscript. When it asks him for my password, he turns the laptop toward me and says, "Password, please."

I hesitate but ultimately type it in for him. It's not that

anything I've written is horrible—or features him, thank God—but it's not there. And he's going to know right away that it's not.

Sure enough, after scanning through once, he scrolls back to the beginning of the new portion and starts typing comments in the margins.

"What are you saying?" I ask, craning my neck to try to read it.

Instead of answering, he continues typing at lightning speed. Then he highlights an enormous section of text and hits the delete button.

"What the heck are you doing?!" I screech, grappling for the computer.

"Saving us both some time later when we have to make cuts. I can tell you right now, that's not going to make the final cut," he answers, relinquishing my laptop to me.

I immediately hit "Control" and "Z" to bring the text back. Reading through it, I suppose he has a point, but I, and I alone, have delete privileges. And I don't delete anything. I cut it and put it in a separate file labeled "Cuts," in case I ever want it back again. That's what I do now, while he smirks at me. Then I read his comments.

Comment: This is pedantic.

Comment: I like this, but I'm not sure it goes here.

Comment: This is good.

Comment: Move this to the end of Chapter Two.

Comment: This is not-so-good.

Comment: It's obvious you don't have anyone here during the day to force you to take breaks when you go on your Kleenex rants.

I look up at him and narrow my eyes. "Very funny."

Again, he confiscates the computer, but this time he closes it and sets it on the coffee table. "Come on. Let's go swimming."

"I don't know."

"It's gorgeous outside. I couldn't believe it when I walked out to the gazebo only to find it empty." He stands and offers me a hand up.

I don't take it.

Using my own power, I rise from the couch and avert my eyes when I tell him in a tone that's as blasé as possible, "Sometimes, especially after lunch, it's too hot out there. I'd rather work in here."

What I don't tell him (and *never* will, because it's pathetic) is that I start to miss him in the afternoons, and there are more reminders of him in this room than out there. Plus, it *does* get hot in the afternoons.

He readily accepts my explanation. "Race you to the pool?"

"I don't think so."

"You don't think so? You mean no racing, but you will go swimming?"

He looks so hopeful that I can't stand to tell him no.

"I'll go swimming," I allow, like it's the biggest imposition ever.

As he leads the way upstairs to the bedrooms, he says, "Oh, good. Because I was going to throw you in, no matter what."

CHAPTER NINETEEN

G us isn't busy this weekend, unless you count staying out of my way and giving me some quiet alone time with Luke. That sounds bad, or like I have shady motives. I don't. But, Paulette has weekends off, and last weekend, after Caroline's departure, it was nice when it was only the two of us. I got a lot of writing done. Good writing. Writing that made Luke smile.

Today, after several hours of isolation in the gazebo, the work I presented to him made him grin and say, "You're so close. So close. Next week, let's talk about blending the old with the new and figuring out where we can get the most emotional bang for your buck. It only needs to be one sentence. That's all it takes. One sentence that knocks the wind out of the reader and says, 'You're my bitch, now.'"

I laughed at that, but he wagged his finger at me. "I'm serious. Did you read that Womack excerpt I sent you?"

"Yes," I replied dully, rolling my eyes.

"Admit it; it made you cry."

"It stung my eyes and nose a little bit," I allowed.

"Liar. You wept like a baby."

He was right, but there was no way I was going to give him the satisfaction of saying so. Because so what? We all know Womack is a master manipulator of emotions. You can see it in the self-satisfied expression on his face in his author photo. If pictures could talk, his would say, *"That's right. You're gonna bawl when you read this, so have your hankie ready, because I'm about to own you. First, I have to go to the bank and count some of my money."*

The point is, I delayed Gus's visit, because I wanted another weekend like last weekend. I wish every weekend could be like that. I *do* miss Gus, though, so by next week maybe I'll be ready for an interruption to the routine that's probably becoming a mite too comfortable. I'm not yet ready this week.

"Why doesn't anyone call you 'Dr. Edwards'?" I ask Luke now while we're cutting up vegetables to put on the homemade pizzas we're making for dinner.

He pops a raw mushroom slice into his mouth and then spits it promptly into the kitchen sink with a *"Blaaaagh!"* before wiping his lips and calmly replying, "I've only had my doctorate for a few months. I guess it hasn't stuck yet."

"It never will, if no one ever calls you 'Doctor,'" I point out while chopping a green bell pepper and precisely placing the pieces on top of the first layer of mozzarella on my pie.

"That's fine. I don't want anyone to call me that."

His indifference is puzzling to me. "Why not? You earned it."

He makes my fastidious topping placement look haphazard as he concentrates on making his pizza perfectly symmetrical. After several seconds of silence, he finally answers, "I got my Ph.D. for one reason and one reason only: to keep me too busy to spend any time with my... with

Caroline. Career advancement was a decent bonus, but... I needed an excuse to be away from her on weekends and to avoid family functions. My thesis was an excellent diversion." He looks up and takes in my open-mouthed expression. Testily, he says, "Don't judge me, all right? You have no idea."

"I'm not judging!" I insist.

"Yes, you are. You're thinking that a doctorate degree is a lot of effort and expense to put forth, when I could have simply gotten a divorce. And you're right."

In his defense and in an effort to soothe his temper, I mention, "Well, there *was* a professional advantage, too."

"Exactly."

"You didn't care about that as much."

He sighs. "No. Okay? I didn't. Actually, I did the math and figured out that it was cheaper to get my Ph.D. than it was to divorce Caroline. There. Happy?"

I toss another layer of cheese over my veggies. "No. Why would that make me happy?"

"Because I'm confirming your belief that I'm a whore." He looks out the kitchen window at the pool. "I stay married to someone I don't love because I don't want to give up the comforts I've become accustomed to as a member of her family. I don't want to give up this house or my apartment or my car or the Patriots season tickets or the reserved tables at my favorite restaurants."

"I'm sure you make enough to support yourself comfortably."

He laughs bitterly. "Not like that. And anyway, she'll bleed me dry. I've tried to leave before. It never works."

"Are you done?" I ask, nodding toward the pizza on the stone in front of him.

Blinking, he looks at me and then down at it. "I guess."

I take both of the pies over to the double oven, which is already pre-heated and ready to bake our dinners. With my back to him, I say, "It sounds like you've explored lots of different ways to try to end things with her."

"I have!" he eagerly confirms. "I truly have. And I want you to see that."

After sliding both pans into their respective ovens and closing the doors, I remain turned away from him when I say, "It doesn't matter what I know or assume or think, though, does it? I mean," I nervously chuckle. "Do you explain your lifestyle choices to Tom Ridgeworthy?"

He makes a frustrated noise close to a growl. "Why the fuck do you keep comparing yourself to Tom fucking Ridgeworthy?" he explodes, making me flinch and whirl around.

My mouth dry, I answer, "I-I don't know. Because he's a big deal! And he gives you gifts. And…"

"Is a high-maintenance pain in my ass!" he finishes hotly. "Oh, and hunting buddies with my father-in-law! And an opinionated son of a bitch. Do you want me to go on?"

I look down at my feet and mumble, "No. I get it."

"Good! Because I'm sick of you bringing him up all the time and implying that you're not as good as he is, when he's half the writer *you* are and even less of a person."

Gulping and blushing, I keep my eyes on my toes and say, "Oh."

"Yeah. 'Oh.' So shut up about Tom Ridgeworthy."

"Fine!"

"Thank you!"

Feeling myself dangerously close to crying, and knowing I have about thirty minutes until our pizzas are ready, I cross the kitchen to the door, muttering, "Excuse me," on my way past Luke.

He snags my arm. "Wait."

When I refuse to look at him, he says gruffly, "I'm sorry. I shouldn't have yelled at you."

"It's okay," I lie, trying to smooth things over as quickly as possible so he'll let me go. His grip loosens just enough for me to take advantage of it and jerk my arm away from him. I push through the kitchen door and hurry down the hall, shutting myself in the library. Fortunately, he doesn't follow me.

~

To say the next few hours are tense and chilly is an understatement of epic proportions. I didn't even eat my dinner at the table with Luke; I took it down to the basement and ate in front of the TV. I'd like to make an important distinction here, though; I'm not pouting. Did it sting that he shouted at me? Maybe, but it would be ridiculous to pout about what he said, even if his delivery left much to be desired.

Tom Ridgeworthy is half the writer I am, in his opinion? Really? That's a phenomenal compliment in the mass market literary world. Sure, Ridgeworthy writes according to a formula that he's devised and perfected in his scores of novels, so I'm sure many people—myself included, when I'm trying to make myself feel better—look down their noses at that. But, his formula is proven. It's successful. It's golden. The only reason I don't have my own formula is that I've only written one book, and nobody knows who the hell I am. But if I could crank 'em out like he does and land on the bestsellers list every single time, you bet your ass I'd do it. It wouldn't matter if some elitists thought my writing was subpar. Their opinions wouldn't affect my bank balance or my self-worth at all.

What's making me keep my distance from Luke isn't his

gratifying comparison of my writing skills to one of the most successful and prolific writers of the modern age. Nope. It's the other part of what he said that's freaking me out. Coupled with what we discussed immediately prior to his blow-up, his statement about my being a superior person makes me feel desperately hopeless, ironically enough. It *should* make me feel good. It *should* even make me contemplate "getting the wrong idea." All it does is give me heartburn. Or maybe that's the pizza.

Anyway, I've already entertained plenty of wrong ideas during the past week. Plenty. Too many. It seems in doing so that I've forgotten my place. I am a writer who works with an editor, who has generously offered me the use of his *wife's* house for the purposes of finishing my manuscript, because I had trouble working anywhere else. This environment suits me and allows me to write well. That is all.

Except... that's *not* all. Because I love that stupid, bad-tempered editor, and he makes me happy. And I make him happy, I think, based on the amount of time he *chooses* to spend with me, even when we're not working. I'm going to come right out and say it: I want him to rip my clothes off and do things to me that they do to each other on the naughty channels in the wee hours of the morning. Some of the things, anyway. I know I'm too meek and skittish and *plain* to make that possible.

Even if he offered, I'd be unable to go through with it. Because he has a *wife*. And possibly a fetus inside that wife. He may seem to have forgotten those things sometimes, but I haven't. I *can't*. Call me an unsophisticated farm girl, or whatever, but just because I've transplanted myself to a big city doesn't mean I left my upbringing on a shelf in the house that burnt down in the middle of Nowhereville in Indiana. My old-fashioned morals and values—as inconvenient as they are—didn't die with the rest of my family.

Maybe when I'm finished with this book (if that ever happens), I'll go wander on the moors of singlehood in the hopes that a less complicated man discovers me and nurses me back to vigor before I perish from sexual inactivity. I've heard it can be fatal.

Okay, so I'm pouting a little bit.

"Are you going to hide down there all night, watching porn?"

I knew it was a mistake to answer my cell phone when his name flashed on the screen, yet... I couldn't resist answering.

"I'm not watching porn!"

"Mm-hm. Sure. Okay."

"I'm not! It's not even on at this time!"

This inadvertent betrayal of my knowledge of such things makes him laugh.

Shit.

"You know what I mean," I grumble. "What do you want?"

"I said I was sorry for yelling at you. Why are you still mad at me?" he asks, sounding more hurt than annoyed. "Was it something I said? Surely, it can't be anything I said. I didn't say anything offensive."

"I'm not mad at you for anything you said," I confirm. "I *am* sick of you thinking it's okay to shout everything at people when you want to get your point across."

His voice sounds tight when he replies, "I know. It's wrong. That's why I apologized."

"It's not okay to shout and think that an apology is good enough."

"What else do you want?"

Oh, gosh. Don't ask me that! I can think of about a hundred ways to answer that question, and none of them is clean, appropriate, or professional.

Finally, I come up with a decent response. "I want you to think *before* you shout so that the apology isn't necessary."

He sighs. "But my temper—"

"You're not a child. You need to learn how to control your temper. Plus, you lose it about the strangest things."

"I don't think I do."

"We'll agree to disagree so it doesn't turn into another argument that ends with you shouting at me."

"Are you *trying* to piss me off?"

"No! The opposite."

"Could've fooled me."

"It's not my fault you're so quick to anger."

"I'm—" He stops abruptly and takes a deep, steadying breath. After a length of time that suggests he counted to at least ten, he says pleasantly, "Are you going to work anymore tonight?"

"I hadn't planned on it," I reply sweetly.

"If I promise not to shout at you anymore—tonight—will you at least come upstairs and watch TV with me, instead of making me feel like a hothead with no friends?"

Well, when he puts it that way, it would seem spiteful of me to say no.

CHAPTER TWENTY

His warm breath against my back, right at the base of my neck, is the first clue that this isn't a dream. The second clue is the weight of his arm across my hip. And it doesn't take a detective to tell me that I'm insane for relishing this moment, however accidental and inadvertent it is. Let me revel in the fantasy a few minutes longer.

"Jayne," he whispers behind me.

I pretend I'm still sleeping. I'm afraid if I acknowledge him, he'll move away from me. Unfortunately, I don't have to talk for that to happen. He scoots to the other side of the bed when I don't answer him, probably hoping I never noticed the contact to begin with. Now what do I do? Do I go along with the act? It's not fair to suffer through an awkward morning after when nothing happened the night before.

Because nothing happened. I still have all my clothes on. The only reason we ended up in this room, in his bed, is that he mentioned the TV in his bedroom was a 3D TV, and I said I'd never seen one (a 3D TV), and so he offered to show it to me (the TV), so we came up here and popped in *Avatar*, so I could get the full effect (of the 3D TV), and as when Gus made me watch the blue people movie, I fell asleep. Luke obviously didn't have the heart to wake me up and kick me out to sleep in my own room—and he's a cuddler. Big deal! (Oh my gosh, that's so sweet!) And anyway, I'm cool. It's not like he was consciously cuddling with me (breathe!) or making a move or—

"Jayne."

This time, he says it louder, so I roll onto my back and turn my head toward him. "What?"

"You fell asleep during the movie," he tells me with a smile as he stretches his arms over his head.

"Yeah, it's still boring, even on a 3D TV. But your TV is cool."

As he brings his arm down, he hits himself in the face. "Ow. Also," he rubs his forehead. "I, was touching you a minute ago, and—"

So he'll stop making this more embarrassing than it already is (not that it's embarrassing, but his explanation is cringe-worthy), I quickly reassure him, "It's okay."

He freezes. "I-it is?"

The way he's looking at me is making my heart race. "Yeah. And, anyway, I hope I didn't talk in my sleep." I said it to make him feel better, but the possibility of it being true makes my heart pound even faster. Considering some of the dreams I've been having lately, talking in my sleep around him would be very bad indeed. "I didn't, did I?" I squeak when he continues staring at me.

He shakes his head and whispers, "No."

"Oh, good." I still can't catch my breath.

"Jayne?"

"What?"

"I want to kiss you."

I babble, "That wouldn't be a very good idea, though, right? Because, well, there are so many reasons." I hate myself. "Like, well…"

"I can't think of any."

"They exist! Lots of them!" I say, as if I'm talking about unicorns. "You're married, for one."

"Only on paper. That doesn't count."

I laugh nervously. "Oh, it counts! It matters to the IRS, and it matters to me."

He edges closer to me, but I don't move. Instead, I keep rabbiting. "And you're going to be a father—"

"No, I'm not. She knows I'm reaching my breaking point and that all of her usual tricks aren't going to work, so she's in desperation mode. She's not even faking it well this time, though. She's not pregnant."

"What if she is?"

"She's not." Closer still. "Is that the only thing stopping you?"

"No." I say it so weakly that it's hardly audible.

"I used to have lots of reasons, too, but right now, I can't think of any of them."

His shaking hand tells a truer story, though, when he lifts it to brush my hair away from my face. And pokes me in the eye.

I flinch and jerk my head back, pinching my eye closed. "Ouch!" I cover the burning, watering socket with my palm.

"I'm so sorry! Are you okay?" he says on a groan. "Shit. I can't believe I did that. I mean, I *can* believe it, but… Let me see."

"I can't open it right now," I tell him as I roll away from him and sit on the side of the bed.

He sits next to me and repeats, "Are you okay?"

"I'll be fine. It's only an eye poke. No big deal." Experimentally, I blink hard and wipe away the tears streaming down my face. "It already feels better," I fib.

"Oh, good. Damn. I am such a moron. You must think I'm so stupid."

"I'm one of the lucky ones, I guess. I still have all my teeth."

He laughs miserably. "You can replace teeth, though. Eyes, not so much. Let me go see if I have some drops in my bathroom."

After he goes into the other room, I hear him muttering to himself, "Real smooth, asshole. 'I wanna kiss you… after I blind you.' What is it about a room with a bed in it that makes you such a spaz?"

"I can still hear you," I inform him while continuing to wick away the tears.

He pauses and then says, "Of course you can. Because I'm not already humiliated enough." He reappears in the doorway, looking chagrined. "I don't have any eye drops. I'm sorry. I can run to the pharmacy for you. Yes. That's what I'll do." He strides to his closet. "I'll get dressed and leave the house to get you some eye drops. And I'll be gone for a while. Or maybe I won't come back."

"Luke."

"Hmmm?" he asks from the confines of his closet.

"Um, why don't you come back over here and kiss it better?" I blush and hold my breath.

A few seconds pass, but then he emerges, looking shy. "Really?"

I nod. "Yeah. I don't think it's serious." I sniff and blink. "See? It still works. One kiss, and I bet it'll be good as new."

He sits next to me on the bed. "One kiss?"

I shrug. "Maybe more than one. Go ahead."

He does. And I almost weep for real at how good it feels.

"Do your lips hurt?" he asks. At my nod, he briefly presses his lips against mine. "Better?"

"They hurt real bad," I murmur.

He smiles and kisses me harder, wrapping his arms around me and then threading his hand up through my hair, which is still slightly sleep-tangled and snags on his fingers.

"Gaaa, my hair! Never mind. It's okay," I frantically tell him when he withdraws from me. "Just keep kissing me."

No pain, no gain, right?

Nothing else happened. My pain tolerance is too low for it to have gone on much longer. Luke wasn't kidding. He's a bull in a china bedroom. And if it wasn't so painful, it would be sweet and cute and kind of a turn-on. It did hurt. A lot. It hurt when he tried to get his hand out of my hair; it hurt when he elbowed me in the ribs; and it hurt when he trapped my hand under his elbow on the bed. The pain was a blessing in disguise, though, because if I didn't have it to ground me, who knows how far I would have let things go? In spite of everything, he's a damn good kisser.

When I sat up, wiped my mouth and said, "We have to stop," he immediately agreed.

"You're right. Tullah's gonna kill me if you have bruises in your author pic."

I acted like that was my main motivation, too. It was easier than repeating all the depressing things we already know.

I had another heart-stopping moment, though, when he

said in a jocular tone, "Hit the showers, Greer," as I was headed toward his bedroom door.

"W-what?" I asked, sniffing inside the collar of my t-shirt. "Do I stink?!" Oh, it would just figure, although I didn't know how it could be possible, considering I'd showered the day before and spent much of the afternoon in the pool.

He laughed in his bathroom doorway. "No! I was... Never mind. You don't smell bad. At all."

"Okay. Good."

Shaking his head and still chuckling, he turned and disappeared from my view, closing the door behind him.

Now, hours later, it's like I imagined what happened earlier. I didn't, though. It was real. Really real. I have the red eye to prove it. If all I had to go on was Luke's behavior, I'd wonder. Not that I expect him to act differently. Well, maybe I do. I don't know. I don't know what I expect. I feel so different. And I don't know how to act.

After alternately staring at my blinking cursor and studying him in my peripheral vision for the better part of two hours, I close my laptop and set it on the coffee table with a thunk. He looks sharply over at me as I stand and stretch.

"I'm going for a walk," I announce. When he moves to get up, I add, "Alone."

He looks surprised, but he doesn't make a big deal about it. Instead, he goes back to reading the manuscript in front of him. "All right. See you in a while, then." *Scritch-scratch, scribble, scribble, scribble, slash.*

Okay, then. That was easy enough.

When I continue to simply stand in the middle of the room, he glances up and half-smiles. "You okay?"

"Fine," I toss, missing "breezy" by a long shot (as in, falling somewhere closer to "leaden").

I don't want him to come with me, but I want him to want to. Oh, shit. I'm losing my mind. I'm becoming one of those scary mind-game-playing women who get all proprietary at the first kiss.

He starts to look up at me again, but before he can even ask a question with his eyes, I bolt from the room. Must have fresh air.

I jog through the yard, scramble up the dunes, and scamper down the other side. I'm not a runner, but for the first time in years, I decide to try it. Barefoot, I pound down the beach on the packed sand, mesmerized by the prints I make that almost immediately disappear again.

When I get into a rhythm and no longer have to think about things as basic as breathing, I'm forced to confront other, more disturbing thoughts. As in, what's the goal here, Jayne? Miss High and Mighty from last night seems to be nowhere around today. No, one careless cuddle session and a slightly less-accidental kissing clinic later, and the moral dilemmas have suddenly escaped me. He has a wife? Big whoop. She could be pregnant with his baby? No prob. He's my editor? So what? I'm horny. Oh, in that case, the rules don't matter. Do whatever feels good and deal with the consequences later. That's the way of the world, isn't it? I've always wanted to be worldlier. This is good practice.

No. I don't like this. I mean, I *do* like it. Too much. I don't like where it's going, ultimately. The pit-stops along the way are fun, but the final destination sucks.

Now that the train's left the station, though, how do I stop it? I don't know if I can. I don't know if I want to.

~

I still don't know what I'm going to do, but I can tell I'm going to have shin splints from my *Baywatch* audition, so I turn around and return to the house, hoping I'll magically figure something out when I hit the back door. That doesn't happen, oddly enough. Maybe some lunch will get my brain working.

As much as I'm trying to avoid talking to him until I figure out what I'm going to say regarding more serious matters, it would be impolite not to ask Luke if he'd like me to fix him something while I'm making my own ooey- gooey peanut butter and jelly sandwich. When I get to his study doors, though, I nearly injure myself when I try to open them and find them locked.

"Aggh!" I cry, gripping my shoulder.

On the other side of the door, I hear Luke say, "Hang on a second, Arthur."

The lock clicks, the door opens, and he winces at me through the narrow opening. "Hey. Sorry about that. I'm on a call."

"I see that," I reply, rolling my shoulder. "I was coming to ask if you wanted lunch."

He suddenly becomes stiff and formal. "No, thank you. I'm busy."

Taking my cues from him, I say, "Okay. Sorry to bother you," but it's barely off my lips before he's closing the door in my face. And throwing the lock home again.

I stare at the wood grain for a second, wondering what that was about. Then I remember that the owner of the publishing company is named Arthur, and it hits me that we probably broke a rule or two earlier this morning regarding publishing staff and their authors, so he's trying to sound ultra-professional so as not to arouse any suspicions.

I've satisfied myself with that explanation, but as I'm

about to walk back to the kitchen, I hear him say, "I'm back. Sorry for that. Yes. I know. It *has* been a few weeks. No, everything's fine, but she's making the edits a bit more slowly than I expected. I know. Yes, I know. But—"

He's quiet for a long time. Then he says with typical temper, "You think I don't know that, Arthur? What is this, my first author? No, not at all! Trust me; she's a lot further along than she would be if left to her own devices. This place is good for her. No, she's not sunning herself on the beach and making me rub suntan oil on her! She's working.

Again, he doesn't say anything for a couple of minutes, until, "I'm well aware of that deadline. No, she doesn't know about it; I didn't want her to freeze up under the pressure. With all due respect, sir, when have I ever let the company down? Never. Would you let me do what I do and stop worrying about it? I *know* what we're sitting on, yes. I'd assumed that's why I was assigned this. I had heard those rumors, too, but she hasn't said anything to lead me to believe they're true, and anyway, that's R&D's bread and butter, not mine. I fine-tune the copy." He sighs. "I have Ms. Greer under control. Can we move on to the next writer, please? Ridgeworthy's latest round of edits is nearly finished."

I move away from the door, taking care not to even breathe too heavily for fear that he'll know I was listening in on his conversation. About me. To the head of the company. What are they "sitting on?" What "deadline" is looming? What rumors are they hearing?

Oh, gosh. I feel like I'm going to throw up. Why do I feel like I'm going to throw up? There's nothing to worry about. Right? Luke was (sort of) standing up for me. And I trust him. Don't I? I think I do. I don't have much of a choice. I can't very well ask him anything without letting him know that I'm an eavesdropper. Maybe I don't care if he knows, though. Maybe I have a right to hear what he's saying about me to his colleagues and his boss.

Maybe I'm going to go hyperventilate out in the gazebo for a while.

CHAPTER TWENTY-ONE

A brisk breeze is preventing the afternoon heat from
becoming too oppressive, so I sprawl on my back on
the padded bench to take advantage of the cross ventilation.
I stare up at the wooden beams and let the endless string of
confused thoughts run in a loop in my brain. I don't worry
much about trying to answer the questions I have or making
any decisions. I merelyexist.

Plus, what's the point in wasting my energy? Seems to
me like any sense of control I have over anything is an illusion, anyway. I'm not saying this is in a spiritual sense, either
(God and I have a bit of a tense relationship since He killed
off my whole family and everything). I mean that Luke is
driving this spaceship. And I'm the alien he's captured to
bring to his leaders for tests and observation.

This thought naturally leads me to dream about aliens
and space travel when I inevitably fall asleep to the soft
whispers from the ocean and the gentle caresses of the wind
in my hair. When I wake up, the light around me is a deep
goldenrod color, and the warmth around my ankle radiates
from a hand that's attached to an arm that belongs to a very

serious-looking man sitting on the bench and gazing down at me.

"Creepy staring is always a sure way to wake someone up," I murmur at him. I bring down my arms, which have been flung over my head for the majority of my stay out here, and rest my hands on my midriff. My shoulder screams. "Owwww," I intone.

"We need to talk," he utters the worst words ever to be arranged together into a sentence.

"Do we have to?" I half-joke. "We *can* sit out here and not say a word. As a matter of fact, I'd prefer—"

"Jayne."

I scowl at him. "Luke."

"I'm serious." Now he looks away from me, out toward the water. "We need to get your manuscript in shape for final editing."

Nervously, I ramble, "We are. You even said it's almost done. All we need is the 'money sentence.' Oh, we have to blend and cut and… oh! I experimented with turning the fire into a tornado, but… I think it's better as a fire…" I trail off when he squeezes my ankle more firmly.

"The fire's fine," he says with uncharacteristic indifference.

"Okay. But you—"

"Yeah. I know." He blinks and focuses on my face. "The thing is… some of the other team members are getting anxious to see a final draft. I'm afraid maybe my suggestions were a bit too ambitious."

"They're doable, though. I didn't think so at first, but—"

Again, he interrupts me. "Well, we don't have time to do them all. I'll need you to email me what you have—in whatever form—by the end of the day tomorrow."

"Tomorrow?!" I sit up and wrap my arms around my knees. "What's the big rush?"

"We'd like to start getting a return on our investment, I guess. We've paid you for this book—and two others—and haven't made a dime."

Having been put in my place and reminded where I fit into this equation, I gulp. "Right. I get it. I guess."

He stands. "Don't take it personally."

"I'm not."

"I don't want you to feel like it's your fault, either. I've permitted your slow pace with this rewrite because… Well, anyway, it doesn't matter why. It was selfish of me. I should have been more like I would have been with any other author." Now he looks incredibly sad when he says, "There's something about you that makes me feel—"

Yes? Yes? What do I make you feel? Do you want me to go first? I can tell you about all kinds of things you make me feel.

"—protective. And indulgent."

Oh. Not really what I was going for. Those are very fatherly words.

When I say nothing, he continues, "That has to end. We have to be more disciplined. Not only with your writing."

"I see."

"No, you don't. You think I'm saying this because I've suddenly come to my senses. But I'm just as insensible as—if not more than—I was this morning. This is *not* something I want to have to say."

I should be relieved. I should be glad that he's taken the decision away from me. I don't have to tell him how much it bothers my Midwestern sensibilities to be in love with a married man. I don't have to confess to anything as strong as love, even. As far as he knows, I kissed him a couple of times so I could say I did. Fodder for future fiction.

But I'm crushed.

I skulk to the gazebo steps. On the top one, I pause and say with my back to him, "I'll work tonight to get a draft to you first thing in the morning."

"You don't have to—"

"Yes. I do. You're right; it's taken me too long. I've abused your patience."

"I don't have any to abuse. You know that. Jayne, please don't be upset."

I laugh bitterly. "You can't scrawl your directives in the margins of my life. 'Don't take it personally.' 'Be more disciplined.' 'Don't be upset.' I'm not a… a manuscript."

"I didn't say you were!"

"For the record," I toss over my shoulder with the last lucid sentence I can muster before I dissolve, "*I* was going to tell *you* that we can't repeat what happened this morning." I stomp across the lawn and don't even pause when I stub my toe on the edge of the flagstone patio on my way into the kitchen, where Paulette, having returned from her weekend, is standing in front of her electric kettle.

"Jayne! What's the matter, dear?" she addresses to the moving target that is me.

"Nothing. I'm fine," I sob as I stalk through the kitchen. "I'm going to work all night upstairs in my room. I'm not hungry. And could you please arrange for Tom to come pick me up first thing in the morning?"

I don't even wait for her to respond or verify that she'll honor my request. I know she will. Tom will be here to take me back to Boston right after breakfast. And from there, it's a three-hour flight back to my old, plain Jayne life.

∾

Both Paulette and Luke honored my wishes to be left alone, so I worked nearly non-stop until three in the morning, when I ceased to be able to think straight. Then I emailed the file to Luke and packed before setting the alarm on my phone for seven, when I dragged myself out of bed, got dressed, and sat at the bedroom window, watching for Tom in the black town car.

I trudged down the stairs and set my bags by the front door so Tom could load them while I said goodbye to Paulette, who was friendly but not overly emotional about my departure, thank goodness. I was also relieved Luke was nowhere around.

I should have known it was all going too smoothly.

Before I even have a chance to take my first complete lungful of air since waking up this morning, I realize with a start I'm not alone in the backseat.

"Leaving without saying goodbye?" Luke asks as Tom starts the car. "Put your seatbelt on."

I automatically comply with his order while asking incredulously, "What are you doing here? I thought you'd already gone to work."

Drolly, he replies, "When Paulette informed me that a car would be here so early to get you, I figured it would be more beneficial to my carbon footprint if we carpooled into the city."

"I'd rather we didn't."

The car lurches forward. "Too late. We're on our way." He pats my knee condescendingly. "It's only forty minutes. But I thought it would behoove both of us to have a chat about the state of things before we get back to civilization."

I coldly inform him, "Don't worry; I won't be raising a stink about my damaged eye."

He suddenly leans forward and looks into my eyes. He

seems relieved when he sees nothing. "For a minute there, you had me worried your eye was still hurt."

"No. It's back to normal. Like nothing ever happened. Because nothing ever did. I won't tell a soul anything about this weekend."

After a sigh, he sits back. "This is exactly what I was worried about."

"What?" I prod, pretending to be bored with the entire conversation.

"I was worried you'd hate me."

I wish I did. Then I wouldn't be in this total agony. Instead of telling him that, I say after a pause, "I don't hate you."

I hate myself. With a passion I used to reserve for difficult, irritable editors.

"As convincing as that is," he says, "it doesn't make me feel any better."

"I'm sorry, but I'm not responsible for your feelings."

He laughs bitterly. "My God! You're ruthless."

I turn my head away from him and blink rapidly as I gaze unseeingly out the window. When I'm sure my voice won't be choked when I speak, I say, "I'd rather not talk. I was up all night—a copy of my manuscript is waiting in your email inbox—so I'm very tired."

"Jayne—"

"Please, Luke!" I hate that I can't keep the begging tone from edging in.

"No, *you* please. I've already received your icicle-laden email. And I'd like to remind you that I'm your *friend* in all this. I'm here for you. Maybe not in all the capacities that we—at least, *I*—would like, but I'm here nonetheless." He lays a hand on my shoulder, but I shrug, and when he doesn't remove it, I purposefully do it myself with my own hand.

"Please, don't touch me." I glance nervously toward the front seat.

When he notices, he says, "Oh, don't worry about Tom; he's used to hearing women tell me that."

I will not laugh. I will not smile. I will focus on getting through this torturous car ride without any histrionics.

Tom drily replies, "What women, sir?"

"Touché, Tom. Touché." Addressing me again, Luke says lightly, "All right then. I respect your wishes, as much as they pain me. But if you need me—for anything—I hope you won't hesitate to call me."

"Whatever."

"Yeah. Whatever."

CHAPTER TWENTY-TWO

The nightmarish vision of me in my Indianapolis apartment, sniffling into my blankie, never comes to fruition. Almost immediately upon returning to the Hoosier State, I received an offer to serve as guest lecturer for a semester at Fairfax College in Annapolis, with the possibility of it becoming a more permanent arrangement. I gave up my apartment, put my things in storage, and moved to a furnished bed-sit near campus, right outside our nation's capital.

Yes, this is the type of relationship I can handle. An intellectual relationship. A high-maintenance intellectual relationship, at that. I haven't had time to think or brood or mope about Luke. Not that I would. Obviously, that was a silly crush my inexperience blew out of proportion and had me convinced was a full-fledged love affair-in-the-making. When I think about it now, I blush and cringe.

Luke and I have exchanged emails regarding drafts of my book, but now that I've made all the changes he wanted, it's in the hands of the other publishing folks. Occasionally, I get things from people whose names I haven't bothered remembering. I've chosen a cover design, but it brought me no pleasure. None of them were that great, to be honest. They were better than the ones Luke showed me the day we met, but that's not saying much. This process's novelty has definitely worn off. If I weren't contractually obligated to write two more books for them (and don't even ask me how I'm going to do that), I'd get through this, check it off my list, and move on. That's what's left of my dream. The joy's been sucked from it.

Oh, there's one other thing: Luke's been trying to get in touch with me—nearly relentlessly—for the past couple of days, but I'm dodging his calls. I have some legitimate reasons for not calling him back (my syllabus is due to the head of the English department tomorrow; I need to wash my hair; I'm sure there are other things), but mostly I simply don't feel like talking to him. I don't want to hear his voice. I don't want to imagine how he looks or what he's wearing or how he smells.

I informed him of my change of address in a mass email to the entire publishing "team," so I can't think of anything else to discuss. He's not even part of the equation anymore. He needs to know when to let it go. Maybe I should have Tullah call him and ask if there's anything she can help him with. Then I can have her request a new editor for me for my next book.

My next book. The mere thought gives me chills up and down the backs of my thighs. I don't know if I have another one in me. I *know* I don't. Not right now, anyway. I'm desperately looking for inspiration, though. It won't be long after *The Devil I Know* hits shelves (maybe even before) that they'll be asking me about my next project. Luke hinted at it weeks ago, on one of our "break" walks. When he asked me if I had any new ideas marinating, I'd coyly said, "A few," but it was a bold-faced lie. I have zip. Which is a potential problem. I'm not panicking yet, though.

For one thing, I have a class to teach to bright, young minds who still believe in the fairytale that is the publishing world. I still haven't decided if I'm going to crush their dreams (which would be the most humane thing to do) or do them the disservice of allowing them to continue to think that a publishing contract will make all their problems disappear. I think I'm going to go with the latter, but only because I don't want to be that bitter bitch who makes them roll their eyes. They won't believe me, anyway. They'll say, "It won't be like that for me."

And maybe it won't be. Maybe they won't fall in lust with their editors. It's statistically likely that they *won't*. And maybe they won't screw themselves over by promising to deliver something that they're incapable of delivering (two books more than the only one residing in their heads). So, who am I to tell them that the experience is a major letdown? I'll let them find out for themselves or do what I couldn't manage to do: enjoy the process.

Speaking of processes, I may not have a very firm grasp on the creative process, but I do know all about language and the mechanics of writing. I know the rules and when to bend them—or when to break them. And I think I'll be good at passing along that information to the next generation of writers. As long as they don't ask me about *my* experience or *my* process or any of those other questions that aspiring writers love to ask published writers, everything will be fine.

My experience: I wrote a book based on the most horrific tragedy of my life, concealed that fact from everyone, made out with my editor, and crawled back to my boring life after being rejected by him afterwards.

My process: Write eight to thirteen hours a day (depending on whether you have to hold down another job to pay the bills). Period. Oh, a blankie helps. And a nice-smelling man. I mean, candle! Candle. A man has nothing to do with it. Which will be a relief to the heterosexual men in my class.

I can't tell anyone either of those things, obviously. I'll have to stick to the vague answers: "everyone needs to find their own system" and "expect to be rejected... a lot." And "don't take it personally." Don't ever take anything person-ally. Nothing. No matter how personal it feels.

Yeah, not sounding bitter is going to be the biggest chal-lenge in this new position, after I get this syllabus written, that is.

"Jayne Greer! Exactly who I was coming to see!" Dr. Miles Brooks, the Head of the English Department, says when he sees me approaching him in the hallway. "Wanted to see if you're settling in okay. Sorry about the small office. We're a little tight on space around here lately. I guess that's a good problem to have, though. Means we're thriving!"

I hold out my syllabus to him. "The office is fine, thanks." It's not like I plan to spend much time there, but I don't tell him that. "Here's my syllabus. Just before deadline."

He smiles encouragingly as he takes the paper from me and tucks it under his arm. "Only a formality. And you're far from the last person to turn in her syllabus," he says cheerfully. "We're absolutely thrilled to have you here this semester!"

Blushing at his effusiveness, I scuff at the floor with the

toe of my shoe. "Thanks. I mean… this is going to be good for me, too, I think. Something to keep me busy."

He laughs at what he must perceive to be modesty. "Yes. I'm sure," he replies drolly. "Speaking of," he produces a pile of pink message slips from his pocket. "Liz was collecting these for you this morning in the main office. I told her I'd deliver them to you when I saw you."

Glancing down, as the pink papers pass from his hand to mine, I see they're all from Luke. I quickly look up at Miles again as I shove the messages haphazardly into my jeans pockets.

His brown eyes crinkle at the corners. "I let my cell phone battery die all the time, too. Nothing to be embarrassed about. That's what Liz is here for. Check in with her regularly, and she'll give you your messages. Or she'll email them to you at the end of the day, if you haven't checked in. She's amazing."

I smile weakly. "Yeah. Okay. Thanks, Dr. Brooks." I back away from him, in the direction of my closet-sized office.

He holds up my syllabus and runs a hand through his rusty hair. "I'll take a look at this and shoot you an email later. I'm sure it's fine, of course. I don't expect to have any suggestions or changes."

"I can take constructive criticism," I assure him while I continue to edge down hall. "You don't have to worry about hurting my feelings. I followed the example you sent me, so your biggest criticism may be that I'm not very original. But since it's my first time and all."

With a general wave at me, he says, "Don't worry about it. It's only an outline, anyway. You'll have plenty of creative license once the semester gets underway and you get to know your students and how they work best. Please, call me

212

or stop by my office if you have any questions, or if you want to talk. I have an open-door policy."

Whatever that means. But I smile and say, "Thanks," before turning around and speed-walking to my office, the messages in my pocket crackling and practically calling out to me to be read.

What on earth could possibly be so important that Luke would resort to calling Fairfax's English office to get in touch with me? I have a cell phone (fully charged, thank you very much) and email. I also have an agent. So, I may not be returning his messages, which are all very vague and curt, but that's my prerogative. His calling the office makes me seem like such a self-important prima donna. Like I told people to contact me there, so I could show off to the faculty that I'm a big deal. Argh! Damn him!

As soon as I'm in the cozy confines (claustrophobic's hell) of my office in the basement level of the English building, with the door closed, I pull out the messages and read them. The good news is that he didn't go into any detail in the messages, so Liz—and Miles—aren't privy to any of my business. The bad news is, he didn't go into any detail, so I still have no idea why he's so aggressively trying to reach me. I check my personal email one more time (*nothing*) before resigning myself to calling him back after I check with Tullah.

Tullah knows nothing. She hasn't heard anything from anyone at Thornfield in more than a week. I'm about to ask her to call Luke and see what the deal is, but it makes me feel too much like a chickenshit, so I bravely tell her, "I guess I'll give him a call back, then."

"That's usually the logical step when someone's left you numerous messages to that effect," she replies wryly. "Is everything okay? Is there a particular reason you're hesitant to call him back?"

"No! Not at all! I'm busy." Irritably, I tack on, "And I don't want to get into some stupid conversation about the implications of choosing to use 'that' rather than 'whom' in a certain context. He's so nitpicky!"

"Well, you could have already called him back by now," she points out unhelpfully.

I sigh and snap, "Fine. I'll call him back. I wish he'd be more specific in his messages so I have some idea of how long the conversation's going to take and if I need to have my manuscript in front of me." I look at the clock. The afternoon is stretching in front of me; I have nothing else to do. But it's the principle of the thing.

"Call him back," she intones blandly. "You're only serving as the logjam in the process by dodging him. I know he's not the easiest person to work with but…"

"He's fine to work with!" I suddenly and instinctively (not to mention, irrationally) find myself defending him. "He's a genius! I mean, he's very good at what he does. I'm not in the mood to talk to him, that's all."

She laughs. "As puzzling as this conversation is, I have a teleconference to join in about three minutes. Regarding the adaptation of your book into a screenplay, as a matter of fact. We have several excellent candidates for the job…"

"Yeah, okay, whatever," I reply distractedly, already trying to figure out how I'm going to act when I talk to Luke. I haven't *spoken* to him since we rode back to Boston together.

Tullah breezily ends the call without another question. She obviously thinks my indifference stems from the same ennui I explained away a few weeks ago when I told her I was sick of the book and the characters after so much writing and re-writing.

Placing my phone gently on my desk, I stare at it like it's a deadly weapon with a mind of its own that could go into attack mode without warning at any second. I really don't want to call him. Because I really *do* want to talk to him.

The last message he left gave me instructions to call him back at a number I know to be his cell phone number. No. Too personal. I'll call his direct office number and be patched through by Sally, like any other author.

Sally greets me brightly and says she'll put me through "right away," which is unusual in itself. I've never waited less than two minutes on hold for him to answer one of my calls. The situation's peculiarity continues when he hardly lets me get out a "hello," before saying, "Call me back on this number," rattles off ten unfamiliar digits, and makes me repeat them back to him before unceremoniously hanging up on me.

What. The. Figgity?

Intrigued, I punch the numbers into my cell phone, but when he answers on the first ring, I say, "Listen, James Bond, I don't know what the subterfuge is all about, but—"

"Be quiet," he interrupts shortly. "Why has it taken you so long to return my messages?"

"I have a life," I reply simply.

"That you do. A very interesting one, from what I've gathered recently."

If he has a private investigator tailing me, the idiot's been following the wrong person, because nothing I've done recently can be remotely described as "interesting." Instead of asking him what he means, I say, "I'm calling you back now, so what's going on? And why did I have to call this other number? I don't have time to play games."

He also ignores everything I say, so it seems like we're having separate conversations when he asks, "Where does your family live?"

"Excuse me?"

"Your family. Mom. Dad. Siblings. Where are they?"

My heart thuds. My mouth dries. "None of your business!"

"Don't mess with me, Jayne," he says in a low growl. "I'm not asking out of idle curiosity. You can either tell me, or I can assume what I've heard is true."

"What have you heard?" I practically whisper, leaning back in my chair and hitting my head on the wall behind me.

"Answer my original question, damn it!"

"Why? I don't understand why you want to know. Or why it matters."

"That's exactly why you need to answer it. God! After all this time, you still don't trust me?" he laments.

"I think our history is precisely why I *don't* trust you."

"I have always been honest with you, Jayne, to a fault. At my own peril sometimes. So stop playing the victim and answer my damn question!" he yells.

My hands are shaking so badly that it's hard for me to hold the phone to my ear. "I won't tell you anything if you're going to shout at me. I don't have to take your abuse. You may think I do, because I'm inexperienced and plain and a bit player in the publishing world, but I don't. If you don't have questions about my manuscript, then—"

"A lot of people have big questions about your manuscript. Myself included. Which is why I ask, again…" He pauses, takes a deep breath, and says calmly, more gently, "Where is your family?"

This is obviously about more than what's going on between Luke and me. Dread grips me by the throat.

I gulp, not sure if I'm physically capable of saying the words out loud. I've almost thoroughly convinced myself that *The Devil I Know* is fiction, a fabrication, and that I sprang from the earth and never had a family, which is what I've basically told myself for years to keep the truth from ever coming to light.

Tenderly, he mutters, "I already know the answer, Jayne, so you don't have to say it out loud, if you don't want to. I'm sorry. I shouldn't bully you."

Pressing my fingertips into my eyes, I squeak, "How did you find out?"

"How did you think nobody would?" he retorts. "In this day and age, nothing is a secret, Jayne. Especially something like your story. A zit-faced intern in R&D put your name in a Google search and hit the jackpot. You never even changed your name."

"Yeah, I'm a dumbass!" I snap. "Anything else?"

"Of course, there's something else. I didn't need to call you to get this information. But I wanted you to know that I cared to hear it from you. And that I think you should be aware that the company is going to use this as a major marketing ploy to sell your book. They're redesigning the cover to state, 'Based on true events,' and—"

"What?! No! I didn't authorize that!"

"You don't have to authorize it."

"Like hell I don't!"

"Jayne, I'm sorry, but…"

"You have to tell them not to do that!"

He laughs bitterly. "I have no say on those matters."

"Yes, you do! You're Lucas Edwards. Everyone thinks you shit gold. I'm begging you! Please! Make them stop."

"If they knew I was telling you all this, I'd be fired. Most likely."

I don't believe him for a second. And even if it's true, I can't help but lash out at him. "Oh, well in that case... Thank you so much for taking such a huge personal risk!" I snap sarcastically.

"It *is* a huge risk," he insists. "But it's worth it. *You're* worth it. I don't agree with their methods. I think you should have a say in how your book is marketed, in how much of your personal, private life is revealed. Jayne..."

When he doesn't continue for several seconds, I prod impatiently, "What?"

"I—I'm so sorry about your family. I—"

"Don't be. It was a long time ago."

"Does that matter?"

"Does it matter that my book is largely autobiographical? Would you have treated it any differently in this process?"

"No," he hesitantly admits. "But I probably would have treated *you* a little differently."

"Exactly. That's why I never told you. Or anybody. I don't want to be treated differently. I'm just a plain, old person."

Artlessly, he blurts, "But you have no one!"

I blink and swallow repeatedly. Finally, I manage, "Thank you for pointing that out so bluntly."

"You know what I mean."

"Yeah. I do. Anyway, thanks for the heads-up. I guess... I mean, maybe I need to contact an attorney."

"Don't waste your money."

"I have to try."

"No, you don't. Your contract is iron-clad. You won't win.

They're not making anything up about you. They're stating facts. And they can travel to your hometown to corroborate everything they've found out on the Internet. Should you let them know you're not happy with this marketing strategy? Yes. Should you voice your objections and ask them not to use this private information about you? Absolutely, if you feel strongly about it, which you obviously do. Should you turn this into a protracted legal battle you have no prayer of winning? No. I didn't stick my neck out so you could take action; I'm telling you all this so you're not blindsided. That's all."

"Oh. Now I see," I mumble. "Don't worry. I won't tell anyone this information came from you."

"That's not what I'm worried about."

"Yes, you are. You said yourself that you could be fired for leaking the information to me. What is this number you had me call? A pay-as-you-go phone registered under a fake name?" I snort. "Puh-lease, Luke. I recognize someone covering his ass when I see it."

"You don't know anything."

"I do! That's a common misconception among you and your colleagues when it comes to me, but I do know things. I know plenty. I definitely know when I'm being screwed over. And when I've been played. Well, done."

"What the hell are you talking about?"

"'I've got Ms. Greer under control.'" I repeat what he said to Arthur Thornfield about me.

He pauses. "I still don't follow. Who said that?"

"Stop playing dumb. You're too smart for that, considering you could write a how-to manual about charming hayseeds into doing what you want them to do. Start with intimidation, then tone it down and become generous, downright protective and indulgent, toss in some flirting and a lot of flattery, a kiss or two is a nice touch, and then snatch it all away—"

"Nothing I ever said or did around you was calculated or manipulative!"

"'You're twice the writer Tom Ridgeworthy is.' 'My wife makes me so miserable, but you're such a good person.' That reminds me—was Caroline in on everything, too?"

"There was no 'everything!' What you saw was my actual life, unfortunately. And I meant everything I ever said to you. And a lot more that I never did say."

"Your commitment to this deceit is admirable. Perhaps you missed your calling in the CIA. Tom Ridgeworthy should consult *you* for his next book."

"Jayne, you're not in your right mind."

"I'm sure that's what you'll tell Arthur and Blanche and all the others, too."

"Don't be this way. Don't think the worst of me. Please."

"What else am I supposed to think? Do you actually expect me to believe that you *care* about me? That you've contacted me out of the goodness of your heart? This is probably part of Thornfield's plan, their way of giving me notice of what they're about to do to me, so I can't say I wasn't warned." Only when a sob breaks up the last word do I realize I'm crying. "I don't know who to trust or what to think anymore. Like you said, I'm alone. I have no one."

"That's not true. You have me."

"Shut up. Stop it."

"No. I can't stand your lumping me in with the rest of them."

"You should have thought of that before you conspired with them to 'control me.'"

"I have no recollection of ever saying that, so I obviously didn't mean it as sinisterly as you interpreted it when you overheard it. Is that what happened? You heard me say that to someone? On the phone, perhaps?"

"Never mind. It doesn't matter."

"It *does* matter to me."

"Well, it shouldn't. I have to go."

"No! Please, don't hang up on me."

"I'm busy," I lie. "And I need to call Tullah to get her advice about this." I wipe the tears that are threatening to drip from my chin. Stiffly, I say, "Thank you for bringing this to my attention."

"Jayne—"

"Goodbye, Luke."

"No! Jayne!"

I hit the button to disconnect the call and collapse across my desk.

My calling him a liar is highly ironic, considering most of what I just said to him was a lie. Biggest lie: "I know plenty." I know nothing. I have suspicions about some things, but everything else? Clueless.

Well, that's not true. I know I'm in deep shit. Not only professionally, either. When Gus finds out—which is going to have to be sooner, rather than later, so that he hears it from me and not from a poster hanging in the window of a bookstore—he's going to be furious. And hurt. I'll call him tonight, after this is all a bad memory associated with a bad day. Unfortunately, that's the least of my worries.

Right now, I have to figure out if there's any way to prevent Thornfield from turning me into the poster child for sad stories. To do that, I have to call Tullah. Because surely she'll know what to do. She'll know how to fix this.

CHAPTER TWENTY-THREE

"There's nothing we can do." She breaks the devastating news when she ends my hour-long wait for her to call me back after consulting the agency's attorneys.

"What do you mean?" I reply disbelievingly. "There has to be *something*."

"There was a way for you to protect yourself from this," she informs me. "And that was to disclose this information when we drafted your contract with Thornfield. Then we could have specifically written a non-disclosure clause into it. As things stand now, you're at their mercy."

"Oh, shoot me now."

"Are you sure you don't want to tell me who let you know about this? It could help, you know."

"No! I promised I wouldn't say. Their job could be at stake."

"All right, then. Well, it sounds like your source had the best advice: request that Thornfield doesn't use this knowledge and hope they respect your wishes," she concurs with Luke.

"And if they don't?"

She sighs. "Like I said, we don't have a non-disclosure clause, so… they can use historical facts however they choose. Unfortunately. I'm sorry."

"It's not your fault."

"No, I know. But anytime something like this—something unforeseeable, I'd like to add—happens to an author, I regret it. It's a shame your experience may be ruined by something as unpleasant as this."

I hate to break it to her, but my experience was ruined way before now. As a matter of fact, this is sort of anti-climactic. I always thought the truth getting out would be the worst thing that could happen to me. It's not even close to the worst thing in all this.

If we weren't speaking on video chat, and I couldn't see my only friend, I'd think we'd been disconnected. But he's merely staring at me.

"You *are* Rose?" he finally asks in the most normal tone of voice I've ever heard him use.

I take a deep breath. "In a way. The things that happen to her happened to me. But Rose is a lot stronger than I am. She's the version of me I wish I could be. She reacts to adversity in ways I could only dream of."

"And I really am Jack?"

"Well… yeah. But you already knew that."

"Yeah, he's too awesome to come from your imagination," he says, rubbing his chin. "But Chicka-Chicka-Boom-Boom! Did that really happen to your family? Did you really have two sisters who died in a fire?" He makes the last word sound like two syllables.

It's probably the only possible way someone could ask

me about it that would make me smile. So, I do, albeit sadly. Then I say, "Yes. And my parents died, too."

He gasps and covers his mouth. "OMG, Jayne!" he muffles. He blinks rapidly. "I—I—I—"

"Please, Gus. Please," I interrupt him. "Don't say it. I know you're sorry. I know it's awful. I lived it. I wrote it. I whored my story out—"

"Now, wait just a buh-donk-a-donk minute, Missy May—"

"I didn't say it so that you'd reassure me it was the opposite."

"I know you didn't! You mean it, which is the most bajiggity part of it. You actually think that! Good guh-ravy!" He fans his face. "Girl, you're gonna make me cry!"

"Why are *you* crying?"

"Well, one of us should be!" he replies defensively. "It's a horrible thing you lived through, and you obviously feel guilty for surviving and for profiting from it, although you should *not* consider this profiting. You will never, ever, ever even break even, not with a bazillion dollars, and not by meeting a thousand movie stars—even Nicholas Hoult. Not even by having someone like Luke-Ass Edwards fall in love with you and sweep you off your feet in his ever-so-awkward, grumpy way. Oh, girl!" He dabs at the corners of his eyes with his pinkies.

Having been semi-distracted throughout this entire conversation by what Luke told me earlier today, and already thinking about him, it takes me a second to realize how out-of-place Gus's mention of him is. When I do, though, I say, "Wait. What? What about Luke? What are you talking about?"

I never told Gus anything about what happened between Luke and me. As a matter of fact, I had to make up a bunch of nonsense to explain having to cancel—yet again —our fun weekend together in Marblehead, when I left earlier than I'd planned. Gus was none-too-pleased about it, too. My lies kept getting more and more complicated as I made up increasingly impossible reasons we couldn't stay at that house, even after my manuscript was finished. It was horrible.

Gus weakly slaps himself in the face. "Oh, shoot! I've done it now!" he says without sounding at all remorseful. "And I promised him I wouldn't tell you. Oh, well. What's done is done."

"Tell me what?" I demand, feeling breathless and panicky.

Casually, on the verge of sounding extremely bored, he explains, "After you went back to Indiana, he stopped by my work one day, and we had a man-to-man. He invited me to stay out at Marblehead the weekend I was supposed to stay, anyway, and I jumped at it." When I make an indignant sound, he says, "Hey! Twice you took back your invitation, which wasn't fair, so I figured it was only right that I get to spend a couple of days at a house like that, even if you weren't there."

"You stayed there alone all weekend?"

"Hells to the no, sister! Luke-Ass was there with me."

This is an even more incredible scenario. "Huh?! You and Luke spent a weekend together in Marblehead? I don't believe it."

He becomes more animated now. "Buh-lieve it, Babushka. Cuz it happened. And let me tell you, it was awkward at first."

"I can only imagine."

"But it got better. I mean, at first, I could tell he wanted to talk about stuff but he didn't know how to get things started, so I finally got the ball rolling and told him how you and I met, which led to your book, which led to him not being able to shut the hell up about you."

My heart stutter-steps. "R-really?"

"Oh, yes! Finally, by Sunday morning, I was like, 'I love Jayne, but can we talk about something else, or not at all?' My ears were tired! What did you do to that man, anyway? He's got it bad!"

"I didn't do anything to him!" I defend myself too vehemently. "Why didn't you tell me any of this before now?"

He thinks about it for a second and then says, "It never came up in conversation. If you had mentioned him, it would have reminded me, and I probably would have said something."

"Probably?"

"Maybe. I dunno. You know how I am sometimes."

"How about mentioning that you went to Marblehead and stayed at the beach house? That would have been a start. For one thing, it would have let me know I was off the hook for canceling on you twice."

"You didn't deserve to be off the hook, sister-friend! But like I said, I just kept forgetting."

"Liar."

He sighs. "Okay, fine. He did ask me not to tell you that he invited me out there. But he kept saying that he'd heard so much about me and that he was disappointed that your finishing your book ahead of schedule meant that I didn't get to spend my weekend at his house." He laughs. "I mean, he didn't say it that eloquently. It was kind of a bumbling, stumbling delivery, but that was the gist of it. I could tell he was fishing for information about you, too, but since you hadn't mentioned his name once since leaving Boston, I figured you didn't feel the same way he feels about you, so I kept mum. Not that it was hard to do, since he hardly let me get a word in edgewise, anyway. He was so busy talk-talk-talking about how wonderful you are."

"Stop it. That can't be true!"

"So he did a good job of hiding it around you."

"Well, there were *some* indications that he tolerated my company, but if you're wondering if we had sex, the answer is no."

"I know you didn't. He told me."

"What?"

"Yeah. He said you were freaked out about his crazy wife, and then *he* had some worries about your professional relationship, but he figured that as soon as the book was out, you guys wouldn't have to worry so much."

My heart takes a nosedive. "He'd still be married."

"You know it's only a matter of time before he kicks that bitch to the curb, though."

"I refuse to stand in the background and wait," I grumble mulishly.

"Good for you! But he told me that he can't continue to live in limbo with that crazy dipshit always interfering in his life."

He's known that for a long time, though, and it hasn't motivated him enough to divorce her. I stare at my laptop keyboard, replaying in my head my most recent conversation with Luke, in light of all this information.

Gus interrupts my woolgathering by trilling, "Woo-hoo!! Hello, Ms. Greer? Are you alive there?"

"Barely," I mumble, too low for him to hear. Then I focus my eyes and smile shakily at him. "I guess I can't be mad at you for not telling me this, all things considered, huh?"

"Damn right. I mean, I had a feeling your parents were

no longer living, but I had no idea their deaths were so… dramatic. I dunno, I never thought to ask. Is that weird?" he asks.

For anyone else, yes. For self-absorbed Gus, no. Instead of putting it that way, though, I say, "I was glad you never asked. Saved me from telling lies."

"You wouldn't have told me the truth, even if I asked?"

"No."

"Uh!"

"If the whole world weren't about to know, I wouldn't be telling you now," I admit. "It's too difficult."

"We don't ever have to talk about it, Babushka, unless you want to," he promises, uncharacteristically gentle.

I tear up. "Really?"

"Absolutely! I won't ever say anything about it, unless you bring it up."

I nod furiously before I can choke out, "Thanks, Gus."

"You betcha. Now what're you gonna do about Luke-Ass Edwards?"

My hand on my forehead, I admit, "I have no idea."

Before Gus could get too carried away with crazy ideas (lounging naked next to the pool at the beach house and waiting for Luke to notice me out there being one of the tamer ones he proposed before I stopped him), I revealed that I wasn't sure I was going to do anything about Luke for the time being. I had my reasons (in addition to the hugest one, his *wife*): classes were about to start at Fairfax; things were about to get extremely tense between several people and me at Thornfield; and I needed to think about why Luke would be so willing to tell Gus—a practical stranger—

all the things he told him (obviously with the intent that Gus wouldn't keep it from me) but not tell *me* any of those things directly.

Gus didn't like my decision, but he seemed content with my promise to let him know if anything noteworthy happens. I don't expect to be giving him a report anytime soon.

Teaching is taking up most of my attention and energy right now. I have a small class, and I'm sure they're not representative of the average American college student (at least they're not like any of the people I went to college with), considering they attend a very small, very selective school, but their enthusiasm astounds me. I guess I was still sleepwalking through life when I was an undergraduate, because I wasn't anything like they are. I expected to spend most of my classroom time lecturing about various styles and techniques and then giving assignments, but these kids like to talk. And ask questions. And discuss my answers. That's great, too. I'm glad. Surprised, but glad.

Also not what I expected: my office hours are busy. I pictured myself grading papers, keeping an eye on the clock, and going home when my office period was over. The reality is that I haven't left campus on time once so far. Students are waiting for me when I arrive at my office; they queue up along the wall outside. Sometimes they're looking for clarification on an assignment; sometimes they want to chat about how to get published; sometimes they want me to look over something they've written in their spare time; and other times they merely want to shoot the breeze.

As long as we're not talking about me, I enjoy the conversations. I only get uncomfortable when they ask me for personal specifics regarding my thoughts, experiences, and feelings about writing and publishing. That's when I find myself very obviously closing up and becoming terse. That's when I enforce my fifteen-minute-per-student time limit.

Conversely, things aren't going so great for me on my personal publishing journey. I've appealed all the way up the Thornfield chain of command to Arthur Thornfield, himself, regarding my plight about their using my personal history as a marketing tool. While the people under him put on a fairly good show of being pleasant and sympathetic to my concerns, Arthur didn't mince words.

"Welcome to the Big Leagues, kiddo," he said condescendingly. "You're not going to get your way all the time, especially when you don't make your wishes known upfront."

The more I persuaded (and eventually, pleaded), the harder he became. He interrupted me two or three times and even mocked me once, after I said, "This is my *life* your trifling with." Using the same plaintive tone of voice, he replied, "This is my *business* you're trifling with, Ms. Greer. And you started it, by writing a book about your life, and selling it to my company."

"I never wanted anyone to know that's what it was about, though," I explained, foolishly thinking he'd finally understand.

He simply laughed and said, "Well, that didn't work out according to plan, now, did it? I'm sorry, Ms. Greer, but I'm afraid that's going to have to be the last word. I have a lunch meeting. Please trust us, though your biography is going to lend a dimension to your book that will probably triple your sales. Your book signings will be packed. Readings will be sold out. And talks with the movie studio are going well, I know firsthand. Try to relax and enjoy the ride. You deserve it. Bye now."

I could think of a few things *he* deserves. Like a slow, painful, lonely death.

I wanted to call Luke and tell him all about it, too, but I didn't see the point in exposing myself as unimportant and ineffectual when I figured he'd find out soon enough from the man himself that I'd been in touch and that I'd been "handled."

Anyway, I didn't want Luke to get the wrong idea and think that I was telling him in the hopes that he'd do something about it. That's definitely not what I had in mind. What *did* I have in mind? Well, I wanted a sympathetic ear, I guess. But then I realized I'd be telling him, in effect, that he was right about my not being able to fight Thornfield, and that killed the urge to call him, once and for all.

Today, I'm saying goodbye to the last student to visit me during office hours (a fast-talking female essayist who reminds me of Gus and who wants to know how to transition from writing personal essays to novels) when Dr. Brooks peeks his head around the door frame and asks, "Is it my turn, finally?" with a comically pathetic look on his face that makes me laugh at its unexpectedness.

"How long have you been waiting?" I ask when I've recovered.

"On and off for about forty-five minutes," he tells me, taking the seat next to my desk. "Jayne Greer, you're a popular lady!"

"An oddity, maybe," I reply, shutting down my laptop and tucking it into its bag.

Now it's his turn to laugh. "I don't know about that. Students here are typically more hands on than at some other universities and colleges. They like intellectual discourse."

"I've noticed."

"Other than the long hours, are you enjoying the experience so far?"

I smile at him. "Immensely. This is nice. It's very comfortable and familiar. I've always enjoyed academia. And it's even better now that I'm not the student with seven papers to write."

He rubs his chin in a Machiavellian manner, closes one eye, and states, "Ah, yes. I find it's much better to give than receive when it comes to term paper assignments." Becoming more serious, he says, "The reason I stopped by, though, was to see if you'd like to maybe, I dunno, join a few of us for dinner tonight."

The way he runs the end of the invitation together makes me laugh.

Encouraged by my reaction, he continues, "It's a little Thursday night tradition some of us English nerds have. We talk about everything and nothing and compare notes about how to most effectively torture our students."

I consider the alternative (going home alone to watch TV alone and eat a frozen dinner alone before going to bed alone and reflecting on how alone I am) and immediately accept.

He grins. "Great! We meet up at a place called Saul's, usually sometime around six. It's close to campus and easy to find, but you can ride with me or one of the others if you want."

"I'll find it, I'm sure," I say confidently. "I'm going to stop by home first, though, to—"

"Oh!" he interrupts me. "That reminds me. There are a few silly ground rules about our Thursday nights at Saul's."

"Okay," I say hesitantly, not sure I like the sound of this.

It's obvious he's trying to suppress a smile at my reaction

when he continues, "Yes. Um, rule number one: first names only. No 'Doctors' or anything fussy like that."

"Got it."

"Rule number two: no fancy clothes. You wear what you wore to work or—even better—what you'd wear if you were going to hang out in front of the TV at your house. Unless, of course, you're an exhibitionist. You get the idea, though."

"Yes. Ultra casual."

"Exactly!" He holds up his hand and displays three fingers. "And, finally, rule number three: what happens at Saul's stays at Saul's. Not that anything ever happens there. It's more like a succinct way of saying we don't hold grudges about conversations that may get heated after someone's had a few glasses of wine with dinner and forgets that politics and religion aren't very pleasant topics. We do a decent job of moderating ourselves, but sometimes we get carried away. Some of us are pretty passionate about certain topics."

"Intellectuals," I say with a snort.

"Yep. Oh! I guess there's a sub-rule associated with rule number three," he adds. "When someone in the group says, 'Subject change!' you must immediately and unquestioningly obey the command. That's how we keep things civil. The person requesting the subject change does not have to explain his or her reasons for wanting one, because that could cause further discomfort. You can call for a subject change on your own behalf or if you simply feel one is in order, based on the reactions of others around you."

"I see. A proactive approach to conflict avoidance."

"Yes! Oh, I can tell you're going to fit in very well, Jayne Greer." He stands. "I'll see you later, then."

"Looking forward to it," I tell him. And I am. It sounds like exactly the sort of nerdy crowd I can disappear into.

CHAPTER TWENTY-FOUR

These people make me look cool. I love it!

Oops. Let me backtrack. Saul's. Very cool hole-in-the-wall-looking place on the outside with an old-fashioned speakeasy atmosphere on the inside. Dim, but not creepy. Very flattering light, actually. I've met or seen most of the people in this group before tonight, but they've never looked better, even in their "ultra casual" attire after a long day at work. It certainly beats the fluorescent lights in the halls and classrooms of the English building.

Our group of nearly twenty occupies several tables pushed together to make one long table along the side wall of the place. I'm smack-dab in the middle of it all, listening to bits of every conversation but not participating in any so far. I'm trying to get a feel for who I'm dealing with.

Based on first impressions and stereotypes (sorry, but it's the most efficient way to go when meeting so many new people at once and when determined not to offend anyone with off-handed comments), we have, among others: the former beatnik who still thinks Jack Kerouac will never be equaled (Karl); the Marxist who sneers at pretty much anything anyone says and turns it into a debate about class (Irene); the sensitive poet who speaks barely above a whisper and constantly jots things in the small journal she keeps at hand (Paige); the no-nonsense former journalist who speaks in short sentences, eschews adjectives, and manages to make everything he says sound like a fact (Dan); and the prim and proper schoolmarm prototype who has cat hair on her cardigan sweater, which she wears year-round, and diagrams sentences in her spare time (Marcy).

Then there's Dr. Brooks. I mean, Miles (*first rule of Thursday nights at Saul's, Jayne: first names only!*). He's harder to pin down. Definitely an intellectual (you can spot that from a mile away, with his perpetually distracted air, hair that's somehow always about a week overdue for a cut, and wrinkled khakis and plain dress shirt with the sleeves rolled up to mid-forearm), but he doesn't seem out to prove anything. Tries to portray a balance of intelligent and down-to-earth and is in touch with what the rest of society values, even if it sometimes perplexes him. Likes to laugh. Likes to make others laugh. He's the peacekeeper. And the cruise director. And the moderator.

"Jayne!" he calls down the table to me now. "You're so quiet and mysterious. You must have something to add to this potentially volatile conversation about pop culture's contribution to the decline of the educational system."

I shrug and smile. "Not necessarily. I agree that there's no motivation to get an education when we've been conditioned to believe that anyone can be the next big reality TV star."

"Can we somehow blame Facebook and other social media for part of this?" he queries with a raised eyebrow.

"Absolutely," I reply. "Facebook, Twitter, blogging—it's all deluding us into thinking our every thought and action is interesting to the rest of the world. 'Why shouldn't I have my own TV show? People love my Tweets.'"

"They are mighty fine," Karl leans closer to me to say *sotto voce*.

After the laughter dies down, Miles winks at me. "Excellent. As long as we can blame social media, I feel okay." He looks around the table. "Okay. Honest answers, now. How many of us are on Facebook?"

Several hands, including mine, go up. Most of us don't feel the need to apologize, but Marcy splutters, "I have a large family, and we're spread out all over the globe. It's the easiest way to keep in touch."

Miles ignores her justification. "Twitter?"

Fewer hands go in the air, but they mostly belong to the Facebookers.

"And who writes a blog? I'm including blogs you may write for professional purposes, too. Doesn't matter. They're all the same." He chuckles when he and I are the only two who don't raise our hands. "My, my, my. How interesting!" Again, he turns his attention to me, "Jayne, why don't you blog? Don't you think you have invaluable information with which to bore—I mean, *educate*—the World Wide Web surfers?"

"Nope," I answer honestly. "But I'm impressed when other people can find topics to feed their blogs. I'm the most boring person on the planet." I turn it around on him. "What's your excuse?"

He considers it for a second. "Too busy. Too lazy. Too dull. Dan, what's your blog about?" he asks, turning to the Mark Twain lookalike next to him.

"Wooden boat building. What's it to ya?" he answers semi-jokingly.

Miles widens his eyes. "Nothing. I'm extremely interested to find this out about all of you. Let's go around the table and say what your blogs are about. No laughing or judgment, I promise. This is fascinating!"

"Knitting."

"Writing, of course."

"Politics."

"Feminist theory."

"Paleo lifestyle."

"Marathon running and training."

"Grief management."

"Yoga."

"British period dramas."

Miles raises his eyebrows at that one but maintains his composure and keeps his "no laughing" promise.

"Antiques."

They skip over me, the non-blogger.

"Cockatiels."

"Hand bells."

"Children's literature."

The easy flow dries up when it's Paige's turn to report. She fidgets, looks beseechingly at Miles, and with an uneasy smile says, "Subject change?"

Wryly, Miles remarks, "It's always the quiet ones," before realizing he's close to breaking one of the gathering's rules. "Okay, Paige. What'll it be, then?"

She looks down at her plate. "I dunno. Anything else, I guess."

I feel so terrible for her—and the ensuing pause is so awkward and uncomfortable—that I blurt, "My upcoming novel is semi-autobiographical."

All heads turn in my direction.

I blush. "Something different to talk about. Maybe."

"Indeed it is!" Miles agrees in his typical easygoing fashion. "You all know that Jayne, here, is in the process of publishing her first novel, which has already been optioned by a film studio." Nods all around and several "Kudos" and "Congratulations." "What parts are real and what parts are fiction?" he asks, resting his chin in his hand.

Wiping the corners of my mouth serves as a way to stall while I cringe at putting myself on the spot and then debate how much to tell before deciding it's pointless to be coy, since I'm the one who brought it up, and it's all about to be public knowledge, anyway. Might as well get used to talking about it.

"Well, the whole story is basically true—my parents and sisters were killed in a house fire when I was out of the house at a post-high-school-graduation party—with some poetic license taken with individual events and conversations, etcetera."

Nobody says a word. Nobody moves. For a second, I wonder if I've harnessed the power to freeze time around me.

Embarrassed at what seems to be an unknown (to me) social faux pas, I laugh nervously. "Sorry. Major conversation killer, I guess. Maybe I need to practice my delivery. Book signings are going to be a real drag otherwise…"

That tickles Irene, who cackles across the table from me. Her laughter breaks the spell over the rest of the diners, who re-animate and seem to remember how to talk.

Dan quips, "We've been conditioned to think that all tell-all books are about sex or drugs. Death threw us for a loop."

Since Miles has done most of the talking tonight, I reflexively look to him for a reaction, but he merely nods thoughtfully at me and looks away, at Irene, who's saying, "Readers will benefit from having read your book and will know this information at a signing, though. Like Dan said, I think none of us was expecting something so… dramatic. Or for you to say it so matter-of-factly."

"It happened a long time ago," I state, trying not to sound too defensive.

"Couldn't have been *that* long ago," Karl counters. "You're still a young thing."

"Fairly," I allow. Uncomfortable with the intense attention, I say, "Anyway, I've spent a lot of time with the topic while writing this book, so I guess I'm somewhat desensitized to my feelings about it. I've had to figure out a way to be more objective about it, or else I would have spent the past five years in the fetal position. Plus, once you hand a book over to a publisher, you have to emotionally detach. At least, I found that was the case for me."

"Editors can be ruthless," Marcy concurs. "I've been through several. I'm like the Liz Taylor of the publishing world. Couldn't seem to find one who understood me… until I was finally assigned to a female editor. It's been smooth sailing ever since."

"What kind of books do you write?" I ask politely, glad to move onto someone else.

"Erotica," she answers simply. "I guess they figured that a male editor would give me the opposite perspective, but it never seemed to work out that way. We always ended up butting heads. My new editor and I are very like-minded. It's quite refreshing."

While everyone else shares their editor horror stories, I push the remaining food around on my plate. It's not that I don't have anything to add to this topic (I probably have more material than I'd prefer), but I don't feel like trashing Luke to these people. To anyone. He's off-limits. And I guess that's pretty telling.

Anyway, I've done what needed to be done: I've changed the subject and gotten Paige off the hot seat (although I'm dying to know what she blogs about that she'd rather not discuss). I'm covertly studying her profile while she listens to someone whose name I can't remember tell a funny story about a news director he used to work for when he was a television news producer when I get the sense that I'm being watched. Sure enough, when I glance at Miles, I see he's the culprit. I smile shyly. He grins back and doesn't look away. I have no idea how to interpret the gleam in his eyes.

The weekends are the worst. I'm not a museum person, but I've already resorted to riding the train into D.C. to visit all the museums and tourist attractions in my efforts to not sit at home alone on the weekends. Strangely, seeing all those things by myself made me feel even lonelier. So, it's not something I'm proud of, but I've taken to spending time at Fairfax on the weekends, sometimes even in my tiny office. It's pathetic, but at least I'm sort of surrounded by people on campus. I know all I have to do is walk a few steps to the door that will take me outside, where I can come in contact with other humans. Knowing I'm part of a community— however peripherally I'm involved—keeps at bay the yawning blackness of depression that threatens regularly.

It doesn't even matter (much) to me that the students with whom I come in contact are in their late teens and early twenties, and I'm usually lost when listening in on their conversations. How is it that only a few years can make such a big difference? Are my contemporaries as mystified by the generation immediately following us, or am I simply out of touch?

The English building has always been deserted on weekends, so it's not like there have been any witnesses to my loserdom. As far as anyone at our Thursday night get-togethers knows, my social calendar is hopping on the weekends. They probably assume I divide my time between cranking out my next book and hobnobbing with interesting people. If they knew the truth, they'd pity me. And suggest I blog about it. Or get a cat.

So today when I hear squeaking sneakers on the asbestos tiles in the hallway outside my office, I brace myself to be caught reading students' papers on a Sunday, and I prepare myself for the inevitable outpouring of sympathy and hobby suggestions. Of course, I guess I can console myself with the fact that this person is also at work on a Sunday. Or maybe it's a student (although that would be even sadder, so I hope it's not). I'd close my door to discourage any social interaction, but I get breathless and faint in the four-by-six room when the door's closed for longer than thirty seconds, so I've resigned myself to facing the consequences of being lame and friendless when Miles stops in the doorway.

"Jayne Greer. What the heck are you doing here?"

I figure the truth is probably the easiest answer, so I give it to him, unvarnished. "I have nothing better to do."

He laughs. "I'm sure. Let me guess: you promised you'd return those papers tomorrow, but you procrastinated, so now you're frantically working to get them done."

I know I should take his out, especially since it's obvious he doesn't believe the truth, but the only person I lie to on a regular basis these days is me. Sheepishly, I insist, "No, really. I am *that* sad." I say it with a smile, though, so he doesn't know how sorry I feel for myself.

"It's a nice day out," he states. "Cold, but sunny. Do you like the outdoors?"

I wrinkle my nose. "Not much. I like the beach." I could kick myself for saying it, but there it is. Damn my need to fill the silence when he's around!

He grasps onto that detail. "Oh? Being a Midwesterner, I wouldn't think you'd have much experience with beaches."

Pretending something on my laptop has grabbed my attention, I look at the monitor and say distractedly, "Only from travel."

"I see." He looks down at his shoes. "Well. Far be it from me to discourage your admirable work ethic, but would you be interested in doing something a bit more recreational?"

"Such as?" I'm not down with 'shrooms or other mind-altering substances, which the word "recreational" always brings to mind.

His head snaps up at my wary tone, and he laughs at what must be the equally leery expression on my face. "Nothing scary."

"Is it legal?"

"Uh, yes. I think it's safe to say that it is. I'm no lawbreaker."

I blush at what he must perceive to be my ridiculous mistrust of him. "I'm sorry," I tell him. "I don't mean to be socially awkward; it comes naturally."

Shaking his head, he replies, "Don't worry about it. I stopped by here to grab a movie coupon I left on the printer Friday, and then I was going to go see said movie… alone. But it would be much better if I had some company. Would you like to join me? You can even have my coupon."

Although it doesn't matter, I ask, "What's the movie?"

He lifts his chin. "I'm not ashamed to tell you that I'd planned to see the new period piece starring all the usual English actors who are in every period piece. But we can see something else, if you'd rather."

"You had me at 'period piece,'" I say, closing my laptop, grabbing my purse and coat, and digging my keys from my coat pocket.

Jogging toward the main office, he says, "Great! I'll meet you back here in a second with that coupon I promised."

No coupon required.

CHAPTER TWENTY-FIVE

Miles has saved me from the interminable weekends from Hell. Since it's so cold and often snowing, we tend to see movies together a lot. That's fine with me. It's casual and on neutral turf, and it doesn't make me feel (too much) like we're doing something the college may frown upon. Because *nothing* like that is going on. Nothing. We're truly just friends. As much as Gus and I are friends. Except I don't point out hot guys to Miles, because I don't think he'd be interested, judging on some things he's said about past relationships with women.

Not that I'd be against dating Miles, if he asked me. He's an attractive, funny, positive, intelligent guy. If nothing else, it'd be interesting to try it out. Maybe it would take my mind off a certain *married* man who continues to plague my thoughts and dreams when I'm not careful to keep myself too busy to think.

But if Miles is waiting for me to make the first move, he'll be waiting a long time. I don't do that, especially to satisfy mere curiosity. I mean, if I had a burning passion for the guy, I might consider it worth the risk of rejection. But I won't put my pride or our friendship in jeopardy simply to see if I feel the same attraction—or stronger—when kissing him as I did when I kissed that other guy in Marblehead.

That *other* guy.

"Hey." I interrupt Miles's analysis of the differences between the movie we just saw and the book upon which it was based.

He stops mid-sentence, holding his mouth open for a few seconds, and then he closes it before asking, "What? Am I being obsessive again? I hate it when they change major plot points. After all, it was written that way for a reason. I understand filmmakers sometimes have to cut things out for time's sake, but in this instance, the changes were gratuitous and offensive."

Even though I didn't read the book in this particular case, I still say, "I totally agree. As an author, I say the screenwriter and the director need to respect the original telling as much as possible. But that's not why I interrupted you."

"Do I have food on my face?" He swipes at his mouth with his napkin.

"No. It, uh, occurred to me, though, that maybe you didn't know something kind of important. Or maybe you do." I swipe the salt shaker from the table and start playing with it.

"Jayne Greer. You're being quite enigmatic!" he says proudly, as if it's a rare skill that I've only now mastered after months of training.

I do my best impersonation of the Mona Lisa. "Well, I'm sure you do know what I'm about to tell you. As the English Department Head, you'd have to know. Maybe you're responsible, now that I think of it." I tap my finger-nail against the metal top of the shaker. "Fairfax has offered me a two-year contract to continue teaching creative writing."

He grins indulgently. "As a matter of fact, I did know that. I was wondering if *you* knew, since you haven't brought it up. I didn't want to step on any toes and speak out of turn by telling you, if you hadn't gotten the offer letter yet."

"How much did you have to vouch for me to make that happen?" I ask him.

Widening his eyes innocently, he says, "Not at all! Obviously, I was consulted. But your work speaks for itself. Your students love you. You're accessible. You get along well with the other faculty members. You're published. What's not to love?"

I smile modestly. "Aw, you're embarrassing me."

"I'm serious!"

"Okay. Enough of that." His effusive praise is only making what I'm going to say harder to say. "The thing is— I can't accept it."

He sits back in his chair and makes a sound like he's been punched in the gut. "W-what do you mean? Why not?"

I avoid eye contact while moving my attention from the salt shaker to my water glass. I wipe the sweat from it. "Well, I have a book tour coming up. And sometime after that, they're going to start filming the movie based on my book. And sometime during all that, I have to figure out how to write two more books, which I haven't even begun to write. I don't even have any ideas." He's the first person to whom I've dared divulge that information.

If he's shocked, he's hiding it well. Or maybe I can't tell, because his dismay at my initial announcement is overshadowing it.

"This is bad news," he says simply.

"Tell me about it." When I realize he's not talking about my lack of ideas but rather about my not taking the job offer, I change tracks mentally. "Oh! That. Yes. Oh, no. You *did* vouch for me, didn't you? And now you're going to look bad when I don't accept."

He waves away my worries. "No. Nothing like that. You have every right to make whatever decision you want to make, and it has no bearing on my status at the school." Leaning forward, he puts his weight on his elbows on the table. "But it's bad news for all of us who have gotten to know you and like you. A lot."

After holding his eye contact for a few seconds, I venture, "Nobody has to *stop* knowing me, just because I'm not teaching at Fairfax. I hope to keep in touch with a lot of people. But… it's not possible for me to do what needs to be done with my writing career and be tied to a classroom. This was a nice break, but that's always what it was meant to be. A temporary break. From reality." I smile to soften what appears to be the worst news he's heard in a long time. I've never seen him look so somber.

Distractedly, he says, "Yeah. I know. I mean, I don't know what I was thinking. Of course, you have to see to things with your book." He licks his lips and attempts a smile that falls slightly flat. "Silly fantasy, I guess."

"Not silly. If I were to be completely honest—and this is just between you and me—I'd rather continue teaching than make appearances and be in front of a bunch of strangers, but I agreed to do all that before I had a clue what I was agreeing to, when I thought it was what I wanted. I was an idiot." I look off into space and try to remember the person who signed those contracts. She's practically a stranger to me.

Trying to capture some of his usual enthusiasm and

optimism, he says brightly, "Well, you're always welcome at Fairfax, as long as I have anything to say about it. So, when you're finished with your glamorous, whirlwind book tour, and if, during filming, a movie star hasn't swept you off your feet and taken you to exotic, overseas locales, come back to see us. We'd be honored."

He reaches across the table and grabs my hand. I let him. We both stare at our hands. He has nice ones, I notice not for the first time. I hope he doesn't notice that winter has not been kind to mine.

"I'm going to miss you, Jayne Greer," he says quietly.

Finding the nerve to look into his chocolate eyes, I tear up at the emotion I see there. "You'll be fine," I reassure him. I clear my throat and continue, "Dan will probably go to the movies with you, if you ask him nicely and only go to the ones based on true stories of political conspiracies. And for the English period pieces, you can always call up Gert. Isn't she the one who blogs about them? You two would have—"

"I don't want to go with anyone else."

Okay, this is a lot less ambiguous than anything he's said to date. As in, not ambiguous at all. As in, I'm pretty clueless, but I think he's making the first move. As in, I have to acknowledge what he's saying, or it'll seem like I'm rejecting him. And I'm not. I sort of wanted this, right? More than sort of. I *have* wanted this. For a while. I want to prove I can move on. I'm not broken. There's more than one person out there for me, and he doesn't have to be a bad-tempered editor who lives in Massachusetts. He can be a sweet, *single*, intellectual, optimistic professor at a liberal arts private college. He can be an avid filmgoer and reader. He can call me by my first and last names and make it sound affectionate.

"I don't want to go with anyone else, either," I tell him, ignoring the irritating voice in my head that's screaming, *"Second choice!"* She can go to Hell. Or be alone for the rest of her life, which seems worse to me at the moment.

His shoulders relax, and he rubs the top of my (scaly) hand with his thumb. "That's excellent news, Jayne Greer." Signaling for the check, he asks uncertainly, "Can I take you home? With me? You don't have to. Never mind. That's crass. I'm getting carried away, and—"

"Miles Brooks. If I didn't know better, I'd say you were nervous!" He laughs at my impersonation of him. "I'd love to go home with you. Unless you've taken back your invitation for real."

He shakes his head. "No, the invitation is still very much out there, exposed and unsophisticated though it may be."

"Then let's go, Professor."

I'm a big talker. But I couldn't do it. I couldn't do *it*. Which I guess isn't all that bad. Maybe it's good. Maybe it would suggest a flaw in my character if I could hop in bed with a guy at a second's notice. Of course, it wasn't a second's notice. We've been friends for months. I've wanted to be more than friends—and so has he, obviously—for at least half of those months, or maybe more. Or maybe less. I don't know. I'm so confused!

The truth is, it felt weird. I barely had my coat off and had looked around his nice, modest house—which, however clean and tidy it was, had very apparently never benefitted from a woman's influence—when he was kissing the back of my neck and steering me toward the sofa, a very large, very leather thing in the middle of the living room. I was tense and robotic as he turned me around so that he could kiss my lips. And when we sank to the couch, I was determined to remain sitting, even though he attempted to push me onto my back every thirty seconds or so, like he was saying, *Now? No? Okay, how about now? No? What about now?*

I finally stopped kissing back and pushed away from him. Smiling gently, I said, "Let's stay vertical for a while, huh?"

Looking sheepish, he replied, "Okay. Sorry."

"No apologies necessary. But it's been a long time for me." It was the truth, so I didn't feel horribly guilty about it being less than the half the reason I couldn't get into our little makeout session.

"For me, too," he admitted. "That's probably why I'm anxious. Do you want to stop?"

That seemed extreme. I worried it'd never feel right if we gave up and stopped. I just had to get used to it, right? That's what I told myself, anyway.

"No. But I don't want to lie down."

He studied my face and then smiled crookedly. "I love that you use correct grammar, no matter the situation." Before I could reply, he kissed me again. I closed my eyes, hoping I could relax, knowing he wasn't going to try to force me to do something I didn't want to do.

No dice. I was as stiff as a wax figure. Eventually, he gave up. He was a good sport about it, because that's his nature, but I felt like a horrible, frigid tease. Before I had a chance to apologize or explain myself more than I already had, he stood and said, "Let me show you around the place. It's not much, but it's home." His upbeat tone made it clear he didn't want to dwell on what had just happened—or not happened.

Now I lie in bed in my own tiny apartment and wonder

what's wrong with me. Or, more accurately, what's wrong with Miles? He meets all the requirements—and then some —of an ideal guy for me. He's even a good kisser. I guess. But when I think about being with Miles (as in, *being* with him), the strongest reaction I can summon is, "Meh. Okay." And that's not right. I should experience that loin-jerking, stomach-fluttering feeling that someone as horny as I am right now should have no problem feeling for the right—or even currently available—person.

It wasn't that long ago that I felt it. But like the cold Maryland winter has dulled the memory of the hot summer temperatures on the Massachusetts coast, months of separation and sadness have made it equally difficult to remember exactly how it felt to want someone so much that it was like another sense. Taste, smell, hear, feel, see, desire. Right now, it's merely a vague recollection. I know I felt it. I remember how it felt. But I can't quite conjure the same feeling for anyone else.

Ambivalence is killing me. I want to stop feeling sad and lonely, and I want to stop missing the man who shall not be named, but when someone hands me what appears to be the solution, I stare at it, like, "On second thought, maybe I don't want that."

But I do!

Unfortunately, any man won't do.

It was a mistake to try to turn Miles into something he's not. We're friends. That's it. That's all we'll ever be. I'm too hung up on that other guy, and Miles is too hung up on someone he thinks he knows but who doesn't exist. I'm not a mysterious and enigmatic and complicated author. I'm just Jayne, posing as the author part and somehow unintentionally giving the impression that I'm those other things. I think the truth is simply too boring for him to believe.

I'm so boring that I can't even muster the interestingness to have sex with someone for the fun of it.

I knock on Miles's open office door. To my relief, he seems glad to see me when he looks up from his computer monitor.

"Jayne Greer! It seems like I haven't seen you in forever."

It's only been three days, but I don't point that out to him. Instead, I say, "End of semester insanity, you know. Nobody warned me about that."

He cocks his head. "You mean, how you have to give an exam or collect on an assignment weighty enough to judge that someone's learned something in your class, but you only have twenty-four hours to grade or assess that work?"

I grin. "Exactly. I never even considered that side of things when I was a student."

"Students generally don't consider anything from their instructors' points of view, I've found."

I edge further into the room and point with my thumb to the door. "Do you mind if I…?"

His smile fades, but he answers, "Not at all!" so I close the door and sit in the chair across the desk from him.

"I know you're going to tell me not to worry about it, but I want to apologize for last weekend." To my surprise, he says nothing but looks at an invisible speck on his desk that must be uber-interesting, so I continue, "I thought I was ready, but I guess not. Well, I *know* not. Obviously." I sigh. "I'm screwed up right now."

This statement gets his attention, including full eye

contact, in a hurry. Brow furrowed, he asks, "Is everything okay? Do you need help?"

I laugh so he'll relax a bit. "Probably. The professional kind. But not for anything serious. Just run-of-the-mill angst typically reserved for people half my age or slightly older."

"There's someone else," he states.

I hate admitting it, but I do with a curt nod.

"Anyone I know? Because, you know, I could beat him up or something."

We both laugh at the image, but then I shake my head. "No one you know. I assume you don't know him, anyway. He's not someone here." After an awkward silence, I repeat, "I'm sorry."

"I am, too."

His quiet intensity makes me gulp. "I mean, I could fake it. I considered it. But that wouldn't be fair to you. You deserve better than that. You deserve more than being someone's second choice." I choke on the last two words.

He rubs his thumbnail. "Bitterness isn't in my nature, but I do have to tell you, being a second choice does get old. I've been there a few too many times, unfortunately."

"It won't always be that way, though," I confidently assure him. Sniffing, I blink rapidly and say, "One of these semesters, your guest lecturer is going to be a stunning model-slash-writer-slash-film-critic with a sharp wit and a shared love of Andrew Davies movies, and you two will fall madly in love and have tons of highly literate babies, who can read before they hit their third birthdays."

My joke gets a soft chuckle and a, "Yeah. I thought I'd already met that woman, but I guess not."

"Not yet, Miles Brooks. But you will."

He humors me with a nod. "And what about you, Jayne

Greer? Are you saving yourself for someone worthy? Or just another asshole who makes life difficult for us nice guys?"

For someone whose personality doesn't allow for bitterness, he has it down. I guess it's only fair to let him have his moment, so I don't call him on it but say lightly, "Oh, this is unrequited love of the highest order."

"A celebrity asshole, then?"

I laugh. "No! I'm not *that* delusional."

"Married?"

Squirming in my chair gives him all the answer he needs. "Ah," he says knowingly, his face tightening. He closes his eyes for a fraction of a second longer than a blink and then turns back to his computer. "Well, good luck with that," he snipes. "I, uh, have a lot to do, so I'll catch up with you later?"

His judgment hurts. And I can't resist defending myself against it.

"It's not like that," I say quietly.

At first, it seems like he's not going to engage, but then he swivels in his chair to face me once more. "Not like what?"

"I didn't have an affair with a married man. It's not all sordid and other-woman-ish."

He pulls his head back. "What is it like, then? One woman's not good enough for this guy? Let me guess: he doesn't love his wife, but he can't leave her for whatever reason—kids, religion, money, all of the above—and he's so miserable, but you understand him, and you can be for him what she can't be. Is that it? Wake up, Jayne!"

"You don't know what you're talking about."

"Unfortunately, I do. Because I'm surrounded by these scumbags. They're all the same. And they all seem to be irresistible to otherwise-intelligent women like you, who don't have enough self-respect or good sense to be with a man who loves you and nobody else." He runs his hand through his hair. "So guys like me are forced to step aside and watch. Anyway—whatever." He clears his throat. "I can't compete with that. I'm too damn attainable."

I stare down at my hands in my lap. "I can't help how I feel."

He clicks his tongue, pauses, and says, "You're right. Something or someone a long time ago taught you that this is the best you can ever expect, that this is all you deserve, being someone else's second priority—if that—while you make him your top priority and get nowhere."

When I stand to leave without defending myself, he turns back to his computer and says, "Don't forget your final grades are due in the system by the end of the day today."

I yank the door open. "You got it, Dr. Brooks."

CHAPTER TWENTY-SIX

It's Week Two of the book tour, and I've made it to the East Coast, a destination I've been both dreading and anticipating. I've been especially wishy-washy in regards to my feelings about the party Thornfield Publishing is throwing for me tonight at a fancy Boston venue, but as I prepare in my hotel room, I realize I've been looking forward to it more than dreading it. I want to see him. That's all. See that he's okay, show him that I'm okay, do that nod thing across the crowded room, and get on with my life.

Gus is going with me as my date to the party. I considered not going at all, considering the way they've treated me lately, but then I thought, *Why should everyone else get to drink the booze and eat the food, when I'm the one who did all the work?* Actually, that's what Gus pointed out to me when he informed me we were going. He has a good point. Plus, how else am I going to see Luke?

A knock on the door informs me my date has arrived. I let him in and go right back into the bathroom, where I put the finishing touches on my makeup.

"If I were a straight man, I'd be all over you, Babushka!" Gus gushes. "Look at you! You're gorgeous!"

"Thanks!" I trill back, nervous energy making my voice higher than usual.

"No, I'm serious! If I had bumped into you on the street, I wouldn't have recognized you. Put your shoes on and let me get the full effect." He thrusts the Jimmy Choo pumps at me and won't stop nudging me with them until I set down my mascara wand and take them from him.

After sliding my feet into them, I stand tall and strike a one-hand-on-the-hip pose.

He whistles. "Lawd have mercy! I think I almost felt the first twinges of a stiffie when you did that." He fans himself while I laugh. "Luke-Ass better do all his eating and drinking before you get there, because once he gets a load of you, his jaw will be permanently on the floor. He'll have to drag it around the rest of the night."

"That's quite the mental image."

"My half-stiffie or Luke-Ass's dragging jaw?"

"Both." I cap the mascara, give myself one final look in the mirror and one final shot of hairspray, and say, "Well. I guess I'm as ready as I'll ever be."

When Gus doesn't move and continues to stare at me, I say, "What?"

He blinks and shakes his head. "Nothing, but... Well, I don't want to hurt your feelings—"

"What? Is something wrong? Do I not fill out the top of this dress enough?" I yank at the bustline and look down into my cleavage, which seems impressive from up here, but maybe that's an optical illusion from this angle.

"No! I already told you that you look amazing!" he snaps. "Stop fussing with your dress! Stop!"

I freeze.

"I've never seen you look like this. Ever. It's unbelievable."

I blush. "It's amazing what a lot of makeup and hairspray can do for someone."

"That's just it. I've never seen you wear makeup. Or do whatever miracle it is you did to your hair." He walks in a circle around me. "I had a feeling that all you needed was a decent makeover to bring out your inner swan, but girl, you're a whole 'nother species of bird altogether!"

"Okay, okay, I get it. I know I'm naturally plain. I've never had a reason to make an effort at my appearance, that's all."

He cocks an eyebrow at me. "Honey, if I looked like you do right now, any old Tuesday would be a good enough reason."

"Stop it. You're going to make us late with all this silly, superficial nonsense."

"You will *not* be coming back to this room alone tonight. Or at all."

Pushing him through the door, I shrug on my coat and pull my keycard from my pocket. "Yes, I will. Unless *you* want to spend the night here with me tonight. A sleepover would be fun."

Adamantly, he says, "No way would I interfere with the other kind of fun you'll be having with Luke-Ass. It's inevitable. It's gonna happen. Don't fight it."

I know better than to argue with him when he thinks he's right (or heaven forbid, having one of his "premonitions"), but he's not right in this case. At all. There's nothing Luke could say to me to change my mind about how things have to be between us. One word nullifies all others: married.

As angry as I was with Miles for what he said to me and

assumed and presumed about me that day in his office, it didn't take much thinking on it to know deep down how right he was, even if he was speaking out of turn and didn't have all the facts. It boils down to this: I deserve better than to be someone's mistress. Period. It doesn't matter that I wouldn't ever wonder who he loved more or that I wouldn't even have to share him with her. She would always be there, between us.

Us.

Ha! Oh, man. I think I inhaled too much hairspray.

My face is starting to hurt from all the fake smiling I've done the past two hours. I also have a repetitive use injury from looking over at the door every time someone new walks in. But Luke has never been the person walking in. He's not here. He didn't come to my party.

Nevertheless, I've limped my way through some painfully dry conversations this evening, trying to remain animated and engaged so that I don't look like a drooping dullard if and when he finally does arrive, but he's never going to arrive.

With that realization, I hardly mutter a reasonable excuse for abandoning the current group that has been boring me for the past ten minutes before shuffling over to Gus, who's back at the buffet table for at least the third time I've seen. I murmur next to his shoulder, "I want to leave."

He looks down at me, finishes chewing, and says, "Oh, Babushka, it's your party!"

"I don't care."

"But look at all the copies of your book scattered

around! Hard copies! Have you sniffed any of them? They smell fantastic."

"Whatever."

He sighs. "I know he's not here, and that's disappointing, but I'm sure there's a good reason. I know he wouldn't miss this unless he couldn't help it."

I narrow my eyes at him. "Is there something you're not telling me? Again?"

With a casual shake of his head, he answers, "No. I can't imagine why he's not here. Maybe someone knows where he is."

Without thinking, I nod over his shoulder at Blanche. "You could ask Jessica Rabbit over there."

He looks around, sees to whom I'm referring, and turns away from me. Before I can make myself believe what's happening, he's halfway across the room, headed toward her. When he gets a few feet away from her, he asks, "Where's Dr. Edwards tonight?" I follow him like a pitiful puppy.

She looks uncertainly from Gus to me and says, "Dr. Edwards? Oh, you mean, Luke?" She laughs and swirls her drink.

Gus waves away her deep chuckle like irritating smoke. "Yeah. I call him Dr. Edwards."

"Gus," I've caught up to him and pull on his elbow. He shrugs me off.

"The doctor and I are good friends, and I expected him here tonight," Gus explains smoothly. "And you are…?"

Blanche stiffens as she answers, "A colleague of Luke's, Blanche Turner." She turns to me. "Congratulations on your book's success so far, Jayne. We don't like to jinx things around here, but it looks like you have a bestseller on your hands." Her smile is surprisingly warm and sincere-looking.

"Yeah. Thanks," I inarticulately reply. "I, too, was sort of expecting Luke to be here." Quickly, I tack on, "Since he's my editor. Of course."

She seems to think about something for a second before pulling Gus and me aside and saying quietly, "Not even Arthur knows this, but I think Luke would want you to know."

"Yes?" Gus asks impatiently.

I nudge him in the ribs. "Sorry," I tell her. "Go on."

"He's been having some problems lately," she practically whispers so I have to strain to hear. "His ex-wife has gone off the deep end, doing some increasingly crazy things to try to hurt him."

"He has a crazy *ex*-wife, too?" Gus breathes incredulously and then mutters, "Sheesh. Well, we know what his type is."

Blanche shoots him a dirty look but returns her attention to me. I hope she can't tell that my heart is in my throat and beating so quickly that it's about to wiggle up and out of my mouth. If she can tell, she's not letting on as she lists, "She tried to run him over in her car, right here at the office, in the parking garage; she came at him with a knife at his beach house; and then she pretended to overdose on some pills. Her family's very powerful, you know, so they've kept it all hush-hush, but they blame Luke for her meltdown. It's been very upsetting to him."

Suddenly, her disclosures feel gossipy. Curtly, I say, "I don't know that he'd want me—or anyone—to know this; he's very private."

"Right, but you guys became close last summer. Right?"

"Not really," I deny. "Not at all. I mean, I stayed at his place in Marblehead, but that's it."

She narrows her eyes at me but lets it go. "Hm. I guess I

misunderstood. Anyway, he wanted to be here tonight, but she tends to show up wherever he is, especially when there's an opportunity to embarrass him in front of a lot of people."

Gus rolls his eyes. "The brother needs to get a restraining order on her ass."

"It's more complicated than that," Blanche says but doesn't explain how it's more complicated, so Gus sighs and wanders away. Blanche seems relieved he's gone. "Listen," she says confidentially, "I don't know what happened between you and Luke—"

"Nothing happened!" I insist too loudly and too firmly.

"—and I don't care. It's not my business. But he's my friend, and I know he was bummed not to be here tonight."

Bummed? What are we, high schoolers? I try to conceal my distaste for her word choice and focus on the meaning. I don't know how to respond. Self-preservation takes over. "It's okay. It's not a big deal. I was just wondering if you knew why he wasn't here. Tell him I said hi." I edge away from her.

"Jayne!" she calls after I've rejoined Gus.

I turn to face her, so she takes that as an invitation to proceed and approaches me. Quietly, she says, "Again, I know it's none of my business, but maybe you could call him while you're in town?"

Gus, ever my protector, steps in. "You're right; it *is* none of your business."

She blinks at him. When I don't contradict his assessment, she says stiffly, "Okay, then. Forget I said anything," and walks away.

As soon as she's out of earshot, Gus says to me, "So, he divorced that crazy Caroline chick."

"You finally puzzled that out?" I snap. "And what's the

deal with you? You're suddenly my bodyguard? My posse of one? Makes me look even lamer than I already am, thanks."

My ire doesn't faze him. "She was getting awfully chummy. Plus, she strikes me as the office gossip."

"She's friends with 'Dr. Edwards.' For real. I've seen them together. I think they have the potential to be more than friends." I can't keep the pout from my voice.

"She's a lesbo."

"Grow up!"

Defensively, he replies, "I'm not saying it as an insult, you bonehead. I mean, she's actually a lesbian. Luke-Ass told me that weekend I stayed in Marblehead with him."

This news—or the question of how Blanche's sexual orientation ever came up in conversation between Luke and Gus—hardly causes a ripple in my consciousness. There are too many other pieces of information vying for my attention. Staring into space, I say, "I should call him."

"I've been telling you that for months."

"Why didn't he ever call *me*?" I ask in my own defense. "If he loved me so much—as he claimed to you—then why didn't he call me the day his divorce was final? Or sooner, even?"

Gus inspects an olive before popping it into his mouth. While chewing, he offers, "Sounds like he's been keeping busy, trying to stay alive. Not to mention, you were a total bitch to him the last time you two talked."

"Well, how do I know whether he hasn't contacted me because he's too busy or because he's plain over me?" I grab a flute of champagne from a passing waiter and toss it back. "I don't want to make an ass of myself. 'Hey, Luke. It's Jayne. Heard you got divorced. Wanna hook up?'"

"Old guy at six o'clock, headed this way," Gus mutters down at me.

"What?" I spin around to see Arthur Thornfield coming at me with arms spread wide.

"Jayne!" Before I can do anything to stop it, I'm enfolded in a smothering hug, and he's kissing both of my cheeks. Wet kisses. Ugh! It's all I can do not to grab the cocktail napkin from Gus's hand and scrub my face with it. I seriously want to gag as I feel the publisher's spit drying below my cheekbones.

"Arthur," I coldly acknowledge him.

"I hope you're enjoying yourself here tonight. This is all for you, you know. *The Devil I Know* is, as we expected, a raging success. I hear from Tullah that your appearances have been packed. Good for you!" He pats my shoulder.

I want to punch him in the face. Instead, I coolly reply, "Yes. Everything's going swimmingly. I'm holding up very well, despite the super-personal questions people feel entitled to ask me, thanks to your decision to splash my tragedy on billboards, buses, and magazine ads. Oh, and the Internet. Don't forget the Internet." Champagne makes me sassy, apparently.

"Now, Jayne. Let's not quarrel about this. Let's not hold grudges. We're like a family here at Thornfield." He points to his chest. "I'm the father who knows best." He rests his hand on my shoulder. "You're the daughter who will blossom under my guidance, if you'll only trust my judgment. I pay you a very generous allowance, after all." He grins proudly at his comparison.

"It's not about money!"

"Oh, yes it is. That's one of the things you haven't learned yet. But you will. It's all about money." Pityingly, he looks down at me. "I know it's been a while since you've had any family to rely upon, so this may be a foreign concept to you, but—"

Gus grabs my hand. "We're leaving," he announces loudly.

I'm glad he can still speak and move, because I'm dumbstruck and frozen at Arthur's audacity.

When Arthur simply tuts indulgently at us as we move toward the door, Gus says, "She has family, you miserable sonofabitch. You, however, are not a member of it." This declaration silences the rest of the room and brings the focus of attention on us more effectively than a spotlight ever could. At the threshold from the ballroom to the lobby, Gus stops long enough to say, "But if you were, you'd be the pervert uncle who molests his nieces and nephews and tries to pay them to be silent. Well, fuck you!"

Two security guards in suits approach us, but Arthur waves them off. "They're already leaving," he informs them in a bored tone.

"That's right, we are!" Gus confirms. "This dysfunctional family reunion is over."

CHAPTER TWENTY-SEVEN

New England loves me. Probably because Thornfield did a major marketing push here, close to home, where they could closely monitor the results and feel most proud of their dastardly efforts. The outcome is that I'm stuck here for three weeks, hitting every bookstore—chain and privately owned alike—within a thirty mile radius of the city center. When I'm not at an event and Gus isn't at work, he tries to keep me occupied and entertained, but the hours of his full-time job happen to coincide with the free hours I have before signings and readings and photo ops, so I spend a lot of time alone stewing—and obsessing.

It wasn't until Gus had delivered me to my hotel room and was running a hot bath for me that I had any reaction to what had happened at my Thornfield party. Even then, all I could do was sit on the side of the cushy bed and cry. Suddenly, I was that eighteen-year-old orphan again. Only I cried much harder in my hotel room than I ever did in the aftermath of losing my family. I couldn't afford the luxury of a breakdown then. Now, I can afford a lot of things my eighteen-year-old self couldn't. I'm not sure that's such a good thing. It would probably be better if I were still in survival mode.

I want to call Luke, but fear of the unknown (what he'll say to me; what I'll say to him) keeps me from tapping that entry in my phone's contacts. I *was* a bitch to him the last time he called me. And he was only trying to help. I blush at the memory as I imagine him dodging Caroline's attempts to kill him, absorbing her family's hatred, and bearing my accusations and verbal barbs. Talk about being everyone's scapegoat! Despite what Gus told me months ago and Blanche insinuated recently, he probably hates me. I'm just one more person who's made his life unpleasant lately.

I'm bored, though. And boredom (combined with cabin fever) pushes you to do some dumb things. So today, I dialed the number Luke gave me when he revealed what Thornfield had discovered about me and how they were going to use the information. I was both relieved and crushed when the voice on the other end told me the number was no longer in service. Damn. If he had picked up, I would have swallowed my pride and apologized for the months of silence. I'm that ready to stop being in limbo with him.

But not ready enough to call him at a number where I can be sure to reach him.

I go online and type in "Marblehead" on weather.com to see how inhospitable it is today. Yesterday, it was in the low 20s and windy, with a chance of flurries. Today, it's 40 (heat wave!) with overcast skies but no chance of precipitation. I'm chagrined to realize I think that sounds lovely. The fireplaces are probably blazing and soup's simmering on the stove. The smell of Paulette's fresh bread in the oven suffuses the entire ground floor. Maybe Luke's sitting at his desk, scribbling on a manuscript.

My quest for information about Marblehead not quite

satisfied, I type the name in a Google search to see if anything interesting has happened there recently or will be happening while I'm in the area. Maybe I can rent a car and drive out there, for something to do, if nothing else.

When the list of links finishes loading, I focus my dreamy stare at the top one. It's from the local paper, the *Marblehead Reporter*, and the preview headline states, *"Magnate's Home Burns in Overnight Blaze."*

I click on it to see if I recognize the house from my walks along the beach, but the photos of the blackened house are too close up for me to put the place in context. Until… a wider shot of the property from almost head-on grabs my attention. Two very distinctive features—an unfocused gazebo in the background and a sporty silver car in the seashell driveway—make my eyes bug and my heart lurch.

"No" I whisper aloud, bringing my nose closer to the computer monitor. I skim the text and the photos' captions without focusing enough to actually glean any information until I force myself to calm down and read. That's when I find out that the house *"…caught fire around 3 a.m. and w,as fully engulfed by the time volunteer fire crews arrived on the scene. Shipping tycoon Malcolm O'Shea currently owns the home. However, the property was in the process of ownership transfer in a divorce settlement between O'Shea's daughter, Caroline, and her ex-husband, Lucas Edwards. Three occupants, including Edwards and Caroline O'Shea, made it out with minor to moderate injuries. Edwards was taken to a Boston-area hospital, where he's being treated for moderate injuries related to the fire. Ms. O'Shea suffered minor smoke inhalation. She was treated and released. The other victim, Paulette McGovern, a family employee, was treated at the scene. The cause of the fire is currently under investigation. Investigators say arson has not yet been ruled out. The house is considered a total loss."*

"Oh, shit," I say behind my hand when I get to the end of the article.

Feeling sick and shaky, I stand and pace the room.

A fire. A fucking fire. She tried to kill him in a fucking fire. Murder him. With flames and smoke. Choking, burning, crackling fire. Tried to melt his flesh and singe his hair and remove him from this earth. With fire, of all things.

The article doesn't say that, of course, but I know it's true. Running him over didn't work. Stabbing him was a failure. Guilting him proved impossible. So she targeted something he truly cared about—that house—in a desperate attempt to get her revenge.

If I ever see her again, I'm going to kill her.

But first, I have to see him.

A Boston hospital? What does that mean? There must be a dozen hospitals in this area. How do I know which one he was taken to? I don't. There's no way for me to find out, either. Damn privacy laws! He may not even be at the hospital anymore. Depends on how bad his injuries were. What does "moderate" mean, anyway? Smoke inhalation? Burns?

I guess I could call Thornfield and talk to Sally. Surely, she'd know something. After the scene Gus and I caused at my party, I'm hesitant to talk to just anyone there, but Sally's an ally. She'd tell me, right? I'd even talk to Blanche, if I had to. It's worth it. I have to find out if he's okay. Really okay. Not newspaper-speak for "okay."

But I can't get through to anyone at Thornfield. The phone lines are jammed. How do you get a busy signal on a multi-line phone system at a company as large as Thornfield? I try his cell phone next, but it goes straight to voice-mail. I knew it was a long shot, but I'm desperate.

I call my publicist, Jules, to see if she's heard anything.

She tells me she'll get back to me in a few, but not before she reminds me to get ready for my reading and signing this afternoon at a place called Vine Street Reads in an affluent neighborhood. Oh, shit! Life has to keep moving? For real?

"Can't we cancel?" I whine.

"Because your editor was in a house fire?" she asks skeptically. "Why would you even want to?"

After a deep breath, I reveal, "He's not just my editor."

"Oh." After a befuddled pause, she croons, "Ohhhhh! Really?! Lucas Edwards? And you?"

And this is why I don't tell people things. But I got a huge lecture from Tullah about trusting my "team" and confiding in them so nobody's blindsided again like they were when my personal history was revealed.

So, I sigh and confirm, "Sort of. Yes."

"Wow." Typical publicist, she barely misses a beat. "Well, we still can't cancel this afternoon. Sorry. I'll find out what I can about Lucas, though."

After we hang up, I go back to my computer, but there's nothing else to learn about the fire from the Internet. I've barely missed the local midday news, so the TV won't be any help, either. I sit on the bed and chew at my chapped lips while I wait for Jules to call me back.

When my phone finally rings after what feels like hours, I'm devastated to hear her say, "I can't get anything. I called Thornfield's PR department directly and got nowhere. They said what you already know: he was treated at a Boston-area hospital. They did tell me what the injuries were, though. Broken leg. Smoke inhalation. They're not releasing any further information at this time."

To my dismay, my frustration makes me start crying. "But I need to know!"

Jules snaps, "Well, I'll keep trying to find stuff out, but

for now, you need to focus. He's fine. And you have to be at a signing in two hours. Your car will be at the hotel in an hour. Are you ready?"

"No. I don't want to go."

"Too bad!" She's using her scary publicist voice, the one that makes my butthole tighten.

"Fine," I back down in a sulk.

"Good. I'll see you in an hour."

"You better have news for me," I assert semi-bravely.

"Don't get all high-maintenance on me, Jayne."

"Sorry," I grumble. "I'm worried, that's all." And that's all I'm willing to admit.

"Yes, I'm getting that impression. But you have obligations. And we're going to fulfill them. And tomorrow, you can drive all over the greater New England area looking for him, if you want, but today, we have things to do."

I'm beginning to despise this published author gig.

I don't know anything new the next morning. I still don't know anything new after waking up Jules to ask her what she's heard. I still don't know anything new after checking the television and online. I still don't know anything new after running downstairs and buying a newspaper.

Then I call Sally as soon as 8:00 finally rolls around.

"Sorry, Jayne. They're not telling us anything."

"Well, didn't you send flowers to him at the hospital or something?" I ask, trying to jog her memory.

"Oh, he's not in the hospital anymore. I do know that," she says, sounding proud that she can help in some way.

"He's not? Well, that's good, right?" I say, grasping at the tiny morsel of good news. "So, he wasn't hurt that bad."

There's a shrug in her voice. "I guess not. He hasn't called once to check in, though, so he may have a traumatic brain injury. He's never been out of touch this long."

"You wouldn't happen to have his address in the city, would you?" I inquire ultra-casually.

"Oh, I can't tell you that."

"Sally, please. I, uh, want to send him a card," I lie.

She brightens. "How nice! You can send it here. I'll make sure he gets it."

I smack my forehead with my palm. "Never mind. Hey!" Again, I pretend we're talking about nothing more sensitive than the weather. "Blanche wouldn't happen to be around, would she?"

"No," she informs me regretfully. "She's taking some personal days. It's so quiet around here!"

"Damn," I can't help but say out loud.

"If you need Luke for something, I can give him a message or have him give you a call when he checks in," she offers generously. "I'm sure it won't be too much longer."

I hate how desperate I sound when I say, "Yes! Please do. Tell him I'm glad he's okay, and I'm sure he's busy, but…" Shit. Now what? What professional reason would I have for him to call me? "I've started my new book!"

"Oh, good for you, Jayne!" she enthuses.

"Yes. And I have a question about grammar and stuff. I've tried to look up the answer, but I'm still not sure, so…"

"Okay. Yeah. Sure, Jayne. I'll pass along the message and have him call you back."

"Don't forget to tell him I'm glad he's okay. Because that's the most important thing. But I need him to call me, too."

She laughs. "Don't worry. He's not gonna think you're a jerk for asking for his help."

I pretend to be relieved. "Whew. Thanks, Sally."

"No problem."

I have no appearances until this evening, at another small store tucked in a tiny town in the 'burbs. Am I supposed to sit here in my hotel room, waiting for my phone to ring? I won't be able to do it. It's a weekday, so Gus can't keep me entertained. Jules is about to wring my neck.

I call down to the front desk. "Hey. I was wondering— could you recommend a car rental place that would bring the car to me here at the hotel?"

CHAPTER TWENTY-EIGHT

Self-Awareness Lesson #1: I am not an attentive passenger. Therefore, I have no idea how to get to Marblehead. Thank goodness for technological intervention (a.k.a., GPS).

Self-Awareness Lesson #2: Being in love sucks. It makes me feel and act like an idiot.

Self-Awareness Lesson #3: I'm an impulsive idiot. What am I going to do when I get to the house? And how is this going to make me feel better? Am I even going to be able to handle seeing another house that I've inhabited—however briefly—burned into mounds of ash, blackened boards, and warped furnishings?

Self-Awareness Lesson #4: Despite all these doubts and reasons that I shouldn't go anywhere near the beach house, nothing could stop me. Therefore, I must be an unreasonable idiot, as well.

Summary of Self-Awareness: I'm an idiot with a poor sense of direction.

When I get to the house, I'm faced with more proof of this. There's yellow tape everywhere. And a police officer guarding the property line. *Pretend like it's completely logical and natural for you to be here,* I instruct myself as I park my car across the street and walk confidently to the police car.

He rolls down his window. "Can I help you, ma'am?" he asks in a heavy Boston accent that makes me want to curl up on his lap and ask him to tell me a story (okay, add "random idiot" to the list).

I pour on the charm. "Good morning, Officer. Hey, I, lived in this house fairly recently. Last summer, as a matter of fact, and I forgot a few things when I left, and I was wondering if... I mean, *when* you'd be releasing the scene, so I could go through and look for my stuff."

Considering I came up with it off-the-cuff, I'm pretty impressed with my story. He's not. "I don't have an answer for you, ma'am."

I remember it was about a week before I was allowed to try to salvage anything from our house in Indiana. Not that I tried.

I smile self-consciously. "Oh. I'm only in town for a couple of days, so maybe I can poke around a little bit now?"

He shakes his head. "Absolutely not. For one thing, it's not safe. Second of all, it's a crime scene."

"What?!" I play dumb. "A crime scene?" I laugh, as if I think it sounds melodramatic. "Good grief! What do you mean? Like, insurance fraud or something?"

Patronizingly, he answers, "As in, attempted murder, Miss. Now, I'm going to have to ask you to move along. The people in this neighborhood don't want a lot of gawkers. I know the owner of the property wouldn't appreciate it."

"I know. He's one of my very best friends," I stretch the truth. "You know, that's why I was staying here?"

He looks nonplussed.

"Well, I see some of the property isn't cordoned off. So… I take it that it's okay for me to walk around and look at the house from outside the yellow tape?" I fold my hands under my chin. "Please?"

"Still private property. No."

He's a bigger idiot than I am if he thinks I'm going to accept that answer, but I sigh and say resignedly, "Okay. Well, thanks anyway. I'll ask Luke to keep a lookout for the really important stuff I'm missing."

"Sounds like a plan," he says dismissively. "Have a nice day now."

I trot across the street and get back into the rental car. As I drive past him, I wave as if he's been most helpful and friendly instead of a big douche-and-a-half. Then I drive where Mr. GPS tells me there's a public access beach not too far (a mile or so) from Luke's house, park my rental car, grab my coat, sunglasses, and keys, lock my purse in the car, and take off on foot up the beach.

Twenty minutes later, I'm sneaking over the dunes like a not-so-graceful Navy Seal and running, hunched over, to the gazebo, which looks incongruously pristine and white against the blackness of the nearby house. Once inside the gazebo, I can't see the police car, so I know he can't see me, either. If he does foot patrols, I may be in trouble, but I'll deal with that if the time comes.

When my heart stops thudding from the exercise and risk, I breathe in through my nose, and close my eyes, and I'm seized by a sense memory so strong, it brings tears to my eyes. That smell. Smoldering house fire. It's distinct. And sad.

I open my eyes and peek through the lattice toward the house, the entire back of which is exposed to the elements. Luke's room (or where it used to be) appears to be the ignition point. Even to my untrained eye, it's obvious. There's nothing left of that area of the house. That's where it's the blackest. The damage radiates from there, becoming less extreme the further out it goes. But the entire house is still a ruin. Destroyed.

I watched porn in that house.

Yes, unfortunately, that's the exact thought that comes to mind first. After that, I think, *I kissed Luke in that house; I finished my book in that house; I fell in love in that house.* But the first thing I think: *I watched porn in that house.*

What an idiot.

I'm marveling at my idiocy when I hear two car doors and voices. Oh, shit. Maybe Deputy Dawg *does* go on periodic foot patrols. But there were two car doors slamming. And who is he talking to? Maybe the arson investigators are here. If that's the case, they won't come near the gazebo. And they won't see me in here. Probably. I lie flat on my belly on the bench, just in case, and watch through the slats.

I hear a woman's voice, followed by a laugh that's familiar somehow, but I can't place it. It's not Paulette or Caroline or anyone else I associate with this house. Who is it? I can't see her! The house is still blocking the arrivals from my view—and vice versa. Now there's a murmury man's voice and more laughter from the semi-familiar female.

Their voices are louder and closer. Help! They must be walking around the side of the house, along the side lawn, surveying the damage from a distance.

"Those crutches are useless! Throw them down and hold my hand."

"The grass is too soggy!" the man grouses.

Before he comes into view, I know it's Luke. I don't know

whether to hide from or run to him. I decide to sit up and do neither.

"You're going to kill yourself trying to walk on those crutches." Now I see it's Blanche with him.

"Well, won't Caroline be overjoyed? I'll finish the job for her."

"Enough of that talk," she scolds.

Chastened, he says, "Okay. Fine. Anyway. This is good enough. I can see okay from here." He sounds out of breath. "Holy shit." He's staring toward his bedroom.

"You can say that again," Blanche agrees. "Damn. What'd she do? Start a bonfire on your bedroom floor with gasoline and newspaper?"

"She may as well have," he answers. "My lawyer says she purchased a blow torch with her credit card last weekend. I'm guessing she simply lit my bed on fire. The heat and smoke woke me up."

"Thank God."

"Yeah. I guess." He doesn't sound very thankful, though. Actually, he sounds miserable and regretful.

After a long pause, Blanche says quietly, "At the party last weekend, I suggested Jayne call you while she's in town."

He shrugs and loses a crutch. She bends down to get it for him.

"It's fine. I don't expect her to get in touch with me. She thinks I was somehow in on what went down with the mess about the autobiographical material, and any contact she had with Arthur on the matter didn't suggest otherwise."

"How could she think that of you?"

He chuckles bitterly. "She's seen me at my worst. And the more I tried to convince her that it was the exact opposite, that I tried to distract Arthur from the truth and lead him in other marketing directions—to the point that I was completely and obviously overstepping my bounds—the less she believed me. So I stopped trying." He snorts disgustedly. "She'd even started believing that Caroline was part of some complicated scheme to trick her into sympathizing with me so that I could get close to her and get information from her or something. I don't even know what she thinks, to be honest. Gus couldn't—or wouldn't—tell me anything."

"That guy's a piece of work," Blanche mutters.

They move even closer to the gazebo. Luke looks a little surer on his crutches. I know at this distance, if I move, they'll see me. I don't want to be seen yet—if ever—so I remain motionless.

"He's a good guy. And a loyal friend. I'm glad Jayne has someone like that who she can count on. I'm also glad he told off Arthur in front of all those people. Arthur deserved it."

Neither says a word while they stare at the house for a while. Then Blanche says, "You better be careful who you say stuff like that around."

"Well, duh."

"No, really. All it takes is one slip-up, and your career at Thornfield is done."

He shakes his head. "You know what, Blanche? I don't give a shit at this point."

"Come on, now."

"I'm serious." Taking his eyes off the house for the first time, he looks at her. "Do you like working for a place that did what it did to Jayne? I don't."

"Yeah, but you can do her more good by working there than you could if you got fired, and she had *nobody* on the inside on her side."

Grudgingly, he agrees but asks, "Why don't we ever screw over numb-nuts assholes like Tom Ridgeworthy, though? Why do we have to screw over good people? Because they're easy targets? It makes me sick."

She says nothing to that. Instead, she nods toward the house. "What're you going to do with this wreck?"

He sounds tired when he answers, "I don't know. My first instinct is to make Malcolm Fucking O'Shea rebuild it for me. But then I think, why? What's the point? Maybe it's better to bulldoze the damn lot, sell the property, and walk away. I've put myself through a lot of grief trying to hold onto this place."

"Why is that?" she asks him, bemused.

Shifting his weight against the crutches, he answers, "I don't know. At first, it was mostly to spite Caroline. It was the only bargaining chip I had. Not that I ever had it. But you know what I mean. I thought I did. I've always loved the house, and I thought I deserved to have one place I could go where she wouldn't be allowed to bother me. Ironic, in light of recent events, huh?"

Blanche nods. "Very. You said, 'at first,' though, which implies that's not why you've held on more recently."

He says nothing at first, but then he finally replies, "I had good memories in this house. And I wanted to make more. I began to think that I would, anyway. Foolish hope, as it turns out. But in a way, letting go of the house feels like giving up on those hopes." Impatiently, he adds, "Anyway, it's stupid and sentimental. I need to reclaim my inner cynic and get on with life, apparently."

"Don't give up hope yet, all right?" She puts her hand on his arm. "I could see it the other night; the divorce was news to her. When I told her about what Caroline'd been putting you through lately, her mind was racing in a thousand directions. She wanted to call you right then. I recognized that look in her eye. She had a very itchy dialing finger. She and her friend were talking a big game and giving me the cold shoulder, but… they both have terrible poker faces. Give her some time to process what I told her. Surely she's heard about the fire by now. Maybe she's already tried to get in touch."

"My phone is melted somewhere in there," he says, pointing toward the charred rubble with one of his crutches. Then he abruptly laughs and says, "Oh, shit."

"What?"

He looks down at the ground while he continues to laugh. Eventually, he stops and tells her, "During one of my first meetings with Jayne, I told her that fires were the biggest clichés in literature. Of course, at the time, I had no idea her book was based on her life and that the fire in it wasn't a random tragedy that she pulled from her imagination. Still. Look at this. Look at *me*! I'm paying dearly for being such an insensitive dickhead, aren't I?"

"Fires *are* cliché," she defends him. "I can't believe you almost died in one. It would have been extremely poor taste."

"Sticking with the poor-taste theme running through my life right now."

She laughs. "Let's get out of here. It's cold. And depressing. Let's grab some lunch at that tavern in town. I'm jonesing for some clam chowder."

He smiles and squints over at her. "I'm not ready to go yet."

"I can wait for you in the car, then, while you have a few minutes alone," she offers.

Shaking his head, he says, "Nah. You know what? You go on back to the city. Tom can come get me."

They argue back and forth for a while, but he eventually wins when he loses his temper and yells, "I'm trying to tell you nicely that I want to be alone, okay? Do I need to take out a billboard?"

With her usual irreverence, she backs away, "Message received, Lukey-pookie. I'll see you back at the office."

"Not today," he corrects her. "I have other things I need to do. Thanks for bringing me out here, though."

She waves and hikes back to the road, where she gets into her SUV and drives off with one last horn honk in Luke's direction. He lifts a hand in a half-hearted wave, turns, and hops toward me. It's immediately apparent that the gazebo is his destination. I brace myself to be discovered.

CHAPTER TWENTY-NINE

H e almost doesn't look surprised to see me. Of course, after the past couple of days he's had, maybe nothing does surprise him anymore.

"Hi," I say simply.

"What are you doing here?" he asks, lowering himself onto the bench closest to the gazebo steps and propping his crutches next to him. He rests his casted foot and leg against the floor and coughs like someone who's smoked two packs a day for the past ten years. Before I can even think of a decent answer, he asks, "Are you really here?"

I shoot him an alarmed look. "Yes."

He shrugs. "I'm on a lot of drugs right now, so… it's possible I'm hallucinating. How'd you get past the cop?"

That's easier to answer than why I'm here, so I say, "I parked at the public access beach and walked."

He smiles weakly.

To save him the effort of the tough guy act I can tell he's going to try to put on, I walk over to him, sit right next to him, and take his hand. "I've missed you," I say bluntly. "When I heard about this, I was so worried. Nobody could tell me anything, and I couldn't get in touch with you, so in order to not go crazy in my stupid hotel room while I waited for you to get your messages from Sally, I drove out here. It's the only thing I could think to do."

He stares down at our hands. Mine still look halfway decent from the paraffin treatment I got at the hotel before the Thornfield party. His are scratched and rougher than I remember them. They also look like they're sunburned, as does his neck, face, and any other skin I can see. I'm guessing first-degree burns.

After he doesn't say anything in response to my emotional monologue, I ask, "Are you okay?"

"I'm fine." He looks up and smiles bravely, but the broken blood vessel in his right eye, the cut above his eyebrow, and the various scratches on the rest of his face tell a different story. "I'm alive, anyway. And, like I said, I'm on a lot of pain medication, so everything seems okay for now." He pulls his hand away from mine and rests it on my knee. "Are *you* okay? Seeing this," he points over his shoulder with his thumb toward the house, "can't be easy."

"I'm trying not to think too much about it," I admit. "The smell is bothering me, but as long as I don't stare too long at it or let myself imagine what it was like when the fire was at its strongest, I'm okay." I gulp. "And seeing you makes me feel a whole lot better."

"Seeing you has vastly improved my day, too," he states matter-of-factly.

"Good."

I want to kiss him. Or at the very least hug him or put my head on his shoulder or something. But he looks like it hurts him to breathe, so I content myself with taking hold of his hand again and squeezing it.

"Is Paulette okay?" I inquire, realizing that as long as I

keep asking questions and dealing with facts, the less I feel like I'm about to fly apart.

He nods. "She's fine, physically. She got out right away and was smart enough to stay out, unlike yours truly." He grins self-deprecatingly.

"Why'd you go back inside?" I wonder, unable to think of a single thing that would be worth returning to a burning building for. Oh. Except for my laptop. I'd totally go back inside a burning house for that, I think with a stab of embarrassment.

Ducking his head, he answers, "Well, for one thing, Caroline was still in there."

"So what?" My heart races, and my elevated blood pressure makes my eyes bulge. "You should have let her burn."

"That's exactly what she wanted, though. And I'd be damned before I gave her the satisfaction of killing herself in the process of trying to kill me. And then for me to live and her to die? No way was she going to be a fucking martyr." He shakes his head firmly.

"But she's the one who started the fire!"

"I know. And the authorities know. And she's going to be put away for it. She's already been charged. I'm glad it's out of my hands. I don't have a choice about whether to press charges, so her family can't try to pressure me not to, like all the other times." He sighs. "But that's not the only reason I went back inside." Wincing, he flattens himself so he can reach into his pocket. He pulls something out that he holds in his closed fist. "You're going to be mad at me when I show you this, but…"

He opens his hand. On his upturned palm is a flash drive. While I'm puzzled as to why the tiny plastic device is so important, I'm not sure why he thinks it would make me angry.

"I don't get it," I admit. "What is that?"

"A bunch of your writing files. Copied—actually, moved —from your laptop onto this." The guilty look on his face tells me he's confessing to something major, but I still don't understand the depth of his revelation.

"Okay."

Holding it up between our faces, he says, "I, uh…" and then stops. He sets his jaw, takes a deep breath, and restarts. "The day I came out here to try to get Caroline to leave you alone, I opened your computer and read your manuscript after I got back from my walk on the beach."

I nod. "Yes. I remember. It pissed me off, hardcore."

He smiles at the memory. "Yes, it did. And I told you to password protect it, and, as usual, you thoroughly ignored me—"

"No, I didn't! I password protected both the document and the computer after that incident."

"Not immediately after," he points out and then declares, "I checked. While you were down at the beach."

Instead of saying anything, I simply clench my teeth together and stare him down.

"You left your laptop unattended quite often," he defends himself. "And with Caroline lurking around. Well, it made me sick to my stomach to think what kind of hell she could unleash on you with one keystroke. I also wouldn't put it past her to plagiarize something and have it published under her own name. Or, like I said, I thought of a thousand horrifying scenarios, so while you were on your walk, I went to the gazebo with this," He flicks the thumb drive with his forefinger, "planning to simply copy your writing files onto it, but I got ultra-paranoid, so I completely moved the bulk of them, when I saw you hadn't accessed some of the files in years. I figured you wouldn't miss them. And I was going to put the drive in a safe deposit box and tell you what I'd done—after Caroline left, and there was no chance of her overhearing me—but I realized the next day that you'd be understandably pissed off at my interference, so... I tried to put the files back on your computer the day you stayed in bed all day, but by then, you'd password protected it." He looks miserably at me. "I should have confessed everything right then, but... I felt like you were finally starting to trust and—maybe even *like*—me."

"So you've had these files all these months? What are they? I don't even know what they could be..."

He swallows audibly. "I wish I could say I don't know, that I didn't look at them, but I did. Of course, I did. Not until after you'd gone, though, and I realized I still had it. I looked at them to see if I needed to send them to you and tell you what I'd done. I was trying to figure out how I could get away with not ever telling you."

Even though he's the one completely in the wrong, I feel bad for him. He looks so remorseful. About a bunch of stupid documents I don't even remember writing. I never would have missed them. But he went back into a burning house for them.

Pressing the plastic rectangle into my hand, he says, "There's some good stuff on there. Obviously. Really, really, really good."

"There is?"

He laughs. "Yes! Stuff you must have written in college, before you started writing your book."

"Wow. I don't remember any of it."

He scratches his chin. "There's a short story about a man having to put his dog to sleep that made me cry."

Now it's my turn to laugh. "Sounds like a knock-off of *Old Yeller*."

"No! It's excellent and original. Anyway, it was worth saving."

I gently tap his cast. "And how did *this* happen to your leg? Obviously, it was after you rescued Caroline and the thumb drive?"

He nods. "Yeah. The stairs collapsed under me when I was on my way back down. Caroline was already out; she went down the terrace stairs and around from the backyard into the front. I found out later that she watched me run back inside. I should have known better than to think she'd still be inside. She never did have the guts to kill herself the easy way, much less in a painful way like burning and suffocating to death." He winces when he sees my reaction to his statement. "Oh, no. I'm sorry, Jayne." He pulls me closer to him and hugs me to his side. "That was such an insensitive thing to say!"

Hugging me obviously hurts, because he takes a sharp breath, which then brings on a coughing jag. I pull away from him but offer my arm for him to hold while he bends at the waist and sputters. Finally, he stops and straightens. Eyes watering, he blinks and smiles wanly. "Sorry. Oh, hell, that hurts. Cracked rib."

"Come on." I stand and hold out my hand to him. "Let's get you home. You can wait in the cruiser while I go get my rental car. It's a good thing I'm here; I don't know how you expected to call Tom to come get you, if your phone burned up in the fire."

He flinches and tilts his head at me. "How?"

I hold up the thumb drive to remind him of his own transgressions while admitting, "Yeah, I was eavesdropping on you and Blanche. So sue me."

For the sake of his ribs, he stifles his laughter but grins widely while grabbing his crutches and hoisting himself to a standing position. "No thanks. I think I'll be getting my fill of legal action in the upcoming months, what with testifying against my ex-wife at her trial, which will be sure to be a media circus, considering who she is. No need to add petty litigious issues, such as eavesdropping, to the docket."

His reference to Caroline sobers me. "I'm sorry life's been so difficult lately. I'm sorry if I've added to it in any way."

"Bah! Fearing for your life on a daily basis adds some excitement." He looks away from me when he continues, "And heartbreak reminds you you're alive."

"In that case, I've been extremely aware of being alive," I say to let him know how I've felt without him.

He smiles sadly. "Yeah?"

"Yeah." I step in front of him and look up into his face.

"I've spent a lot of time lately wishing I wasn't."

"All you had to do was stop moving out of the way of speeding cars, stabbing knives, and blazing blowtorches," I point out.

His lips inches from mine, he says thickly, "The will to survive is oddly subconscious. And extremely difficult to fight."

Our lips are nearly touching when I say, "I'm very glad about that. And don't ever risk your life again for something like a thumb drive with a bunch of my forgotten ramblings on it. Understand?"

"But the guy and the dog and... Tears streamed down my face when I read it, Jayne."

"I don't care. Promise me you'll never do something stupid like that again."

He rolls his eyes. "I promise the next time my insane ex-wife tries to burn me in my bed that I'll only worry about saving my own ass. And yours. Since I fully expect you to be in that bed with me."

Finally, our lips touch, first softly and tentatively and then firmly and hungrily.

There's that tummy-jolting, heart-jerking feeling I've been missing so much!

CHAPTER THIRTY

"It's coming along quite nicely," I say, getting into the car after our latest look at the beach house's construction. "How much longer are they saying it'll take?"

Luke buckles his seat belt and turns the key in the ignition. "A few more weeks. It'll go quickly from here on out. Mostly cosmetic stuff. And Malcolm O'Shea's money gets things done more quickly than normal people's money."

In settlement talks (out of court, of course) nine months ago, Malcolm had tried to appeal to the Luke he'd been dealing with all the years he'd been married to Caroline, demanding, "Isn't it enough that my only daughter lives in a loony bin and will forever be looked upon as a criminal?"

But that Luke doesn't exist anymore. He got lost somewhere in the smoke and ashes overlooking the beach. Instead, Malcolm's ex-son-in-law had matter-of-factly replied, "No. I want my house back, and since your only daughter—who tried to kill me on more than one occasion —was responsible for its burning down, I think it's reasonable for you to pay to rebuild it. Maybe you should have locked her up sooner—perhaps the first time she tried to kill me?—and saved yourself some money—and face. Not to mention, you would have been doing *me* a huge favor."

Malcolm had forked over the dough, however grudgingly.

"I'm dying to get back into that gazebo," I half-joke. Actually, I'm not joking at all. I'm praying it'll work its magic, and I'll be inspired to start—and eventually, finish—the book that Thornfield is seriously pressuring me about. I have enough money to pay them back the advance I received so that I can get out of my contract with them, but Tullah says that won't work in my favor if I ever want to publish another book sometime in the future (ha!). I'm not going to have a choice for much longer, though. I'm going to have to put out or pay up. I've never been great at putting out on demand.

Turning from the driveway onto the road, Luke sighs. "You don't need the magic gazebo. You have the thumb drive. Why won't you look at the stuff on it? I'm begging you."

Yes, he's been begging me for months, to no avail. I want nothing to do with that thing.

"When we get home, I'm loading those documents onto your laptop," he says in a tone that leaves no room for argument.

"Why?!"

"Because. This is ridiculous. You have two dozen good starts right under your nose, but you're too stubborn to look at them. You'd rather be a one-hit wonder."

"That's not true! I've been busy, that's all. Too busy to be bothered. Too busy to be inspired. Now that we've finished the screenplay and cast the movie, and they're scouting filming locations, they don't need my input for a while. I'll have some time to relax and think and—"

He reaches over and grabs my hand. "I'm not Arthur Thornfield, so stop trying to blow smoke up my ass."

I know better than to continue lying to him. He knows I have nothing. He knows I feel like a fraud. He knows I'm worried I'll never have another idea.

Letting my head fall back against the headrest, I stare out my window. "You'll see. There's nothing on that flash drive that can help me."

He lets go of my hand and says hotly, "I'm sick of you ignoring my instincts on this! Would I have gone to the trouble to run back into a burning house if there were nothing on it?"

Ironically, that's part of why I can't bear to look at it. It freaks me out to think he could have died retrieving a bunch of my crappy college writing assignments. I would have never forgiven myself. Not that I would have known. Anyway! I hate thinking about it; I don't even want to look at that flash drive (that's why it's shoved into a desk drawer in our apartment). And I definitely don't want to touch it long enough to plug it into my computer and retrieve the files from it.

I hate making him mad, though, so I relent. "Fine. But I'm not touching it. And I'm still pissed off at you for taking such a risk to get it."

"So damn stubborn," he mutters, rubbing his chin and staring straight ahead through the windshield. "I told you; I'll copy the files to your laptop. Promise me you'll read them."

"Is that an order?" I listlessly turn my head to look at him.

"Yes. I'm pulling rank and ordering you to read them, if that's what it takes."

"'Pulling rank'? What the hell is that supposed to mean? You don't out-rank me!" Outraged, I stare at his profile.

He stifles a sudden grin. "I broke my leg and almost died for those files. The least you can do is read them."

"I never would have asked you to do that. Ever."

"And I did it anyway. More reason for you to do as I say."

"I already said I would."

"Just making sure you understand how important it is to me."

I clench my teeth when I feel the tears of frustration threatening. "I get it. Can we please change the subject?"

He glances over at me and does a double-take when he sees that I'm becoming emotional. "Hey," he says gently, offering me his hand again.

I take it and squeeze his fingers. "I'm fine," I claim. And I am, but I get easily upset when I think too much about what could have happened. And I hate when he makes light of it. I know too well how it could have turned out. It's far from funny.

"I was only kidding."

"I know."

"I'm sorry. It's not funny."

"No, it's not."

He knots his fingers through mine. "That's how I deal with it, though. It still scares me, so I joke about it."

"I know."

"Don't be mad, Jayne."

I sniff and say curtly, "I'm not," but I don't say anything else for the rest of the drive home. When we get to the apartment, I ride the elevator with him in silence, and as soon as it spits us out into our living room, I stride to the bedroom, where I strip and then shut myself in the bathroom to soak in a hot tub of water.

He's so sure that the answer to my problems lies on that stupid piece of plastic and metal. What if it doesn't? What if I read through it all, and nothing comes of any of it? He makes it sound like any dipshit with an eighth grade education could make something out of what's on there. But what if I can't? Won't that be the ultimate proof that I'm a hack? Or at the very least, that a gift I once had is now gone? I'm terrified to find out that I don't know how to write anything other than the book I've already written, no matter how many inspirational ideas are tossed my way.

When I emerge from the bathroom, wrinkled and wrapped in Luke's robe (which he hasn't had a chance to wear in months, since I've commandeered it), he's sitting up, fully clothed on top of the bedclothes with his back against the headboard, scratching his way through a crossword puzzle, which he immediately sets aside.

"Do you feel better?" he asks hopefully.

"A little," I acknowledge. "Cleaner."

He smiles. "I'm sorry I upset you."

"It doesn't take much. Don't worry about it." I slide a pair of panties up my legs and under the robe. After fishing a t-shirt from the dresser, I go into the bathroom, hang the robe on the hook on the door, and pull the shirt over my head. Returning to the bedroom, I slip under the covers on my side of the bed, reach up to kiss Luke's chin, and burrow down into my pillows. I close my eyes so I don't have to see the worried look on his face. "Good night," I say as normally as possible.

"It's not even seven o'clock!"

"I'm tired," I tell him. "Jet lagged."

"In that case, your body would think it's even earlier. Plus, you've been home for two days."

"I know. It's finally hitting me." It's true that until now I've been too glad to be back with him, after being out in L.A. for a week and a half, to be tired. Now exhaustion is crushing me. Reality is crushing me.

My eyes fly open. "Shit," I mutter. "I forgot—"

"I'll do it." He rolls off the side of the bed and leaves the room. I hear him open the pantry. After a few seconds, a shrill beep sounds from the kitchen, where he's pressed the "test" button on the smoke alarm with the handle of a broom. The chirp of the carbon monoxide detector's test tone follows. I listen for the same sounds from the devices in the other rooms. Finally, he appears in the bedroom, where he jabs at the alarms on the ceiling. They dutifully participate in the nightly roll call, after which I can truly relax.

"Thanks," I say with a sleepy smile.

"No problem." He flicks off the lights and stands next to the bed, broom in hand. He seems ready to say something, but then he simply bends down, kisses my lips, and says, "Good night. I'm going to… stay up for a few more hours. I guess."

"That's fine. I'm just too tired."

"Yeah, well if I go to bed right now, I'll be up in the middle of the night."

"I know. I'll see you in the morning."

"Okay." Finally, he moves toward the light on the other side of the doorway.

"I love you," I tell him.

He pauses with his hand on the doorknob and says, "I love you, too," before pulling the door closed.

∿

Wishing to avoid another tense conversation, I wait until I hear Luke leave for work in the morning before I get out of bed. I know I'm a coward. But he's a persistent a-hole sometimes, and I'm not in the mood to be harassed about my "career" right now. After the couple of weeks—months— I've had, I deserve to take at least a week off to relax and restore my energy.

And to get used to sharing living quarters with someone again.

It's an interesting dichotomy that when I'm traveling I miss him so much, but when I return home, it takes me a few days to adjust to being around him again. I love being around him, so it's not *him* so much as it is taking into consideration someone else's wants and schedule.

Last night was the perfect example. When I'm on the road, it doesn't matter what time I want to go to bed (as long as I'm not in the middle of a public appearance; that would be weird). I'm all by myself in a hotel room, and I don't have to worry about what time it is or if my going to bed— or staying up late—is going to be a disappointment or an inconvenience to anyone else. I simply do it.

On the flip side, when I'm traveling, nobody gives a damn what I do or when I do it, as long as I fulfill the obligations I've promised to fulfill. My free time is very lonely. And that's why I get in the habit of sleeping a lot when I've been on the road. There's nothing better to do. Which is ironic, considering I'm traveling all over the country and could see some cool sights. But just like when I taught at Fairfax and lived a short train ride away from our nation's capital, I've discovered it's no fun seeing all those places alone.

Now that I'm home, though, "alone" is sounding pretty

good. Especially if the price of Luke's company is talking about my gasping-for-breath writing career.

The first thing I notice when I go into the kitchen to get some much-needed coffee and breakfast is my laptop, open and turned on (albeit hibernating), sitting on the breakfast bar. The barstool is pulled out, as if inviting me to take a seat. A sticky note on the keyboard says, *"Files are copied. I made a shortcut on your desktop. LOOK AT THEM! XO Luke."*

"Bossy," I mutter, shutting the computer so I don't have to look at his note or think about writing. I know he thinks he's helping, but I wish he could see that he's only adding to my stress levels.

As I'm pouring myself a bowl of cereal and waiting for my coffee to brew, the elevator bell sounds to let me know someone's on their way up. Since it's a Monday, I expect it's Paulette, so I'm not surprised when she appears in the kitchen doorway a few minutes later.

"And there she is, returned from her travels," she greets me warmly with a quick squeeze of my shoulders from behind. "You should have waited for me; I'd have whipped up some brekkie for you, Luv."

"I'm not that hungry," I tell her, pushing the computer out of the way so I can sit at the bar and eat while she unloads her canvas bags of groceries.

"And how was Hollywood?" she asks enthusiastically.

I smile sheepishly. "The hotel was nice."

"Oh, you! You've got to get out there and see some of the sights!"

"I did, when I went to New York, and Gus went with me," I defend myself. "That was fun. And Luke and I had a good time in Seattle. But it's not the same when I'm alone somewhere. Plus, by the end of the day, I was so tired. I didn't care to gawk at a bunch of big houses behind gates and walls."

"Your publicist must be a real stick-in-the-mud to not want to hang out with you," she posits.

I laugh. "Jules is fine. I don't make friends easily. I'm a solitary person."

Her expression softens as she tilts her head at me. "Who could blame you, considering..."

Before she can get all misty-eyed at the thought of my past, I swallow a bite of cereal and say, "Anyway! I'm home now. And if you love laundry, do I have a present for you!"

"Oh, goody." Her statement sounds so sincere that it makes me laugh. Folding her empty canvas bags, she says, "It's good to have you back, Jayne. Luke is quite grumpy when you're away. But don't tell him I told you that."

He has no one to boss around, I think sullenly before checking myself. Actually, it's sweet that he misses me so much that it affects his moods. I grin at her. "Aww."

"Yes. One day, before I was leaving for the evening, he told me to never again make what I'd made the night before for dinner, because it was disgusting. And then he said he'd take the leftovers to a homeless shelter, but he doesn't like to kick people while they're down."

I gasp. "What?! No, he didn't!"

She nods and chuckles. "He did."

"What an asshole!"

She waves away my condemnation. "Ah. I knew he was simply missing you and taking it out on the only person around."

"Yes. That would be the definition of 'asshole,'" I insist. "Paulette, I'm so sorry."

"No need for you to be sorry, Dear. He apologized the

very next day. And he gave me Friday off so's I'd have a long weekend."

"Did he give you a raise, too?"

Now she gets very serious. "No! And you'd better not try, either. My salary is burden enough on the two of you, now that I don't work for the O'Sheas." She pulls her shoulders back and straightens her shirt. "Not that I would, after the way they treated Luke. Shame on them, who have no shame. Detestable, ungrateful—"

"Well, we don't want to share you with anyone, anyway," I interrupt before she gets too worked up. "And your salary isn't a burden. We wouldn't know what to do without you, Paulette."

This statement makes her fidget and stammer. Finally, she says, "I'll be seeing to that laundry, then. Unless you want me to do the washing up in here first."

I look around and note that my cereal bowl and spoon and Luke's coffee mug comprise the "washing up."

"No. I think I can handle putting three things in the dishwasher. But thanks."

After she leaves, I do just that, pour myself a cup of coffee, and sit down at the counter.

Tapping the shiny cover of my new laptop with my fingernail, I bite my lip and consider the consequences of *not* looking at the files while Luke's at work. He has no right to order me around like I'm some sort of freshman author under his tutelage. It's my career. If I want to let it die, I should be allowed to let it die.

Plus, if I decide to buy out my contract, it will be a blessing for him. He won't have any reason to stay at Thornfield, and he'll be free to go work for a company that he respects more. Maybe somewhere in New York. Or Connecticut. I love Connecticut.

I think of the house on Marblehead that Luke's rebuilding, mostly at my urging. Oh, yeah. That thing. I couldn't stand the idea of a place with such important—if not always "good"—memories no longer existing. And I do want to make more memories there, but I wish there were a way for us to move it with us somewhere else.

Because *when* my writing career goes up in flames, I wouldn't mind going back to teaching. You know the old saying: "Those who can't, teach." I never believed that before now. Now, I'm a living example.

So, again—what's the worst that will happen if I ignore Luke's directive to look at those writing files today? He'll sulk. Or raise his voice. Or give me the silent treatment (no, I won't be that lucky). I envision a bit of a rant, followed by sulking, followed by the appearance of agreeing with me while he actually tries to use reverse psychology on me to get me to do what he wants me to do.

As Paulette would say, "Oh, goody."

CHAPTER THIRTY-ONE

To my surprise, Luke doesn't say a word about the files when he gets home. As soon as he steps from the elevator, he glances around and asks me (the nearly permanent fixture on the couch), "Is Paulette still here?"

I set my magazine on the coffee table. "No. She left a couple of hours ago. Why?"

He crosses to the couch in economically large steps. "Because I want to make sure I have you all to myself," he says suggestively.

"Oh, I see," I flirt back. Reaching up, I let him pull me against him and wrap his arms around me. "Yes. I'm all by my lonesome."

"Not anymore." He grabs two handfuls of my butt and lifts me off the floor.

When I yelp and laugh, it knocks him slightly off-balance, so he steps backward to regain his footing, but his leg meets up with the corner of the coffee table, and before I know it, we're on the floor in a laughing heap.

"What happened?" I ask incredulously.

He answers while staring at the ceiling, "Apparently, I fell down."

His over-simplified assessment makes me giggle. "I see."

"Well, nothing that embarrassing has happened in a while," he points out proudly.

"No, I thought maybe you'd outgrown your coital clumsiness. I haven't said 'Ow' during sex in months." I unbutton his shirt and kiss his chest. "But I suddenly had a flashback to trying to have sex while you had that stupid leg cast."

After a groan, he says, "Yes, I think that was the last time there were any serious injuries. That thing was dangerous." He rubs my back. "Oh, man...! Now we're going to have to change the OSHA sign in the bedroom. 'Zero days since last reportable incident.'"

"I won't tell anyone," I whisper against his skin.

"Oh, you're so naughty."

I let loose a dirty laugh to match my supposed naughty nature.

He rolls me over and slides on top of me. "I'm so glad you're home."

"Me, too," I agree.

"Are you?" he double-checks. "You seem tense."

This observation makes me stiffen.

"Like that," he asserts.

I try to relax. "I'm fine."

"Are you sure?"

"I'd be better if you'd shut up and finish what you started," I allow.

"All right, then." Without further hesitation, he follows my orders.

Who's pulling rank now?

∽

Quite a while later, Luke pulls on his underwear and hops up from the floor. On his way to the kitchen, he asks casually, "Did Paulette happen to make anything for us to eat for dinner?"

Drolly, I reply while donning my t-shirt and panties, "No, I told her we didn't want any disgusting food that we wouldn't even feed homeless people."

He freezes with his back to me but then spins on his heel to face me. Eyes wide, he says, "I can't believe she told you! I told her not to tell you!"

I laugh at his humiliation. "You are such a dickhead. How could you say that to her?"

Wincing, he explains, "It slipped out, okay? I was in a horrible mood, and Jayne!"

"Luke!"

"It was seriously the grossest thing I've ever eaten. Worse than anything I've ever cooked."

"That's saying something."

"Exactly! I think she made a mistake when she was measuring ingredients, or something. Distractedly, he scratches his nipple. "I'm not even sure what it was supposed to be. Some sort of meat and vegetable concoction, but it was, like, bitter? Or something." He makes a face as if he can taste it right now. "Anyway, I wanted to make sure she never made it again, whatever it was."

"I hope she spit in the next thing she cooked for you."

"Hey! I apologized and gave her an extra day off."

"Too little, too late. I bet she cried herself to sleep when she went home after you insulted her cooking."

"You're trying to make me feel like a jerk."

"You *are* a jerk," I proclaim, joining him on his walk into the kitchen. I open the fridge and start taking out sandwich fixings and placing them on the counter.

He pulls the sandwich bread from the breadbox and works at the twist tie. "Okay, so I wasn't very diplomatic about it, but she knows that's not my strong suit. I was being honest! How would you have told her?" Without waiting for me to answer, he accuses, "You probably wouldn't have said anything, and then she would have kept making it for us, thinking we liked it. At least with my method, we know we'll never have to eat it again. You should be *thanking* me for saving you from the horror."

I wrap my arms around his upper arm and watch around his shoulder as he slaps meat and cheese onto two pieces of bread in front of him. "No mayo for me," I tell him and then say, "I'll tell you what. You be Paulette, and I'll be you."

"Wha…?" He sounds skeptical but intrigued.

"We'll role play, and I'll show you how to be nice."

"Role playing. Kinky."

"Be serious!" I implore him while not doing a very good job of it myself. "So how did this topic come up? Who started the conversation?"

He thinks about it while pressing the top slices of bread on our sandwiches. "She did. She—"

"No! Show, don't tell."

Shooting me a dirty look for throwing in his face one of the most worn-out editor's commands, he nevertheless says in a high quasi-English accent, "There's chicken soup simmering on the stove, Lyook. I'll pop round to the shops in the morning to get something a bit heartier for tomorrow night. The weather's turning cooler."

"Your English accent sucks."

"I would never say that to her!"

"Shut up. I'm saying it to you!"

"This was your idea, so stop breaking character." He slaps my sandwich onto a plate and holds it out to me.

I take it and say in a deep voice, "This looks great, Paulette. Thanks."

"You make me sound like a doofus."

"Shh!" I slap his arm and continue, "Speaking of food, the dish you made last night…"

"Yes?" he replies, slipping back into character. "The Alpo Surprise? Did you enjoy it, Lyook?"

I rub the back of my neck and then bring my hand around to cover my mouth and hide the grin I can't suppress.

He raises his eyebrows expectantly. "If you liked it, I can make that once a week for you and Jayne. I'm sure she'd love it!"

Recovered somewhat, I clear my throat and intone, "Actually, Paulette, it wasn't my favorite."

He makes his bottom lip and chin wobble. "Oh?"

"No. And Jayne's pickier than I am, so I'm not sure it would be to her liking, either. Where'd you get the recipe?"

Tearfully, he answers, "'Twas an old war-time favorite. We served it all the time at the inn. But if you don't like it…" He breaks down "sobbing" in earnest now, covering his face and making his shoulders shake.

"She would *not* be crying at this point."

He stops suddenly, uncovers his face, and looks up at me, blinking. "Oh, she's very sensitive."

"Then she must have been rending her clothing after what you said to her."

"This is styoopid," "Paulette" says, grabbing her sandwich and taking it to the breakfast bar.

"My point is, you don't have to be so blunt all the time. You'd have more friends if you'd learn to use some tact."

"I have plenty of friends."

"Name two, and I don't count."

Shooting me a sympathetic look, he chews, swallows, and says, "Ah, Jayne. You count! Don't sell yourself short."

I plop down next to him and reply. "You know what I mean. You can't count me as one of your friends."

"But you're my BFF," he claims, examining his sandwich at close range.

"Name two others," I demand, taking a big bite and watching him while I chew.

Smugly, he answers, "Blanche and Gus."

"Gus is *my* friend!" I object before I've quite finished chewing and swallowing.

"So? He's my friend, too, now."

"He calls you Luke-Ass!"

"You started that, though, so it's not his fault. He's obsessed with asses, anyway, so I'm sure that's why the name stuck."

"The name stuck because of stunts like the one you pulled with Paulette."

He considers this while eating his sandwich in silence. After his last bite, he says, "Anyway, I don't need a lot of friends. Friends are work."

"Spoken like a true sociopath."

"Hey!"

"Okay, maybe that's a bit harsh," I concede, "but you do tend to get all dictatorial and insensitive and then hide behind honesty and efficient communication. As if, as long as something is honest or efficient, it's okay."

He pushes his plate away and crosses his arms over his bare chest. "Are we still talking about Paulette, here, or is this about something else?"

I avoid his eyes when I reply, "Still applies to what you

said to Paulette, but it's also something that applies to your social skills in general."

His voice is rock-hard when he says, "And my social skills when dealing with you. Right?"

Pretending not to get what he's driving at, I nod and say lightly, "Yeah. Of course. With everyone, including me."

"Is this about the note on your laptop this morning?" He snatches my plate from me and stacks it on top of his before walking around the counter and taking them to the dishwasher. Nodding to the computer, which is still sitting on the counter in front of the same barstool as this morning, he snaps, "Excuse the hell out of me for trying to help."

My plan to deny this has anything to do with the note or the files collapses as I plead to be understood. "But you're not helping. Can't you see that? You're bullying me. You're making me feel lazy and defeatist and... and... ridiculous for not looking at those files. And guilty! Because you could have died trying to save that stupid flash drive. I wish you had let it burn!"

"I don't! There's good stuff on there. It was worth the burns and the lung damage and the broken leg and the itchy cast and the agonizing physical therapy."

"You're crazy!"

"I'm not, Jayne! Your next book—*books*—are in that folder. Why don't you trust me?"

I stand up so quickly that I knock over my barstool. "It's not about trusting you, okay? It's not about you at all!" When he simply glares at me across the counter, I choke, "Why don't *you* trust *me* when I say that I'm screwed? I've lost it. I know. I know what it feels like to have it, and I don't. I don't have it anymore. It's gone. So stop pressuring me to keep looking for it!" I adopt the very pose he struck when he was pretending to be the heartbroken Paulette, only I'm not acting. I weep into my hands, my hunched shoulders shaking violently.

I hear the dishwasher door slide open and the soft clank of china against the rubber-coated racks, followed by the soft whoosh and click of the appliance closing. Then the air around me shifts, and Luke's warm arms wrap around my shoulders.

He rests his chin on top of my head and says quietly, "Jayne, Jayne, Jayne. I've never seen someone take writer's block so personally."

"What am I going to do?" I despair into his chest.

"I thought you didn't want me to tell you what to do."

"I don't!"

He sighs. "Okay. Uh… I don't know. I guess you'll either get past it or not. We'll figure out a way to appease Thornfield, though. Don't worry about—"

"I'm not worried about my stupid contract!" I cry, frustrated that he's not getting what the real problem is. "To hell with Thornfield. I've already made them fifty times what they paid me."

"I don't know about that," he chuckles indulgently.

"Then I'll use the money my dead parents left me. Whatever. I'm not being exact, okay?" I push away from him and wipe my face on the inside of my t-shirt collar. Dejectedly, I ask, "What am I going to *do*, Luke? If I can't write, what can I do? My life is yawning in front of me, this huge, black space with endless empty hours and nothing to do to fill them. Since I finished my book and the tour, I've been lost. The movie is a slight diversion, but it's not mine. It's someone else's project, and I stand on the sidelines and say, 'Good job' about every ten days or so. They don't care what I want or what I think, but they have to pretend they do. I don't care what they do, but I'm expected to care. I'm supposed to play the part of the temperamental author who insists that not a single word of dialogue change, who throws a fit when a scene is cut or added or altered. But I don't care. It's a completely separate animal to me. And I keep having to remind myself why I'm involved at all."

"You're exhausted."

"I'm impotent."

"Potato, potahto."

"The point is…" I clench my fists at my sides, bordering on enraged that I have to continue to spell it out for him. "The point is, I don't know how to do anything else but write. It's been my answer to everything from PMS to boredom to insomnia to *everything* since I could hold a pencil and form the letters of the alphabet. It sounds stupid and dramatic, but I don't feel like a person if I can't write. And I can't write."

"Right now."

I laugh bitterly. "What's going to change, Luke? What's going to make ten years from now different from right now?"

"Sleep, maturity, experiences, love, hate, marriage, children, grief, joy, *life*! I don't know! Anything can happen. You're no stranger to the creative process. It's not logical. It's not methodical, and it certainly doesn't follow any rules or laws of a scientific nature." He pulls me against him again. "Cut yourself some damn slack!" He kisses the top of my head. "I don't mean that in a dictatorial way, either. It's merely a suggestion."

I give him a watery smile.

"There," he practically croons. "Deep breath."

I obey.

"We need a vacation," he declares. "You and me, alone.

Somewhere that neither of us associates with any form of work." He kisses my nose. "A honeymoon."

My eyes widen.

He's too busy brainstorming to notice my reaction to that word, though. "I can probably get away from work in a week or two. We'll go away for two weeks, and by the time we get back, the house on Marblehead will be ready for us to move in. We'll get reacquainted with it, take long walks on the beach, swim, play, relax, make love, and not worry about a damn thing. Then life won't seem so daunting. You'll see." He looks down into my face. "What say you?"

His solution doesn't solve anything, but it stops me from trying to solve everything, even if only temporarily.

"A honeymoon?" I ask, repeating the last word I truly heard and comprehended.

He smiles crookedly. "Yeah. Unless you think that's too corny. Or too soon. I don't want to rush you or—"

"Rush *me*? I thought you never wanted to get married again. And trust me, I don't blame you. I understand."

I've even told myself a few hundred thousand times that I'm okay with it. Lord knows I don't want to be the *next* crazy Mrs. Edwards.

"You've made me eat my words on so many occasions, Jayne, that I don't even keep track anymore. How about we forget everything I ever said before you woke up in my arms the morning after you fell asleep watching what you call 'the blue people movie'?" He shakes his head ruefully. "Because I didn't know anything before then. And I said some really stupid things."

"You've said some really stupid things since then, too," I point out, making a face and poking at his lower lip with my index finger. "But I don't want to forget anything."

"That's your choice."

"And I would love to be your wife."

"Do you have good health insurance? Because you're going to need it, if you're shackled to me as I stumble through life."

"I'll take my chances. Now, take me to bed, after we check the detectors."

He lets me go, bends down to right the barstool I upended, and says, "I'd like nothing better."

CHAPTER THIRTY-TWO

Three weeks away from everything—first in Key West and then in Marblehead—helped put things into perspective for me. I didn't even take my laptop with me on our honeymoon; yet, I survived. It was liberating. I had no access to email or social networking sites, and I would have left my cell phone in the apartment if I thought I could get away with it, but Tullah and Jules would have had my head. They were nice about leaving me alone the first week, but there was no dodging our daily status calls longer than that. After all, it's so important for me to know that *nothing* new is happening, which I already know, because I'd have to be writing something new for new stuff to be happening.

In spite of that, though, I feel more serene (a.k.a., "resigned") about things than I did before we took a break. Before my daily walk on the beach this morning, I even sent an email to Miles, asking him how he's doing and getting caught up. I hope there's an answer waiting for me when I get back. I want us to be friends. I want him to see that I'm happy now, but I'd be happier if we were on good terms. I'd be even happier still if I knew I was welcome back at Fairfax or he'd be willing to give me a reference to another school when I decide sitting around the house all day while Luke goes to work isn't my thing.

I've already decided that, actually. I've made up my mind that teaching at the university level (maybe even furthering my own education; after all, it's not fair that Luke gets to be the only Ph.D. in the house) is where my future lies; I simply haven't informed anyone else yet. Putting out feelers to Miles is my first step. It's a baby step. But it's a step, at least. I guess I could do charitable work or pop out some kids, but that doesn't appeal, either. I want to *work*. I want to use my brain and challenge myself. I want to challenge others. I want to help someone else learn the best way —for them—to express to readers what they're thinking and feeling.

It's chilly on the beach, so my walk is a short one today. When I get back to the house, I enter through the back door and stand just inside the kitchen as I take off my sandy shoes and leave them under the shoe bench. Paulette turns with a cup of coffee in hand and holds it out to me.

"Mite blustery for a walk by the water, don't you think?" she asks. "Wouldn't want you to fall sick, now."

Lightly, I reply, "Why not? It's not as if I have anything to do or anywhere to be."

"You still don't want to be sick!" she counters.

"I guess not," I concede with a mutter.

"Anyway," she continues, "you *do* have something to do. I noticed when I was dusting the office that Luke left something for you on your desk."

I shoot her a puzzled look over the rim of my coffee mug. "Something for me to do? Like what?"

Casually, she answers, "It looks like a manuscript. But I didn't read the note stuck to it."

Her preemptive denial makes me laugh. "I don't care if you did. I'm sure it's nothing secret or important."

"In that case," she says eagerly, "he wants you to read something he promised to read as a special favor for someone who knows someone who knows someone who knows him, but he hasn't had time, because he's so busy getting caught up from being gone on holiday."

I groan. "Personal favors are the worst!"

He complains about them all the time. It's so clever of him to have figured out a way to pawn them off on his idle wife.

Paulette cringes sympathetically, "I'm afraid so. But, anyway, at least you won't be bored! I'll make some bean soup for lunch and come get you early, so you can take a break."

I drain the rest of my coffee and harrumph like a surly teenager. Paulette intercepts my cup on its way to the dishwasher and murmurs something encouraging that I can't quite make out.

"This is true love," I gripe as I push against the door that leads to the dining room. "Reading the trash that Arthur Thornfield's daughter's friend's ex-husband's girlfriend wrote."

When I get to the sitting room, I see the stack of paper on my desk and breathe easier. It's not an epic tome, thank goodness; it may not take me long to read at all. And as I read the first page at arm's length, like I'm worried it'll transmit a literary STD, I note that it doesn't seem to be the style of writing that lends itself to scene after graphic sex scene of gag-inducing euphemisms for sexual organs.

As Paulette reported, the sticky note on the top page features Luke's chicken scratch and tells a sad tale about being buried at work and forgetting all about this favor he'd promised Arthur (I knew it!!) months ago and how much "you'll be pulling my chestnuts out of the fire" and how much he loves me.

The last part makes me smile while I roll my eyes. With a big sigh, I say "Fine!" out loud and retreat to the sofa with a blanket, a pen, and the sheaf of papers.

When Paulette pokes her head through the doorway later, I blink up at her and say distractedly, "You need something?"

"Soup's ready," she tells me.

Confused, I ask, "Already? What time is it?"

"Nearly noon. I would have been in sooner, but—"

"Noon?!" I shift my position under the blanket and, sure enough, notice that I'm stiff, as if I've been sitting for three hours without moving, but it doesn't seem possible that that much time has passed since I sat down with this thing.

"Is it awful?" she asks, nodding toward the manuscript.

I shake my head. "No. It's not. I mean, there are some rough parts and some mixed metaphors and a few analogies that don't work, but for the most part, it's good stuff." I stand and stretch my arms over my head. "Unfortunately, I read something very similar to this a long time ago. I think. I can't remember what it was, probably something in college that I had to read for a class that I don't remember. But I distinctly remember this plot. I know what's going to happen next. And that's a bummer, because this is good writing. In my opinion, which isn't worth much."

As I follow her into the kitchen, Paulette says, "You have thousands of fans who would beg to differ, I'd think. You know the good from the bad, surely."

I shrug while she fills a bowl of bean soup for me. "I guess. It's bothering me, though, that I can't place where I've read this before. I'd like to read the original so I can see if it's similar enough that it would prevent this person—whoever she is—from being published."

Disdainfully, she says, "Doesn't stop Tom Ridgeworthy from publishing the same book over and over again. Virtually."

We snicker about that over our steaming bowls.

After a few bites, Paulette says, "You said, 'she.' What's this writer's name?"

I swallow and shake my head. "Dunno. There's no name on it. Dumb. This person obviously doesn't know her way around the publishing industry, or she'd guard her intellectual property with her life. All it takes is this thing falling into the wrong hands, with no name on it, and someone else gets to write their ticket on her hard work. But I can tell by the way it's written that it's a woman. I'm making some sexist assumptions, I guess."

She nods pensively. "I find that it's usually easy to tell if the author's a man or woman. Except in the case of that Blake Redmond-Womack. Although I have a theory that his wife writes his books, while the novelty of a man writing so romantically is what sells them."

I grin at her. "I like that theory. There's something not right about him."

"I agree," she states unequivocally. Then she admits sheepishly, "I've read every single one of his books, though. They're like drugs, they are!"

Grudgingly, I concur. "Yeah, yeah. I know. I find, though, that as long as I don't open his books, I can't get sucked in. So, I avoid them."

With a mischievous glint in her eyes, she reveals, "Luke reads them."

Assuming she's referring to the time he brought one home for me to read the passage that illustrated the emotion he was looking for in my manuscript, I say, "I know. That one time…"

"No. All the time. Every time."

I snort. "Whatever."

She widens her eyes at me. "I'm serious. He gives them to me when he's through with them."

Still not sure whether to believe her but also equally unsure of her motives for lying about such a thing, I point out, "I've never seen him reading one."

"Womack hasn't written a new one in a while! But when he does, mark my words, Luke will buy it and read it." She stands. "Can I get you more soup, Dear?"

I shake my head while staring into space. "You think he'll read it in front of *me*?"

"I don't see why not," she replies, taking my empty bowl to the sink. "It's not exactly *shameful*. Ever-so-slightly unmanly, but I think it's sweet."

This information makes me see my husband in a whole new light. I thought I knew everything about him. And it doesn't make me think less of him (I don't think), but it makes me think differently about him. He's read every single Blake Redmond-Womack book? I have a vagina and can't claim that. And how has this emotional education via Mr. Womack colored his perceptions of love and romance? Does he channel Womack's protagonists when trying to think of ways to compliment me or when picking out the perfect Christmas or birthday gift? It's too hilarious to even consider.

Luke Edwards, *my* Luke, Mr. Anti-Sentimentality, a Blake Redmond-Womack fan? How does he justify that? It's like a dietician going home and eating ice cream for dinner.

Now, I say, "I can't wait to give him shit for this."

Paulette whirls and nearly gasps. "Oh, no. You can't!"

"Why not? He'd be all over me if I admitted to reading..." I grasp in my mind for the female equivalent of Womack and land on, "Jessica Creed!"

"She writes smutty romance novels, though."

"So does Womack! But because he's a man, they're not perceived or marketed as such."

"No, there's a definite difference. Womack's not smutty. He's deep and emotional and—"

"Puh-lease!"

She purses her lips. "Promise me you won't tease him about this."

"No way. I don't promise that at all."

"I shouldn't have said anything." But she looks like she's proud of herself, in spite of all her protestations.

"No, you shouldn't have. You should have let me discover this dirty little secret all on my own. You should have waited until Womack released his next book and let me walk in on my husband sitting up in bed, reading it. You would have heard me laughing all the way down in your room." I rise, anxious to get back to reading, but at the kitchen door, I pause, turn, and say, "Don't worry, though. I'll choose my moment wisely so he won't know you told on him."

"Oh, you!" she squawks and waves her towel at me, like she does to Luke when he's teasing her. This simple gesture makes me feel like a member of a true family for the first time in more than a dozen years and almost knocks the wind out of me.

"What is it, Dear?" she asks, suddenly serious. "You look peaky."

"I'm fine," I mumble unreassuringly. I shake my head and try to smile the emotion away. When my attempt fails, I simply exit the room and return to the sitting room and the anonymous manuscript. But I stare off into space for a long time before reading any more.

Because, in addition to the obvious warm glow this familial sense of belonging brings, it also intensifies a fear in me that I've never been stupid enough to think would ever leave me, but I've done a decent job of keeping at bay with my nightly smoke detector and fire alarm and carbon monoxide detector checks.

Now that I have so much, I have so much to lose.

CHAPTER THIRTY-THREE

Throughout the afternoon, as I've scribbled on the manuscript (which I came to find out was unfinished), I've shifted position several times on the couch in an effort to get comfortable or to facilitate long stretches of writing notes out by hand. Eventually, when I was finished writing and merely wanted to peruse critical sections, I ended up on my stomach, the manuscript on the floor below my head. That's how I fell asleep, spinning through my mind numerous possible endings to the story, trying to remember the original story I read in college so that I could figure out a way to advise this author to write it and make it different.

I wake up to the sound of ruffling paper and the feel of a finger tracing a line down my spine and coming to rest slightly above the rise of my rump.

"Mmmph!" I protest the tickle and arch my back.

"Wake up," Luke softly commands. "I believe I gave you some work to do, and you're sleeping on the job."

I roll onto my back and glare up at him. "I did your crap work, thank you very much. I finished it and then some. So I earned my nap."

He smiles crookedly down at me. "I'll be the judge of that." He gives the stack of papers in his hands a perfunctory flip-through. "My, my, my. This is quite the mark-up."

I sit up, my excitement for the manuscript waking me up. "Yeah. I know. I think it's a great idea. And well-executed. But…"

"What?" He sits next to me but keeps his eyes down on the pages as he skims my comments.

"It's been done before."

Dismissively, he declares, "Yeah, well, there's no such thing as a new idea, right? Only variations on themes."

I shake my head regretfully. "No. I mean, I've read *this* story before. If it's published as-is, it'll be plagiarism."

His head snaps up at one of the most serious words in his line of work. Calmly, he asks, "Oh? And what work is it plagiarizing?"

Rubbing my eyes, I admit, "I don't know. I can't remember the name or the author, but I *know* I've read this before. How is this writer related to Arthur, anyway?"

His intense study of my face is obviously distracting him from our conversation, because he slurs, "Wha…?" and then after blinking and giving his head a tiny shake, he quickly says, "Oh. Arthur. Yeah. She's not related to him. I never said that."

I grab his note from the coffee table and re-read it. "'I promised Arthur months ago that I'd take a look at this and give the author my thoughts.' Okay, so not a relative of Arthur's, but your read-through is something he requested on behalf of someone else?"

He slaps the manuscript onto the coffee table and snaps, "What does it matter, anyway?"

"I guess it doesn't," I concede, startled by his sudden irritation. "I was only wondering."

"Maybe we should focus more on figuring out where you've read this before, that's all."

"Maybe you should relax and let me do some research on it tomorrow. I've put in enough unpaid hours in your little literary sweatshop today," I snipe.

Hotly, he replies, "I wasn't suggesting you had to figure it out right this second. I only meant that it was more important than the name of the writer."

"It sounded to me like your typical whip-cracking." I snatch the manuscript from the table and take it over to my desk, where I set it precisely in the center of the otherwise-empty surface.

"As usual, you're putting words in my mouth and taking things the wrong way."

"I've learned to anticipate your demands in order to keep the peace."

"You haven't learned very well, apparently. I'd hardly call this peaceful."

"Screw you!" With that less-than-witty retort, I sweep from the room and run up the stairs to our bedroom, where I slam the door and then flop breathlessly onto the bed.

What an asshole! When I think the Luke I met in his office at Thornfield all those months ago doesn't exist anymore, he acts like this, and I'm reminded of one of the few pearls of wisdom my mom ever bestowed on me regarding love: "You can't change someone, so don't ever go into a relationship with change in mind."

And I didn't, in this case. I thought Luke had already changed by himself. I thought his experiences with Caroline had changed him. I thought falling in love with me had changed him. But every once in a while, the old angry, mean editor I loathed reemerges and makes me want to scream. This instance is particularly disheartening, because I haven't seen that douchebag in such a long time that I thought he was gone for good. Foolishly, I thought marriage had changed him.

Even though there's no possible way it could be true, I pretend to be asleep when I hear him enter the room a few short minutes later. If nothing else, maybe he'll get the hint that I don't want to continue our conversation. The sound of fabric gliding against skin and the bounce of the mattress tell me he's sitting on the bed and changing out of his work clothes—mercifully in silence. I hear the click of the closet light and the sound of hangers sliding on the metal rack. Something falls from the shelf, eliciting a muted "Ouch" before landing with a clunk on the wooden floor.

My closed eyes are like bouncers at an exclusive club. And Luke's not on the list. As I'm thinking he doesn't have the guts to even approach and ask for admittance, his side of the mattress sags again, and he says, "I'm glad you remember that story."

This statement is confounding enough that it makes me open my eyes and wonder aloud, "Why? I'd think it would be a major complication."

He mistakes my verbal response as permission to touch me. Sliding across the bed, he rests his chin against my hip and says, "It's not a complication; it's a blessing."

"Then why are you being such a dickhead about it?"

He doesn't have a quick answer for that one. I don't rush him. Finally, he answers, "I didn't realize I was being one. Your preoccupation with the name of the writer seemed irrelevant and a waste of time."

I bristle anew. "'Preoccupation'? I asked one time. I'd hardly call that preoccupied. But you bit my head off."

"Sorry." He sounds anything but. "I'm also glad you like

the story and had a lot of ideas about the direction in which to take it."

Sullenly, I mutter, "So glad you approve."

He chuckles at my sarcasm.

"It's not funny." I flop onto my back. He braces himself on his elbow and looks down at me while I continue, "I know it seems like I'm an idle waste of space and that since I don't have any ideas of my own, I should be grateful to you for allowing me to help other people with *their* ideas—"

"Now, wait a minute—"

But I'm not an editing robot. I should be allowed to ask questions and give feedback without worrying about being shouted at or treated like a nuisance. You asked for *my* help. If you don't want me to bother you with the things I have questions about, then don't ask for my help. Frankly, I'd rather watch British cartoons and eat Magnum bars all day."

"No, you wouldn't."

"Yes, I would." I'm gathering steam now. Looking straight into his green eyes, I say, "Anyway, Miles Brooks emailed me back today—"

"Why'd you email *him*?"

"—about my interest in getting back into teaching at the collegiate level, and he seemed pleased to hear from me—"

"I'm sure he was…"

"—and said he'd be glad to give me a reference *or* even find a place for me on the faculty at Fairfax, so—"

"Hang on a minute!" He doesn't look the least bit amused anymore. Nor does he seem to be willing to let me talk over him. "Hang on! Teaching? I don't think so."

"Excuse me? It's not your call."

"Of course, it's not, but… What I mean is… Well, for

one thing, Fairfax is in Maryland! In case you didn't know, we live in a completely different state."

"We can move."

He doesn't even dignify that with a response.

"And I know you're fond of pretending it's not true, but you still have contractual obligations with Thornfield. I'd suggest you focus on those before you commit yourself to a mind-numbing life in academia!" His jaw hardens and his nostrils flare.

"My contract with your employer is the least of my worries, in the grand scheme of—"

"I beg to differ!"

"Beg all you want, but it's true. All I have to do is write a check and—"

"All you have to do is give up, you mean? Writing becomes a little bit of work for you, and suddenly, it's not worth it? Is that how you want to approach life? What about when marriage gets difficult, Jayne? You gonna throw in the towel and write me a damn check? Is that what I have to look forward to?"

I push him away from me and cross to the window. Looking down on the gray, wet beach, I say, "Stop being so self-righteous and dramatic. They're totally different things."

When he doesn't argue—for once—I take advantage of his silence and continue, "Listen. It's my career, and I know you work for Thornfield, so that puts you in an awkward position when it comes to my decision to break my contract with them, but—"

Sitting up on the bed, he explodes, "I don't give a damn about them or what any of them thinks of me or you!"

"Then why are you so intent on my fulfilling my contract?"

"You owe it to yourself not to give up on something you love to do, Jayne! You love writing. You're good at it. Just because it's not coming easy right now doesn't mean it's not worth it." He stands and, despite my protests, joins me at the window, pressing his chest against my back and cupping my shoulders in his hands. "Didn't it feel good to read through that manuscript and have it reawaken your imagination? Don't you remember the thrill of getting a sentence exactly right?"

I blink at my tears. "Yeah. It felt great to read someone else's work and say, 'I used to be able to do this,' and 'If this were me, I'd say it this way.' It felt awful, actually. It felt like looking through an old photo album full of dead people I dearly loved and miss so much that it physically hurts. It made me feel nostalgic and jealous and... and... horrible!"

He kisses my ear. I bring my shoulder up to nudge him away, but he's not deterred. Goosebumps raise my hair follicles as he murmurs next to my ear, "Jayne, don't be a dumbass. *You* are the author of that manuscript. Or a younger facsimile of you. *You* wrote that your freshman year in college."

"*You're* the dumbass, thank you very much. I think I would have remembered that."

"That manuscript was an assignment for a class. A class taught by a Dr. Wallace Nichols. Creative Writing 101. The assignment was to write a 5,000-word novel start. You wrote 30,000 before you ran out of time and had to turn it in. You always turned in your assignments, after all, no matter what was going on or how you were feeling. You got things done. Gus told me that much."

I spin around to face him. "Gus gave it to you?" I can't imagine how he got hold of it, but it at least lends some credibility to the claim that it's truly my writing. I want so much to believe it is.

Luke shakes his head and rolls his eyes. "No. It's one of the files you refuse to look at on the flash drive. But Gus gave me the background on the assignment. You two met in that class."

I suddenly get a very vivid picture of Dr. Nichols. He looked like a goat, with his sculpted beard and his jutting chin. I remember how Gus used to swear the professor's pupils were vertical obelisks, if you could ever get close enough to see them.

"He was annoyed that I didn't follow the assignment parameters," I say spacily. "Dr. Nichols. I got a C on this assignment, mostly because I overachieved."

"Sounds right."

"Why don't I remember writing it? Why does it feel like the work of a stranger?"

Luke smiles down at me. "You do remember it. A little. You said it's familiar to you. Your logical brain is trying so hard to make you recognize it, but your emotional brain won't allow it. You wrote it at a time when life was too hard to experience, too hard to undertake, when it was easier to walk through life on auto-pilot."

I relax at the truth of that assessment and choke, "How do you know that?"

"I know *you*, Jayne." His smile has a guilty tint to it. "You told me that yourself once. Something you said in Key West reminded me of it and gave me the idea to test the theory by showing you one of your old files and seeing if you recognized it."

"By tricking me, in other words?"

He closes one eye and thinks about it. "Not really. I didn't lie. And I didn't say it *wasn't* your writing."

"'A favor for Arthur'? How do you explain that red herring?"

Ultra-seriously, he insists, "Arthur *has* been on my case for months about getting you to produce something. I wasn't exaggerating about my chestnuts being held firmly in the fire. They're roasting."

I smile sadly. "We can't have that. I'll march into his office and kick his old, wrinkly ass."

"It'd probably be better if you just finish that manuscript."

"Not as exciting, but okay. I might be able to do that."

"I *know* you can."

I gulp and try to temper the hope in my chest when I say, "I believe I can, too."

"I respect your space and your 'process,' but I haven't seen you—or been invited to the house on Marblehead—in months, and I'm starting to feel neglected and unloved. Not that I don't have other friends, Babushka; I do. I don't want you to get the wrong idea there. But they're not *you*, and they don't have houses on Marblehead, if you get my drift. Especially with summer getting into full swing, I want to sit on the beach and drink Mai Tai's and hang out in town, checking out all the gay married men who are trying so valiantly to be straight with their blue blood wives and their broods of bratty kids. All the openly gay men anymore are in committed relationships—or worse, married to other openly gay men—so I've resigned myself to being someone's mistress. I think I can handle it."

I un-mute my phone long enough to say, "I wouldn't recommend that."

"You never were, so what would you know? Anyway, what do you say? How much longer am I going to have to wait for an invitation? I know I'm not a low-key houseguest, so I understand why you want to be finished with your work before I come out there for a visit, but seriously! How much longer is it going to take you? Glaciers move faster, honey!"

"Soon," I answer vaguely. "Hey, it was great catching up, but I have to get back to it."

"Wait! Before you do, has Nick said anything about me since, you know, we met on the *Devil* set? I felt a connection. I know you weren't there, but trust me..."

I sigh inwardly and lie, "Ah, yes! As a matter of fact, he said you were... 'fascinating.' But... I think he's straight," I inform him regretfully.

"He probably thinks he is, too," Gus says. "That doesn't mean anything. All right, then, Babushka. Au revoir!"

And like that, he's gone.

Luke marks his place and closes his Blake Redmond-Womack book. "After listening to that, I'm thoroughly exhausted and am going up to bed." He stands and stretches. "You coming?"

I barely glance up at him while shaking my head. "Nope. Gotta keep at it."

I was on a roll before Gus called. He has "writing groove radar" like that. But I've screened his calls for weeks, so I felt an obligation to answer this time.

After bending down to kiss the top of my head, Luke leaves the room and shuffles up the stairs.

Now, where was I?

∾

The last piece of paper rasps from the printer and lands, warm and facedown, on the two-inch stack already in the output tray. I straighten the edges and hug the ream to my chest while tiptoeing up the stairs to our room, where Luke lies, warm and facedown, in our bed.

I poke him with my foot.

"Grrrr," he growls into his pillow.

"Luke!" I hiss. "Wake up!"

Turning his head toward me but keeping his eyes closed and remaining still, he says, "If the house is on fire, just leave me. God's trying to tell me something, obviously."

I kick him harder. "That's not funny. Wake up."

He cracks an eye but then quickly squeezes it shut again when I turn on his bedside lamp. "What the …? Jayne! What time is it?"

"Never mind," I say, not wanting to admit it's nearly 4 a.m. "I need you."

"Then turn off the light and get in bed," he replies. "Since when do we have to have the lights on? And do we have to do this right now? We can have sex when the alarm goes off."

Laughing, I say, "I don't need you for sex. I finished the book!"

This gets his attention much faster than a middle-of-the-night delight ever would. He pushes up to a sitting position and wiggles his fingers at the fresh, clean manuscript in my arms.

"That's what I thought," I mutter, handing it over and then going into the bathroom to get ready for bed.

When I slide between the covers a few minutes later and nuzzle down into my pillow and up against his side, he's nearly finished reading the two chapters I've most recently completed. My eyes are burning and blurry from the strain of staring at my laptop monitor for fourteen hours, so I close them. It's pointless to watch his face for a reaction, anyway. He never gives away anything while he's reading.

Soon enough, he's setting the manuscript on his bedside table, turning out the light, and scooting down under the covers again.

"Well?" I ask eagerly when he doesn't volunteer any feedback.

"It's good," he says in the same tone one would probably use at receiving a crayon drawing from a young child.

My heart sinks. "What do you mean? What's wrong with it?"

He sighs. "I mean, 'it's good.' And there's nothing wrong with it. Well… I saw a couple of things that you'll need to change, but nothing major. The usual. You really don't know how to use semi-colons, do you?"

"I thought I did…"

"You don't."

"Fine. But what about the *content*?"

"Jayne, it's 4:00 in the morning. I'll give you a full critique tomorrow, complete with fancy red pen marks."

Grudgingly, I accept, "Fine. I'm just excited." I know it's good, anyway. I don't necessarily need his stamp of approval. I simply wanted to share my good news with someone. "I already have an idea for the next one… It'll be told in first person from the point of view of a guy who works at a—"

"Jayne!" He pulls me against himself and kisses my forehead. "Tomorrow."

"Okay, okay." I rub his chest with my palms. "I'm sorry. I had a lot of coffee tonight."

Already sounding half-asleep, he says, "Don't apologize. You're inspired. That's a good thing. But I'd rather hear about it when the sun's up." He gives me a final hug. "I love you. G'night."

Before I can return the sentiment, he rolls over and, in the process of rearranging himself and getting comfortable, elbows me in the face.

The *Underdog* series (chick lit/sports romance):

- *Out of My League* (Book 1)
- *Rookie of the Year* (Book 2)
- *Opportunity Knox* (Book 3)
- *Ready or Knox* (Book 4)

The *Secret Keeper* series (chick lit/Christian romance):

- *The Secret Keeper* (Book 1)
- *The Secret Keeper Confined* (Book 2)
- *The Secret Keeper Up All Night* (Book 3)
- *The Secret Keeper Holds On* (Book 4)
- *The Secret Keeper Lets Go* (Book 5)
- *The Secret Keeper Fulfilled* (Book 6)

The *Nurse Nate* series (chick lit/romantic comedy):

- *Let's Be Frank* (Book 1)
- *Let's Be Real* (Book 2)
- *Let's Be Friends* (Book 3)

Stand-alone novels:

- *Daydreamer*
- *The Family Plot*
- *Quiet, Please!*